College life 201;

Sophomore Studies

J.B. Vample

Book Three

The College life series

COLLEGE LIFE 201-SOPHOMORE STUDIES

Copyright © 2016 by Jessyca B. Vample

Printed in the United States of America

First Printing, 2016

ISBN-10: 0-9969817-5-6 (eBook edition)
ISBN-13: 978-0-9969817-5-0 (eBook edition)

ISBN-10: 0-9969817-4-8 (Paperback edition)
ISBN-13: 978-0-9969817-4-3 (Paperback edition)

For information contact; email: JBVample@yahoo.com

Website: www.jbvample.com

Book cover design by: Najla Qamber Designs

To all of my amazing supporters/readers/fans! Thank you, thank you, thank you! Your questions, your comments, and your enthusiasm about my books make this journey so much more fun. Thank you for being as passionate about these characters and their stories as I am. I promise to keep the drama and the laughs coming.

Chapter 1

"Damn Sid, how many bags do you *have*?" Marcus Howard griped at his younger sister as he struggled to maneuver two suitcases at once.

Sidra Howard rolled her eyes. "Marcus, you asked me that same question when you helped Daddy load the bags in the van this morning," she returned, turning the doorknob to her new dorm room. Another semester was upon the students of Paradise Valley University, and once again the campus was flooded with new and returning students eager to start the new school year. Sidra, for one, was extremely excited to be a sophomore.

"Yeah, yeah," Marcus grumbled as he stepped foot into the room. With a thud, he dropped the bags on the cream-carpeted floor.

Sidra's bright grey eyes roamed around the space. "Wow, this is nicer than Torrence Hall," she gushed. The two extra-long twin beds, dark-wood dressers, large mirrors, desks, cushy swivel chairs, and accent chairs complemented the large space. Paradise Terrace was certainly a step up from the freshmen dorms. Sidra rushed over to a closet door and flung it open. "Nice," she beamed, admiring the space. She then hurried over to another door and opened it. "Check out this bathroom."

Marcus exhaled loudly as he headed over. "Sid, I'm tired," he groaned. "Can you come on so we can get the rest of the stuff out the car?"

She cut her eye at him. "Can you stop whining for just a second?" she bit out. He made a face at her in retaliation. It wasn't rare for one of Sidra's brothers to annoy her. That came with the territory of being the youngest and only girl of four children.

Marcus looked around the bathroom. "Nice double sinks though...and two showers? You and your roommate get your own shower?"

A frown fell over Sidra's pretty brown face as she came to a realization. "Damn it, we're sharing a bathroom with the room next door." Sidra was so used to only sharing a bathroom with her former roommate, Chasity Parker. She didn't know how to feel now that she had to share with three other people, including her new roommate. *I hope those girls next door aren't nasty,* she thought. She closed the door and began dragging one of her suitcases to her chosen bed.

Marcus watched as she began unpacking the contents. "So you're just gonna sit there and unpack when there's more stuff in the car?"

Sidra glared up at him. "Boy, can you just go and help Daddy with the rest?" she barked, pointing to the door.

Just as Marcus opened his mouth to say something, the door opened and in walked their father, carrying a forty-two inch flat-screen TV. "Marcus, go down and grab her mini-fridge," he ordered.

Sidra shook her head as Marcus walked out of the room without another word. "Daddy, your son is being a pain," she grumbled, pushing her long ponytail over her shoulder. A signature style for her long hair, Sidra's ponytail fell almost to the middle of her back.

Mr. Howard chuckled. "As always," he joked. "Decided to bring your TV back this year, huh?"

Sidra placed a few neatly folded items on her bed. "Yeah, well, I used Chasity's TV last year. But my new roommate doesn't have one, so I'm sharing mine," she informed.

Mr. Howard smiled. "Okay, let me go get the rest of your things so we can get out of your hair," he said.

"*You* can stay, but Marcus has to go," she giggled.

Alexandra Chisolm let out a loud huff as she struggled to drag her bags up the front steps to Paradise Terrace. "Where is a damn man when you need one?" she muttered. As if on cue, she heard a familiar male voice shout her name. She closed her eyes and chuckled; a voice that loud could only mean one person.

"Hey Mark," she smiled as he approached, arms outstretched.

"Give me my hug, my curly, curvy friend," Mark teased as they embraced.

"You're so silly," she laughed, parting from him. "How was your summer?"

"I was bored out of my damn mind," he grunted, bending down to grab one of Alex's bags. "I barely did shit."

Alex slung an overnight bag over her shoulder. "Well, if you were *that* bored, you could've gotten a job," she pointed out, walking through the glass doors with Mark following close behind.

"Naw, that wasn't happening," he returned, earning a snicker from Alex.

Navigating the hallway of her assigned floor, Alex smiled and waved to her fellow dorm mates. *This place is huge*, she mused to herself. "Mark, are Josh and David back yet?"

Mark was so preoccupied with glancing behind him at a voluptuous resident who sauntered past, he didn't hear Alex's question.

"Hey," she called.

"Huh?"

Alex shook her head. "Already losing focus," she ground out. If sophomore year was anything like their freshman year, Mark would lose focus more times than she could count. "Are Josh and David back?"

"Josh is coming later tonight, and David is in the room unpacking all his nerd shit," he scoffed.

"So who's your roommate this year?" she asked, curious. Mark shot her a side glance, then rolled his eyes. Alex laughed. "You mean that—"

"Yes, David the glasses man is my roommate this year," he sneered of his childhood friend. "He corny."

"Aww, leave David alone," Alex chided, approaching her room door. "I'm sure he's not too thrilled to be *your* roommate either." Alex ignored Mark's mumbling as she pushed the door open. "Sidra!" she screamed when she saw Sidra walk out of the bathroom.

Sidra let out a squeal of delight as she hopped over to her new roommate. "See, I told you that you would like your roommate," she boasted, hugging Alex.

"I *love* my roommate," Alex returned as the two women parted from their embrace.

When the girls came to the realization that they would have to switch roommates for the new school year, the news was met with some worry; they didn't know what or *who* to expect. But the room assignment letters that arrived to their homes over summer break were met with relief.

"Really, with all the sappy mess?" Mark bit out, folding his arms. "Y'all act like you didn't see each other a couple of weeks ago."

"Mind your business and give me a hug, boy," Sidra demanded, holding her arms out.

Alex unzipped her duffle bag, then pushed some of her thick, brown, shoulder-length, wavy hair off of her face. "I talked to Emily the other day," she announced. "She's not happy."

"Yeah, I can imagine," Sidra sympathized.

"Have you talked to Malajia or Chasity yet?" Alex asked, sitting on the floor.

"Oh God, why did you mention that parasite's name?" Mark sneered of Malajia. "I just ate and would *like* to keep my damn food down."

Sidra waved her hand at him dismissively, focusing her attention on Alex. "No, not since this morning. But I know that Malajia should be on her way here."

Malajia Simmons sauntered through the fourth floor of Paradise Terrace, scanning each door for her room number.

"Hey Malajia," a girl greeted in passing.

"Hey girl, good to be out of the freshman dorm, huh?" Malajia smiled.

"You know it," the bubbly girl replied. "Where are all your bags?"

"In my parents van so my dad can bring it up. I wasn't carrying that shit up here," Malajia replied, still maintaining her pace. "I'll catch up with you later, gotta check out my new room." Once Malajia arrived at a door at the end of the hallway, she stopped and eagerly rubbed her hands together. She had been waiting for this day ever since she received her room assignment letter in the mail. Twisting the knob and pushing open the door, Malajia walked in and struck a seductive pose. "Heeeeyyyy biiiitch!"

A visibly annoyed Chasity Parker turned around from hanging up her clothes and threw her head back in agitation. "Fuck my life," she groaned.

"We're roommates, we're roommates, go roommate, my roommate," Malajia sang as her slender body gyrated to imaginary music.

Chasity's hazel eyes narrowed, watching Malajia in disgust. When she received her room assignment, she hoped that the office had made a mistake in putting her in a room with Malajia. Sadly for her, it was no mistake. "I fuckin' hate you," she seethed as Malajia clapped her hands in delight.

"No you don't, you *love* me," Malajia teased, tossing her purse on the remaining empty bed. She walked over to Chasity, arms outstretched. "Hug me, Satan."

"Don't touch me. Don't touch me," Chasity warned, backing away from Malajia who just kept coming at her.

"Just let it happen," Malajia gushed, throwing her arms around the disgusted Chasity.

"Get off," Chasity hissed, jerking Malajia off of her.

Chasity's attitude didn't faze Malajia. She was used to it. "Oh my God! Our room is huge," she observed, looking around. "Yeeeeesss, our own bathroom and no damn bunk beds." The private bathroom was icing on the cake for Malajia. She didn't have the luxury that Chasity and Sidra had the previous year. The community bathrooms in her old dorm at Wilson Hall had to be shared with half of the floor.

Chasity went back to hanging up her clothes, while Malajia continued to look around. "Yes, you got that HD TV action. This is bigger than the one you had *last* year." she beamed, eyeing the fifty-two inch TV on a wood stand. "I *knew* you were gonna come through for us."

"You touch it and I'll break every last one of those damn fingers off," Chasity cautioned.

Malajia flagged her with her hand. "Ain't nobody scared of you Parker," she shot back. "I *will* be watching that TV." Chasity slowly folded her arms and glared at Malajia. Unfazed, Malajia kept talking. "And I'll be listening to that *stereo* and typing on that laptop and—"

"Did you bring *any* of your *own* shit?!" Chasity exploded.

Malajia smiled. "I brought my clothes and my gorgeous self."

Chasity sucked her teeth.

"Why would I bring stuff when I know *you* got everything? That makes no sense."

Chasity nearly lost it, scowling at the wide-mouthed grin on Malajia's brown face. Without saying a word, she walked over to the door and snatched it open, sticking her head out.

"Where the hell do you think *you're* going?" Malajia frowned.

Chasity ignored her, eyeing someone across the hall. "Hey Marilyn," she called. "I will pay for you to get your teeth fixed if you let Malajia be your roommate," she proposed when the short, busty girl turned around.

"Whatever, Chasity," Marilyn hissed.

"Yo, Chaz, you ignorant as shit," Malajia laughed, darting for the door. "Marilyn, pay her no mind. I'm staying my ass right in *this* room."

Marilyn sucked her teeth. "You wasn't moving in here *any-damn-way*," she bit out, earning a glower from Malajia. "And my teeth aren't that damn bad for y'all to be clowning me about them."

"You don't think so?" Chasity sniped, earning a snicker and a light backhand from Malajia.

Two doors down, a door opened. Alex and Sidra poked their heads out just as Marilyn walked back into her room and slammed the door.

"I knew I recognized the voice of the devil," Alex teased, grabbing both Chasity and Malajia's attention.

"Oh my God, we live on the same floor," Malajia shrieked, clapping her hands.

Sidra and Alex walked out of their room. "Chaz, I'm so sorry you're stuck with *that* all year," Sidra joked of Malajia, pointing to her.

Chasity shook her head. "Please kill me," she begged, voice flat.

Alex peered into the girls' room. "You got the room with the private bathroom huh?" she mused. "I guess that's the perk of having a room at the end of the hall."

"Ahhh, y'all gotta share a bathroom with people you don't know," Malajia teased, smoothing her hand over her wine-colored, shoulder-length, curled hair.

Sidra narrowed her eyes. She didn't appreciate the teasing. "Nice tracks," she sneered at Malajia's new hair length.

"Thank you," Malajia returned, a phony smile plastered to her attractive face. "And when I get the money from that hoe tail I'm about to cut off *your* head, I can buy *more*."

"Okay ladies, we just got back, let's not start taking digs at each other," Alex cut in, putting her hands up. "Didn't we just go through something serious?" Having just faced a stressful meeting with President Bennett over a brawl with Jackie Stevens and her friends and walking away still students at the university, Alex thought that the experience would bring the girls a little closer.

"Shut the hell up," Malajia barked, waving her hand. "That don't mean we gotta stop arguing."

Alex shot Malajia a confused look before shaking her head. "Anyway, I just spoke to Emily," she proclaimed. "She's back, so let's go see her new spot."

"Naw dawg," Chasity refused.

"Chasity, don't be rude," Sidra chided. "She's our friend and I'm sure she'll be happy to see us."

"Not trying to hear it, baby Alex," Chasity sneered, running her hand through her long, layered black hair. "I have shit to do," she continued, heading back into her room.

"Yeah, *we* have shit to do," Malajia agreed, placing her hands on her hips as Chasity shut the room door. Sidra busted out laughing.

"Sid, what's so funny?" Malajia asked, confused.

"You just got locked out of your room," Sidra informed.

It took a few seconds for Sidra's words to register in Malajia's head. "Shit!" she exclaimed, grabbing for the door knob. "Damn it Chasity," she fussed, trying to twist the locked knob. "Open the door. I gotta pee! You play too damn much."

Chapter 2

"Is that Court Terrace?" Sidra asked, eyeing the dorm directly across from Paradise Terrace. "The new men's dorm?"

"Yeah girl," Malajia confirmed, adjusting the straps of the red tank top on her shoulders. "I'm glad we got in this dorm, 'cause we can look outside and see some gorgeous men."

A half-hour later and after much persuasion, Alex finally got a reluctant Malajia and Chasity to accompany her and Sidra on an excursion to Emily's dorm.

Malajia rolled her eyes when she saw Mark Johnson, Josh Hampton, and David Summers walk out of the dorm. "Oh Jesus, Mary, and Joseph," she huffed.

"What's up ladies?!" Mark shouted from across the path.

"Out of all of the damn dorms on this campus, they have to be in the one across from *us*," Malajia scoffed.

As Mark passed Malajia, he gently palmed her forehead, making her head jerk back.

"Come *on*!" Malajia yelled, delivering a punch to his toned arm.

"That's what you get for talking shit," Mark retorted, rubbing his arm.

Josh gave out hugs. "It's good to see you ladies," he chuckled.

Brown-skinned David held a warm smile on his face. "Where are you ladies headed?" he asked, pushing his silver-framed glasses up on his nose.

"To go visit Emily," Alex answered.

Josh frowned in confusion. "Oh, she's not in the same dorm with *you* girls?"

"No, unfortunately she's *not*," Alex sulked, shoving her hands into the pockets of her jeans.

Chasity rolled her eyes as Mark slowly walked over, looking her up and down. "Mmm, look at you," he crooned, licking his full lips. She folded her arms. "You lookin' all sexy and shit." He reached for her arm.

"Boy, back up off me," she barked, jerking her arm out of his reach.

Mark laughed. "Girl, stop being so damn mean and give me a hug," he ordered, pulling her into an embrace.

"Ooh, don't let Jason see that," Sidra teased.

"Don't let Jason see that," Mark mocked, earning a giggle from Sidra. "Man ain't nobody scared of no damn Jason," he boasted.

"You sure about that?" Jason Adams asked.

Startled, Mark turned around and smiled at him. "Yo Jase, my homie, what's good man?" he sputtered.

"Yeah, yeah, what have I told you about touching my woman," Jason chortled, giving Mark a playful shove.

As Jason gave Chasity a hug, Mark walked over to Sidra and grabbed her. "You can keep her," he joked. "*This* is my woman right here."

Mark rubbed Sidra's arm and she shook her head. "Mark, have a seat," Sidra giggled.

Josh wasn't amused. With a scowl frozen on his handsome brown face, he walked over and accidentally-on-purpose bumped into Mark with his tall, solid frame, sending him stumbling into a nearby bike rack.

"You scuffed my new sneaks dawg!" Mark hollered,

bending down to examine the damage done to his name brand black and red sneakers.

Malajia rolled her eyes. "Always so damn loud," she huffed.

"How are you?" Jason asked Chasity, gently holding onto her hand. He couldn't care less what Mark or any of the others were doing at that moment. His focus was on the one thing he couldn't stop thinking about during summer break—Chasity.

"I'm fine," she returned, pushing some hair behind her ear. She narrowed her eyes when he continued to stare. "Stop staring, Jason."

"Sorry," he chuckled. *I can't help it, you're beautiful Chasity*. Even though he saw her over the break due to the fact that he only lived ten minutes from her, he missed the luxury of seeing her every day. Every time he didn't see her, he thought of her, recalling the delicate features of her beautiful face, her light-brown skin, the slight curves of her toned body, the silk look to her black hair which fell past her chest. He found himself staring again and quickly turned his attention to the others.

"All right ladies, let's get going," Alex urged.

"Ugh, don't nobody *feel* like this," Malajia complained, stomping one of her high-heeled sandals on the ground.

A frown was prominent on Alex's dark brown face. "Can you zip it for five minutes?" she seethed, giving Malajia's arm a poke.

"We'll catch y'all later," Mark cut in. "There's gonna be a party in the clusters later on, swing through."

"A party?" Malajia's mood instantly perked. If it was one thing she loved, it was a party. "Oh, you know *I'll* be there."

"Wasn't nobody talking to you," Mark spat, earning a middle finger from Malajia.

Emily Harris read the note that was stuck in her suitcase.

"*Have a good semester sweetheart. Keep away from distractions and study hard,*" and rolled her eyes.

"Please," she mumbled to herself, tossing the handwritten note on her bed.

Sitting on the bed, Emily sighed and ran her hands through her relaxed, shoulder-length sandy brown hair. Looking around her small room, a wave of sadness hit her. Even though she was already in her new room, she read the room assignment letter just as she had every day since she received it over the summer: *Room assignment for Emily K. Harris. Apartment complex B, Floor 2 room C, room type: single.*

As Emily began to remove the folded clothes from her suitcase, she heard a knock on the door. Darting over, she snatched it open and smiled brightly at the girls standing in the hall. "Hey!" she squealed, wrapping her arms around Alex, who was first to walk in. "I'm glad you stopped over." She shut the door as the last girl filed in.

They scanned the room. The small space didn't allow much room for anything other than the bed, pine wood dresser, desk, and swivel chair that occupied it. Emily's room was one of three in the complex. Not only did she share a tiny den, but a bathroom as well.

"Sooo, this is the apartment huh?" Sidra asked, peering out of the small window.

Emily sighed. "Yeah, this is it."

"This room just screams 'lonely'," Chasity sneered, producing a loud snicker from Malajia and a glare from Alex.

"Really Chasity?" Alex ground out. "Couldn't keep it to yourself for five minutes, huh?"

"Absolutely not," Chasity returned, unfazed by Alex's anger or the sadness on Emily's light face.

"I mean, they could've at *least* repainted the outside," Malajia added, voice full of laughter. "It's all dry and old. It's a shame you didn't get in the new dorms with *us*."

Yeah, a huge shame, thanks for rubbing it in, Emily silently seethed. "I *wanted* to but—"

"Mommy said no?" Chasity taunted, folding her arms.

Embarrassed, Emily looked at the floor, pushing some of her hair behind her ears.

"Naw, Mommy put her name on that list," Malajia joined in, giving Chasity a tap on her arm.

Chasity scowled at Malajia. "Don't touch me," she warned. Malajia made a face at her.

"Want to hear something hilarious?" Sidra asked, sitting on Emily's half-made bed.

"Yes please," Emily replied, curious.

Sidra pointed to Chasity and Malajia, who were making threatening faces at one another. "Those two got stuck being roommates."

Emily's mouth fell open as laughter bubbled up. "Oh," she replied. She knew firsthand how much Chasity and Malajia argued and exactly how much Malajia worked Chasity's last nerve. *That should be hilarious.*

Alex sat down on Emily's bed beside Sidra. "Sweetie, I know that you're not happy with your new living arrangements, but you *do* know that you're always welcome to come chill in our rooms whenever, right?" she said, eyeing Emily sympathetically. "Be quiet, Chasity," she hissed, sensing Chasity's protest.

"Damn, she knows you well Chaz." Sidra giggled at the annoyed look on Chasity's face.

Emily forced a smile. *I wish I knew how true that was.* "I know. Thanks Alex."

Alex suddenly hopped up from the bed. "Em, why don't you take a break from unpacking and come with *us*," she proposed. "We can order some food and then go see my friends, Victoria and Stacey."

Chasity and Malajia shot glances Alex's way. "No, *you* can go see Victoria and Stacey by your-damn-self," Chasity sneered.

Alex frowned in confusion. "What's your problem?"

"Victoria is a bitch," Chasity bluntly stated.

"Damn!" Malajia laughed.

Alex folded her arms as she glared daggers at Chasity. She wanted to slap her. "Oh what? Are you mad because *you're* not the only one anymore?" she shot back.

Chasity smirked. "Ouch," she threw back, holding a middle finger up.

Alex waved her hand at Chasity. "Why do you *always* have to be so damn mean?" she asked, irritation in her voice. "Victoria didn't even do anything to you."

"I don't like her." Chasity answered matter-of-factly, drawing her words out slowly.

Malajia, put her hand up. "Alex, I'm sorry, but Chaz has a point," she put in. "I mean Stacey is cool and all, but that other one...something's not right about her."

Alex rolled her eyes. She knew that her high school friend didn't give off the best first impression when she had introduced her to the girls last semester while they were visiting her house in Philadelphia. But she didn't want them to hold that against her before even getting to know her. "Look, I know that she came off a little..."

"Jealous?" Malajia finished.

"*Standoffish*," Alex amended. "It just takes her a while to get used to new people. *Especially* my friends. But if you just give her a chance, I know that you'll love her as much as *I* do."

"I don't even love my own *parents.* How do you expect me to love a bitch I don't like?" Chasity spat. "Hell, I barely like *you.*"

Alex pointed at Chasity; she was fed up. "You've got one more—"

"Make me break that finger, Alex," Chasity calmly warned.

"Okay ladies, let's drop it," Sidra interjected, grabbing Alex's arm, and guiding her toward the door. "Let's not let some girl that we don't even know come between us. Let's just agree to disagree."

Malajia eyed Sidra with disgust. "Why is there a ponytail talking?" she bit out.

Emily put her hands over her face and snickered at the irritated look on Sidra's face. "God, I missed you girls," she grinned.

"I still can't believe that you had to meet with President Bennett over the summer," Emily said, shoving a fork full of beef lo mein into her mouth. "I know you were freaking out."

"That was an *understatement*," Sidra replied, reaching for an eggroll. "I was close to a nervous breakdown."

Alex, Sidra, and Emily parted from Malajia and Chasity and headed back to their room where they fulfilled on the promise of ordering take-out. Emily sat in anticipation while the girls filled her in on their meeting over last semester's much talked about fight.

"I'm sorry that you had to go through that," Emily sympathized. "But at least it all worked out. You didn't get kicked out of school like you *thought* you would."

"I know, and trust me I count my blessings every day," Alex assured, opening a bottle of juice.

"I hope Jackie and those rats stay as far away from us as possible." Sidra was livid as she remembered the ordeal. "Those bitches *jumped* me and I won't ever forget that."

"I know, but let's just *try* to move on," Alex cut in. She understood Sidra's anger, but she knew that dwelling on the past wasn't going to do her any good. "So anyway Em, I know we didn't get to talk much while we were on break. How was your summer?"

Emily looked down at her food and sighed. "It was…" *So boring!* she wanted to scream. "It was okay…I guess it wasn't *too* bad hanging out with my mom every second…of every day." She shook her head in an effort to shake the snide remarks forming in her throat. "I went to visit my Grandmom for a few weeks, which was nice."

Sidra stared at Emily for several seconds. She couldn't let another moment pass without saying what she needed to say. "Em, you really need to talk to your mom about loosening the reigns on you," she began. "You're eighteen and a sophomore now…she was wrong for adding your name to that apartment list."

Emily sat her take-out carton on the floor and rubbed her hands on her baggy, pale blue jeans. "I know," she muttered. "I just…I can't say anything to her…she's my mom."

Sidra stood from her bed and walked over to the bathroom. "Mom or not sweetie, she's wrong," she insisted, opening the door. Sidra turned on the light and sucked her teeth. The mess of balled up tissues and personal products littering her neighbor's side was hard to miss. "Nasty heifers," she quietly vented, washing her hands.

"Alex, I swear, I'm going to end up having words with those girls next door," Sidra seethed once she emerged from the bathroom.

"What's the matter?" Alex asked, wiping her hand on a napkin.

"Their crap is all over the damn place," Sidra griped, shutting the door.

Alex shook her head. "Try not to get up in arms about the bathroom just yet, Princess," she advised. "It's only the first day. Maybe they're just unpacking."

"Yeah for *their* sake, I hope so," Sidra bit out.

Emily was about to say something when the room door flew open and slammed against the wall.

"What the hell?!" Alex exclaimed, spinning around.

"Shut up and get your shit, we're going to the party in the clusters," Malajia ordered as she and Chasity walked in.

"I'm not going to those damn clusters with those upper-class heathens," Sidra scoffed. "All they do is drink and act stupid."

"Exactly. It's gonna be fun," Malajia smiled. "And *we're* upperclassmen now *too*. So we must partake in the stupidity…I'm ready to get some drinks in this sexy body."

"You're not drinking anything tonight, do you hear me?" Alex protested, pointing at Malajia.

Malajia looked over at Chasity, who was pinching the

bridge of her nose with two fingers. She felt a headache coming on "What?" Chasity snarled when she noticed Malajia's stare.

"Who does Alex think she's talking to?" Malajia asked, gesturing to Alex.

"Oh my God, why are you talking to me?" Chasity snapped, fed up with the sound of Malajia's voice. "You have *not* stopped talking since you walked in the fuckin' room earlier. Shut up."

"What the hell are *you* so damn cranky for? You pale-faced asshole," Malajia threw back. "Girl, go get laid so you can calm down."

"I'll lay my fist on your damn face, if you keep bothering me," Chasity threatened.

Alex shook her head at the byplay. "I can see that I have no choice but to go to this party," she concluded, grabbing a fresh top out of her drawer. "Something tells me that either Malajia is going to get drunk and act a fool, or she and Chasity will end up killing each other."

"I'll take the *first* scenario," Malajia joked. She paused, eyeing the shirt that Alex laid on her bed. "Um Alex, I know you're not gonna wear that shirt tonight," she scoffed as Alex took off the old shirt.

Alex's head snapped towards her. "What? What's wrong with my shirt, Mel?" she asked, agitation in her voice.

"It's all ashy and baggy," Malajia countered, face scrunched up. "And what is with you and that shitty, dirty ass, yellow color? I *know* you worked over the summer, you couldn't buy no new clothes?"

Alex took a deep breath. "Malajia, I've told you before about talking about my clothes." She drew her words out slowly in an effort to keep calm. "I wear what I can afford and what's comfortable." Being tall with a thick frame, Alex made sure that her clothing provided room, while accentuating her God-given curves.

"Oh, so *our* eyes gotta suffer 'cause *your* broke ass can't buy no new shit?" Malajia hissed. "I gotta hear people come up to me talkin' 'bout 'why your girl be wearing those baggy ass shirts'? Then *I* gotta get into an altercation, defending *your* non-dressing ass."

Malajia's animated rambling was met with confused and annoyed stares from the girls. "Nobody even *said* that to you," Sidra commented.

"Well, I know people be thinkin' it," Malajia shot back.

"Malajia, you're an idiot," Alex concluded, pulling the short sleeved top over her head.

"Just hurry up, big titties," Malajia urged, flicking her hand in Alex's direction.

"Can we go before I change my mind?" Chasity asked impatiently. "I need a damn drink myself, if I'm gonna deal with *this* all night," she added, motioning towards Malajia.

"Look, if you girls plan on drinking, *please* eat something first," Alex insisted. "We don't need another episode like we had on your birthday, Chasity."

Chasity rolled her eyes as she remembered the episode. She had gone to a party with Malajia and Alex, gotten drunk, and ended up with a killer hangover accompanied by the flu.

"Yeah, I doubt that Malajia will clean up your vomit all night," Sidra chuckled, remembering how she had to play caretaker to her drunken roommate.

"Shit, her ass will *lay* in it," Malajia grumbled, patting her head.

Chasity took a deep breath. She was trying to keep her looming headache from getting worse, but Malajia's constant talking was bringing her to the boiling point.
"Shut…up…Malajia," she put out, voice eerily calm.

Sidra looked at Emily, who was sitting on the floor fiddling with the beaded bracelet on her wrist. "Emily, are you coming?" she asked, already pretty sure of the answer.

"Well—"

"You don't have to if you don't want to," Alex quickly interjected, sensing Emily's hesitance.

"Yes, she *does*. Em, let's go," Malajia insisted, signaling for Emily to get up. "You might as well, because nobody is staying in the room with you this time."

Emily slowly stood from the floor. "Okay...let's go," she quietly put out. The last thing that Emily wanted to do was miss out on fun, no matter how uncomfortable she knew she would be.

Chapter 3

The clusters were a group of small resident houses towards the end of the campus, four houses made up one cluster. With seven clusters, the spot was a popular hangout for upperclassmen, and the perfect place for back-to-campus night parties.

The music blared through all four houses of the cluster that Malajia and the rest of her friends were in. Malajia downed her fourth shot and threw her hands up in the air. "Yeeeeeeesssss! This is my song," she yelled over the music, then danced on the grass.

Chasity was on her way into one of the houses to get some water.

Seeing her pass by, Malajia grabbed her arm. "Come on and dance with me," she ordered.

Chasity sighed loudly. She wasn't in the mood for Malajia's antics. She wasn't feeling well. "Get off me," Chasity barked, jerking out of Malajia's grasp.

"I said dance with me," Malajia demanded, getting up in Chasity's face. Chasity gave Malajia a shove, sending her stumbling to the ground. Intoxicated, Malajia laid there laughing as she kicked her legs wildly in the air. "Partaaaaaayyyy!"

Sidra, who was standing near a bench with Alex and Emily, sucked her teeth. She walked over and extended her hand. "Mel, get up off the ground," she reprimanded. "You have a skirt on, for Christ's sakes."

Malajia reached for Sidra's arm and allowed the help from the ground. "At least my underwear are cute," she slurred, smoothing down her short, black skirt.

"Have some morals," Sidra commented, sauntering off.

"I told that girl to change her skirt," Alex said in a quiet aside to Emily. "She always has to be the one to show her behind…*literally*."

Emily shook her head. "Chasity, are you okay?" she asked when she saw Chasity approach the bench, a bottle of water in her hand.

Chasity plopped down. "I think I hit the shots too hard," she admitted, putting her head in her hands.

Alex took the bottle from her hands and opened it. "Drink a couple bottles of water and you'll feel better," she assured, handing it back. Chasity held on to the bottle, not bothering to take a sip. As Alex tried to guide the bottle to Chasity's lips, Jason walked over, parting ways from some of his football teammates. As the star football player since his freshman year, Jason normally traveled to parties with his team.

Emily rose from her seat. "Hey Jason," she smiled, giving him a hug.

"Ooh, football players!" Malajia shrieked, following their progress. As she took a step, she tripped over a twig and stumbled forward, falling into Jason's chest.

Jason steadied her with his arms. "Don't embarrass yourself," he laughed.

"Who put that twig there?" Malajia looked at her shoes before glancing up at Jason. She touched his arms. "Ooh, did you put on more muscle over the summer?" she cooed, pressing her hand against his broad, toned chest.

"Malajia," he warned, voice stern.

"My fault," she giggled. Malajia remembered the brief

crush that she had on Jason first semester. His tall, solid frame, light-brown skin, clean-cut dark hair, and handsome face made crushing easy. *You're lucky you like my girl, otherwise you'd be mine, you sexy bastard, you,* she mused to herself.

"Jase, about time you showed up," Mark greeted, giving Jason a fist bump.

Malajia rolled her eyes at the sight of Mark, but changed her expression when she eyed the plastic red cup in his hand. "Whatchu got?" she asked, reaching for it. "Gimme some."

"Get out my face! Get out my face!" Mark shouted, moving the cup out of her reach.

Sidra smacked her palm against her forehead. "You two are so childish," she ground out. They both looked at her. "Malajia stop grabbing at his cup, you know he's not going to give you any." Malajia rolled her eyes, while Mark smiled boastfully. "And besides..." Sidra added. "If *anybody's* getting any of his drink...It's gonna be his *sister*," she laughed, snatching the cup from Mark's unsuspecting grasp and hurrying off.

"Yo, chill, I just made that," Mark yelled after her.

"Sidra, save me some," Malajia called, skipping off after her, with Mark tailing.

Jason laughed to himself over his friend's antics, taking a seat next to Chasity. Her head was still in her hands. He stared at her; moving her hair behind her shoulder. The gentle touch made her slowly lift her head. She stared back at him, blinking slowly.

"You okay?" he asked.

"I think I'm drunk," she slowly answered.

Jason smiled. "Couldn't wait for me, huh?" he teased, grabbing the water bottle from her hand and putting it to her lips. "Drink up."

"Maybe *you* can make her drink it, Jason," Alex fussed. "She's just been holding the damn thing."

"I got her," Jason nodded. As Chasity finally took a sip,

Jason saw a teammate approaching.

"Jase, try this," he urged, handing Jason a cup full of drink.

"What the hell is *this*?" Jason frowned.

"Some hot shit," his teammate confirmed, smiling.

"Naw, I'm cool," Jason declined, handing the cup back.

"*I'll* take that," Malajia cut in, appearing out of nowhere. She reached over Jason's shoulder and snatched the cup from him.

Jason fixed a stern gaze on her. "Mel, you don't even know what that *is*," he called after her as she danced away.

"Whatever it is, it's gonna get me drunk, so I'm good," Malajia threw over her shoulder. She took a long sip, coughing as the strong liquid poured down her throat.

"It's been two hours, and half of our friends are drunk," Alex joked to Emily. Having had enough with the growing crowd outside, both girls took their conversation inside one of the houses. "You having a good time?"

Emily nodded. "It feels good to get out," she replied, smoothing her pale pink t-shirt with her hands. She was telling a half-truth. She was glad to be out, but she felt like she couldn't unwind.

"Alex, my beautiful natural sistah, you want a drink?" Praz, a well-known upperclassmen and Malajia's friend greeted.

Eyeing the cup in his hands, Alex shook her head in amusement. "No, thank you," she returned. "If what you have in that cup is the same stuff you made for your reggae party that had my friends on their behinds all night, you can keep it."

The dark skinned man shrugged. "Suit yourself," he replied, turning to Emily. "Do you wanna try one?"

Before Emily could get a word in, Alex put her hand up. "No Praz, she doesn't drink."

Emily shot Alex a side glance. *I could've told him that*

myself.

"Oh well, more for the other drunks around here," Praz shrugged again, holding the cup up. "Hey Malajia! I got another one for you," he yelled, walking off.

"Yeeeeeeessss!" Malajia hollered over the music.

"I tell you Em, these fools will try to feed you drinks all night," Alex cautioned. "Watch out for them."

Emily simply nodded.

Emily left Alex in the house ten minutes later, looking for the rest of the scattered group. She glanced over and saw Malajia along with Sidra, dancing in Mark's face as he laid sprawled out on an outdoor wooden table. Walking over, she giggled.

"Please, please get out my face," Mark begged, grabbing his stomach.

"Nobody told you to mix that nasty dark liquor with that light stuff," Sidra teased. "You always have to take things overboard."

"If you hadn't stole my damn drink, I wouldn't have *drank* the dark one," he slurred.

Malajia got close to his face and started swinging her hair. "Ahhhh, you gonna be sick in the morniiiiing."

"Fuck you, Malajia," Mark hissed.

"Is he okay?" Emily asked, peering at Mark, whose eyes were closed.

A tipsy Malajia faced Emily. "Emily!" she screamed, startling her. Unfazed by Emily's reaction, Malajia wrapped her arms around her and squeezed tight. "How is my little, mousy friend?"

Emily just eyed Malajia with confusion.

"Girl, get off her," Sidra commanded, grabbing the strap of Malajia's top and giving it a tug.

Emily smoothed her hair down once Malajia released her from her grip and scanned the grounds. Everyone around her seemed to be having a good time. Everyone looked relaxed. *I need something, I want to have fun like everybody else.* Seeing Praz over on the steps of another house, she walked over and gently tapped his shoulder. When he turned around, she whispered something to him. He nodded and gave her the thumbs up sign, then walked off.

"Chasity, have you seen Emily?" Alex asked Chasity, who was finishing up another bottle of water.

Chasity, having sobered up a bit, shook her head.

Alex put her hands on her hips. "That's weird," she mumbled. "I haven't seen her in like a half-hour. Maybe she went back to her room. I would've hoped that she would say 'bye' first."

Chasity eyed Alex skeptically. "Are you talking to *me* or your*self*?"

Alex playfully tapped Chasity on her arm in retaliation for the smart question. "Come on, walk me inside to get some water."

"Girl, you go back in that hot ass house by yourself," Chasity sneered, turning to walk away.

"Walk me inside, evil," Alex chuckled, grabbing Chasity's arm. Both girls headed inside, only to be greeted by a blast of heat and a crowd of guys huddled around something.

"I can't Alex, it's too damn hot in here," Chasity griped.

Alex pushed hair off of her face. "I know, come on, let's go," she agreed.

The sound of guys chanting, "Go Emily! Go Emily!" made them stop in their tracks.

"Are they saying, *Emily*?" Alex asked Chasity, who was craning her neck to get a better look. "No, they *can't* be."

Without saying another word to Alex, Chasity pushed her way through the crowd and stared in shock—Emily was wildly dancing with two guys.

"Oh my God! Emily?" Alex exclaimed, joining Chasity in front of the crowd. "She has lost her damn mind." When more guys gathered, Alex felt herself being nudged behind them. "Chasity, grab her," she ordered.

Annoyed, Chasity stormed over and took hold of Emily's arm, giving it a yank. "Chasity, what are you doing?" Emily slurred.

"Don't make me embarrass you," Chasity hissed, pulling her away.

Alex grabbed hold of Emily's other arm and pulled her the rest of the way outside. "Emily are you out of your mind?" Alex scolded, nudging Emily in front of her.

"Why are you two upset?" Emily asked, folding her arms across her chest. "What did I do wrong?"

"First off, you're drunk," Alex spat, taking in the delayed speech and glazed over look in Emily's eyes. "*Second*, you were in a house full of drunk guys who you don't know, *by yourself.*"

"But…I just wanted to have fun. I needed to loosen up," Emily reasoned.

"You're a dumbass," Chasity spat out, eyeing the naïve girl with disgust. "You just don't get what could've happened. You could've been somebody's damn train tonight. Stupid."

"Exactly," Alex agreed, folding her arms. She shot Chasity a side glance. "You don't have to call her stupid though—"

"She *is* stupid," Chasity maintained, cutting Alex off. Alex put her hands up in surrender.

Emily looked at the ground in shame, shifting her weight from one foot to the other. Alex's eyes were full of disappointment as she shook her head. "I expected Malajia to act like a fool, but at least *she* knows to stay around people she *knows* when she drinks."

"I'm sorry," Emily sputtered.

"I'm taking you home, you need to sleep it off," Alex simmered, grabbing Emily's arm yet again. "Chasity, tell the others that I took little miss party girl home," she threw over her shoulder.

Chasity watched the girls walk off, then looked at Jason as he approached. "Feeling better I see," he commented.

"Didn't mean to leave for that long, the damn line for the bathroom was long."

"Its fine," she replied, rubbing the back of her neck. "I'm about to get out of here, I'm done."

"Yeah me too," Jason concurred. "I'll walk back with you."

Taking a step towards the front of the gate, they heard someone shout, "Yo, we gotta get outta here, the campus police are coming through the gates!"

No sooner than those words were uttered did people scatter. Nobody wanted to be apprehended for drinking outside on campus. The sound of the sirens sent people into a panic.

Mark hopped up from the table that he was laying across and tossed his cup on the ground. "Hell, I'm sober now, let's be out," he said, signaling for Sidra and Malajia to follow him.

"Shit, they're trying to lock us in!" Malajia yelled, seeing several officers close the large iron gates.

Chasity looked around. "There's a fence back there," she observed, pointing to a gate in the distance.

"We gotta hop it," Jason decided as the group jogged away from the panicking crowd.

They approached the back gate with haste and began to carefully scale the fence. Malajia was having a hard time in her high heeled sandals, and hung on. "I can't climb in these shoes!"

"We don't have time for your bullshit, Malajia," Mark barked, hopping off the fence and landing on the other side.

"Can somebody help me?" Malajia yelled, swinging her legs.

"Stop being so damn loud," Sidra seethed through clenched teeth as she carefully stepped down on the other side. Lucky for her, she elected to wear capri pants instead of one of her pencil skirts. The latter would have made maneuvering the fence more difficult. "You'll draw attention to us."

"I don't give a shit, I need help," Malajia fussed.

"Malajia, I will leave you and you *know* it," Chasity argued, having made it down.

"Look, just climb up. When you get to the top, jump, and I'll catch you," Jason promised. He wanted to get away from that scene as quickly as possible. He could only imagine the trouble he would get into from his football coach if he was caught.

Malajia let out a loud sigh. "All right, fine." She carefully resumed her climb.

Jason looked behind her and saw a few cops running up. "Mel, you gotta move faster than that, they're coming," he urged.

"What! Oh shit," Malajia panicked, climbing faster.

"Malajia come on, damn!" Mark shouted, his hands on his head. "You about to get left."

"Hey, get off that fence," an officer warned, flashing a light in their direction.

Malajia screamed as she hopped over the fence and landed in Jason's arms.

"Damn you strong," Malajia gushed as she was placed on her feet.

"Let's be out!" Mark hollered, then they took off running.

Chapter 4

Emily groaned as she held the covers over her face in an attempt to block out the sunlight peering through the open blinds. "Ugh, why didn't I shut those last night?" she moaned, rolling over. The loud ringing of her room phone made her jump.

She reached for it. "Okay, okay," she hissed at the pink phone. "Hello?" she answered, voice groggy.

"Hey Em, its Alex."

Emily rubbed her eyes with the back of her hand. "Hi Alex."

"How are you feeling?" Alex asked, noticing Emily's low tone.

"Really bad," Emily admitted, laying her head back to the pillow. "My head and stomach hurt."

"Uh huh. See, I told you that's what drinking does to you," Alex scolded. "You should've listened, but you wanted to experiment."

"Well…" Emily curled into the fetal position. "At least I was relaxed...if only for a little while."

"Maybe *so*, but the aftereffect isn't worth a few moments relaxation," Alex pointed out, voice stern. Emily let out a long sigh. "So I take it you're not well enough to come with me to see Stacey and Victoria?"

"I think I'll be lucky *just* to make it out of bed today," Emily chuckled. "At least it's Saturday."

"True," Alex responded, not hiding the disappointment. *First Chasity and Malajia backed out, and now Emily*, she thought. "Well, get some rest sis. We'll meet up later for dinner if you're up to it."

"Okay," Emily agreed.

"So, how does it feel to be back at Torrence Hall?" Alex asked Sidra as they made their way up the building steps.

Sidra giggled. "This dorm wasn't bad to live in," she replied, pushing her ponytail over her shoulder. "I miss it a little."

"Yeah, Wilson Hall wasn't that bad either," Alex put in before dissolving into laughter. "That is a whole lie. That dorm was terrible." After a quick breakfast with Sidra, the girls journeyed to Sidra's old stomping grounds to visit Alex's friends, who had just moved in a few days ago.

As the girls walked down the hall towards the door, Alex gave Sidra a soft nudge. "I can't wait until we can all hang out together," she gushed.

Sidra just returned Alex's big smile with one of her own. Alex's smile never faded as she knocked on the door.

"Alex!" Stacey Addison exclaimed, opening the door. Sidra was amused, watching the two friends embrace. She'd almost forgotten how many inches shorter Stacey was than Alex. The light skinned, bubbly, curvy girl with the freshly done, long braids and cute baby face looked more like Alex's little sister than her friend.

Victoria James stood from her bed and folded her arms. "You were supposed to come over *last night*," she spat.

Alex looked at her, smile fading. "Sorry, I got held up," she replied, full of remorse.

Victoria didn't reply; she just stood there, a scowl held on her face. *I guess you got held up, hanging out with your new little friends,* she thought, fuming.

Sidra walked into the room behind Alex and noticed Victoria cut her eye at her. Not wanting to immediately go off on the girl, she forced a smile. "Nice to see you again, Victoria,"

"Hey," Victoria mumbled, rolling her eyes at her.

Victoria remembered the slender, well-dressed, prissy girl from when she visited Alex in Philadelphia last semester. She took in Sidra's outfit of white capri pants, royal blue, short sleeved top with matching pumps. That, along with the long, straight ponytail and side-swept bangs just screamed 'stuck up' to Victoria. *What's up with the damn high heels so early in the morning?* she thought, tugging on the baggy grey t-shirt that she had on.

Sidra squinted her eyes at Victoria, desperately trying to contain her temper. *I swear to God, I'm two seconds from smacking her.*

Witnessing the childish response from Victoria, Alex shook her head. *Damn Vicki, don't start.* Victoria had always been the jealous type. But in Alex's eyes, she didn't have to be. Victoria's tall, lean frame, long, thick black hair twists and glowing brown completion wasn't a cause for her to be jealous of anyone. But for some reason, the girl never could share attention.

Stacey, also noticing Victoria's behavior, walked over to her and tapped her arm. "Stop being mean, it's not that serious," she whispered to her. Victoria rolled her eyes and flopped back down on her bed.

"So what *did* you ladies do last night?" Stacey asked, twisting her braids into a bun. "I'm sure it was more fun than unpacking."

"We went to a party in the clusters," Sidra answered.

"I'm sure she was asking *Alex*, not *you,*" Victoria mumbled.

Sidra, having heard the snide comment, turned to Alex and whispered, "Alex, your little friend is on my last nerve, I'm *so* serious."

Alex put her hand up to silence Sidra's complaining. "Vicki, what's wrong with you?" she asked, frowning.

"Nothing," Victoria lied.

"Don't lie," Alex chastised. "*Clearly* you have an attitude about me not coming over last night and I'm sorry for that. But you don't get to take it out on Sidra by being rude."

"Alex don't worry about it, it's *not* that serious," Stacey put in, cutting her eye at Victoria. "She's just being her normal salty self."

Alex resisted the urge to chuckle at Stacey. She looked at Victoria, who looked like her feelings were hurt. "Let me make it up to you," she proposed. "I'm starting work again at the Pizza Shack, and my boss said that I can bring whoever I want in for a free dinner tonight, why don't you both come?"

"Sure," Stacey beamed. "You know my greedy butt wants some free food," she giggled, soon joined by Sidra.

Victoria wasn't impressed with the offer. "So you mean to tell me that you already planned on going with *them* and now you want to invite us to *tag along*?" she sneered. "That's insulting."

Alex took a deep breath, trying to keep calm. She was used to this behavior; she remembered dealing with it when Stacey first came into the picture freshman year of high school. "Yes, I *did* invite the other girls to come, but that's not to say that I wasn't going to invite you two…I'm just getting over here *today*."

"What's wrong with your phone?" Victoria groused.

Sidra let out a quick sigh; she couldn't take it anymore. "Alex, I'll be waiting outside," she threw over her shoulder, walking out.

Alex put her hands on her hips. "Seriously Vicki?" Victoria just stared at her short nails, ignoring Alex's gaze. Alex sucked her teeth. "Stacey, when you're finished unpacking, come over to my dorm."

Stacey nodded.

"I'm done with *this* one," Alex hissed in Victoria's

direction before walking out.

Stacey flinched at the loud slamming of the door. "Girl, what's your damn problem?" she snapped at Victoria.

"I don't like those girls," Victoria barked.

"Why *not*? They didn't even *do* anything to you," Stacey threw back. "I hate this side of you."

Victoria just shrugged, unfazed.

Alex kept her thoughts about Victoria to herself while she and Sidra made their way back to their dorm. "Let's go see what these two are doing," she said, finally breaking the silence as they approached Chasity and Malajia's room.

"Hopefully they didn't kill each other," Sidra joked, knocking on the door. She placed her ear to the door. "I hear Chasity yelling, so they're still alive."

Chasity snatched open the door. "Sidra, get your fuckin' friend," she bit out, pointing to Malajia who was dancing near her dresser to no music.

"It's only been a day sweetie," Sidra laughed. "Just give it time. She'll get on your nerves even more as each day passes."

"I heard that," Malajia ground out.

Chasity stared at Sidra, who found Chasity's agitation amusing. "Sidra, I will pay you a thousand dollars right now if you switch rooms with Malajia," she offered.

"Okay!" Sidra exclaimed, turning to head back out the door.

Alex stopped her by grabbing her arm. "Oh no you don't," she put in. "There's no switching roommates. Grow up and deal with who you were assigned with."

"Nobody asked *your* fat ass anything," Chasity threw back, tone nasty.

Alex made a face at her. "Snapping at *me* isn't gonna change your roommate situation," she pointed out, earning an eye roll from Chasity. "And I keep telling you heifer's, I'm not fat…I'm *curvy*, there's a difference."

Sidra walked over to Chasity's bed. "So Chaz, if you're still feeling generous, you can still put that thousand into my bank account," she teased.

"Go to hell," Chasity sneered.

"All right, fine," Sidra chuckled, sitting down.

Alex shook her head as she watched Malajia rifle through Chasity's jewelry box. "God girl, do you ever quit?" she laughed.

Chasity spun around to see Malajia holding a pair of her diamond drop earrings to her ears, staring at herself in a full-length mirror.

Chasity pinched the bridge of her nose. The girl had been irritating her ever since she woke up that morning. "Malajia," she called, teeth clenched.

Malajia spun around, her full, glossed lips curved into a wide smile. "Yes, sunshine?" she taunted.

"If you don't put my earrings down, I swear to—" Chasity was so annoyed that she couldn't even get the rest of her threat out, before lunging towards Malajia.

"Oh no, no, there'll be none of that," Alex quickly interjected, wrapping her arms around Chasity.

As Chasity struggled to get out of Alex's grip, Malajia pointed at her, "You come near me and I'll smack your damn clothes backwards," she barked.

"Get off me, Alex," Chasity warned, trying to pry the girl's hands off of her waist.

"You'll smack her *clothes* backwards?" Sidra asked, confusion on her face and in her voice.

"Mel, you better put her earrings down because my arms are getting tired," Alex advised, trying to keep her arms locked in place. "This girl is strong."

"Alex don't you let her go!" Malajia shouted, seeing Chasity pull away. "Don't you da—" she screamed and began running around the room with Chasity chasing after her. "Chaz quit it! I put them back, I put them back," she wailed, running into the bathroom and slamming the door.

"Mel, open the door," Chasity ordered, banging on it.

"Do I look stupid to you?" Malajia shouted from the other side.

Sidra slowly raised her hand. "Can I answer that?" she joked.

"Shut up, Sidra," Malajia huffed.

"Chasity, calm it down cranky, you know she's stupid," Alex commented, hearing a knock at the door.

"Stop talking shit about me when I'm not out there," Malajia barked.

Ignoring Malajia's comment, Alex opened the door to find Mark and Jason standing there. "Ugh, *you* guys huh?" she scoffed, moving aside to let them in.

"You rude as shit, and this isn't even your room, bee," Mark spat out.

"Who the hell is *bee*?" Alex asked.

"Some bullshit he made up on the way over here," Jason chortled, leaning up against Chasity's dresser.

"Whatever man," Mark ground out, waving his hand dismissively. "It's gonna stick, watch."

"Please, this gonna be just like that 'penguin with shades on' shit that he tried to make stick in high school," Malajia commented from the bathroom.

Mark rolled his eyes. "Aye Mel, shut up and bring your ass out here," he demanded.

Malajia cautiously pulled the door open and peered out. Sensing that Chasity was nearby, she sucked her teeth. "Chasity, I'm not stupid," she fussed. "I'm not coming out until you move."

"Fine, stay in there," Chasity smirked before hitting the door with her forearm. The force from the hit almost caused the door to hit Malajia in the face.

"Damn Chasity!" Malajia wailed. "You tryna take my nose off?"

"It would be an improvement," Mark laughed.

Malajia snatched the door open and walked out. "I heard what you said, you black bastard," she hurled at Mark as she sat on her bed.

"Okay, enough with all the nonsense," Alex cut in, trying to cut short the impending argument that was about to happen between Malajia and Mark. "So about dinner tonight—"

"Brace yourself," Sidra chimed in, brushing a piece of lint from her shirt.

Alex shot Sidra a warning glance before turning her attention back to the other girls. "Anyway," she began. "So, you remember how I invited you out to a pizza dinner at the Pizza Shack?"

"Yes, free food," Mark rejoiced, holding his hand up for a high-five from Alex.

"I wasn't talking to you," Alex quickly threw back, pointing at him.

His mouth dropped open as he put his hand down. "Damn, that's rude yo," he griped.

"No, what's *rude* is the fact that you're always looking to freeload," Alex scolded, placing her hands on her hips. "Now if you don't mind, I'd like to continue talking to my girls."

"Damn. She told *you*," Jason teased.

"Shut up," Mark returned.

Alex rolled her eyes, then focused her attention on Chasity and Malajia. "So…I invited Stacey to come with us," she revealed, "…and Victoria," she mumbled, turning away from the girls piercing gaze.

"For *what* though?" Malajia asked as Chasity shot Alex a glare. "Alex, ain't nobody tryna deal with her all night."

"Come on girls," Alex pleaded. "She's not that bad once you get to know her."

"Alex, I'm sorry, but that attitude that she gave off earlier isn't helping your argument," Sidra cut in, standing from the bed.

Alex exhaled loudly. "Look…she just isn't used to dealing with a bunch of different girls," she explained. "She'll get used to you. I just don't want there to be any problems tonight."

"Oh there won't be any problems at all," Chasity assured, pushing some hair behind her ear.

Alex smiled as Malajia shot Chasity a quizzical look. "Really?" Alex beamed.

"Yeah…Because I'm not *going*," Chasity hissed, heading for her closet.

"God, can you not be difficult for *once*?" Alex fussed.

"Nope," Chasity returned.

"Please? I'm standing here practically *begging* you three to just give my friend a chance," Alex pressed, voice calm.

"Alex, I don't like her," Chasity reminded.

"I *know* that," Alex replied, fixing her eyes on Chasity. "But I'm asking you to put your feelings aside for one night for *me*." The three girls exchanged glances with each other. "If things don't go right tonight, then…you don't have to worry about me asking you again."

"Well, that's reason enough for *me* to go," Malajia put in, enthused. "'Cause when Victoria pisses everybody off…and she *will*, we don't have to worry about Alex whining about it anymore."

Alex just made a face at Malajia.

Mark put his hand up. "So…I'm really not invited?" he asked.

"What part of 'no' did you not get?" Alex sneered, fixing a confused gaze upon him.

"The 'no' part, 'cause you never actually *said* it," Mark returned sarcastically.

"God, Mark will you get the hell out?!" Malajia snapped, slapping her hand on the bed repeatedly. "I'm tired of seeing your damn face."

"It's not just *your* room," Mark shot back, folding his arms, a smug look on his dark brown face. "You don't get to just make me leave without your roommate's say so."

"Mark, get the fuck out," Chasity demanded, voice calm. Jason snickered at the salty look on Mark's face.

"Well damn," Mark groused.

Chapter 5

"I wonder where they are," Stacey said, glancing at her watch. "You said seven, right Alex?"

Alex sighed. It was now a half-hour past when the girls were supposed to meet her at the Pizza Shack for dinner. Nobody answered their phones and Alex was beginning to worry. *I hope they're okay…or that they didn't decide to back out at the last minute.* "Yeah, I said seven," Alex confirmed to both Stacey and a sullen Victoria, who just played with a piece of straw paper. "I'm sure they'll be here soon, I know traffic is pretty rough around this time."

Victoria sucked her teeth. "Go ahead and make excuses for them, Alex," she scoffed. "Bottom line…they're late and that's rude."

"You act like *you've* never been late for anything," Stacey threw back, interrupting the words that Alex was about to speak.

"Oh so now you're on team *them*?" Victoria sneered.

"I'm on team whoever is Alex's friend and *acts* like it," Stacey argued.

"What is *that* supposed to mean?" Victoria barked.

Alex put her hands up. "Girls, that's enough. Chill out," she abruptly cut in. The last thing she needed was for

Victoria and Stacey to be at odds with each other. She looked at both girls who were now quiet. "This arguing is unnecessary…and so is your attitude, Victoria."

Victoria tossed the paper she was playing with, on the table. "No, your *new clique* is unnecessary," she grumbled, sitting back in her seat.

Alex checked her reply once she heard the girls' voices.

"Hey everybody," Emily greeted, sitting down in one of the empty seats.

Alex smiled back. "How's that hangover?"

"It's better," Emily replied, rubbing her eye. "The aspirin and ginger ale that I had a little earlier helped."

"I hope you learned your lesson," Alex said, earning a slight nod from Emily as she looked down at the table.

"Sorry we're late," Sidra apologized, sitting down along with Chasity and Malajia. "The heel on Malajia's sandal broke when she was running down the steps. So of *course* we had to suffer through all the whining and complaining she did while she changed her shoes…and the entire *outfit* to go with it."

Malajia glared at Sidra for several seconds. "Didn't nobody ask you for the full recap," she spat out, slamming her purse on the table. "You need to stop bitchin' about waiting. I would do it for *y'all*."

"No, what *you* need to do is stop buying those cheap ass shoes," Chasity chimed in as she looked at a menu.

Malajia's head snapped towards her. "Buy me some expensive ones then, rich bitch," she demanded.

"I'm not your man *or* your daddy, you fuckin' freak," Chasity nonchalantly shot back, earning two middle fingers and a face from Malajia.

Stacey placed a menu over her face to conceal her laughter, as Alex slammed her hand on the table in anger.

"Ladies, can we get through *one* meal where you're not throwing insults?" Alex griped, before pointing to Chasity. "Chaz, that was rude. Stop it. We have company."

Chasity shot Alex a confused glance. "Did she *not* just

call me a bitch in front of *company*?"

"Oh, you should be used to the title by now," Malajia scoffed with a wave of her hand.

Alex rubbed her temples with her fingers. *This is going to be a long dinner,* she thought.

Surprisingly for Alex, Chasity and Malajia were behaving for the most part. It was only an hour into dinner, but for those two, that was a miracle. The one who wasn't behaving was Victoria. The eye rolls and the comments under her breath were beginning to wear thin with her and the other girls, who had yet to address it.

"So, homecoming will be here in a few weeks," Stacey said, before taking a bite of her pizza. "How is it here? Is it fun?"

"Yeah, they usually do activities of some sort. Then we have a big football game," Sidra informed.

"Yes, girl, I can't wait. We're supposed to be playing Prime State University, our rival school," Malajia eagerly added. "Their team may suck, but those players...talk about fine. I can't wait to get my hands on one of those chocolate drops."

"And they'll ignore you like every *other* guy on the face of this earth," Chasity put in, poking at the lettuce on her plate of half-eaten salad.

Alex giggled. "Chaz, you were doing so well."

Malajia flagged Chasity with her hand. "Her damn comments don't faze me," she assured. "Besides, she's a whole liar. I'm too sexy for *any* guy to ignore."

"Sounds like something a ho would say," Victoria mumbled.

"You think nobody heard you say that shit?" Chasity hissed, fixing her with an angry gaze.

"Obviously she thinks *so*," Malajia seethed, folding her arms. "Did you just call me a ho?"

"I hope for her sake, she *didn't*," Sidra jumped in.

"Okay, okay, now I'm sure she didn't really say that," Alex interjected, holding her arm out in front of Victoria.

"Yes she *did*," Chasity argued. "Just like she's *been* saying little smart shit for the past damn hour."

"Alex, you better get your friend, because she don't know me like that," Malajia fumed. As far as Malajia was concerned, she might banter with Chasity, but at the end of the day they were friends. Victoria didn't know her, therefore the insulting comments weren't going to fly.

Alex ran both hands through her hair. "Can everybody just calm down?" she pleaded.

"No," Chasity replied, pushing her plate back. The smug look on Victoria's face nearly sent her over the edge. "Alex can I *please* slap her?" Chasity snarled.

"No, violence won't be necessary, Chaz," Alex replied, voice full of disappointment.

"Necessary my *ass*," Malajia returned, furious. "It wasn't *necessary* for her to make that smart-ass comment. Shit, let her slap the bitch. Hell, let *me* do it."

"Nobody is slapping *any*body!" Alex wailed.

Victoria shot Chasity a challenging look. "Girl, I wish you *would* try to slap me," she bit out.

Sidra rested her elbow on the table and leaned her head on her hand. "Aww shit," she mumbled, knowing her friend and her temper all too well.

Chasity smirked as her eyes burrowed through Victoria's face. Any other time, she would've jumped across the table and taken the girls head off. But for Alex's sake, Chasity decided to give Victoria a reprieve. "Trust me when I say, that's not a wish you want fulfilled, bitch," she hissed.

"Chasity don't leave," Alex pleaded, watching Chasity get up from her seat. "Let's just talk this out."

"*You* talk. *I'm* done," Chasity spat out, before walking out.

Alex sighed when both Sidra and Malajia rose from their seats. She knew that there was no chance of them ever giving Victoria another shot.

"See you back at the room, Alex," Sidra said, tucking her clutch under her arm. "Stacey, *you're* welcomed anytime."

Stacey nodded as Sidra walked out.

Malajia fluffed her curls with her hand. "Yeah, and I'm—"

"Malajia, just come on!" Sidra called after her.

The bass in Sidra's voice startled her. "Damn, I was coming," Malajia fussed, walking off. "Can a sistah finish her sentence? Rude ass."

"Are you okay?" Emily asked Alex after a few moments of strained silence. Even though she rode with the other girls, she couldn't just leave Alex sitting there, knowing that she was upset.

"No, not yet," Alex replied, glaring at Victoria, who was looking down at the table while tearing up a napkin.

"Lay her ass out, Alex," Stacey prompted, folding her arms.

"No Stacey, before I talk to your ignorant ass friend, I'm going to have to calm myself down," Alex replied. "Because the way I feel right *now*...I can choke the hell out of her."

Emily, walked into her room later that evening and grabbed the TV remote. All she wanted to do was lay in bed and drift off to sleep to the sound of her favorite TV show. With her hangover nearly gone, she was looking forward to a peaceful rest.

She grabbed her pillow and propped it under her head, then closed her eyes. She groaned when she heard the phone ring. "This can only be one person," she said to herself, reaching for it. "Hello?"

"Emily sweetie, where were you? I was calling for the past hour!" Ms. Harris exclaimed into the phone.

Emily rolled her eyes and sat up, cradling the phone between her ear and her shoulder. *I knew it*, she thought. Having just left Alex mere minutes ago, she knew it wasn't her calling. "Um, I was in the library," she lied.

"Emily you know better than to be out this late by yourself," Ms. Harris scolded, she heard Emily's soft sigh come through the phone. "But, at least you were studying and not hanging out with those little hood rats."

Here she goes again! Emily screamed to herself. "No Mommy, I wasn't," she lied again. The last thing Emily wanted to endure after a long day of feeling like crap was her mother hollering at her about the company she was keeping. It was a well-known fact that Ms. Harris didn't like the girls and thought they were bad influences on her youngest daughter.

"That's my girl," Ms. Harris gushed. "I would hate to make you come home every weekend again."

Emily felt a chill go down her spine as she recalled the events of last semester. After getting caught in a lie that allowed Emily to go to Miami for spring break with the group, her overprotective mother punished her by making her come home every weekend. Emily was miserable. She was elated when her mother granted her a reprieve at the start of the school year. Emily figured that having her own room away from the girls satisfied her mother.

"Hey, how about you come home next weekend?" Ms. Harris suggested, breaking into Emily's thoughts.

Emily's eyes widened. *Is she serious? I just left home yesterday.* "Mommy, my classes start this week and I know I'll have a lot of homework to do during the weekend," she protested. She closed her eyes tight, hoping that her mother would not try to press the subject further. "Maybe some other time."

Ms. Harris sighed. "Well…okay sweetie, I'll just hang by myself then," she replied, not hiding her disappointment.

Emily hated to hear the disappointment in her mother's voice. "Sorry," she sputtered.

"It's fine," Ms. Harris assured. "Anyway, I have something on the stove. I'll call you tomorrow."

"All right, I love you."

"Love you too, bye."

Emily slowly placed the phone back on the receiver. "I'm sorry. I hate lying to you, but you leave me no choice," she sighed to herself.

Chapter 6

Monday morning arrived and Malajia was none too happy. "God, why do I have to have freakin' Algebra 2 first thing in the damn morning?" she complained loudly as she and Chasity walked through the crowded campus towards their respective class buildings.

"The same reason why I have Accounting with Mark…life's a bitch," Chasity replied in an even tone, glancing at her watch.

Malajia looked at her. "Ooh, you got class with *Mark*?" she laughed. Chasity slowly turned her head and narrowed her eyes at the laughing Malajia. "Ooh, good luck with that. He'll work every last nerve you have, trust me."

Chasity shook her head, looking ahead. Seeing Mark jogging towards them, she sucked her teeth. "And here comes nature's mistake now," she griped.

Malajia stomped her foot on the ground as Mark nearly tripped over his own feet. "Look at this fool," she scoffed.

Mark dusted his sneaker off and continued his approach, stopping right in front of them. "Y'all ain't see that," he joked.

"Damn, *everybody* knows we hang out together," Malajia fussed. "Stop doing stupid shit to draw attention to yourself."

Mark looked at Malajia for a second before taking his hand and wiping the sweat from his forehead.

Malajia flinched as he flung his hand at her. "Oh God, I'm about to die," she gasped, frantically wiping his sweat from her cheek.

Chasity was growing tired of the banter. "What do you want, you freak?" she sneered.

Mark flashed a winning smile. "If I told you what I *really* want, Jason would kick my ass," he joked.

Chasity turned her lip up in disgust. "Eww."

Malajia huffed loudly. "Man, don't nobody wanna sleep with your ugly ass," she barked, putting her hand up near his face.

Mark threw his head back in agitation. "I'm *far* from ugly," he boasted. "You already *know* that, and you mad 'cause you want me."

"Yeah, whatever," Malajia mumbled, turning away. Sure Mark was tall, dark, with a solid build; and if she didn't despise him, she'd find him attractive; but Malajia wasn't about to let *him* know that.

"Anyway Chasity, come on. Let's leave big mouth to walk by her-damn-self," he directed to Chasity. "Our Accounting class awaits."

"Don't remind me," Chasity complained, running her fingers through her loose curls.

Mark chuckled as he placed his arm around Chasity's shoulder. "Come on evil, let's get our learnin' on."

"Fine," Chasity sighed, allowing herself to be led away.

"You're gonna fail the class *anyway,* you bastard," Malajia hurled at Mark's back.

"Just like your *parents* failed when they created *your* wack ass," he threw over his shoulder.

Malajia's mouth fell open at the insult. A smirk formed

on her face after a second. "Good one," she mused to herself, heading off to her class.

Sidra panted as she hurried up the stairs to Paradise Terrace. Having left the textbook that she needed for class on the bed, she only had a few moments to spare before she was going to be late.

Finally making it to her room, she collapsed on the bed. "Never do that again," she heavily panted. She grabbed the book from her bed and tucked it under her arm. As she headed for the door, she searched in her purse for a tissue and shrieked when she felt something prick her finger. Pulling her hand from the bag, she groaned at the sight of blood. She rolled her eyes when she pulled the cause of the prick from her bag.

"Freakin' Malajia, sticking these damn earrings in my bag," she seethed, eyeing the large hoop earring in her hand. Irritated, she tossed the book and her purse on the bed.

She stomped over to the bathroom and opened the door. The pain in Sidra's finger was the furthest thing from her mind once she laid eyes on the clutter littering her neighbor's side.

"Why the hell are their freakin' clothes all over the shower?" she fussed to herself. "And they can't clean the damn makeup off the sink when they're done?" Spotting the trash on the floor nearly sent her over the edge. Anybody who knew Sidra, knew that messiness was her biggest pet peeve. Sidra took a deep breath as she knocked on her neighbors adjoining door, forcing a smile once it opened.

"Yes?" a voluptuous dark skinned girl answered.

"Hi, so, I know you and your roommate got settled the other day, so I wanted to come and introduce myself," Sidra politely put out. "I'm Sidra." She stuck her hand out for the smiling girl to shake, but immediately pulled it back when she noticed a greasy substance covering her hand.

The girl looked at her hand and laughed. "Sorry, I was spraying oil on my hair and it got on my hand," she explained, wiping her hand on her black tights. "I'm Deidre. People call me Dee." Dee Parlor was built like Alex, her thick shape was proportioned in the right places and she wore her naturally kinky hair cut short.

Sidra returned Dee's greeting with a smile.

"Sidra huh?" Dee asked, coming to a realization. "Your name sounds familiar. Are you one of the girls who got into that big, talked about fight last semester?"

Sidra put her hand over face from embarrassment. She was tired of being known for the fight. "Yeah I *am*," she confirmed. "Not one of my *classiest* moments. But it was necessary at the time."

"Well, shit happens," Dee replied, scratching her head. She scanned Sidra from head to toe. *She's pretty and seems nice enough....not like the snobby chick that people say she is.* Sidra was about to open her mouth to say something but Dee quickly cut her off. "So I just transferred here at the end of last semester from Cal University."

Chick, I don't care that much. "Oh so you're from California," Sidra concluded, feigning enthusiasm.

"Originally yeah. My family moved to Virginia, so I decided to transfer schools to be closer to them."

"Aww isn't that sweet." Sidra's smile was bright, despite what she was thinking. Not that she didn't think the girl was nice, she just wasn't interested in small talk.

"So, homecoming is coming up, how much fun is it going to be?" Dee asked, enthused.

Sidra looked at the silver watch on her wrist. "Um, it should be pretty fun. Listen before I get to class, I wanted to ask you about this mess in the bathroom."

Dee frowned slightly. *Damn just change the subject why don't you?* "That's my roommates junk," she replied.

"Oh okay," Sidra nodded. "I'm just saying, it looks a little tacky when one side is spotless and the other side, is you know...disgusting."

Dee just stood there, staring at Sidra as she continued to talk. *And there's the snob that everybody talks about.*

"So if you could please just ask her to clean up her mess, that would be great," Sidra politely said.

"I really don't think it looks that bad," Dee threw back, folding her arms.

Sidra raised an arched eyebrow. "*Really?*"

Dee narrowed her eyes at Sidra's smart tone. "Anyway, she was in a rush this morning so she didn't get a chance to clean."

Sidra held a smile on her face as the patience left her body. "Was she in a rush *yesterday* too?"

"Not sure. But I'm sure she'll clean it when she gets *ready* to," Dee returned.

Sidra let out a chuckle. "If you could just let her know what I said, that would be great," she said, completely done with the conversation.

"Sure, no problem," Dee responded, all traces of politeness gone from her face. She glared at Sidra's back as Sidra walked out of the bathroom, shutting the door behind her. "Stuck up bitch," she seethed to herself before heading back inside of her room.

Chasity stretched her neck before focusing her eyes back on her laptop screen. "I hate essays," she complained to herself. After a long day of classes, she, like many students, was in her room doing homework. She peered at the notes in her notebook before looking back at her screen. "Think girl," she coaxed herself. The sound of her cell phone ringing offered a welcomed distraction.

"Hello?" she answered without looking at the caller ID.

"Hey beautiful," a deep voice crooned through the phone.

She ran a hand over the back of her neck. "What's up Jason?" she returned, voice unenthused.

He chuckled. "Not excited to hear from me, huh?"

"I never *am*," she joked, then smirked when a gasp came through the phone. "No, I'm just stressing over this essay," she amended. "This English Literature class is the devil."

This time Jason laughed. "I had it last semester, it isn't that bad."

"Maybe for *you*, but I hate writing essays and shit. Literature is stupid and it bores me," she fussed. "I hate it *almost* as much as I hate Calculus."

"You have Calc 3?"

"*Unfortunately*," Chasity griped. "All my classes this semester are some bullshit. I mean, Calculus, this dumbass Lit class, Econ 2, Computer Language 3, Public speaking, *and* Accounting…I see some stressful days ahead of me."

"Why are you taking six classes?" Jason asked, curious. "It's not like you repeated anything from last year."

"'Cause I'm out of my damn mind," Chasity realized. "Just want to get as many out of the way as I can *now*, I guess."

"Chasity, you're a bright student and your grades always prove that. And Computer Language should be a breeze for you, you know computers like the back of your hand," Jason assured, tone comforting. "Just do what you've *been* doing and you'll be fine…Now, if you need me to tutor you in Calculus again—"

"I *don't*," Chasity quickly shut down. The last thing she wanted was to admit that she needed help again. "I'll be fine."

"Okay…just let me know if you change your mind. I'll be happy to help."

"Uh huh, it'll just give you an excuse to be in my face," she teased.

"Well, that's a perk," Jason threw back, voice filled with amusement. "Listen, I'm about to grab a bite to eat and you seem like you can use a break. Do you want to join me? No cafeteria food, my treat."

"No, not really hungry," she declined, repeatedly hitting a key on her keyboard.

"Okay then," he murmured, not hiding his disappointment. He just wanted one chance to take Chasity out and she was turning him down every chance that she got. "I'll check on you later."

"Yep," she replied before ending the call. She sat the phone on the desk and put her head in her hands. Truth was, she could've used the break, but spending alone time with Jason was not a pressure that she could handle at that moment. Not when he'd been on her mind more often than not.

The door swung open and Malajia barged in. "Chaz, you wanna go to a get-together in the clusters?" she asked, tossing her purse and books on her bed.

"I don't wanna go *anywhere* with you," Chasity spat, tone even, rising from her seat.

"Come on, there'll be drinks," Malajia pressed.

Chasity looked at Malajia as if she was crazy. "It's *Monday,* you drunk," she jeered.

"Oh so *what*. My Algebra class killed me today with all their formulas and shit," Malajia griped, with a wave of her hand. "Hell, I *need* a damn drink."

"Find another way to de-stress," Chasity suggested, reaching into her mini-refrigerator for a bottle of juice.

"Pass me one," Malajia demanded, holding her hand out.

"Fuck you and no," Chasity threw back, twisting the top off.

"Are you really gonna be that damn stingy?" Malajia fussed, folding her arms. "You know I ran out of my *own* juice last night."

"Sounds like your thirsty ass has a personal problem," Chasity replied, sitting back at her desk.

Malajia stared at Chasity's back in anger. Between being denied a juice and being told 'no' at her request for Chasity to come hang out with her, she felt like getting back. Malajia stomped over to Chasity, reached over her shoulder and started pushing keys on the laptop.

"Girl!" Chasity wailed, delivering a stinging slap to

Malajia's exposed arm as she pushed herself up from her chair. "Are you out of your damn mind?"

"Your work is messed up, now let's go," Malajia taunted. She then winced and grabbed her arm. "Damn, that shit hurt," she whined, rubbing it. "Do you *have* to hit so freakin' hard?"

Chasity stood with a frown on her face and was about to retort but her words were interrupted by a knock at the door.

"What?!" both girls barked in unison.

Alex walked through the door holding a large pizza box, and a smile on her face.

"I didn't hear either *one* of us tell you to come in," Malajia sneered.

Alex sucked her teeth. "As many times as you barge in *my* damn room unannounced? Girl please," she bit back. "At least *I knocked.*"

Malajia rolled her eyes, but decided against making a comment for once.

"Anyway, I bought this pizza home from work. Do you want some?"

"No," Chasity grunted.

"You always tryna feed somebody that pizza," Malajia scoffed.

Alex put her hand up at Malajia. *I was just enjoying her damn silence.* She focused her attention on Chasity. "I barely saw you eat today," she pointed out, voice stern.

Chasity shot Alex a quizzical look. "So?" she ground out. "And you weren't with me all damn day, so you don't know what you're talking about."

"Yeah okay, you can be a smart ass all you *want*," Alex returned, sitting the pizza box on Malajia's nightstand. "And granted I *wasn't* with you all day, but when we went to breakfast *and* lunch in the cafeteria, you barely ate, so…eat this pizza before you fall out."

Chasity flagged Alex in a dismissive gesture, as she sat down in her seat.

Malajia busted out laughing, "Ahhhh, Chasity got told

off like a two-year-old," she teased. "And her homework looks like trash."

"Alex, Malajia's trying to go to the clusters by herself for some drunk ass party on a Monday night," Chasity revealed, tone dry.

Malajia's mouth fell open as Alex regarded her with a stern look. "Malajia, there's nothing going on in those clusters tonight but foolishness," Alex chided.

"You can't stop me from going, you fat mop," Malajia hissed, earning a snicker from Chasity.

Alex's eyes became slits. "Call me fat one more time, hear?" she warned, pointing a finger at Malajia. "And *I* may not be able to stop you, but your *parents* will when I call them."

"Bitch, you ain't gonna call my parents," Malajia shot back, tone confident. "You said you lost the number."

"Oh *I* have it," Chasity chimed in, grabbing her phone.

Malajia look at her. "You roommate traitor," she seethed.

Alex flashed a satisfied grin Malajia's way. "Sit your butt down and do some homework," she ordered before heading out of the room.

"Snitch," Malajia hurled at Chasity.

"Yeah? I bet you stay your ass in and do that homework," Chasity returned, unfazed by Malaria's betrayed feelings.

Malajia flopped down on the bed. "Oh I'll *do* it," she mumbled. "But not 'cause *she* said it…that party is probably dry anyway."

Chapter 7

"I get to see some fine ass men in tight football uniforms," Malajia sang as she danced in Sidra's face.

"Contain your hormones, Mel," Sidra said, thumbing through her daily planner. Two weeks had passed and homecoming week was finally approaching Paradise Valley University.

Malajia stopped dancing and regarded Sidra with disgust. "You are so *dry!*" she hurled, flopping down next to her on the bench outside their dorm. Malajia for one, couldn't wait for next week's activities to begin. She was ready to let loose and relieve some stress.

"That is your opinion and it's a stupid one," Sidra replied in an even tone, eyes not leaving the pages.

"No, your dryness is a *fact*," Malajia threw back, earning a side glance from Sidra.

"I hope you know *just* how gross that sounds," she sneered.

Malajia, having caught on after a few seconds, made a face. "Eww, wasn't nobody talkin' about your lady parts," she scoffed. Sidra shook her head. "You *need* to get hype. This is gonna be fun...think of the parties, the sexy alumni men. In fact, there's a party on Saturday."

"How much partying do you think you'll be doing while your parents are down here?" Sidra asked, looking up from her book.

Malajia's head snapped toward her. "What are you talking about?"

Sidra fixed her bangs with her fingers. "Family weekend is this weekend," she answered, much to Malajia's horror.

"Oh come *on*!" Malajia barked, slamming her hand on the bench.

Sidra closed her planner, uncrossed her legs, and stood up from the bench. "Yeah, so you better watch yourself this weekend," she advised.

"I'm not watching *shit*," Malajia huffed. "My parents aren't tryna come down here for some stupid family weekend mess. They *barely* want to come down here to drop my ass off."

"If you say so," Sidra shrugged. "You just better pick out some 'mother appropriate' clothing just in case."

Malajia didn't respond as Sidra walked off. Mood dampened, she just sat there and folded her arms in a huff.

Alex held the cordless phone to her ear as she sat on her bed. "Yeah Ma, are you coming down this weekend?" she asked.

"Yes, me and your sister will be there," Mrs. Chisolm gushed through the phone. "Sahara is so excited."

Alex giggled. "I know, I talked to her yesterday. She can't wait," she replied, propping a pillow behind her back. "And neither can *I*. I miss you guys. It's a shame that Dad and Semaj can't come."

"Child, your brother has been talking about that sleepover he's going to this weekend for months now…getting on my nerves," Mrs. Chisolm grumbled. "There was *no* way I was going to make him miss it."

Alex laughed out loud. Her little brother did have the tendency to go on and on when he was excited about something.

"And you know that your father has to work."

"I know." Alex's tone was somber. "I wish he didn't have to work so much though. I know he's tired."

"You don't concern yourself with that," Mrs. Chisolm urged, voice stern. "Your father works hard for his family, and he never wants you or your siblings to feel bad about that...So *don't*, do you hear me?"

"I hear you Ma," Alex assured, twisting a few strands of hair around her finger. "So are you riding down with Aunt Karen?"

"Yeah, I'm riding with that crazy fool," her mother joked. "She's been running her mouth about seeing her first niece at college...*she's* on my nerves too."

"You leave my auntie alone," Alex teased. "But I have to get ready to head to class, so I'll call you later."

"All right my love, see you this weekend."

Alex smiled as she hung up the phone. She couldn't wait to get her arms around her mother and little sister. Looking at the clock on her nightstand, she hopped up from the bed.

Alex darted out of the dorm door and jogged down the steps. Hearing her name being called made her stop and turn around. "Hey Stacey, what's up?" she smiled, seeing Stacey walk up to her.

"On your way to class, I take it," Stacey chortled, noticing the hurried expression on her friends face.

"Girl yes, on my way to this Spanish class," Alex returned, rolling down the sleeves of her grey and maroon school sweatshirt. The weather was taking a chilly turn. Fall was surely on its way. "What's up? You look like you want to ask me something."

Stacey shrugged as she moved some of her braids out of her face. "I was hoping that I could tag along to lunch with you and the girls a little later," she put out. "I don't want to go by myself...Victoria is getting on my nerves."

"*Sure* you can," Alex smiled. She was happy that Stacey

had taken a liking to her friends, and vice versa. "Come over around one…and try not to be too hard on Vicki."

"No Alex, she's on my nerves," Stacey bit out. "I'm regretting rooming with her…We put each other's name down as a preference when we both got accepted senior year...I wish I knew then what I know *now*."

Alex folded her arms across her chest. "Victoria may be petty at times, but she's a good person overall," she swore. "I certainly don't think a little jealous behavior is basis for a roommate switch."

Stacey stared at Alex, who was making light of Victoria's issues. She, for one, didn't find them humorous. "Alex…that's not um…"

Alex stared at Stacey in anticipation. Her friend looked troubled. "Has she done something *else*?" she asked.

Stacey looked at the concern on Alex's face and just shook her head. "Don't worry about it," she dismissed, smiling. "Get to class, I'll see you later."

Alex stared at Stacey's back as she walked off. *I wonder what Victoria did to her,* she thought before heading off in the other direction.

Chasity opened her room door. "You're not really coming to this family weekend thing are you?" Chasity asked into her wireless earpiece device. Upon entering, she set her book bag and grocery bag on the floor.

"Why *wouldn't* I come?" Chasity's Aunt Trisha Duvall asked, a sternness in her tone. "I *am* your family. I'm like a parent to you."

Chasity rolled her eyes while proceeding to brush her hair into a ponytail. "Yeah I know that," she replied, tone lacking enthusiasm. "But…I kinda don't *want* you to come."

"Why not? You're not embarrassed by me, are you?" Trisha joked.

"Trisha, I'm not laughing," Chasity returned with seriousness that her aunt wasn't expecting.

"Chasity, what's wrong with you?" Trisha asked, voice full of concern.

Chasity sat on her bed and sighed. She pinched the bridge of her nose with two fingers, wondering if she should say anything more. On top of her classes stressing her, Chasity's mind had been clouded with thoughts about her life that she wished would just go away.

"You're not going to answer me?" Trisha asked, picking up on the silence.

"Look Trish..." Chasity began, trying to gather her words in the most respectful way possible. "No matter what you do for me or what you *say*...you are *not* my parent," she put out. "Don't get me wrong, I'm not saying that I don't appreciate anything but...I just don't want to walk around here pretending that you're my mother because...you're not...and pretending that I have a mother—it doesn't..." she paused. "Forget it."

Trisha sighed, sensing Chasity's struggle to express her feelings. She had a feeling that family weekend would stir up some bad feelings in Chasity because of the fact that she was adopted. She also felt that maybe that reality wouldn't have been so bad for Chasity, if she actually had a good relationship with the woman who raised her, Trisha's sister. All Trisha could do was try to keep her mind off of it.

"Look...I can't stop you from feeling hurt," she replied. "But I can only hope that you can try not to let this bother you so much. *I'm* still here and you know that I love you like a daughter."

Chasity frowned; that's not what she wanted to hear. "That's fine but—"

"Just listen to me, Chasity," Trisha cut in, voice stern. "I need for you to not let this whole mess stress you out."

"I'm trying *not* to," Chasity hissed. "But it *is* something that's bothering me and I just want to vent." It seemed like every time Chasity brought the topic up, which had been quite often recently, Trisha never fully let her talk it out. She always tried to make Chasity see the bright side, but that was not what she wanted. What she *wanted* was for her aunt to understand how she felt.

"Venting won't change the situation," Trisha dismissed. "It's just going to make you even more angry…It's not healthy for you."

Chasity let out a loud sigh. *Shut up!* "Whatever Trisha, I'll talk to you later," she ground out, before abruptly disconnecting the call. She then removed the wireless device from her ear and tossed it on her dresser.

Malajia barged through the door and slammed it. She glanced over at Chasity who was sitting on her bed deep in thought, paying her no mind. Malajia, in an effort to make Chasity look at her, took off her heels and tossed them against the wall, creating a loud noise. Not getting a reaction, she then began huffing loudly.

"What?! What is it?!" Chasity snapped, looking up at her.

"Hey! Don't yell at me."

"You're like a big ass child looking for attention, what the fuck do you *want*?" Chasity ranted.

Malajia sucked her teeth and folded her arms. "My mother is coming down this weekend for stupid family weekend and she's bringing my stupid sisters Geri and Maria," Malajia fussed. "Can you believe that bullshit?"

Chasity stared at her, a blank expression on her face. "Wow, your mom is coming down to spend some time with her daughter. Oh the horror," she sarcastically drawled, standing up from her bed.

Malajia frowned. "What's up *your* ass?" she sneered.

"You complain too fuckin' much," Chasity threw back. Malajia's mouth fell open in shock. "You complain about stupid shit. So *what* if your mom and your sisters want to come down? What are you so damn mad for? If you weren't down here showing your ass, *literally*, you wouldn't have anything to worry about, now *would* you?"

"Whatever Chasity," Malajia hissed. "You just don't get it."

"No, *you* don't." Chasity rolled her eyes.

Malajia stared at her for a moment. "Look here damn it. You're my roommate and my best friend," she declared, pointing. "You're supposed to be on *my* side."

Chasity was confused. "Since *when* have I become your best friend?...and for *what*?"

"You don't need the details," Malajia barked, flicking her hand in Chasity's direction repeatedly.

Still confused by Malajia's revelation about their friendship, which she had no clue about, Chasity shook her head and walked into the bathroom.

"I can't believe my mother is bringing Jazmine down here," Emily said to Alex as both girls walked along the path towards Emily's apartment. While getting ready for class earlier that morning, Emily received a call from her mother, letting her know that she would be bringing her older sister along to the family weekend.

"That's rough Em," Alex sympathized, knowing all about Jazmine from many conversations with Emily. "Maybe it won't be that bad."

Emily pushed some hair behind her ears and sighed. "It *will* be," she sulked. "She'll be picking on me the whole time."

Alex just looked at Emily. She really didn't know what to say. Between her mother's hovering and her sister's teasing, Emily was sure to have a rough time. "Well...maybe you can ditch them long enough to hang out with us a little bit," she placated. "I mean, our mothers won't be with us the *entire* day."

Emily shot Alex a knowing look before shaking her head. "I don't think I'll see much of you girls this weekend," she concluded.

"She still hates us, huh?"

Emily nodded hesitantly. "If I even so much as *mention* you girls, she goes off," she said. "I have to lie about what I'm doing when I'm out with you guys."

"That's not healthy, Em," Alex pointed out. To Alex it seemed that the vendetta that Ms. Harris had for the girls wasn't really about *them*. It was almost as if she wouldn't want Emily being friends with anybody who wasn't *her*.

"She's just being overprotective…she thinks that you girls are a bad influence," Emily muttered.

No, I think she just doesn't want you to branch out on your own, Alex thought, but remained silent.

"I almost wish I hadn't told her about this weekend."

Seeing how down Emily already was, Alex decided not to lecture her on her mother's behavior. Alex put her arm around her. "You'll be fine, it's only two days."

Emily offered a slight smile up at Alex as they approached the steps to her building.

Chapter 8

Sidra flipped through the channels on her television. "I'm so over this day," she griped to herself. The quizzes that she had in three of her five classes had her tightly wound. A loud knock at the door startled her.

"Who the hell is banging like that?" she frowned, muting the television. She heard the knock again as she approached the door. Snatching it open, Sidra came face to face with an angry young woman.

"Can I help you, Dominique?" Sidra asked, tone not hiding her agitation.

"Uh yeah, you wanna tell me to my *face* what you been saying behind my back?"

Sidra frowned in confusion. She and Dominique, her neighbor and Dee's roommate, barely exchanged two words on a daily basis. So why she was spewing this accusation out of nowhere was beyond her.

"Okay..." Sidra drew out slowly. "You want to tell me what you're talking about?"

"I don't appreciate you talking shit about me!"

"*What* shit are you *talking* about?" Sidra asked, raising her voice. "You come over here banging on my door like you're the freakin' police. You're accusing me of something that I *don't* do...you want to fill me in here?"

Dominique, who was Sidra's height and complexion, put both hands on her hips. "You told Dee that I was some dirty bitch!"

Sidra put her hand up. "*First* of all, you need to lower your damn voice when you speak to me. I'm *not* a child and I'm *not* deaf," she hissed. "And *second*, I never called you dirty nor did I call you a bitch. I rarely use the word," she added. Dominique rolled her eyes. "But I *have* said that it was tacky to leave your crap all over the bathroom. We share it, and you need to be considerate."

"Is that so?"

"*Yes*, it *is*," Sidra maintained, livid. "And I *would've* said it to your face but you never come to the damn door when I knock."

Dominque pointed her non-manicured finger at Sidra, earning a warning look from her. "Look, if I wanna leave my mess in there, I *can,* because it's half *mine*."

Sidra was more focused on the obvious fake ponytail sitting atop Dominique's head than on what she was saying.

"Let me hear you say something else about me, and I'll—"

"You'll do *what*?" Sidra snapped, staring daggers at her. "Don't let these dress clothes and these updo's fool you. I will drag you, chick."

"Whatever," Dominique snarled.

"Yeah whatever, freak," Sidra retorted, before slamming the door in Dominique's face. Sidra was still fuming as she backed away from the door and began pacing. "I don't know who her ugly self thinks she's dealing with," she vented to herself. "Damn troll."

A few moments later, Alex entered the room and looked over at her roommate, who was still in mid-rant. "You okay?" she asked, amusement in her voice.

Sidra looked over at her. "I am so sick of these damn neighbors," she vented, pointing to the bathroom door.

The amusement left Alex's face once she heard the anger

in Sidra's voice. "What happened?"

"Can you believe that that dirty girl next door had the *nerve* to come over here and get in my face?" Sidra raged.

"Get in your face about *what*?" Alex asked, tossing her book bag on the floor.

"Talking about 'I called her a dirty bitch'," Sidra ranted, mocking Dominique's voice. "I never called her ugly ass dirty. But I *should* have because she *is* dirty."

Alex stood in silence as Sidra continued to pace the room with her hands on her hips. "With her tacky looking self. Looking like somebody threw up her ponytail and slapped it on that nappy ass head of hers."

Alex was shocked; she hadn't seen Sidra that angry since after she was jumped by Jackie and her friends last semester. "Calm down sweetie," she pacified. "Don't let her get to you."

"Yeah well, it's too damn late for that," Sidra seethed.

Alex shook her head. "Come on, let's go meet the others and head to the cafeteria for dinner," she suggested, retrieving her ID from a small pocket in her book bag. "Maybe some food will help."

"No, some *new neighbors* will help," Sidra ground out, reaching for her purse that was hanging on the closet door.

"Can't do anything about that right now, let's go," Alex chuckled, giving Sidra a soft nudge toward the door.

Sidra's temper seemed to calm a bit during her walk with Alex to the cafeteria. "I hope they have lasagna for dinner tonight," Alex mused, shoving her hands into the pockets of her brown sweat jacket.

"I'm in the mood for seafood for some reason," Sidra chortled.

On her way up the steps, Alex spotted Victoria making her way out of the cafeteria. "Vicki!" Alex called, waving her arm.

Victoria stopped, glanced at both girls, then rolled her

eyes and continued her pace down the steps.

Alex frowned. "Are you freakin' kidding me?" she complained in an aside to Sidra, who just shook her head and continued her journey inside the cafeteria.

The last thing that Sidra needed after her run-in with Dominique was to argue with Alex's surly friend.

Refusing to be ignored, Alex turned to face Victoria's departing back. "Victoria!" she called.

Victoria stopped abruptly and spun around. "What do you want, Alex?" she spat.

Alex held her angry gaze as she walked up to her. "So, first you give me attitude, and *now* you're flat out ignoring me?" she observed, tone not hiding her frustration.

"I don't have time for this, I have homework to do," Victoria sniped, turning to leave.

Alex quickly grabbed hold of her arm, stopping her. "Victoria, we've been friends way too long to let *whatever* this is that you're dealing with affect us like this."

Victoria faced Alex. "Oh, don't act like we're friends *now*," she ground out. "You've barely paid any attention to me since I *got* here."

Alex sighed. "Vicki, I've *tried* to spend time with you. But your attitude towards my other friends is uncomfortable for me."

"I don't give a shit about your *other* friends," Victoria barked. "You keep trying to force them on me and I just want it to be like old times. With just me, you, and Stacey."

"I've been here for a whole year!" Alex snapped, holding her arms up. "What? You didn't expect me to make any new friends? You expected me to stay to myself and wait until *you* got here?"

Victoria folded her arms and looked away as Alex continued.

"Come on, you of *all* people know me better than that," Alex said. "I've *always* made friends."

"Yes, you have, and every time you make a new friend, your old ones get pushed aside," Victoria threw back.

Alex narrowed her eyes. "That's not true and you *know* that."

"Oh no?" Victoria challenged. "It was me and you, then Stacey came along...then it was *you and Stacey* for a while before I started hanging back around—"

"Don't try to turn this mess around on *me* because you're a jealous person," Alex interrupted, folding her arms.

"*Jealous?*"

"Absolutely," Alex confirmed confidently. "You're jealous of anybody who gets *any* of my time that isn't spent with *you*." Alex ran her hand over her hair. "This is childish and petty and you need to grow up. If you keep acting like this, you're gonna end up by yourself and I don't want to see that happen. Because despite what you may think of me, I still love you."

Victoria slowly shook her head. "No, you don't love me, you love *them.*"

"I love *all* of you," Alex stressed, voice rising. "I have a big heart. I have room for more than one friend in my life."

"Whatever Alex, just leave me alone," Victoria grunted. "Stacey's trading on me with them...so I guess I really *am* alone."

"This self-pity act is tiresome," Alex groused, rubbing her temples. "You wanna act that way, fine. Stacey isn't treating you any differently than she did *before*."

"Yes she *is*," Victoria maintained. "She's been giving me attitude ever since you brought those bitches to Philly last semester."

"Don't call my friends bitches," Alex warned, pointing her finger at Victoria.

Victoria shot Alex a piercing look. As if she wasn't angry enough, Alex had to go and defend the people she was annoyed with. Victoria was over it. "You know what? To hell with you *and* Stacey for that matter," she hissed, adjusting the hood on her sweatshirt. "She *thinks* she still has a place with you, but it'll just be a matter of time before you dump *her too*...Just like *me* and just like *Paul*."

Alex was taken back by Victoria's accusation. Shock and hurt resonated on her face. "Did you just bring up Paul to me?" she asked in disbelief. "Did you just throw my relationship with him up in my goddamn face?"

Victoria stared Alex down, unfazed by her hurt feelings.

"Are you kidding me?! You of *all* people know why I ended things with Paul. He cheated on me!"

"And you know what? I don't *blame* him either," Victoria threw back. "You left home and forgot about him. You gave him attitude when he called you, you—"

"That's a lie."

Victoria stared at her, eyes wide. "What?"

"I didn't give him attitude when he called me," Alex contradicted. "He gave *me*, attitude."

Victoria shook her head. "I find that hard to believe," she bit out. "You treated him like shit and that was wrong."

"So, what? You're now gonna tell me that he had a right to cheat on me because I wouldn't talk to him on the phone every five damn minutes?" Alex questioned, tone angry. "That's funny, because you didn't make it *seem* that way when you called me and *told* me that he cheated," she recalled. "Now because you got a damn attitude with me, you wanna change your story?"

"No…I just see things better now," Victoria shot back. "Enjoy your dinner, Alex."

Alex watched in disbelief as Victoria stormed off. *Unbelievable!* She couldn't wrap her mind around what had just taken place. Victoria, one of her best friends, just threw her doomed relationship with Paul up in her face, and made it seem like the demise of it and his cheating was *her* fault.

"Somebody *please* tell me how I'm gonna ditch my parents this weekend," Malajia huffed, taking a bite out of a dinner roll.

"Shit, when you find out, let *me* know," Mark replied,

cutting into his lasagna. "Man, why they always stingy with the cheese?" he complained, lifting some noodles with his fork.

Sidra, ignoring Mark's outburst over his dinner choice, looked up as Alex approached the table. Seeing the troubled look on her face, she frowned slightly. "You okay?"

Alex sat down in the booth with a huff and folded her arms on the table. "I'm fine," she replied.

"Had a run-in with Victoria, huh?" Stacey assumed. "Sidra told me y'all saw her."

"I'm so over my so-called *friend* right now," Alex bit out, scratching her head. "What were you guys just talking about?" She was desperate to talk about anything other than Victoria.

"Malajia and Mark were running their mouths about some bullshit," Chasity sneered, pouring dressing on her chicken salad. "As *usual*."

"Funny, Lucifer," Malajia sarcastically returned.

"So…who's gonna let me hide out in their room for the weekend while my wack ass parents are here?" Mark asked, looking around the table.

Sidra shot him a glance. "You better stop talking about your parents like that, boy," she teased. "They are not *wack*, they're pretty cool."

"They *corny*," Mark reiterated, earning a giggle from Sidra. "To be honest, my dad isn't even the problem, it's my *mom* man," he added. "She's gonna come down here trippin'. Smackin' me all in the back of the head and shit." He ran his hand over his freshly cut, black hair.

"You have and will *continue* to deserve every one of those smacks," Sidra said, pointing her fork in his direction. "You're always showing your behind."

Mark rolled his eyes. "Whatever, she not gonna be down here playin' me. That's all *I'm* sayin'," he mumbled.

"My dad is actually looking forward to coming," David put in, taking a bite of his turkey sandwich.

Mark threw his head back and let out a loud groan.

"Dave man, your dad is corny *too*," he barked.

"Call him what you want," David returned, voice deceptively calm. "But remember that the next time you need me to help you with one of your assignments."

Mark turned in his seat and pointed his finger in David's face. "I'll say what I *want* and you'll help me *anyway* and you'll—" Mark was caught off guard when David grabbed his finger and twisted it. "Oooooowwww!" he howled.

Alex put her hands over her ears. "Come on with all that damn noise," she complained.

David finally let go of Mark's finger and smacked it away. "Keep your hands out my face," he said.

"Fuck you *and* your face," Mark bit back.

Josh let out a little laugh. "Nice comeback," he teased. Mark just gave Josh the finger.

"So, anybody else besides Mark and Mel trying to ditch their people this weekend?" Sidra asked, trying to diffuse any more tension.

"To hell with *them*, y'all still haven't helped me with *my* parent problem," Malajia cut in, holding her arms up in the air.

"Please put those down," Mark joked.

"You don't have a parent problem. They have a *you* problem," Chasity sniped.

Malajia shot her glance. "Keep on with the comments, hear? I'll try on all your damn clothes, including the drawls," she warned. Her off the wall threat earned disgusted looks and snickers from the table.

"The fuck?" Chasity questioned, disgusted.

"Yo, Malajia you trippin'," Josh laughed.

"What? She buys cute underwear," Malajia reasoned with a shrug. "I don't *want* the girl, I just want her clothes."

"Please, somebody shoot me," Chasity requested, pinching the bridge of her nose.

Mark, not happy with his dinner choice, eyed Chasity's chicken salad. He wasn't normally a salad person, but the crisp veggies, grilled chicken pieces, shredded cheese and salad dressing was a better sight than the flat, greasy, cut up lasagna on his plate.

"Aye Parker, let me get a bite of that salad," he demanded, reaching his fork across her bowl.

"Boy, get away from me," Chasity hissed, knocking his hand away.

Jason, fed up with Mark's mouth and antics, frowned as he watched him reach for Chasity's food yet again. "Mark, will you stop with the bullshit and eat your own damn food?" he barked.

Mark slammed his hand on the table. "This shit is nasty cuz!"

Jason stared at him. "Who...the fuck are you yelling at?" he drew his words out slowly.

Mark jumped up and pointed in Jason's face. He was so close that he accidentally poked Jason in the nose and immediately regretted it. "Oh shit!" he exclaimed, pushing his way out of the booth. "David move! Moooove!" he panicked, pushing the cursing David out of the way.

Ignoring David's complaints, Mark darted out of the booth with an angry Jason chasing after him. "My bad Jase! My bad," he yelled on his way out the room.

Chapter 9

Emily took a bite of her toaster pastry and stared through her blinds, chewing. Knowing that her mother and sister were merely minutes from arriving, Emily was in a funk. She sighed, taking another bite of the dry pastry. *I'd much rather be at breakfast with the girls*, she sulked. Seeing her mother's blue sedan pull up in a nearby parking space through the window, Emily resisted the urge to roll her eyes. "Here we go," she coaxed herself.

It took only a few moments from when Ms. Harris pulled up to when she reached Emily's door. Emily darted to the door and opened it, a smile plastered to her cute face.

"Hi sweetie," Ms. Harris beamed, hugging Emily tightly. She pulled away and brushed the crumbs from her child's face. "Just finished eating, huh?" she chuckled, smoothing some loose hair strands back into Emily's low ponytail.

Jazmine Harris's reaction to seeing Emily was opposite her mother's. She walked into the room, brushing past Emily with an overnight bag in her hand. "Where do I sleep, Pasty Face?" she bit out, tossing the bag on Emily's bed.

Emily looked down at the floor before glancing at her sister. *Hello to you too Jaz.* To Emily, Jazmine looked like she didn't even bother to look presentable. The girl had her relaxed brown hair snatched back into a tight bun, she had on sweat pants that looked like they belonged to one of their brothers, a faded t-shirt and run down sneakers. The scowl on her brown face didn't add to her beauty at all. In fact, it made her look much older than twenty-two years old.

Ms. Harris regarded Jazmine with a stern look as she straightened out her long sleeved, floral print dress, which fell to her ankles. Emily glanced at her mother. She was relieved that the woman stopped buying dresses like that for *her* to wear. Emily's baggy, frumpy wardrobe still left a lot to be desired, but at least she didn't have to be subjected to those God-awful dresses.

"Jazmine, she has asked you to stop calling her that," Ms. Harris chided. "There is nothing pasty about your sister's complexion, she's just lighter than we are."

Jazmine shrugged, she couldn't care less about Emily's complexion, or *her* for that matter. She didn't want to be there in the first place.

"So," Ms. Harris began, pulling a piece of paper out of her pocketbook. "I have a whole itinerary planned for us."

Oh God, please not the itinerary. I'm not gonna get a moment to myself all weekend. Emily stared at her mother as she ran down the list of activities that she had planned for the girls. A smile stuck to her face, it almost looked deranged.

"Mom, nobody wants to go to the aquarium," Jazmine protested. "Unless you're dropping Emily off and leaving her there with the *other* spineless eels."

Emily's smile faded as she felt her jaw tighten at her sisters' words.

"Stop talking about your sister."

"Mom, you dragged me down here to this stupid college, at *least* let me go see some games or go to a party or something," Jazmine griped, ignoring her mother's request.

"We're not down here to party," Ms. Harris hissed through clenched teeth. "We're here to spend some time with Emily, so stop complaining."

Jazmine flopped back on Emily's bed. "Why couldn't you have dragged Brad and Dru down here with you?" she fussed of her older brothers. "I mean, they don't like Miss Baby *either,* but at least *I* wouldn't have to look at her."

Feeling tears well up in her eyes and a knot in her throat, Emily headed for the door. "Excuse me," she said, walking out and shutting the door behind her. The last thing she wanted was for Jazmine to see her cry. It would just give her another reason to look down on her.

"Should I wear my silver heels or my red ones?" Malajia asked Chasity, holding both pairs of shoes in her hand.

Chasity, who had just finished curling her hair, glanced over. "Why are you wearing heels? We're only going bowling with the guys."

"Why did you curl your *hair*?" Malajia threw back.

"'Cause I wanna look cute."

"For *who,* Jason?" Malajia teased. Chasity flipped her the finger, inciting a laugh from Malajia. "Seriously, which ones?"

Chasity eyed both pairs of shoes. "You might as well throw dirt on your face *now* because every time you wear either *one* of those shoes, you fall on your ass," she sneered.

Malajia rolled her eyes. "I don't fall...I *trip*," she corrected, tossing both pairs in the closet. As she went in search of her best pair of flats, Alex walked through the door with Sidra and Stacey in tow.

"You two *still* not ready?" Alex asked, voice filled with amusement.

"That's *her*." Chasity pointed to Malajia.

"Oh shut up. Just because *Alex* is okay with getting dressed in two seconds and looking like trash doesn't mean that *I* need to," Malajia jeered.

"Keep talking your mess, hear?" Alex warned, nudging Malajia. "Just hurry up and put your damn shoes on."

Malajia flagged Alex with her hand, while heading over

to her dresser. "Stacey, get ready to watch the guys lose tonight," she boasted.

Stacey giggled. "I don't know Malajia, they seem like they could be good bowlers."

"Nope, they suck," Malajia confirmed. *"Especially* Mark."

Sidra stared as Malajia moved scattered pieces of jewelry around on her dresser. Something caught her eye, so she walked over. As Sidra approached, Malajia looked up, grabbed an item and tried to stuff it in her underwear drawer.

"No, I saw it!" Sidra exclaimed, reaching over her. "Stop trying to hide it, Malajia."

"Back up off me, Sid," Malajia warned, nudging her away. Sidra moved around Malajia and began pulling at the drawer handle while Malajia tried to keep it closed. "Why you wanna see my drawls?" Malajia barked.

Sidra, pinched Malajia's arm. She let out a scream and dropped her arm from the drawer.

"You cheatin' Sidra," Malajia bit out, examining the red mark on her arm.

Ignoring Malajia, Sidra pulled the drawer open and retrieved the item she was searching for. "I *knew* I recognized this," she seethed, holding up a silver and blue bangle bracelet.

"What's *that?*" Malajia frowned, feigning shock.

Sidra stomped her foot on the floor. "My sapphire bracelet," she barked. "You thief, I thought I lost this."

"You said I could borrow it," Malajia shot back.

"No, I said that if you *touch* it, you'll lose your teeth," Sidra contradicted. "Do you know how much my father spent on this?"

Malajia rolled her eyes, rubbing her arm. "Look, if you *don't* want me to wear your shit then *don't* leave it out," she argued. "You already know if I see it, I'm gonna want it." She directed her attention to Chasity. "Isn't that right, roomie?"

"Stop talking to me," Chasity calmly put out as she

applied her tinted lip gloss in the mirror.

Sidra placed the bracelet on her wrist and Alex chortled, "Malajia, I'm convinced, you need help." A light tap on the door sent Alex over to open it.

"How you just gonna open our damn door?" Malajia griped.

"My God, shut up," Sidra hurled at her, still annoyed by Malajia's sticky fingers.

"Emily," Alex smiled, stepping aside to let Emily in. The girls turned around. Nobody expected to see any part of Emily all weekend with her mother hovering around.

"What lie did you tell to get your mom to let the leash go?" Chasity mocked, Alex shot Chasity a warning glance.

"I told her that I had to run to the library for a few," Emily shrugged. "I figured I would come over and see what you guys were up to."

"You salty you had to lie just to get out of your room," Malajia teased, opening a bottle of water. "*Our* mom's aren't coming until tomorrow morning." Emily looked down at the floor as Malajia began laughing. "Ahhh, you salty your mom came down on a Friday."

"Malajia, kill it," Alex scolded.

"So," Emily began, hoping to get the attention off of her. "What are you up to? Looks like you're about to go out."

"We're about to meet the guys and go bowling," Sidra answered.

Emily glanced over at Stacey, who was sitting on Malajia's bed. "You going too?" she asked her.

"Yeah, they invited me to tag along," Stacey smiled. "It seems like fun."

"Oh." Emily's tone was low and somber. "I can't come."

"We *know*, that's why nobody invited you," Chasity rudely spat.

Malajia nearly spit out the water that she was drinking. "Oh shit!" she coughed at Chasity's bluntness. Stacey turned her head in an effort to block out the hurt look on Emily's face.

"Stop being rude," Sidra chided through clenched teeth as she gave Chasity a poke.

"Yes, I wish she *would*," Alex bristled, shooting Chasity a death stare.

Chasity looked back at Alex. "I hope you don't think you staring at me with those big ass eyes is intimidating," she hissed.

"Ahhh, Alex got big eyes," Malajia teased, much to Sidra's annoyance.

"Put a lid on your mouth for five seconds, okay?" Sidra snapped.

"I say what I want. I say what I want," Malajia taunted, staring at Sidra with wide eyes.

Alex shook her head at them, then turned her attention back to Emily, who looked like she wanted to cry. "Look sweetie...You know we would've invited you. But we knew that your mother..." Alex wasn't sure if her words were providing any comfort to Emily. "I mean, there will be other outings...hey, how about we go on Sunday after everyone's parents leave?"

Emily continued to stare at the floor as she scratched her neck. "I just...I just wish that you guys would've at least invited me," she stammered. "I mean...I know I can't go...but the invite would've been nice."

The four girls looked at her. "Ooh I think she's tryna tell us off," Malajia instigated.

"How's she gonna do *that*, looking at the damn floor?" Chasity taunted. She didn't have a problem with Emily being upset, she had a problem with the wimpy way in which she was addressing it. "A word of advice, when you wanna clap back at someone, look them in the face."

Emily slowly looked up. "I—I'm sorry, I didn't mean to—"

"What the hell are you apologizing for?" Chasity snapped, interrupting Emily's stammering. "You're pissed that we didn't invite you. I mean, I don't *give* a fuck—"

Malajia snickered as Sidra put her hand over her face and shook her head.

"But if you wanna tell us off, don't be a punk about it, *do it*," Chasity continued, tone nasty.

Emily wiped her eyes with the back of her hand as tears began to fall. Alex went to hug her, but Emily just scampered out of the room.

Alex shut the door behind her and pointed at Chasity. "That was uncalled for, rude ass!" she erupted.

"Your friend is a punk," Chasity declared.

Alex gritted her teeth. She could've slapped Chasity right across her face. "How can you continue to be so nasty to her?"

Chasity looked at Alex as if she was crazy. "She's a punk," she reiterated.

"That's not right, you *know* she's afraid of you," Alex simmered, turning away from Chasity. She was so angry, she couldn't even look at her.

"Okay, okay, everybody just calm down," Sidra stepped in, putting her hands up. "Alex, Emily will be fine…Chasity, you *could* stand to be a little nicer to the girl." Chasity rolled her eyes. "Alex, Chaz *does* have a point," she added. "Emily needs to stop this scared, little girl nonsense…and *you* need to stop talking for her."

Alex's mouth fell open. "I don't—"

"Yes, you *do*," the girls returned in unison.

Alex was stunned, she looked over at Stacey, who had participated in the group response. "*You too*?"

Stacey put her hands up in surrender. "I mean, from what I've *seen*…you do," she confirmed. "But I know it comes from a good place," she amended when she heard Alex's loud sigh. "You always try to look out for everybody."

"What she *need* to look out for is a store with better shirts in it," Malajia scoffed, gesturing to Alex's tan and orange, off the shoulder top. Alex gritted her teeth.

Chapter 10

Early Saturday morning, the campus was flooded with the families of the attending students of Paradise Valley University. Being the first year that the school decided to host a weekend for families before homecoming week, many of the students were enjoying an opportunity to blend their campus life and home life together. Children ran across the grass with balloons, parents toured the grounds, while students took advantage of their parent's generosity by loading up on groceries and toiletries.

Malajia was one student who wasn't excited for this weekend. As far as she was concerned, her family being there was going to ruin the weekend for her. She let out a sigh as she tossed yet another clothing item on the floor.

"Damn it! Why are all my clothes so damn short?" she complained, kicking the short, red skirt across the room. Reaching back into the closet, she pulled out a pair of black tights, bright red corset top and black high heeled pumps. She held the top up to her slim body and shrugged. "Hell, if they don't approve, at least I'll look good," she boasted to herself.

Malajia cut the radio on and turned the volume up, then began singing along to the tunes blasting through the speakers.

Chasity opened the room door just as Malajia was in mid-note. She walked in, followed by Sidra and Alex, and covered her ears while making a face. "You look *and* sound like trash," she teased.

Malajia spun around and laughed. "You're too cute to be a hater," she threw back, turning the volume down. Chasity shrugged.

"Did you find anything 'mother appropriate'?" Sidra asked, sitting on a small accent chair.

"Nope," Malajia answered honestly, putting her corset on. "Can one of y'all tie this for me?"

As Sidra walked over and began strapping Malajia into her top, Alex frowned. "Do you have anything *fall* appropriate?" she scoffed.

"Do *you* have anything..." Malajia racked her brain for a snappy comeback. "Mind your goddamn business," she huffed, unable to come up with one.

Alex sucked her teeth. "Go ahead and catch a cold, nobody is gonna take care of you," she replied.

"*You'll* do it and you'll *like* it," Malajia mumbled, examining herself in the mirror.

Alex looked down at her hands, ignoring Malajia's ramblings. Although she hadn't mentioned anything, she was still reeling from her argument with Victoria a few days ago. She hadn't planned on telling Stacey or the other girls about the conversation that transpired. But she knew for her sanity that she needed to talk about it. "So...I still haven't spoken to Victoria since our last little spat," she revealed. She frowned when Malajia loudly snickered.

"She said 'spat'," Malajia joked, riffling through the jewelry littering her dresser.

Sidra waved her hand dismissively in Malajia's direction. "She still acting like a...."

"Bitch?" Chasity finished, laying down on her bed.

"Thank you, oh blunt one," Sidra chuckled. "What is her problem anyway?" she directed at Alex.

"I wish I *knew*," Alex answered honestly, running her

hands over her hair. "I mean, I know that she's always been a little…possessive when it came to my friendships with other people, but she's going overboard. She's just being plain nasty and she even had the nerve to make it seem like it was *my* fault that Paul cheated on me."

"She did *what*?" Sidra frowned. "She's supposed to be one of your best friends. In fact, wasn't *she* the one who told you that Paul cheated?"

Alex nodded.

"Which means that she knew first-hand how devastated you were over the whole thing," Sidra continued. "How could she say that?"

Alex shrugged. "I guess she was just angry," she reasoned. "I don't think she really means it…at least I *hope* she doesn't."

"I hope you gave her one of those intrusive-ass lectures that you give *us* all the time," Chasity put in, looking at her cell phone.

Alex rolled her eyes. "Funny," she hissed.

"Alex, not to sound like I'm bashing your friend, but…that kind of possessiveness is weird," Sidra hesitantly put out.

"Meaning?" Alex asked, curious.

Malajia let out a squeal of delight as a familiar song played on the radio. She darted over and turned up the volume. "Sorry Alex, as juicy as this drama is, this is my damn song," she beamed, dancing around the room.

Little did Malajia know, Alex was grateful for the interruption. The topic of Victoria was bringing her down, and that was the last thing she wanted when she was mere minutes away from seeing her mother and sister. Alex smiled as she watched the other girls, including a reluctant Chasity join in on the dancing and sing along. Feeling the music, she stood up and joined them.

Geri Simmons peered through an open door as she

passed by. "Ooh, nice," she gushed of the room's colorful interior.

"Child, stop being nosey," Mrs. Simmons scolded, giving her a light backhand.

"I'm just seeing if Malajia is in there," Geri explained, amusement in her voice.

Mrs. Simmons offered her daughter a stern look. "Quit playing with me, you already know that's not your sisters' room," she chided. "That's room 418. She lives in 422."

"Yeah, I know we're close anyway," Maria Simmons commented. "I hear loud music and Malajia's loud voice. The girl never *could* use an inside voice."

As the three women approached the door at the end of the hallway, they saw another woman standing in front of it, getting ready to knock.

"Hello," Mrs. Simmons smiled.

Trisha turned around, a warm smile on her beautiful light-brown face. "Hi, you're Malajia's mother right?" she asked.

"I am," Mrs. Simmons confirmed, extending a hand. "Evelyn."

"I'm Chasity's Aunt Trisha," she returned, shaking Mrs. Simmons hand. "I recognize you from pictures."

Mrs. Simmons chuckled. "Ahh, the infamous Trisha huh?" she quipped. "Malajia's always talking about how much she wants you to adopt her...I swear if she didn't work my nerves so much, I'd be jealous."

"There is no need to be," Trisha laughed, smoothing her hand down her black hair, which was styled into a trendy bob. "Malajia is a sweetheart, but I have no plans on adopting her."

"Girl, you *can*," Mrs. Simmons joked. "Save me the headache."

Trisha giggled, then finally knocked on the door. Not hearing an answer, she went to knock again, but Geri reached over and twisted the knob.

"Girl!" Mrs. Simmons barked, delivering a tap to the

back of Geri's head.

"Ow! Mom, I just got my braids done," Geri whined, rubbing her sore head.

Hearing the commotion, the girls turned around. "Oh God," Malajia jeered, heading over to give her mother and sisters hugs. Like Malajia, the three women were tall in stature with the same flawless brown complexion. However, her sisters had more hips and breast than she did. Her mother's shape rivaled all three, as she had hips for days.

"Real funny," Mrs. Simmons sniped, moving around Malajia to give Sidra, who was on her cell phone, a hug.

"You just gonna bump me out the way to hug the ponytail?" Malajia groused. Sidra stuck her tongue out at Malajia.

Chasity glanced down Trisha's tall, hourglass shaped frame. "You copied off my outfit," she joked, eyeing the trendy look, consisting of dark skinny jeans, black form-fitting top and black high-heeled designer boots, a look that nearly mirrored her own.

Trisha put her hands on her hips and shot Chasity a glance. "Yeah well, we have the same taste. What do you want me to say?" she replied with amusement. She touched her niece's curled hair. "I missed you, smart ass," she gushed, giving Chasity a hug.

Malajia frowned at her mother's outfit. The grey tights paired with a blue long-sleeved top and matching slide on shoes wasn't to Malajia's liking. Neither was her shoulder-length dark hair, which was pulled back into a ponytail. "Eww, Mom," she griped. "You could've put on something cuter. You're embarrassing me."

Mrs. Simmons glared. "Look little girl, I have a husband and *seven* children who run me ragged," she groused. "I could care less about being cute. I'm more concerned with being comfortable."

Malajia rolled her eyes.

"You're worrying about *me* being cute, meanwhile *you're* dressed like its summer time."

Malajia waved her hand at her mother dismissively. "Look here, unlike *you*, my clothes flatter me okay," she replied. "And I'm not cold."

"I'll be back, my mom just got here," Sidra announced, heading for the door.

"Ooh, sweetie, tell Vanessa to stop over," Mrs. Simmons called after Sidra. Sidra nodded as she walked out.

Trisha glanced at Chasity, who was playing with her phone. "You look tired," she commented.

Chasity narrowed her eyes at her. "Thanks," she spat, voice filled with sarcasm.

Trisha chuckled. "You don't look *bad*, you just look…tired," she amended.

"Went to bed late," Chasity said, tone even. "Was trying to finish a paper."

"On a Friday night?" Trisha asked.

Chasity shot Trisha a look, telling her to drop it.

"So…" Trisha began, sitting down on a chair. "Where's Jason, Chaz?"

Here she goes with this Jason shit. "Okay, time to go," Chasity huffed, grabbing her laughing aunt by her arm. "Didn't you say you wanted to take me shopping?"

"No, I want to talk about Jason," Trisha teased. It was no secret that Trisha thought that Jason was good for Chasity. Chasity only wished that she would stop mentioning him every chance that she got.

"No, we're going," Chasity demanded, pulling Trisha out of the door.

"Take me with you," Malajia called after them.

Mrs. Simmons folded her arms. "I'm standing right *here*, you know," she groused.

"So," Malajia said under her breath.

"What did you say?"

"She said 'so'," Geri instigated.

"Will you shut your ugly ass up?!" Malajia barked at her sister.

"Did you just cuss—You know what," Mrs. Simmons

hissed through clenched teeth as she removed her shoe.

"Oh my God, she took off her shoe," Malajia panicked, moving toward the door. "Move, moooove!" she hollered, pushing Geri out of the room to make a break for it.

Jason, having just returned from having lunch with his parents and younger brother, was on his way to his room to retrieve his gym bag before heading to football practice. The star player ever since his freshman year, Jason knew that the pressure was on for the following week's big homecoming game.

He nearly collided with Mark on his way to the door.

"My bad, Jase," Mark grumbled, rubbing the back of his head.

"It's cool," Jason assured. "What's up with you man?" he asked, noticing the annoyed look on Mark's face.

"Yo, my mom has been smacking me in the back of my damn head, *all day*," Mark complained.

Jason busted out laughing.

"It's not funny man, she trippin'."

"What did you do, bro?" Jason questioned. Knowing Mark, he had to have done something.

Mark held his hands up. "I *may* have said that I've always hated her cooking," he revealed.

Jason stared at him, a blank expression on his face. "Seriously?" he said. "You told a woman that you hate her cooking? Your *mother,* of all women?"

"I ain't *mean* the shit. She was just gettin' on my damn nerves," Mark explained, rubbing his head. "Buying me all these damn ugly sweaters that she *know* I'm not gonna wear and shit."

Jason shook his head. "Tough luck with that one," he teased. "I gotta get my stuff for practice."

"Jase wait," Mark said, halting his progress. "You gotta let me hide out in your room while you're at practice."

Jason frowned. "What? No!"

"Please? She don't know where your room is, so she can't find me," he pleaded. "She already found me in Josh's room earlier."

"Nooo," Jason repeated, this time slowly.

Mark stomped his foot on the floor. "I swear, I can't take this parent shit," he huffed. "If it's not my mom being all up in my face, smacking me and shit, David's *dad* is here and he won't leave our damn room."

Jason stared at Mark as he continued to ramble.

"He keeps trying to lecture me on politics and shit, and he don't get the fact that I don't wanna hear it. I don't *care*!"

Jason opened his mouth to protest further, but spotted Chasity walking along the path to her dorm. He smacked Mark on the arm. "Stop being an asshole, and be nice to your mother," he ordered before trotting off to catch up to her.

Mark sucked his teeth before stomping into his dorm.

"Hey Chaz, wait up," Jason called.

Chasity stopped and turned around. "What's up?" she answered, pushing hair behind her ears.

"Just wanted to say 'hi'," he smiled. "And actually to see how your visit with your aunt is going…I know you had your reservations about her coming."

How cute, he's concerned. "It's going fine," Chasity replied nonchalantly. She told Jason about her issues with family weekend a day after her conversation with Trisha. Like always, Jason was worried for her. "Thanks for asking."

"Anytime," he replied. Jason stared at her, wondering if he should put himself out there again and ask her out.

"Did you want something else?" she asked after a few seconds of silence.

You, as always, he thought. "Well…when your aunt leaves…do you wanna go out?" he put out.

Chasity turned away. "I…can't," she slowly declined.

"You *can't*?"

Chasity shook her head. As much as she wanted to go out with Jason, she just couldn't bring herself to accept his invitation.

Jason successfully hid his disappointment. "Zero out of a hundred, huh?" he joked. "It's cool, I live to try another day," he promised.

"Later Jason," she smirked before walking away.

Jason watched her saunter into her dorm. He meant what he said, he wasn't going to give up.

Gotta try a different approach.

"Alex, when are you gonna introduce me to your guy friends?" Sahara Chisolm asked, staring up at Alex from the floor.

Alex laughed as Mrs. Chisolm shot her young daughter a stern look.

"Girl, stop concerning yourself on meeting guys," she reprimanded. "The only thing you need to concern yourself with at your age, is school."

After a full day of spending time with her mother and sister on campus, Alex was relaxing in her room later that evening, taking part in some much needed girl chat.

"All right Ma, dang," Sahara muttered, returning her eyes to the book that she was reading.

"Excuse me?" Mrs. Chisolm barked.

Alex touched her mother's shoulder, successfully concealing a laugh. "Ma, she didn't say anything," she lied.

"Oh," Mrs. Chisolm said, looking away.

Alex gave Sahara a look, silently telling her to watch her mouth. Sahara mouthed the word 'sorry'. Alex held her gaze on her curvy fifteen-year-old sister for another moment. A sophomore in high school, Alex wasn't surprised that Sahara had an interest in boys. Most teenage girls did.

"It was nice of Sidra to stay in the hotel with her mother," Mrs. Chisolm said, tucking some of her curly hair into her satin scarf.

"Yeah, she wanted to give us some alone time," Alex smiled. She was grateful for the kindness and consideration that Sidra showed for her family, who couldn't afford a hotel room.

"If your aunt didn't get called into work at the last minute and would've come down with us like she was *supposed* to, we could've stayed in her hotel room."

"Ma, don't sweat it. I prefer this anyway." Alex stared at her mother and smiled. Although she inherited her glowing dark skin and curvaceous body from her mother, she got her height from her father. She and Sahara stood several inches taller than their mother. As Mrs. Chisolm spread the colorful comforter out on Alex's bed, Alex sighed.

"I want to talk to you about something," Alex began, bringing her bare feet up on the bed.

"What's the matter?" Mrs. Chisolm asked, noticing the sullen tone in Alex's voice.

Alex took a deep breath. "It's Victoria."

"What's going on with her?"

"I wish that I knew, Ma," Alex admitted. "She's been acting like this nasty, jealous person. I can't deal with her when she's like this."

"Is it the other girls?" Mrs. Chisolm asked, knowing Victoria all too well. "'Cause you know how she is when it comes to dealing with new people."

"I think that the girls are *part* of it…" Alex paused to gather her thoughts. "I honestly feel that there's something else going on with her that she won't tell me about."

A knock on the door interrupted Mrs. Chisolm's thoughts.

"Come in!" Alex bellowed.

Stacey walked into the room. "Alex can I borrow—Hey Ma!" she exclaimed, seeing Mrs. Chisolm sitting on the bed. She darted over and gave her a hug. "I'm sorry that I didn't stop by earlier, my parents had me running all day," she apologized, sitting down on the bed next to Alex.

"It's no problem," Mrs. Chisolm assured with a wave of her hand. "Are you having problems with Victoria too?"

"Wow Ma, just came on out with it, huh?" Alex teased.

"Well, I know that you three have always been close,"

Mrs. Chisolm shrugged. "I just figured I'd ask."

Stacey glanced at Alex. "Um...yeah," Stacey replied.

Alex looked at her. "You mean she's *still* giving you attitude, *too*?" she asked.

"Yep," Stacey confirmed. "I'm not pressed over it, trust me."

Alex sucked her teeth. "This is ridiculous," she seethed. "*She's* being ridiculous."

Mrs. Chisolm sighed as she took hold of both girls' hands. "Listen girls, you three have been friends for years," she said. "You can't let this friendship go down the drain because of one person's attitude...Now unless she did something devastating, there's no reason why this friendship can't be fixed."

Stacey once again glanced at Alex, who simply nodded at her mother's words.

"You're right Ma," Alex replied. "She may be acting like a jerk, but she's still a good person...I'll talk to her." She gave Stacey a playful nudge. "You wanna come with me when I talk to her?"

"Nope," Stacey bit out, earning a confused glance from Alex.

Hmm, I wonder why Stacey seems so much more disgusted with Victoria than I am, Alex thought.

"I'm gonna get going," Stacey announced, standing up.

"Wait Stacey, can we meet *your* guy friends?" Sahara asked, looking up wide-eyed.

"Girl!" Mrs. Chisolm barked.

The weekend passed quickly, too quickly for Alex, who was still reflecting on the conversation that she had with her mother just two days ago. Alex bundled her coat up to her neck while she sat on the chilly steps of Torrence Hall.

She was soon joined by Victoria, who walked down the steps and stood in front of her without saying a word.

"Thanks for coming out," Alex said, standing up. "You

could have sounded a little nicer on the phone though."

Victoria rolled her eyes. "What do you want to talk to me about that can't wait?" she wondered, tone not masking her disdain.

Alex shook her head. "I don't know why I thought that we could have a civilized conversation when you *clearly* have issues," she ground out.

"Save it," Victoria sneered, turning to walk away.

"No, hold on." Alex stepped in front of her. "Look, honestly I didn't come over here to fight with you," she said, putting her hands up. "I still want us to get past *whatever* this issue is…I'm willing to try even though I'm pissed at you."

Victoria stared at Alex in disbelief. "You're pissed at *me*?"

Alex narrowed her eyes. "Yes," she confirmed. "You had the audacity to stand in my face and tell me that Paul cheating on me was *my* fault."

"I know what I said," Victoria scoffed, folding her arms.

"How could you say that to me?" Alex fumed. "You *knew* how much he hurt me. What kind of friend are you?"

"The kind of friend who is tired of your nonsense, Alex," Victoria snarled. "Truth is…I don't blame Paul for what he did. He was lonely and angry."

"Are you fuckin' kidding me?!" Alex exploded.

"Alex, all you did was put him down because he didn't graduate on time," Victoria threw back, unfazed by Alex's loud voice. "How do you think that made him feel?"

"I was *hoping* that it would motivate him to do better," Alex replied defensively, folding her arms. "This is real funny. You couldn't *stand* him when he first came around and now all of a sudden you're pro Paul…You're not the person that I thought you were."

"It doesn't matter, I'm over you anyway," Victoria shrugged. "Go head and get back to your little college family. Those girls are just as fake as *you* are."

"Victoria, I'm not fake, I have *never* been fake," Alex sighed. "I may have grown as a person, but I haven't changed. *You're* the one who changed."

"I really don't care."

Alex stared at Victoria. This mean-spirited person in front of her was not the friend that she grew up with, nor was she someone who Alex felt that she could be around anymore.

"I'm glad that you don't care anymore Victoria…'cause now, neither do *I*."

Victoria watched as Alex turned on her heel and stormed off.

Chapter 11

"Ooh girl, look at all these sexy men," Malajia crooned, watching the football players from both the home and opposing teams as she made her way to the massive football field. The homecoming game at the university was the much anticipated highlight of the week.

"Girl focus *less* on those tight—"

"Tight asses? I sure *will* focus on those," Malajia joked, interrupting an annoyed Sidra.

"Malajia, put your tongue back in your damn mouth, and let's just find a freakin' seat," Chasity griped, looking at her watch. They'd been standing around the over-crowded concession stands for the past twenty minutes, and she had grown tired.

"Don't rush me, Parker," Malajia replied, checking her appearance in her pocket mirror. She looked up and locked eyes with a tall, dark, handsome player on his way inside the stadium. "Hey, cutie," she smiled, offering a slight wave.

Chasity, noticing the interaction, rolled her eyes. "He's not even paying *attention* to you," she observed, flinging hair over her shoulder.

"Bet money I get his number," Malajia challenged.

"I don't give a fuck," Chasity snapped.

Sidra put her hands up. "Chill out, you two," she urged. "Malajia come on, let's go get these damn seats before all the good ones are taken."

Malajia flagged them with her hand. "Y'all are on my damn nerves," she grumbled, speeding up her walk.

In her haste, Malajia didn't notice the glob of nacho cheese on the floor, and stepped right in it, nearly slipping in the process. The incident caused Chasity and Sidra to bust out laughing.

"That's what your dramatic ass gets," Chasity laughed.

"I *meant* to do that," Malajia threw over her shoulder, trotting towards the ladies room.

"She looks so stupid," Sidra laughed in an aside to Chasity.

"She always *does*," Chasity concluded.

Sidra turned toward Chasity and pointed to her. "That's *your* roommate," she teased.

Chasity sucked her teeth. "Shut up."

Emily counted the change in her hand while waiting to be called up in the hotdog line. She was so preoccupied that she didn't notice Stacey walk up next to her.

"Hi Emily," Stacey smiled, opening a bottle of soda.

Emily glanced up and forced a smile. *Oh goodie, my replacement is here.* Emily wasn't in the mood to socialize with Stacey. She hadn't spoken to her or the other girls since she left their room in tears a week ago.

"You here with the other girls?" Stacey asked, removing money from her jeans pocket.

Emily shook her head. "No…I walked over by myself."

The sullen reply wasn't missed by Stacey, who shot her a sympathetic look. "Well, I'm here with a friend of mine, do you want to sit with us?"

"You mean, you didn't come with *them*?" Emily asked, pleasantly surprised.

"No, but I'm gonna see them later tonight," Stacey revealed.

How nice, Emily thought. "Oh?"

"Yeah we're supposed to go for pizza with the guys," Stacey added, unaware of Emily's feelings. "Are you coming?"

Emily pushed hair behind her ears and looked at the ground. "I'm not sure," she stammered. "I—I wasn't invited."

Embarrassment resonated on Stacey's face. "Oh." She racked her brain for something comforting to say. "Um…well I'm sure they'll invite you," she said, giving Emily a pat on the shoulder. "They're probably just waiting until after the game. I only heard about it this morning when I saw them at breakfast."

They didn't even invite me to breakfast. "Yeah I guess," Emily replied, moving up in line.

"Well…do you still want to sit with me and my friend?" Stacey asked.

Emily glanced at her. "Really? You'll let me sit with you?"

"Sure," Stacey smiled. "You're a friend of Alex's, so that makes you a friend of *mine*."

"This school cheap as shit," Mark complained, making his way up the bleacher steps. "How they not gonna give us trays to carry our food?"

"Don't blame the school because *you* decided to buy the whole concession stand," Josh teased before taking a bite out of his hotdog.

Mark sucked his teeth. "Always minding my damn business, with your one hotdog."

Josh busted out laughing.

"Let's grab these seats over here," David suggested, pointing to a few empty seats in the row ahead of them. "I'm gonna call Sidra and let her know that there are some empty seats behind us."

"You didn't need to tell us all that," Mark mocked, sitting down in a seat.

David rolled his eyes at Mark and placed the cell phone to his ear.

Mark groaned as he struggled to arrange his two hotdogs, burger, cheese fries, fried sandwich cookies and large soda in his lap. "Shit!" he exclaimed when his cup of soda fell over, landing on the floor by his feet. He smiled when the top held its position, keeping the contents from spilling.

"Good deal," he beamed, handing some of his food to Josh. "Hold these right quick." Mark bent down to retrieve the cup, only to have the top fall off, spilling the drink to the floor. "Are you fuckin' kidding me?!" he hollered.

"That's what your smart ass gets," David chuckled as Josh broke into loud laughter.

Mark stared at both guys in anger for several seconds. "Just give me my shit," he seethed, snatching his food from Josh.

"Hey greedy, did you buy the whole stand?" Alex quibbled, taking a seat behind the guys, along with the other girls.

Mark threw his head back and groaned, "It was corny when Josh said it, and it's corny *now*."

"And *your* problem *is*?" Alex frowned at Mark's attitude.

"He's salty because his drink spilled," Josh informed.

"Ahhh, you gonna be thirsty," Malajia teased, giving the back of Mark's head a nudge. "You got all those dry ass cheese fries and shit."

"Malajia, isn't there some mud you should be playing in, you pig?" Mark shot back.

"Boooooo!" Malajia hollered in dramatic fashion. "That comeback was weak."

"Shut up," Mark grumbled through clenched teeth. *I should take my damn sock off and stick it in her big ass mouth.*

Malajia nudged Chasity, who was sitting beside her. "Wasn't that comeback corny?"

"Oh my God, why are you touching me?" Chasity snapped, turning to face her. "Sidra, I'm gonna choke this bitch, switch seats with me."

"Nope, I'm already comfortable," Sidra giggled.

"Ahhh, you stuck sittin' next to me and shit," Malajia teased, unfazed by Chasity's irritation.

Chasity clenched her jaw. Refusing to be drawn into a verbal altercation with the silly Malajia, Chasity faced forward and concentrated on the field in front of her.

"The players are coming out now," Alex announced, pointing to the field.

Mark turned to face Alex. "You hype as shit," he said, earning an eye roll from her. "You act like you never seen a damn game before."

"Boy, will you turn your irritating behind around?" Alex demanded, pointing at him.

"I wish he *would*," Malajia added. "His ugly is drying my face out."

Mark glared daggers at Malajia. "How's your face dry when I jizzed all over it last night?" he sniped. Malajia's eyes widened in shock. "I thought protein was supposed to moisturize."

Chasity busted out laughing.

"You gross bastard!" Malajia wailed, giving Mark's arm a hard slap.

Ignoring the stinging pain on his arm, Mark turned to the laughing Chasity and gave her a high-five. "How was *that* comeback? Good?"

"On point," Chasity confirmed.

"Fuck y'all," Malajia fumed, folding her arms and sitting back in her seat.

"That was disturbing," Sidra scoffed. "Ugh, images, images!" she complained, putting her head in her hands.

Alex turned to Sidra, who was busy trying to shake the

images of Mark ejaculating on Malajia's face from her head. "I'm a little worried about Em," she began. "I haven't spoken to her since last Friday. Have *you*?"

"No," Sidra replied. "I called her a few times, but I didn't get an answer."

"Yeah, I've been calling her too," Alex said. "I even went by her place, but she didn't answer."

"I'm sure she's fine," Sidra assured. "Maybe she's been wrapped up in studying."

"Maybe," Alex replied, facing forward. Despite the answer that she gave Sidra, she wasn't sure if she actually believed it herself.

As the players positioned themselves on the field, Malajia sat up in her seat and began frantically tapping Chasity's arm. "Ooh, ooh, look," she urged, leaning close and pointing to someone.

Chasity backhanded Malajia on the arm. "Girl, stop breathing on me," she barked.

"Look at number fifty-eight," Malajia cooed, paying Chasity's reaction no mind. "That's the guy I was looking at by the stands. The guy from the other team."

Chasity rolled her eyes and looked at the player who had Malajia acting giddy. "And?" she scoffed.

"Isn't he sexy?"

"Nope," Chasity returned, tone even.

Malajia sucked her teeth. "You're full of shit," she ground out.

"Or, he's *just* not sexy," Chasity returned.

"Whatever you say Mrs. Adams," Malajia threw back. "I forgot you like em' light skinned, and not chocolate."

Chasity made a face at her.

"That game was intense," Sidra breathed, fanning herself. The football game ended merely minutes ago, with Paradise Valley winning by two touchdowns. As the crowds of students and alumni filtered down the bleachers and onto the field, the group stood off to the side, hoping to catch Jason in passing.

"Where is he? Where is he?" Malajia asked, craning her neck every which way.

"Who, Jason?" Alex asked.

"Naw, my future boyfriend," Malajia answered.

"Didn't that *used* to be Jason? In your *mind*, anyway," Sidra laughed, recalling Malajia's short-lived crush on Jason last fall.

Malajia shot the giggling Sidra a glare. "Always gotta bring up old shit," she ground out.

Jason was hurrying past the group with the rest of his team when Chasity reached out and grabbed his arm, stopping him. He smiled when he saw her. "I'm sorry, didn't see you," he said, tucking his helmet under his arm.

"Good game bruh," Mark commended, giving Jason a high-five.

"We're so proud of you," Sidra grinned, clasping her hands together.

"You looked good out there Jase," Alex gushed, giving his arm a light tap. "Way to win for the home team." Her compliment was met with eye rolls and groans from some of the group. "What?" she asked, voice filled with amusement.

"You always gotta be on some ole' jolly shit," Mark griped. "'Way to win for the home team'," he mocked. "Just say good game."

David shook his head. "You've been angry ever since your soda spilled," he teased, pushing his glasses up on his nose.

"It should've spilled on those *glasses*," Mark returned.

"Thanks guys," Jason replied, ignoring the sniping. He looked at Chasity, who was staring at him. "What did *you* think of the game?" he asked, "Are *you* proud of me too?"

"I mean…you did okay," she jeered.

Jason chuckled. "I guess that's a good thing, coming from *you*."

"No, you did really good…as always," Chasity amended. *God, even all sweaty he's still sexy.* Chasity rubbed her eyes in an effort to rub the sexual image of Jason out of her head. *Girl! Get your shit together.*

She's actually being nice to you, ask her out again. Jason opened his mouth to speak but was interrupted by his teammates calling his name. "We still hanging out later?" he asked the group, eyes not leaving Chasity.

"You know it," Mark replied. "Pizza on the winner."

"No, pizza on the *freeloader*," Jason returned, before heading off to join his team.

Malajia tossed her arm up in the air. "I can't believe it. I've seen every other damn player pass by here, but not my man," she fussed. "Where *is* he?"

"In the toilet with the other shit logs," Mark answered, still salty from Jason's dig.

Malajia flagged him with her hand. Mark and his smart comments were the last thing on her mind as she continued to search the crowd with her eyes for the mysterious player.

Sidra spotted a familiar figure standing just a few feet away from them. "There's Emily, Alex," she announced, giving Alex a nudge. "She's over there with Stacey."

Alex glanced over. Eyes lighting up, she shouted for them at the top of her lungs.

"And y'all say *I'm* loud," Mark grunted, rubbing his ear as the two girls approached.

"Where were you two sitting?" Alex asked, ignoring Mark's comment.

"At the bottom of the bleachers," Stacey answered.

Sidra looked at Emily, who was looking at the floor. "Emily, long time no see," she said.

"Sorry, I've been um…studying."

Sidra eyed Emily skeptically. "I figured that," she replied after a few seconds. Sidra couldn't put her finger on it, but Emily's attitude seemed a little different to her. Standoffish even.

"Emily, we're all going out later on," Alex announced.

"You should come with us."

Emily successfully contained her frustration. *Thanks for asking me at the last minute.* "Um…I can't," she slowly put out. "I have a few tests coming up this week that I really need to study for."

Alex was taken back. Recently, Emily had only denied outings with them when her mother was around. Mother nowhere in sight, and Emily was still declining an invitation to hang out with the group. Not to mention the fact that Emily hadn't been answering her calls or the door.

Something's wrong. Alex smiled as she walked up and gently took hold of Emily's arm. "Come talk to me real quick," she urged, guiding Emily away from the group.

When they were out of range, Alex looked at Emily, a sympathetic look on her face. "Em, is something wrong?"

Emily stared at her short, unpolished nails. *I feel like you guys are replacing me.* "No," she lied.

"Are you sure?" Alex pressed. "I mean, you seem like…I don't know, like you're upset with us, with *me* maybe."

Emily continued to focus on her nails.

"I've been calling you all week and you never pick up," Alex continued. "I come by your apartment and…I don't know, I just want to make sure we're good."

"We're fine." Emily's answer was barely audible.

Disturbed by the fact that Emily had not made eye contact with her the entire time, she gently took Emily's chin in her hand and lifted it up. "Emily?" she said.

Emily forced a smile. "We're fine," she assured, voice louder. "I'm just stressed over my classes. I've been having a crazy amount of assignments…That's all."

Alex stared at Emily, *I swear it feels like you're lying.* "Emily, you know we love you right?"

Emily was confused. *That was out of nowhere.* "I know," she replied, pushing her bangs to the side.

"Good," Alex smiled. "Next time we do something, make sure you come okay? Don't think that because you're not living with us, that we won't include you."

That's exactly what's happening. "I will," Emily promised, despite what was going on in her head.

Chapter 12

"This rain is horrible," Stacey griped to a dorm mate in route to her room. Stacey flung the water from her hand, then opened the door. Relieved to find the room empty, she tossed the soaked umbrella and coat on the floor. Stacey retrieved her mail from her book bag, then flopped down on her bed and began scanning the letters.

"Damn, people sure do miss me from back home," she mused to herself, eyeing the return addresses from friends and family.

She noticed that one letter didn't have a return address. Frowning, she ripped open the letter and began to read it.

'Stacey, I know it's weird that I'm writing you, but I don't have Alex's new room information. I know after everything that has happened, you probably hate me just as much as she does. But I need a favor, I need to talk to her. Can you please tell her to call me? It's important.'

Stacey put her hand over her mouth as she continued to read.

'Please, whatever you do, don't tell Victoria that I sent this, thanks – Paul'

"Shit," Stacey panicked, placing her hand on her forehead. She quickly balled up the letter and threw it into her book bag when she heard the doorknob turn. Her eyes locked with a talking Victoria, who abruptly ended the call on her cell phone without saying goodbye.

"Why do you look so nervous?" Victoria asked, noticing the wide-eyed look on Stacey's face.

"Why do *you*?" Stacey threw back. "You hung up on somebody pretty quick."

"It was Mom," Victoria replied, tossing her book bag by her closet.

Stacey eyed Victoria suspiciously. *You would never hang up on your mom like that, you liar.*

"What's your problem?" Victoria sneered, picking up on Stacey's vibes.

Stacey shook her head as she stood up. "Don't worry about it," she spat, walking out the door.

The rain no longer concerning her, Stacey hurried to Paradise Terrace and up to Alex's floor. She knocked on the door and waited for a response, sighing when she didn't get one after the third knock. Preparing to make the journey back to her dorm, she figured she would try one other room first.

"Coming!" Stacey heard Malajia call from inside the room after she'd knocked.

Stacey gave a half smile once Malajia opened the door. "Hey Malajia, is Alex here by any chance?"

"Naw, she's in the library I think," Malajia panted. "You look like a wet dog, you wanna come in and dry off?"

Stacey chuckled. "Yeah, my simple butt forgot my umbrella," she admitted, stepping inside and removing her rain boots, leaving them by the door.

Malajia turned the TV down with the remote and grabbed a bottle of water from the fridge. "You can sit your coat by the vent," she offered, trying to catch her breath.

Stacey thanked her as she removed her coat. She then sat down on the floor by the vent. "What were you in here doing that has you breathing all crazy?"

"Girl, I was watching videos and trying to get those damn dance moves," Malajia revealed, sitting down on her bed. "They doin' too much. Got me in here sweatin' my perm out."

Stacey laughed, pulling her wet braids into a ponytail. "Thanks for letting me chill for a minute."

Malajia waved her hand in Stacey's direction. "Don't mention it," she replied. Noticing that Stacey's face took a gloomy turn, Malajia frowned. "You cool?"

Stacey looked up. "Oh, yeah I'm fine." *Or at least I will be once I talk to Alex.*

Malajia shrugged, then went back to drinking her water.

As Stacey relished the heat hitting her back while she waited for her clothes to dry a little, she began letting her mind wander. The letter that she'd just received, as well as prior events, were plaguing her and if she didn't say something, she felt like she was going to explode.

"Malajia, can I ask you something?"

Malajia nodded as she fanned herself.

Stacey took a deep breath. "What would you do, if…" she paused as she tried to gather her words. "If you knew about something that happened to a friend…but the friend didn't know?"

Malajia frowned. "What *kind* of something?"

"Something bad."

"*How* bad?" Malajia asked, curious.

Stacey took a deep breath. "If this friend found out…it would devastate them," she hesitantly put out. "Would you tell them? Or would you keep it to yourself to avoid hurting them?"

"If you want me to tell you to keep it to yourself, then you got the wrong person," Malajia replied. "My mouth is huge so I'd tell every-damn-body."

Stacey put her head in her hands. "God, I hate this," she mumbled.

"Whatever it is, it sounds like you need to say something," Malajia pointed out. "Things always have a way of coming out, and if this person finds out that you knew about *whatever* it is and didn't say anything...well, you may just get cussed out."

That's what I'm afraid of, Stacey thought.

"Is this secret about Alex?" Malajia asked, coming to a realization. "Whose ass do I gotta beat about my girl?"

Stacey stood from the floor and grabbed her coat. "No, it's not about Alex," she lied. "I gotta go."

"Oh." Malajia almost seemed disappointed. "Well, at least give me a hint about who it's *about*. Is it someone on campus?"

"Bye Malajia," Stacey chortled, heading out the door.

"Aww come on, you know I'm nosey!" Malajia called after her.

Grabbing her cup of hot tea, Alex took a sip before highlighting yet another line in her textbook. She'd grown tired of the library after being in there for over two hours, and decided to finish her studies back in her room.

A light tap on the door broke through the quiet. "It's open," she called. Seeing Stacey walk through the door, Alex sat her book on her bed.

"I won't be long, I know you're studying," Stacey announced, sitting on the bed.

"No it's okay, I needed the break," Alex assured. "What's up? You seemed so serious when you called me earlier."

Stacey rubbed her hands across her jeans, peering at the notebooks sprawled across Alex's bed. *I wish I could concentrate long enough to study*, she thought. Ever since receiving that letter from Paul earlier that day, books were the furthest thing from her mind.

"So...Paul contacted me," Stacey drew out, earning a confused look from Alex.

"Wait...he contacted *you*?"

Stacey nodded. "Yeah…he can't get in touch with you personally, and he really wants to talk to you."

"For *what*?" Alex bit out. "I have nothing to say to him."

"Clearly he has something to say to *you*," Stacey pointed out. "I mean, have you two really sat down and talked after your break up?"

"Nope, what would be the point in that?" Alex dismissed. "He cheated, end of story."

Stacey ran her hand along the back of her neck. "Look…I know that you're still angry at him," she began, trying to carefully put out her words. "And rightfully so. But, I just think that maybe you should talk to him…I mean, maybe you can get some closure."

Alex stood from her bed and walked over to the microwave. "I don't need closure," she barked, grabbing a bag of popcorn from a box. "When he stuck his damn penis inside of someone else, that closed the damn relationship for me."

"Wow," Stacey commented.

Alex turned the microwave on and sighed. "I'm sorry, I don't mean to snap at you," she apologized. "I just wish he would leave me the hell alone…I mean, first it was that stupid letter that he brought to my house when I came home that time, and now—"

"Did you ever read that, by the way?" Stacey asked.

Alex shook her head. "It must've gotten thrown away by accident. I don't remember seeing it after he left."

"Oh, okay," Stacey mumbled.

"You know what's weird though?" Alex asked, after moments of silence. "You just reminded me of something."

"What's that?"

"I ran into Sherry over the summer," Alex revealed to a surprised Stacey. "I forgot about it because I had the whole 'am I gonna get kicked out of school' thing on my mind then, but yeah…I saw her and I confronted her and…"

"And *what*?" Stacey pressed.

"I don't know, it was weird," Alex admitted, recalling

the encounter. "She said that she left Philly not long after we graduated and that she never got with Paul."

"Didn't Victoria tell you that she *did*?" Stacey asked, already knowing the answer.

Alex removed the popcorn from the microwave and faced Stacey. "Yeah, which is what makes me think that Sherry is a liar, just like she's *always* been," she replied. "She probably bought that fake engagement ring to throw me off."

Stacey stared at Alex momentarily. "Alex...why would she go through that trouble?" she asked. "I'm sure she had no idea that she was going to run into you that day."

"I mean, I get that but—"

"I'm sorry sis, it doesn't make sense," Stacey interrupted. "I haven't seen the girl since you graduated and she used to live around the corner from me."

Alex stood there, a confused look on her face. "Are you trying to tell me that Victoria lied about seeing him with Sherry?"

Stacey looked down at her hands. "I'm saying...just talk to Paul," she urged, standing from the bed.

"Stacey," Alex called, prompting Stacey to turn around. "Is there something that I should know? Did he not really cheat?"

"Talk to him," Stacey insisted and walked out, leaving behind a bewildered Alex.

Malajia retrieved a box of tampons from a shelf and examined the box closely. "Super absorbent my black ass," she griped, tossing the box into a shopping cart which was already half full with toiletries and snacks.

She threw her head back and groaned once she realized how many bags she would have to carry. Having to take the shuttle bus to the Mega-Mart which was a fifteen minute ride off campus, had Malajia's mood shot. "Stupid Chasity and her 'not driving me 'cause she has class' ass," she grunted, placing some of the items back on a shelf.

She pushed the cart out of the aisle and nearly collided with another shopper.

"Yo, watch where you're going!" the young man barked.

"Man, fuck outta here with that tone dawg," Malajia shot back, waving her hand at him dismissively. She was about to delve into her vocabulary of profanity when she recognized the tall, dark-skinned, built man frowning in front of her.

"Have we met?" she asked, voice calm.

The man relaxed his frown. "I don't think so," he replied, roaming up and down Malajia's frame with his eyes. The tight jeans, red top, and black leather jacket that she had on, failed to conceal her shape. "But I'd like to *get* to know you, with your sexy self."

Malajia blushed slightly. His presence was overpowering. "You sure?" she pressed. "You don't go to Paradise Valley University?"

He shook his head. "Nah, I recently played there in the homecoming game though," he confirmed.

Malajia snapped her fingers as she made the connection. "That's right, you're number fifty-eight."

He frowned in confusion. "Who?"

Malajia giggled. "Your jersey number," she clarified. "Prime State University right?"

He nodded. "Yep, that's my school."

Malajia stared at him while he spoke. He was just as handsome as she remembered. His broad arms, strong features, and smooth dark skin made her lose her breath.

"So, you were checking me out, huh?"

"Who *wasn't*?" she cooed, eyes fixed on his chest. "I'm Malajia Simmons," she introduced, holding out her hand.

He took hold of her hand and held it. "Tyrone Edmonds."

Malajia giggled as she flipped some of her hair away from her eyes.

He glanced into her cart. "Stocking up, huh?" he teased.

Malajia looked down and noticed the large box of

tampons in her cart. *Nooooo!* "Um, those aren't mine," she stammered. "I'm holding them for someone."

A laugh erupted from Tyrone. "Listen, how about you give me your phone number," he suggested, pulling out his cell phone.

Anything you want you tall, sexy, black candy bar. Malajia quickly went into her handbag and pulled out her phone. Once she gave him her number, he texted her straight away.

"Wanted to give me yours *too*, huh?" she smiled.

"*That*, and I wanted to make sure you didn't give the wrong number," he replied, shoving the phone back into his pocket. "I'll call you later," he promised, walking away.

"You *better*," she returned, following his progress with her eyes. Just like that, her day was looking up.

Chapter 13

Stacey shoved some papers into her book bag. As she slung the heavy bag over her shoulder, she heard a knock at the door. Thinking it was a dorm mate she was expecting, she smiled as she opened the door.

"Girl, I can't wait for this class to be over," Stacey proclaimed.

Surprise registered on her face; it wasn't who she was expecting. "What the hell?!" she exclaimed, her wide eyes fixing on the man in front of her. "Paul? What are you—"

"Alex hasn't called me," Paul spat, walking in to the room.

Stacey was in panic mode and it showed on her face as she quickly shut the door behind her. "It's only been a few days, maybe—"

"She has no intention of calling me," Paul interrupted. "I need to talk to her, I can't take this anymore."

Stacey was at a loss for words. As she tried to figure out what to say, Victoria walked through the door and nearly screamed at the sight of Paul.

"What the hell are you doing here?" Victoria barked, tossing her book bag to the floor. She stormed over to him.

Paul put his hand up. "Victoria, I'm not for it today," he replied, voice stern.

"No, what are you doing here?"

Paul grabbed Victoria's hand as she went to slap him. "I'm going to talk to Alex," he promised.

"You son of a bitch!" Victoria wailed.

"This shit is over!" Paul yelled, pointing at Victoria.

Stacey couldn't believe what was transpiring in front of her. While Victoria and Paul were arguing, Stacey seized the opportunity and ran out of the room.

Stacey ran all the way to Paradise Terrace, reaching the dorm within record time.

I can't believe this is happening, she panicked, knocking on the door, "Alex!" she called.

Malajia opened her room door and stuck her head out. "Stacey, she's not back from class yet," she frowned.

"Shit!" Stacey panicked, putting her hands on her head.

"What's the problem?" Malajia frowned.

Stacey turned to Malajia. "Alex is about to get gut-punched real bad," she revealed.

"What?" Malajia exclaimed. "Somebody got beef?"

"Malajia, I gotta find her."

"No, you need to come in here real quick," Malajia ordered, signaling for Stacey to come into the room.

Stacey breathed heavily as she walked inside. "This whole shit is about to blow up."

Malajia opened her mouth to speak when Chasity walked through the door. "Ooh! Chaz I met number fifty-eight earlier," Malajia beamed to an unenthused Chasity.

"Mel, I have a damn headache," Chasity tiredly returned, tossing her books on her bed. "I don't feel like your pointless bullshit."

Malajia made a face at Chasity. "Um, you *will* listen to my awesome news later on," she promised. "But for now, I think it's something going on with Alex."

"Something like *what?*" Chasity asked, searching in her drawer for some aspirin.

Malajia looked at Stacey. "You might as well spill it, 'cause we're gonna find out eventually," she urged. "*Especially* if somebody is tryna fight her."

Chasity looked at them, confused. "*Who's* trying to fight Alex?" she barked. "They don't want that problem."

"Girl, that's what *I'm* talking about," Malajia added, heading for her closet. "We ridin'. Where's my sneaks?"

"Nobody is fighting Alex," Stacey interrupted. "But...she *is* about to find out..." *You might as well get it out, you're about to go crazy.* "You guys know the whole story about Paul, right?"

"Yeah," Malajia said. "I got my ass cussed out over it," she added, recalling the verbal lashing that she took from Alex the day that she found out about his infidelity.

"Anyway...the whole story about Paul cheating with some girl named Sherry is..." Stacey paused when she heard Alex's voice from the hall. Jumping up from her seat, she darted out of the door.

"Oh uh uh," Malajia griped. "There's *no* way I'm not gonna find out what's going on," she said, following Stacey out of the room with Chasity in tow.

"Alex, I need to talk to you," Stacey announced.

Alex, having just said something to Sidra, looked over. Her smile faded at the seriousness in Stacey's tone and face. "What's wrong?"

"A *lot*," Stacey vaguely replied, walking into Alex's room, with the girls following. Stacey sat on Alex's bed and gestured for her to sit next to her.

"What's going on?" Alex asked, voice full of concern. "Is something going on with your family?"

Stacey shook her head.

"Is it *my* family?" Alex asked, voice filled with fear.

Stacey once again shook her head.

"Yo, *whatever* it is, you need to tell her," Malajia prompted.

"Tell her *what*?" Sidra asked Malajia, who just signaled for her to be quiet.

Alex glanced at the girls, then looked back at Stacey. "It's okay, whatever it is, you can say it in front of them," Alex assured, seeing the troubled look on Stacey's face.

Stacey took a deep breath. "Alex, Paul is here," she blurted out.

"Here, *where*?" Alex questioned in disbelief.

"On campus," Stacey confirmed. "Remember when I told you that he wanted to talk to you the other day?"

Alex nodded.

"Well, when you didn't contact him, he came *here*." Stacey shook her head. "He has something to tell you, and before he does, so do *I*."

"Aww shit now," Malajia commented in anticipation.

"Just spit it out," Alex ordered.

"When you asked me the other night if there was something you needed to know…I should've said this *then*, but I couldn't." Stacey grabbed hold of Alex's hands and held them. "Sherry wasn't lying about not sleeping with Paul…Victoria made that up."

Alex was confused. "Why would Victoria do that?"

"Because she—"

"I don't get it," Alex rambled, upset. "I mean, did he not cheat? Did I break up with him over nothing?"

"No, he *did* cheat," Stacey confirmed.

"With *who*?" Alex asked, frustrated with conversation.

When Stacey hesitated, Chasity pinched the bridge of her nose with her fingers. "Shit," she commented in a quiet aside to Malajia and Sidra. She knew exactly where this conversation was headed.

"He cheated…with Victoria," Stacey revealed.

Her revelation was met with a gasp from Sidra.

"What?!" Malajia exclaimed as Chasity shook her head in disgust.

Alex looked like someone had just stabbed her in the heart. "Wait, what do you—No, she wouldn't do that," she sputtered.

Stacey wished that she could block out the pain on

Alex's face. "I'm sorry, Alex."

"No, seriously," Alex muttered, tears filling her eyes. "She wouldn't—she did? She slept with Paul?"

Stacey nodded.

"Triflin' bitch," Malajia seethed.

"Hold on," Chasity cut in. "How the fuck did *you* find out?" she directed at Stacey.

"The letter that Paul left at Alex's house," Stacey revealed.

Alex was in so much shock, she couldn't speak. She just repeatedly fanned her face with her hands in an effort to keep the tears from spilling over.

"Victoria took the letter," Stacey said. "I saw it on her desk when I went over her house later that night. I snuck and read it…It told everything."

Alex ran a trembling hand through her hair. "I thought the letter—" she looked at Stacey. "Exactly *what* did that letter say? What did she do with it? Where is it?"

Stacey looked at the floor. "She threw it away but—"

"But *what*?" Alex barked.

Stacey retrieved the cell phone from her pocket and clicked something before handing the phone to Alex.

"You took a picture of it?" Malajia assumed, shocked.

Stacey nodded in shame.

"Why didn't you say anything?" Chasity fussed.

"I don't know," Stacey answered honestly as Alex began to read it. "I guess…I thought I was protecting her."

"And that bitch had the nerve to catch an attitude because Alex hung out with *us*," Malajia fumed. "Like *we* were the bad ones."

Tears fell from Alex's eyes as she read the words on the screen.

'Alex, I know you probably don't want anything to do with me after what happened, and, I don't blame you. But I just can't go on any longer with you not knowing the whole truth. Yes I cheated, and I was wrong for that, for hurting you. But, I'm not the only person in your life who wronged

College Life 201; Sophomore Studies

you. When I cheated on you, it wasn't with some random chick. It was with Victoria.'

Alex wiped her eyes as she continued to read.

'She's not your friend Alex, she's been trying to get with me even before you graduated. When you went away, she would call me all the time and tell me about the conversations that you would have. She made it seem like you were moving on with someone else and I let her get to me. I played right into her and for that, I'm sorry. I still care about you and I couldn't stand around and watch you be loyal to her, when she doesn't give a damn about you.

I hope that you can find it in your heart to forgive me one day- Paul'

Alex slowly handed the phone back to Stacey. "I can't believe this," she sniffled.

Sidra walked over and wrapped her arms around Alex, who looked like she was about to break down. "I'm sorry sweetie," she sympathized.

"No. She was supposed to be my best friend." Alex's voice trembled. "She made me feel like I was treating her like shit, and this whole time, she was treating *me* like shit."

"Can I fuck her up now?" Chasity asked.

"Yes! Please?" Malajia added, clapping her hands.

Alex wanted to respond, but couldn't. She broke down crying in Sidra's arms. Devastated, she felt deceived and betrayed. This girl had been in her house. She had confided in her about everything that had to do with Paul and Victoria used it to get him behind her back.

Chasity felt her headache worsen, emotion building up inside at the sight of her friend breaking down.

Malajia nudged Chasity. "Go hug her," she urged, sensing Chasity's hesitation.

Chasity walked over, and as Sidra moved aside, to allow her access, Chasity wrapped her arms around Alex, who leaned on Chasity's arm as she continued to cry.

Malajia wiped a tear from her eye as she shook her head. She felt horrible for her friend, she couldn't imagine what

Alex was going through. "Alex about to snot on Chasity's sweater and shit," she teased, trying to break the sad vibe in the room.

Sidra gave Malajia a stern look as Stacey shook her head.

Alex just continued to cry as she held on to Chasity.

Stacey watched Alex pace her room. "Are you okay?" she asked her.

"I *will* be once I see her face to face." Alex was boiling as she continued her pace. After having a long cry on the shoulders of her friends, she and Stacey walked back to Torrence Hall and waited for Victoria to return.

"I'm so sorry I didn't tell you," Stacey apologized for the fifth time.

"I wish that you *would've*," Alex admitted. "But, I'm not mad at you. I'm mad at *them*."

"I had every intention of calling Victoria out on it," Stacey continued. "I knew that she would just lie—"

"It's irrelevant now," Alex replied, bite in her voice.

Alex stopped her pacing and faced the door once she heard keys jiggling. Stacey sat back on her bed and waited. She knew that this confrontation wouldn't be pretty, and she had no intention of intervening. As far as she was concerned, Victoria had everything coming to her.

Victoria gasped as she came face to face with an angry Alex. "Alex? What are you doing here?" she hesitantly put out.

Alex stared at Victoria, eyes flaming. *No, she didn't.* "Since you wanna play like you don't know what the fuck I'm doing here, I'm just gonna get this shit started," she seethed. "You fucked my man?"

Victoria was caught off guard. *Shit!* She'd made sure to stick with Paul the entire day to keep him from tracking Alex down on campus, so she knew Alex couldn't have spoken to him. "I don't know what you're talking about," she maintained.

Alex stormed over and stood close to Victoria's face. "Don't play dumb with me, Victoria!" she boomed. "I know *everything*! I know that Sherry never slept with Paul, it was *you*! *You* slept with him. *You* broke us up, you backstabbing, lying bitch!"

Victoria flinched at the bass in Alex's voice. "Who— who told—"

"*I* told her," Stacey revealed, angry. "I read that letter that you took from Alex's house. You're disgusting."

Victoria's head snapped towards Stacey. "So *that* explains why you've been giving me attitude since that day," she bit out.

"This is not about Stacey." Alex pointed in Victoria's face. "This is about *you*. How could you do that to me? I trusted you!"

Victoria felt tears well up in her eyes just as tears filled Alex's.

"How long has this been going on? Huh?" Alex asked. "Was it before I graduated? Before I left?"

"No...it didn't happen until you came here," Victoria sobbed, no longer able to keep up the lie.

"So you sat there and listened as I confided in you about what we were going through, and you—you used that to go after my boyfriend." Alex shook her head as Victoria cried. "No, you don't get to do that," she barked. "You don't get to stand here and cry about this, *I* should be the one crying."

Alex felt like exploding as she stared at the woman she once referred to as her sister. "You lied and told him that I was up here dealing with other guys?" she asked.

Victoria put her hands over her face as she continued to weep.

"Oh, *now* you can't speak?" Alex taunted. "You bitch! You sat on the phone and lied to me...you sat there while I cried to you. You—you offered me words of encouragement when I felt like my world was falling apart and the whole time *you* were the one *tearing* it apart!"

Victoria sniffled. There was no excuse that she could come up with that would justify her betrayal. "I—I'm so—"

Alex pointed her finger in Victoria's face once again. "Don't!" she hollered, making Victoria flinch. "Don't you dare fix your fuckin' mouth to say that you're sorry," she fumed. "You can keep your sorry. You're dead to me."

Victoria's crying only fueled Alex's anger. Feeling herself about to lose control, Alex backed up. "I swear, I should drag your skinny ass up and down this campus by your fuckin' neck," she threatened. She smirked at the scared look on Victoria's face. "Oh don't worry, I'm not gonna put myself in a position to get kicked out of school for beating your ass. You're not worth it."

Alex headed for the door. "And since I'm pretty sure your nasty ass is gonna run to *wherever* Paul is later, let him know that I have no words for him *either*," she added, turning to face Victoria once again. "You can both rot in the hell that you created. Enjoy my leftovers, you piece of garbage."

"Alex, wait," Victoria called as Alex grabbed for the doorknob.

"You don't want to say another word to me right now," Alex warned, stopping in her tracks.

Ignoring Alex's words, Victoria slowly approached. "I know that nothing I can say, can make up for what happened—"

Before Victoria knew what had happened, Alex delivered a stinging backhanded slap across her face, sending her stumbling back into her dresser.

"Shit!" Stacey exclaimed, jumping up from the bed. *That's definitely gonna leave a mark.*

Without saying another word, Alex stormed out of the room, leaving Victoria holding her face, crying out in pain as she tried to keep the blood from her busted lip from dripping on the floor.

Chapter 14

Chasity slammed her textbook shut and shoved it into her book bag. *Dumbass class, I hate Calculus*, she complained silently, heading out the door.

"Miss Parker," Professor Dodson called.

Chasity stopped suddenly. "Why are you talking to me?" she mumbled to herself before turning around. "Yeah?"

"I'm not pleased with your test scores," she said to Chasity once the classroom was empty.

"*You?*" Chasity muttered. Seeing the big red 'F' on yet another test that the professor handed back in the beginning of class made Chasity want to scream, or better yet, throw a chair through the classroom window.

"I remember you, Miss Parker," Professor Dodson said, shuffling papers on her desk. "You struggled in the beginning of both of your Calculus classes last year, but you turned it around in the end," she pointed out. "I suggest that whatever help you received then, you get *now*."

Chasity fought the urge to roll her eyes. *How did I end up with the same Calculus professor for three semesters in a fuckin' row?*

"I mean it, Miss Parker," she insisted. "You're a smart young lady…Your attitude could use some work."

This time Chasity *did* roll her eyes.

"But smart, none-the-less, and I want to see you excel in your field," Professor Dodson added.

"My field is *computers*," Chasity spat, fixing her book bag on her shoulder. If the heavy book bag or her professor's talking wasn't irritating her, her tension headache and menstrual cramps certainly were.

"And *Calculus,* as well as other math courses, are a *part* of that field."

Chasity let out a loud sigh. "Are we finished?"

"Yes, for now," Professor Dodson smiled. As Chasity made her way to the door, Professor Dodson had a thought. "You know Jason Adams right?"

Chasity once again stopped short. *Please God, stop talking to me before my insides fall out.* "Yes."

"He's an excellent math student, maybe you could ask him for help."

"Great," Chasity sneered, walking out of the door. *I'm not asking for any more damn help. I should know this shit by now.* As if on cue, she saw Jason heading past her, on his way into the classroom.

"Hey, my day just got better," he smiled. His smile faded when he saw the pained look on Chasity's face. "Is something wrong?"

"Nope," she lied, continuing her pace.

Jason gently caught her by the arm, stopping her. "Somehow, I find that hard to believe."

Chasity gritted her teeth. She was irritated and in pain, the last thing she wanted was to stand in the hallway and have a talk.

"I'm fine, Jason," she bit out.

He frowned. "Then why do you look like you're about to pass out?"

"Because my head hurts, I'm tired, and my fuckin' uterus is contracting," she snapped, clutching her stomach.

"Oooooh," Jason slowly put out. *Poor baby, no wonder she's pissed.*

"Nice reaction," Chasity hissed.

Jason put his hands up. "I'm sorry," he replied. He hated the fact that she was in pain and he couldn't do anything to stop it. "Let me walk you back to your room," he offered.

"Don't you have class?" she asked, agitated.

Jason shook his head. "No, I was just dropping something off to Professor Dodson," he answered. "Come on, I'll walk with you."

"Why?" she threw back, exasperated.

"Because, I *want* to," he replied, gently taking her book bag from her hand. He put his arm around her, and, surprisingly, she leaned her head on his shoulder as he guided her towards the exit.

I wish I could crawl into a hole and disappear, Emily thought as she made her way down the library steps and proceeded on the brick-lined path to her apartment. Having spent hours in the library trying to study for three tests in classes that she was already struggling in, after learning that her mother would be popping in for yet another visit later that week, Emily's stress level was at an all-time high. Having gotten visits from her mother several times within the past few weeks, Emily was at her wits end.

Why is she coming down here again?! Why doesn't she have her own life!

Emily was so preoccupied with her own burdening thoughts that she didn't see the person walking in the opposite direction.

"Oh!" she exclaimed, nearly colliding with the person.

Praz placed his hands on Emily's shoulder to steady her. "Whoa, my bad," he apologized, amusement in his voice.

Embarrassed about the awkward encounter, Emily looked at the ground as she pushed some hair behind her ears. "Sorry."

"In a hurry?" he chortled.

Emily shrugged. "Just heading back to my room."

Praz nodded at the shy girl in front of him. She looked so lost without the other girls around. After exchanging goodbyes, Praz went to walk away, but remembered something. "Hey, are you gonna see Malajia later?" he asked.

Probably not, Emily thought. She hadn't been hanging with the girls as much lately. After being the last to hear about what happened with Alex and Victoria, a week after it happened, Emily felt left out.

"Um, maybe," she answered. "Do you want me to give her a message or something? Is everything okay?"

Praz sat his book bag down on the ground and unzipped it. "Oh yeah, it's nothing important," he replied, searching inside. "I'm on my way home for a few days and I wanted to give her this before I left."

Emily stared, uncertain, as he pulled out a juice bottle full of red liquid. "You want to give her juice?"

A deep laugh erupted from Praz. "Nah, it's not juice. It's my special drink," he affirmed. "She's been blowing up my phone asking me to make some…Can you give it to her for me?"

Emily eyed the bottle. "Um…okay."

"I was gonna stop past her room before I left, but it's in the other direction."

Emily gently grabbed the bottle. "No problem, I can give it to her," she smiled, stuffing the bottle into her pink and grey book bag. After Praz headed off, Emily continued on her way.

"I hate Spanish," Malajia groaned to herself while staring at her textbook. After trying to study for her midterm for the past two hours, she was at her wits end with her foreign language requirement.

She slammed the book shut and let out a loud sigh. Then she heard a tap on the door. "Whoever it is, I hope you know some damn Spanish," she hurled.

Sidra walked through the door, amusement written on her face. "I'm no expert at it, but I *did* pass my class last semester," she answered.

Malajia made a face. "Didn't nobody ask you that," she griped.

Sidra giggled. "I stopped over to bring your bracelet back," she revealed, handing Malajia the wide, sparkly, bright red cuff bracelet.

"Did you even *wear* it?"

"No," Sidra admitted. "The gaudy look is more *your* thing," she teased.

Malajia rolled her eyes, gesturing towards her dresser. "Just toss it there," she ordered, then flopped back on the bed.

"What's wrong?" Sidra asked, noticing Malajia's depressing demeanor. "Spanish on your nerves?"

"*That*, and…" Malajia sat up, while trying to decide if she even wanted to reveal what was really bothering her. "You remember that guy I told you about, a few weeks ago? The one who I gave my number to?"

Sidra looked confused. "Mel, you give your number to *a lot* of guys."

Malajia narrowed her eyes. "I really *don't*," she bit out, earning a giggle from Sidra. "Anyway, he was the football player that I was checking out during homecoming," she explained. "He hasn't called me yet."

Sidra frowned. She did in fact remember who Malajia was referring to; she spent the next few days after their encounter running her mouth about him.

"Um…you gave your number to him *weeks* ago," Sidra reminded.

"Yes, I'm aware."

"And you're bothered by this, *why*?" Sidra questioned.

Malajia looked at Sidra as if she was crazy. "Because he didn't call, *duh*," she barked. "Haven't you been listening?"

Sidra shook her head. "The smartness isn't necessary," she scoffed. "What I meant was, if this fool hasn't taken the time to call you, *why* are you wasting your time worrying about him?" she clarified. "Screw him, there are plenty of men who would *love* to call you."

"See, I know that and all," Malajia replied, scratching her head. "But…Sid you know some of these dudes on this campus be dry as shit."

Sidra busted out laughing.

"And he is the finest piece of chocolate that I've seen in a while and…I guess I just wanted to get to know him." Malajia waved her hand dismissively. "Whatever, you're right. Fuck him."

"Exactly," Sidra agreed, reaching for Malajia's textbook. "And if you're looking for something chocolate, there's always *Mark*," she joked.

Malajia eyed Sidra with disgust. "Sid, I will punch you in the boobs," she warned.

Sidra waved her hand at Malajia. "Anyway, enough about that, let me quiz you on some of these words. Midterms are next week."

Malajia threw her head back. "Don't remind me."

"How do you say, 'what school do you go to?' in Spanish?" Sidra quizzed.

Malajia stared blankly for a few moments. "Um…Donde estas la escuela de pollo?" She drew out her words slowly.

Sidra returned Malajia's blank stare with one of her own. "Do you really want to give that answer?" she asked.

Malajia shrugged. Frustrated, Sidra pushed the book at her. Malajia flipped through the book and settled on a page.

"Wait, did I just say school of chicken?" Malajia laughed.

Sidra shook her head. "I can see where this is going," she uttered.

Malajia followed her progress to the door. "Where are you going?"

"To go study, *away* from your nonsense," Sidra retuned, opening the door. "Adios."

Malajia stomped her foot on the floor. "I don't know

what that *means*!" she hollered at the closed door.

Chasity rubbed her temple as she stared at the Calculus problems in her notebook. She sighed.

Get your shit together, Chasity.

Escaping to the library a half-hour ago for some quiet, Chasity was trying her best to complete her Calculus homework. She checked her answer to the problem she had just finished against the back of her Calculus textbook. Her work was incorrect, again. She took a deep breath, and slammed both hands on the wooden table.

"Fuck!" she snapped, shoving the notebook across the table. As the book slid to the floor, she put her head in her hands and closed her eyes, silently berating herself, until a deep, familiar voice made her look up.

"You *do* know that the library isn't the place for loud outbursts, right?" Jason joked, standing over her.

She glared up at him. "Does it *look* like I'm in the mood for your bullshit right now?" she fumed.

Her reaction wiped the grin from Jason's face. "What's the matter?" he asked, removing his book bag from his shoulder and setting it on the floor as he took a seat across from her.

"What are you doing over here?" she asked, ignoring his question.

Jason folded his arms over the table top. "I just left a study group," he answered. "I heard your outburst on my way out, so I figured I'd come see what's up." He fixed his eyes on her angered face. "What's the matter?" he repeated.

She moved her bangs out of her eyes. "Nothing."

Jason shook his head. "Yeah, lying's not gonna make me go away," he assured.

Chasity felt like she was about to explode as she looked down at her textbook. "I'm failing Calculus," she blurted out.

"What do you mean, you're failing?" he asked, confused.

Chasity looked at him in disbelief. "The fuck do you mean? 'what do I mean'?" she barked. "It's a simple statement."

Jason raised his eyebrow at her snarky response. If he was any other man, her attitude would scare him off. "Okay, let me rephrase that," he began, putting his hands up. "Why do you think that you're failing? Is it the homework, the tests?"

"Both," she answered.

"How many tests have you failed?"

"Four," she spat.

Jason winced. "Damn," he admonished. "Why haven't you asked for help?"

"Because after a year of this shit I shouldn't *need* any more damn help," she argued.

"Chasity, this class is far more advanced than the other ones. There's nothing wrong with needing help," Jason chided. "You should know better than that."

"What I *know* is that I'm fuckin' stupid when it comes to this math shit," she bit out, folding her arms.

Jason shook his head. "You're *far* from stupid," he assured, voice sincere. "You just don't have the patience for math. But it's just numbers, and with practice, you'll get it."

"What do I need this crap for, anyway?"

"Your *major*, Miss Computer Science," Jason chuckled.

Chasity rolled her eyes. "Funny," she drawled, sarcastic. "The only numbers I need to know, are the ones used for binary codes…ones and freakin' zeroes."

Jason stared at her; it was clear that her pride was getting the best of her. While he understood her hesitation, he wasn't going to sit by and let her fail because she was too proud to ask, he cared about her too much to let that happen.

"I don't want to see you fail," he said. "Let me help you, Chasity."

She shook her head. "I don't want you to," she mumbled.

"Do you want to repeat the class?" he threw back, voice

stern.

"No."

"Then let me help you."

Chasity ran her hands over her hair. She hated asking for help, but knew she had no choice. "Can...can you tutor me...*again*?" she asked finally.

Jason's smile could have lit the entire library. "You know I will," he returned, reaching out and rubbing her arm. "As a matter of fact, we can start right now."

"No, no, can we start tomorrow? I'm tired," she pleaded as Jason retrieved her notebook from the floor.

"No, no, we can start *now*," he insisted, sitting back down. "The sooner we get through your homework, the sooner you can take a nap."

"Fine," she sighed, leaning forward when he placed the notebook in front of her.

"Let's work on these problems," he proposed.

Chasity pointed to her book. "I'm not doing that first problem again," she refused.

Jason rubbed his forehead with his hand. "Chasity, this is not the time for you to be stubborn."

"I don't care," she threw back, folding her arms defiantly. "I've been working on that bullshit for the past twenty minutes and it keeps being wrong. *You* do it."

Jason shook his head. "Fine, I'll solve it, then walk you through how I got the answer," he amended. "You can try the next one."

Chasity sat there and watched as Jason effortlessly scribbled on her notebook. Not more than a minute later, he passed the work back to her. She glanced at it and slapped the book with her hand. "See? What the hell is all that?" she snapped, pushing the book away from her. "How did you come up with that?"

Jason laughed at her outburst. "Calm down, I'll show you," he promised. "Don't worry so much. You'll pass, I'll see to it."

"Please," she scoffed. "You're about to be real

disappointed."

Jason looked at her. "Not *only* am I confident in my abilities as a teacher, I'm confident in *you* as a student," he replied, tapping his pencil on the table. "You'll pass your midterms, no problem. Just like the *last* two times."

"Wanna bet?" she mumbled.

Jason raised his eyebrow as he had a thought. *Perfect!* "You know what? I *do* want to bet," he said, much to her confusion.

"What are you talking about?" she asked. "Bet what?"

Jason leaned forward in his seat. "*When* you pass your midterms, you have to go out with me," he proposed.

Chasity narrowed her eyes at him. "Are you serious right now?"

"Absolutely," he boasted. "And I don't mean on some group outing shit," he clarified. "I mean a *real* date. The kind where I pick you up, take you somewhere nice and we talk…and I mean have a *real* conversation, where you *actually* participate and not give those little smart ass responses you usually give."

Chasity stared at him, successfully concealing her laugh. *He knows me too well.*

"Just you and I, one on one…a *date* date," he concluded. "Deal?" he asked, extending his hand.

Chasity rolled her eyes as she pondered his proposal. She looked at him, taking in the bright, hopeful smile on his handsome face. Fighting the urge to smile back, she just shook his hand. "Fine," she agreed, teeth clenched.

"Well, it's settled," he beamed, opening his textbook. Suddenly, he pointed at her. "And don't try to fail on purpose so you don't have to go out with me, either," he added.

Chasity busted out laughing.

Chapter 15

Emily rubbed her eyes before closing her textbook and shoving it on the floor. After staring at the book for an hour, the words were beginning to run together. She couldn't get her professors words out of her head as she laid on her pillow.

Your grades are low Emily, you need to pass these midterms if you're going to have a chance of passing this class.

Having met with all five of her professors after her last test scores, that was pretty much the consensus going around.

I can't believe I'm failing.

Emily chalked her bad grades up to stress. But knowing that her mother would be looking for her scores soon just added to it. Emily sighed, and picked up the book from the floor. "Two more chapters, and you can sleep," she prepped herself, opening the book.

A knock at the door, startled her. Hopping up from the bed, she darted over and pulled it open. "Alex?"

Alex giggled at the wide-eyed look on her friends face. "Were you expecting someone else?" she teased, walking in.

Emily shook her head, then shut the door. *I wasn't expecting anybody actually, nobody comes to see me.*

"Studying, I see," Alex mused, eyeing the books and papers strewn across Emily's bed.

"Yeah, midterms," Emily sullenly replied.

"Trust me, I get it," Alex chortled, leaning against Emily's desk. "Everybody has their faces glued to their books nowadays."

Emily gave a slight smile as she ran her hand up her arm.

Alex looked at Emily, she looked sad. "You haven't been around in a while, sweetie," Alex said.

Emily looked at her. She didn't know if she should tell Alex that the reason why she distanced herself was because she felt like nobody really cared enough about her to want her around anyway. That it hurt her to be left out of things just because she didn't share a room with one of them. That she wondered if the other girls *actually* liked her, or if they only tolerated her last year because she was Alex's roommate.

"Um…I've just been studying a lot, that's all," Emily answered, finally.

Alex was skeptical. *I swear, I think it's more than that.* "Well, I came over to not only check on you, but to see if you wanted to take a little study break and go to the movies with me," she offered.

Emily glanced at the floor. "Um sure…Are the other girls going?"

"Nope, just you and me," Alex confirmed. "Sidra is in full on cranky, study mode. I don't think Chasity is feeling well, and Malajia is getting on my nerves."

So I'm your last resort, huh? Emily thought, insulted. "Why is Malajia on your nerves?" Emily asked, unenthused.

"She has a Spanish midterm coming up, so she keeps walking around, saying stupid things in Spanish," Alex replied, voice filled with amusement. "I swear, earlier she was trying to say 'let's go to dinner' in Spanish, and she ended up saying something like, 'let's go to a chicken and rice doctor'."

Emily let a giggle come through, despite how she was

really feeling.

"I'm serious, Em. The girl is gone," Alex added with a wave of her hand. "So, what do you say? Wanna go?"

Despite the fact that Emily was annoyed at being last choice for Alex's movie partner, she did need the break. "Sure," she smiled, grabbing her coat from the back of her chair.

David tapped the keys on his laptop, an intense look frozen on his face. The English Literature paper that he was typing had a hold on his attention and his nerves.

Suddenly, Mark barged through the door and threw his gym bag to the floor, making a loud thud. David spun around in his chair and stared up at him, confusion on his face.

"What's—"

"Shut up," Mark rudely interrupted, walking over to his roommate. David nearly had a heart attack when Mark suddenly closed his laptop.

"Mark, what the hell are you doing? I was typing my paper!" David exclaimed, putting his hands on top of his head.

Mark grabbed his wallet off his desk. "I'm bored, let's go out," he replied nonchalantly.

David stared at Mark, his brown eyes flashing. "Are you insane?!" he exploded.

Mark looked confused. "Whatchu mean?"

"Are you kidding me?" David couldn't believe how nonchalant Mark was acting. "You just closed my damn laptop, man!" he thundered, slamming his hand on the desk. "I didn't even get to save my work. I probably lost everything!"

"So whose fault is *that*?" Mark sneered.

"Excuse me?" David fumed, straightening up in his seat.

"It's not *my* fault you didn't save your work," Mark argued, pointing to himself. David continued to stare at him in disbelief. "Damn, I thought that you were smarter than that

Dave," Mark laughed. "You don't have auto save?"

"Not on *this* old laptop!" David hollered, pounding his fist on the table.

Mark shrugged. "Again, whose fault is *that*?"

David put his head in his hands. "Oh my God, I live with a complete imbecile," he seethed.

Mark frowned. "Did you just call me an impotent seal?"

David threw his head back and let out a loud groan. Mark's stupidity was getting to be too much for him to bear. He opened his laptop and after clicking his mouse a few times, he breathed a sigh of relief. *It didn't shut off, thank God.*

"Count your blessings," David threw out, saving his work.

"Man, stop crying over your fuckin' dickhead ass paper and let's go to the movies," Mark ordered, tossing a pillow at him. "Josh and Jason are on their way over."

David caught the pillow in midair. "Movies? I *got* your movies," he bristled, running over and striking Mark with the pillow.

"Come on man, chill!" Mark bellowed, backing against the wall, then sliding down it. "David, you trippin'." Mark shielded himself as David continued to strike him with the pillow.

Josh walked into the room and stared at the commotion taking place. "What's going on?" he asked, laughter in his voice.

"Josh, get him!" Mark howled as the pillow thrashing continued. "He mad, 'cause his glasses closed the laptop and lost his work."

David delivered one last hit before throwing the pillow to the floor. He stepped over Mark and walked over to a laughing Josh. "You ready to go?" David asked.

"Fuck you David, you ain't invited no more," Mark seethed, standing up from the floor.

"Not *only* am I going, but *you're* paying for my ticket, you freeloading, annoying prick," David demanded, heading out the room.

"Dork," Mark grumbled, smoothing his shirt down.

Josh leaned against the wall and folded his arms. "You got your ass beat with a pillow," he teased.

Mark flipped Josh a middle finger as he made a face.

Chasity was slowly navigating the steps to her dorm floor when she felt a wave of dizziness fall over her.

"Not now, not now," she pleaded, putting her hand on her head. She leaned against the wall, waiting for the spell to pass.

"Chasity, are you okay?" a passing resident asked.

"I'm fine," Chasity mumbled, feeling the dizziness pass. Pushing herself up from the wall, she continued her slow pace down the hall. On top of her usual tension headaches, Chasity had been feeling fatigued for the past few weeks. Only recently did the occasional dizziness start. Chalking it up to stress over her classes, she didn't feel any reason to worry.

As soon as Chasity opened the door, she saw Malajia sitting on the bed with her face in her books. "Hi Chaz," she muttered, flipping the page.

"Hey," Chasity replied, removing her coat.

Malajia looked up at her. "You all right?" she asked. "You lookin' all drained and shit."

"I'm tired," Chasity huffed.

"Take a nap."

"I *can't*, I have too much shit to do," Chasity spat, grabbing a bottle of aspirin off her dresser.

"How's Calculus tutoring coming?" Malajia asked, drawing circles in her textbook. "Meaning, how is your alone time with Jason's sexy ass?"

Chasity rolled her eyes and flopped down on her chair. "Leave me alone, Malajia," she ground out.

"So, are y'all gonna get it in this year, or *what*?" she

asked, ignoring Chasity's request. "Might as well get it over with so you can tell me how it is."

"What part of 'leave me alone' did you not understand?" Chasity barked, running her hands through her hair. Malajia's voice wasn't helping her headache.

"The 'leave me alone' part," Malajia mocked, giggling when she heard Chasity suck her teeth. Malajia continued to glance at her Spanish textbook when she pointed to Chasity. "Hey Chaz, quieres pollo y arroz para la cena?"

"No, I *don't* want chicken and rice for dinner," Chasity replied nonchalantly.

Malajia's mouth fell open. "The hell?" she yelped, completely caught off guard. "How did you know that?"

Chasity just shrugged.

Malajia looked back at her book. "Okay fine, get *this* then." She hesitated while she formed the sentence in her head. "Tiré mi falda en la basura."

Chasity frowned. "Why the hell did you throw your skirt in the trash?"

Malajia slammed her book closed. "Bitch, you speak *Spanish*?" she exclaimed.

"Yes."

"Since *when*?!"

"Since middle school," Chasity replied, tone even.

Malajia sat up on her bed. "This is some bullshit!" she wailed, slapping the bed with her hand.

Chasity eyed Malajia with confusion. "Why are you yelling?"

"'Cause! All this time you could've been tutoring me on this nonsense," Malajia argued, folding her arms. Although her reaction didn't show it, Malajia was impressed.

"Malajia, there is no way in hell that I would tutor you," Chasity threw back. "You don't focus and I don't have time for it."

Malajia grabbed her book. "Oh you *gonna* help me you...perra," she demanded, flipping through the pages.

"Calling me a bitch *definitely* isn't gonna get me to do

it," Chasity returned, rising from her seat.

"Shit!" Malajia hollered as Chasity went into the bathroom. "Help me, damn it."

"Go fuck yourself," Chasity shot back from the bathroom.

"Yeah? I bet you can't say *that* in Spanish," Malajia challenged.

"I don't *need* to."

"Te odio!" Malajia hollered.

"I hate you too," Chasity threw back.

Malajia sucked her teeth.

An hour of being in the room with her fatigue getting the best of her, Chasity laid down to try to take a nap. She tried in vain, for Malajia wouldn't stop talking.

"Ooh, what does *this* mean?" Malajia asked the annoyed Chasity.

"Leave me the fuck alone, Malajia!" she snapped, tossing a pillow at her.

Malajia ducked out of the way, sending the pillow to the wall. "Last one, last one," she promised, waving her hand in her direction. "Donde estas la bano de pollo?"

Chasity stared at her in disbelief. "You're just making shit up!" she roared, exasperated. "You're not even *trying*."

"I didn't say that I was *trying*," Malajia confirmed. "I just wanted to know what it *meant*."

Completely done, Chasity jumped out of bed and headed over to Malajia. Malajia laughed as she tried to stop Chasity from grabbing her textbook.

"No! I need it," Malajia laughed.

"I'm about to make your stupid ass *eat* it," Chasity fumed.

Sidra knocked and opened the door when she heard Malajia's loud voice. "Mel, I can hear you all the way in my room," she informed.

Malajia smacked Chasity's hand. In retaliation, Chasity

mugged the side of Malajia's head before heading back over to her bed.

"Sid, you live two doors down, whatchu mean 'all' the way?" Malajia pointed out, fixing her hair with her hands.

Sidra flagged Malajia with her hand. "I'm about to throw my books out the window and jump after them," she joked. "I need a break, let's go to the movies."

"You paying?" Malajia asked.

"No," Sidra bit out.

Malajia sucked her teeth. "Fine, I'll go anyway," she huffed, standing up.

Chapter 16

"That food was good," Emily mused, rubbing her stomach. "Thanks for the treat, Alex."

Alex smiled as the two girls walked into the Paradise Valley movie complex, later that day. After leaving campus, instead of heading straight for the movie, Alex decided to take Emily to the Pizza Shack for lunch so they could talk.

"I get it for free, so no need to thank me, really," Alex joked. "I'm glad that we got to spend some time together. I missed you, sis."

Emily smiled. "I missed you, too." The time that she was spending with Alex was what Emily needed. She was enjoying the time out of her room and even let go her feeling of resentment for Alex.

The girls approached the counter and examined the movie titles. "What are you in the mood for?" Alex asked.

"Something funny," Emily replied.

"Comedy, it is," Alex concluded. Paying for their tickets, they headed for the theater. "I hope all the good seats aren't taken," Alex hoped. "This is supposed to be a good movie."

Malajia unhooked her seatbelt. "I'm starving, can we

stop and eat first?" she pleaded, rubbing her flat stomach.

"We don't have *time* to go to a restaurant before the movie starts because you took forever changing your damn clothes," Sidra griped, stepping out of Chasity's black Lexus. The three girls didn't have long before their chosen movie was to start.

"I already told you that I wasn't leaving the room in those damn sweats," Malajia returned, fixing the red bracelet on her wrist. "Do I *look* like Alex?"

"Well, thanks to your vain butt, we're just going to have to settle on movie snacks," Sidra chided.

"I don't care *what* we eat, let's just get *something*," Malajia said.

"I'm not hungry," Chasity informed, clicking the automatic alarm on her key ring.

"So, what does that have to do with the *rest* of us?" Malajia bit out.

Sidra giggled as Chasity glared daggers at Malajia. "Chaz, you really need to eat something, you look like you're about to fall out."

"I'm just *tired*, it's not that serious," Chasity argued. "Maybe if y'all wouldn't have dragged me to this fuckin' movie, I could've gotten some sleep."

"You already knew we weren't coming without you," Malajia teased.

Sidra was about to say something when she saw the guys heading in their direction.

"Hey ladies," Josh smiled. "Decided to take a movie break too, huh?"

Mark shot Josh a side-glance. *He cheesin' hard as shit at Sidra.* "You smilin' hard as shit, Joshua," he bit out.

Josh rolled his eyes. "I swear, we should've left you home," he griped.

"Coming here was *my* damn idea, and *I* drove," Mark barked, pointing at Josh. "How was y'all gonna come without me?"

"God, can we just go in?" Chasity snapped, exasperated.

The pointless arguing was on her last nerves.

"This movie better be funny, yo," Mark warned, as he and the others approached the ticket booth.

"If it's *not*, it's *your* fault since you picked it," Jason returned, retrieving his wallet from his pocket.

"Look how long that line is," Sidra complained of the many patrons waiting to purchase tickets.

"One person should just go get the tickets, so we don't have to crowd around up there," Josh suggested.

"Who's gonna volunteer?" Malajia asked. All eyes fixed on Chasity as she pulled a credit card from her purse.

"Fuck outta here," she returned, catching their glances.

Jason laughed at the response. "I could take everyone's cash and go up, but you'll still have to come with me," he offered.

"No, you'll just be breathing all on my damn neck," Chasity griped, holding her hand out. "Give me y'all cash."

As the group began to hand Chasity their ticket money, Malajia turned away while playing with the curls on her head.

"Malajia," Sidra warned, noticing what she was doing.

Malajia looked at them, eyes wide. "Huh?"

"Give Chaz your money, before she beats you," Sidra urged, adjusting the purse strap on her arm.

"I don't know what you're talking about," Malajia replied, scratching her head.

Chasity sighed loudly. "Malajia, give me the goddamn money!" she exploded. The loudness of her voice caused Malajia to flinch and other patrons to stare.

"Everything's okay, we're just dealing with an idiot over here," Sidra announced to the curious.

"Why you gotta be so damn stingy?" Malajia mumbled, slapping her money into Chasity's outstretched hand.

Tickets in hand nearly ten minutes later, the gang marched up to the concession line. Mark rubbed his hands together. "I'm starving," he said.

"I guess *I'll* go up and get stuff, this time," Josh offered, holding his hand out for everyone's money. "Orders?"

"We can just split two large popcorns," Sidra suggested, handing Josh some money.

"*Just* popcorn?" Mark griped. "I just said I'm starving." He shook his hand at them. "Nah, get me two orders of pretzel bites, a hotdog, a box of chocolate covered raisins and um…some cinnamon twists." Mark's order was met with blank stares.

"Who in the hell is *paying* for all of that?" Josh asked.

"Come on man, I got you," Mark beamed, patting Josh on the shoulder.

David shook his head. *The freeloader strikes again.* "*I* wouldn't buy him *shit*," he sneered.

"Don't worry, I'm *not*," Josh assured. "You better hope that somebody left food in your seat, Mark, because that's the *only* way you're eating if you don't come up with some money."

Mark's mouth fell open. "You really gonna be like that, bee?" he asked.

Malajia frowned in confusion. "Who the fuck is *bee*?" she scoffed.

Mark, realizing that he wasn't going to get anywhere with the guys, turned to Sidra. "Hey, my sunshine," he smiled.

"No, *sunshine* away from me. You already owe me money," Sidra bit out, pointing at him.

"Come on, I spent my food money on David's dork ass ticket," Mark complained, gesturing to an annoyed David. "I don't got no more money and I'm starving."

"That's on *you*," Malajia put in. "You shoulda ate before you got here. Always tryna get over on somebody…Wit your broke ass. You bum." As Mark fixed an angry gaze on her, Malajia smoothed some hair from her face and turned to Chasity. "Aye girl, you gonna put some candy on that credit card of yours?"

"Fuck you and no," Chasity spat.

"Damn, why you gotta say all *that*?" Malajia exclaimed.

"Guys, can we just get the food so we can go to our seats?" Jason sighed, looking at his watch.

"Look, nobody's telling me how I'm gonna get my food," Mark barked, holding his hands up. "This is bullshit, I'm hungry."

Jason raised his eyebrow. "Now because of that loud, ignorant ass comment, nobody's *really* not gonna buy you shit," he threw back.

Mark pointed in Jason's face. "You're *gonna* buy me something and you're gonna—" Seeing the anger on Jason's face, Mark took off running, with Jason chasing after him.

"Kick his ass, Jase!" Malajia called after him.

"Man, this theater smell like old corn chips and shit," Mark commented with disgust as he and the others walked into the dimly lit theater.

"Please don't start your crap, I'm serious," David warned, sliding into an empty seat in the back of the theater.

As the rest of the group took their seats in the same row, Mark sucked his teeth. "Man, go fuck your glasses and get out my face," he ground out.

"Go head with that corny mess, dude," David shot back, as Josh laughed.

Mark gestured to David. "He mad 'cause his glasses is holdin' out on him," he teased.

David stared at the screen and let out a loud, heavy sigh.

"Mark, shut up," Malajia hissed, removing her coat. "You about to go sit up front by yourself."

"I wish I *would* move," Mark threw back, leaning back in his seat.

Alex, sitting a few rows ahead, spun around once she recognized the others' voices. She waved to them, trying to grab their attention. Seeing that they didn't notice her, she turned to Emily while gathering her belongings.

"The others are here, let's go sit with them," she proposed.

Emily shook her head and sipped her soda. "You go ahead, I'd rather stay here," she replied.

"Come on Em," Alex pressed enthusiastically. "I'm sure they'd love to see you."

Emily felt herself getting angry. She sighed. *They don't care. Why would I want to go sit with them just to be ignored?*

"Alex if *you* wanna go sit with them, then go ahead," Emily replied, bite in her voice.

Alex was taken back by Emily's tone and reaction. *I knew it. I knew there was more to her being standoffish. She's upset with us.*

"Emily…is there something that you want to say to me?" Alex asked, folding her arms.

Emily once again sighed. "No Alex, everything's fine," she lied. "I'm just comfortable right now. Don't really want to move…that's all."

Alex eyed Emily skeptically as the girl shoved popcorn into her mouth. *Uh huh.* "Okay Em," she relented, facing forward.

Twenty minutes into the movie and Mark was far from impressed. "Boooo," he jeered, tossing a few pieces of popcorn towards the screen.

Sidra tapped him on the arm. "Boy, you better not waste that damn popcorn," she scolded. "Especially when *you* didn't pay for it."

"He wasn't even supposed to *get* none of that," Malajia commented, putting a few pieces into her mouth.

"Get your hand out my lap Malajia," Mark joked, voice loud.

Hearing snickers throughout the audience, Malajia

looked around, embarrassed. "Boy there's nothing in your lap to grab *anyway*, pencil dick," she threw back.

Chasity nearly choked on her drink, trying to conceal a laugh.

"Will you two chill out?" Josh whispered.

Mark sucked his teeth when the audience began laughing at a scene. "Yo, that shit wasn't even funny, bee," Mark griped once the laughter subsided.

Chasity and Sidra silently laughed.

"It really *wasn't* though," Jason chuckled, taking a sip of soda.

"I'm saying though," Mark added. "My man up front was laughing all loud and shit like we at a comedy show, bee."

Malajia slammed her hand on the arm of her seat. "Man who the fuck is *bee*?" she snapped. "I wish you'd stop saying that shit."

Noticing that some of the movie goers were shooting glances their way, Sidra put her hand over her face. "You guys have to keep quiet," she whispered.

"I wish they *would*," David added, voice not hiding his disdain.

"Hey, shut up back there," someone from the audience barked.

"Boooo," Mark hissed, tossing popcorn in the annoyed man's direction.

"Stop wasting it," Sidra once again warned. "You're about to be banned from eating it."

"Fuckin' popcorn tastes like tree bark and shit," Mark complained after a few moments of silence.

A half-hour later, the movie that was supposed to be a comic hit left a lot to be desired. Mark threw is head back in frustration and groaned. "Man this shit is *corny*, bee!" he bellowed.

Malajia threw a few kernels at him. "Oh my God, will you shut up?" she spat out.

Mark sat quietly for a few seconds. "Yo, Malajia's ugly as shit, bee," he joked.

Malajia sat back in her seat and let out a huff.

"Mark, next time, we're leaving your stupid self home," David assured, folding his arms.

Mark shot him a side-glance. "Shut up dingus—"

Chasity and Jason busted out laughing as Sidra snickered.

"If *I* didn't come and get you, your dork ass would've never known we were goin'," Mark reminded.

"Stop talking to me," David hissed.

"Fuckin' mad scientist lookin' mutha fucka," Mark commented, facing forward.

Chasity, who was laughing, began coughing as a result of some of her juice going down the wrong pipe.

Jason patted her back. "Man, shut your corny ass up," he directed at Mark.

"Come on Jase, this movie is corny, you *know* it is," Mark threw back, pointing to the screen.

"Maybe *so,* but we paid for it. Let us watch it in peace," Malajia cut in.

"If y'all don't shut up, I'm coming back there," a guy from the audience warned.

"Come on back here," Mark goaded, unfazed. "Ain't nobody scared of you. Come and get me, I'm the one with the glasses."

Sidra nudged Mark.

"Cut it out, you jackass," David fumed.

"You're gonna get us kicked out," Malajia wailed to Mark.

"Kick out these *nuts*," Mark threw back.

"That's it, I'm leaving," Chasity said, standing from her seat. She wasn't going to be the one to sit around and wait to be kicked out over Mark's antics.

"Wait for me, Chaz," Sidra said, following her out of the row.

"Damn, you smell good," Mark crooned to Chasity as she walked pass.

"Leave me alone, boy," Chasity replied, heading towards the door.

"You *too* Sid," Mark added as Sidra passed him. "Can y'all give some of whatever y'all wearing to Malajia so she can stop smelling like an ass crack?"

Malajia sucked her teeth.

One of the movie workers headed up to their row and shined a flashlight in the remaining groups' faces. "I'm going to have to ask you all to leave," the portly worker ordered. "You've been making noise throughout this entire movie."

Mark looked at him. "Man, why you so hype?" he scoffed. "You mad 'cause you work as a flashlight boy and shit."

The group gathered their belongings and headed out of the row. The worker held a stern gaze on them.

"We can't take you *no*where," David ranted, passing Mark.

"Why you so mad, Dave?" Mark mocked. "Your *glasses* was the one making all the noise and shit."

"You're not funny, dude," David shot back.

"You mad 'cause your name is dingus," Mark countered, walking out the theater.

"So damn embarrassing," Malajia fumed, storming out the door.

Alex, having come back from walking Emily to her apartment later that evening, headed into her room to find the others there, playing cards.

"Come on man, you cheatin'!" Mark bellowed, slamming his cards on the floor.

"Fuck you and pick up the damn cards," Malajia teased, pointing to the cards in the pile.

"Ooh, I got winners," Alex called, removing her coat and sitting on her bed.

"David, it's your turn," Josh informed, rubbing his chin.

Mark watched as David studied his cards. "Just throw out a fuckin' card, four-eyed jack," he snapped.

David glared at Mark. "So you're really gonna make glasses jokes all night long?" he bit out.

"Damn right, goggles," Mark confirmed, studying his card.

Sidra looked at Alex. "Where were you earlier?" she asked, throwing a card out. "We went to the movies."

"I know," Alex chuckled, removing her gold hoop earrings. "I was sitting in the same theater as *you* were."

"So, you heard the jackass, huh?" Malajia commented, taking a sip of water from her bottle.

"Yeah, Em and I *both* did."

"Oh, Emily went with you?" Sidra asked, shocked. She'd barely spoken to Emily, let alone hung out with her. "Why didn't she stop over here with you?"

Alex shrugged. "She had studying to do," she replied. "But, I think it's something else...I think she's mad at us or something."

David looked at her. "Why would she be mad at us?" he asked.

"Pay attention to the cards, windshield wiper lenses!" Mark shouted.

Fed up, David threw his cards down, stood up and stormed out of the room.

"Why you mad, bulletproof glass eyes?" Mark laughed as the door closed.

Sidra shot Mark a glance. "You're being mean to him," she chided.

"He mad 'cause he wear glasses," Mark sniped, ignoring Sidra's scolding.

"Anyway Alex," Malajia began, ignoring Mark's antics. "What makes you think that Emily is mad at us?"

"Well, when you guys came into the theater, I tried to get her to come with me to sit with you and she damn near snapped at me," Alex responded.

"Well, I don't know what her problem is," Malajia griped, tossing out a card. "I barely talk to the girl anymore."

"Maybe *that's* the problem," Alex pointed out.

Malajia waved her hand at Alex. "Not my fault or anyone *else's* that she hides in her room all the damn time."

Alex flopped back on her bed and sighed. She hated the separation between Emily and the rest of the group. *I gotta try to fix whatever this is.*

"I'm winning the game, bee," Mark boasted.

"Shut up!" Malajia snapped.

Chapter 17

Malajia walked into her room, kicked her shoes off and tossed her book bag on her bed. Cradling her cell phone between her shoulder and her ear, she opened her refrigerator and pulled out a container of yogurt.

"Geri, family weekend won't be back until next homecoming," Malajia informed, peeling back the foil lid.

"Okay fine, then why don't I just come down on a random weekend?" Geri proposed.

Malajia made a face. "Hell no," she sneered. "I don't want you all up in my damn face."

A laugh came through the phone. "You're an ignorant ass, you know that right?"

"Absolutely," Malajia laughed back. An incoming call beep halted any other words that Malajia was about to speak. Pulling her phone away from her ear, Malajia's eyes widened as the name 'boyfriend' flashed across her screen. Malajia put her ear back to the phone.

"Geri, I gotta go," she quickly put out.

"Okay but—"

"Bitch I ain't got time for your stallin' ass, I gotta take

this call," Malajia barked, before hanging up the phone on her annoyed sister. Malajia cleared her throat. "Hello?"

"Can I speak to Malajia?" a male voice answered.

Malajia smiled brightly even though the man couldn't see her. "Speaking, who is this?' she coyly threw back.

"Tyrone," the guy answered.

About damn time! "Wow, nice to hear from you after all this time, Tyrone." Although Malajia was relieved to finally hear from Tyrone after giving her number to him weeks ago, she was still irritated that he actually took so long to call her.

"Yeah, sorry about not calling back then," he apologized. "I was handling some stuff."

A simple phone call was stopping you from handling stuff? "Oh…okay," was all that Malajia could say. Her tone was sultry and polite, despite the fact that she wanted to curse him out. "Well, you called *now*, so that's what's important."

Tyrone chuckled. "I knew your sexy ass would understand."

Malajia blushed. Relaxing on the bed, she engaged in a fun, flirty conversation for almost two hours with the man.

"So when are you gonna come see me?" she asked, twirling a strand of hair around her finger. *Please say soon, please say soon.*

"How about we chill tonight?" he suggested, much to Malajia's excitement.

Yes! "Sure, that sounds great," she agreed.

"I'll pick you up at ten."

Malajia frowned. *That's a bit late for a date*, she thought. Not wanting to question Tyrone and run the risk of him changing his mind, she just smiled and agreed. When the call ended, she tossed the phone on the bed and kicked her legs wildly in the air. "Yes!" she squealed.

Chasity stepped out of her Calculus class to be greeted by Jason, who was waiting for her to emerge.

"Hello, stalker," she joked, adjusting the book bag on her shoulder.

"Funny," he chortled. "So? How did you do?"

She hesitated for a moment before a bright smile crept across her face. "I passed my midterm," she informed.

Jason clapped his hands before giving Chasity a hug. "See, I told you you'd pass," he beamed. Ever since he learned that Chasity took her midterm over a week ago, he'd been anticipating her results. "The rest of the class and your final will be a piece of cake."

"I don't even want to *think* about that damn final right now," she replied, pushing hair behind her ears. "I'm just going to enjoy this midterm victory."

"I'm here if you need me for more sessions."

"I appreciate it," she replied sincerely. "Thank you...*again*."

"You're welcome," he returned.

 The two briefly stared at each other intensely, before Chasity turned away. "I gotta go, I'll see you later," she said.

Jason watched her progress for a moment. "Just a second," he called after her.

Chasity turned around. "Yeah?"

He walked up to her, smiling.

"Shit," she scoffed, having an idea about what he was about to say.

He laughed. "Oh really?" he returned. "You *that* disgusted that you're about to go out with me?"

She made a face before smiling. "No, not really," she admitted. "A deal is a deal."

"Can I take you out tonight?" Jason asked, hopeful.

"Sure, why not?" she replied. "I'm in a good mood."

Jason folded his arms. "Wow, that's rare," he joked.

Chasity rolled her eyes. "Was. I *was* in a good mood," she sneered, walking away, leaving Jason to laugh.

"I'll pick you up at eight, okay," he called after her. Without responding, Chasity threw up the 'okay' sign with her fingers, continuing towards the building exit.

Heading off to his next class, Jason silently rejoiced.

Mark took a bite of his Italian hoagie while punching the keys of his game station. "Come on, dawg! That's some cheatin' bullshit," he barked at the game character on the screen.

Hearing a knock, he paused the game. "Cheatin' ass game," he mumbled. "It's open," he called to the door.

Jason walked in and shut the door behind him. "I could hear your loud ass all the way down the hall," he chuckled.

"Man, fuck that hall," Mark ground out, taking another bite of his hoagie. "Whatchu doing later? Wanna go play some ball?"

Jason shook his head. "Naw, I actually came to ask a favor."

"I ain't got no money dawg," Mark joked.

Jason shot him a knowing look. "When have I *ever* asked you for money?" he replied. "In fact, don't you owe *me* money?"

Mark shook his head. "Naw, bee."

Jason narrowed his eyes at Mark. Not wanting to engage in a pointless battle with him over owed money, he decided to let it go and take the conversation to its original topic.

"Anyway, can I borrow your car tonight?" Jason asked.

Mark looked at him. "What do you need it for?"

"I'm taking Chasity out on a date."

"What? The ice queen finally said 'yes'," Mark teased. "Was she high?"

"Very funny, jackass," Jason shot back, earning a laugh from Mark. "So, can I borrow it?"

Mark scratched his head. He was happy that his friend was about to take out the woman of his dreams and was happy to help him. But he wasn't about to make it easy. "Doesn't *she* have a car?" he asked. "Why can't *she* drive?"

Jason stared blankly at him for a second before saying, "See, that's why no girl wants to go out with you *now*."

Mark's mouth fell open. "What I do?!"

"Why the hell would I make *her* drive around, when *I'm* the one who asked *her* out?"

"You ain't gotta get no attitude over no question," Mark returned.

Jason pinched the bridge of his nose with his fingertips. He wasn't about to let Mark make him angry, not today. "Can I borrow the car, or not?" he asked, trying to remain calm.

Mark frowned at Jason before breaking into a smile. "Sure, you can borrow it," he said, grabbing the keys from his dresser.

"Good lookin'," Jason replied, grateful, catching the keys in midair.

"You gotta put gas in it though," Mark informed as Jason headed for the door.

"Just take it out of the twenty bucks you owe me," Jason joked, walking out of the room.

"That's not funny dude," Mark called after him as the door shut.

Chasity was running on the treadmill at the gym. She decided to get a quick workout in before her date, which was three hours away. She adjusted the earbuds in her ears when she felt a wave of dizziness, accompanied by the dull feeling in the back of her head, telling her that one of her headaches was on the way.

"Shit," she whispered.

She turned the treadmill off and rested her arms on the bars as the wavy feeling passed. *I'm not even stressed right now! What the hell?*

She carefully stepped off of the machine, grabbed her towel and water bottle, and headed for the exit.

Upon reaching her room, Chasity opened her door and tossed her things to the floor.

"Ugh, what's *your* face all mad for?" Malajia scoffed at

the strained look on Chasity's face.

Chasity laid down on her bed. "I have a headache," she replied, voice low.

Malajia frowned. "What's up with you and all these damn headaches?" she sneered, opening a bag of chips.

"I honestly don't know," Chasity mumbled, burying her face into her pillow.

"You have one like every damn day," Malajia pointed out.

"Yes, I know," Chasity agreed.

"You don't think you need to see a doctor about that?"

"I just need a nap," Chasity replied. "Please shut up so I can take one."

Malajia rolled her eyes. "Fine, but if you die, just make sure you do it in the room so I can get straight A's," she joked.

Chasity just flipped Malajia off.

Malajia fiddled with her hands. She wanted her roommate to get her much needed rest, but she was bursting with excitement at her news.

"Okay, before you go to sleep, I have to tell you my news," Malajia began, voice brimming with excitement.

"Can it wait until I'm sleep so I don't have to hear it?" Chasity spat out, turning over.

Annoyed with Chasity's comment, Malajia rose from her bed, walked over to Chasity and clapped loudly in her face. The loud noise made Chasity wince as she felt her head pound.

"Asshole," she hissed, grabbing her head. Not having the energy to retaliate, and knowing that Malajia wouldn't leave her alone until she said what she needed to say, Chasity sat up and leaned her back against her pillows.

Malajia sat on Chasity's bed and smiled brightly.

Chasity slowly folded her arms and waited for Malajia to speak. When she didn't, Chasity took a deep breath. "Bitch, if you don't start talking, I swear I'm going to choke the bullshit outta you," she slowly put out, tone even.

Malajia waved her hand. "No need for all that," she teased. "Guess who called me earlier?"

"I don't have time for this shit right now!" Chasity barked. The loudness in her voice caused Malajia to flinch.

Malajia reached for the bottle of aspirin on Chasity's nightstand. "Here girl, take these and calm your ass down," she urged, pushing the bottle into Chasity's hands. "Anyway, Tyrone called."

"Who the fuck is Tyrone?" Chasity asked, before popping the pills into her mouth.

Malajia rolled her eyes. "You *know* who I'm talking about."

Chasity thought for a moment as she took a sip of water from her bottle. "I know you're not talking about that idiot who you gave your number to *weeks* ago."

"Yep," Malajia confirmed. "And before you say something smart, I *know* this is the first time he's called me since I gave him the number. I'm not happy about that, but I'm glad that he called, so shut up."

Chasity put her hand up in surrender as she downed her water.

"Anyway, we had a really nice conversation. We talked for like two hours," Malajia gushed. "Girl, the way he talks is soooo sexy."

Chasity rolled her eyes. Malajia getting worked up over some guy who treated her like an afterthought for weeks was irritating her.

"So, long story short, we're going out tonight," Malajia beamed, clasping her hands together.

"Oh okay," Chasity replied, unenthused.

"Yep, he's picking me up at ten," Malajia added, ignoring Chasity's tone.

Chasity frowned. "*What* time?"

"Ten."

"Ten?" Chasity scoffed. "As in ten, at *night*?"

Malajia nodded.

Chasity looked confused. "You don't think that's

weird?" she asked. "He calls you out the blue, you have this *sexy* conversation and he asks you out...at ten...at night?"

Malajia rolled her eyes. "Save whatever you're about to say, okay," she replied, annoyed. "Not *everybody* goes on dates at seven or eight."

Chasity shook her head. *This chick is beyond clueless.* "You're stupid," she spat.

Malajia stared blankly at Chasity. *I knew I shouldn't have told her. She's always so fuckin' negative.* "Thanks, friend," she replied, voice filled with sarcasm as she stood from the bed. "Enjoy your date with Jason tonight."

"Oh really, you're just gonna deflect like that?" Chasity bit out as Malajia opened the door.

"Yup," Malajia hissed, walking out. "Hope your headache feels better." She punctuated her words with a sharp slam of the door.

Chasity clenched her jaw and let out a sigh as she put her hand on her head.

Chapter 18

Jason took a deep breath while standing in front of Chasity's room door. *Why are you nervous, Jason?* Although Jason had been alone with Chasity on more than one occasion, this particular time he was nervous, *more* than nervous. Shifting the single red rose from one hand to the other, he knocked on the door. Running his hand over his freshly shaped-up hair, he anxiously waited for Chasity to answer.

His smile was dazzling as Chasity opened the door. *She looks perfect as always.* His eyes roamed over her. Chasity wore her hair straight, with a part down the middle. Her chosen outfit of black skinny pants, black lace turtleneck top, and high-heeled boots complemented her figure. The sparkly jewelry and makeup perfected her look.

"Hey beautiful," he crooned.

Chasity returned his smile with one of her own when he handed her the rose. Her eyes subtly roamed over him. Jason was normally clean cut and neat, but tonight he looked even better than he normally did. His black dress pants, paired with a matching button down shirt, shoes, and grey tie made him look older, sophisticated even.

He's so damn sexy! Ugh, focus Chasity. Chasity shook her head in an effort to stay in control as she shut the room door.

"You okay?" Jason chuckled, at her awkward reaction to him.

"Huh?" she looked up at him. "I'm fine."

While making their way down the hall, Jason extended his arm, and she took hold of it. "Nice outfit," he complimented.

"Thanks," she replied, pushing some hair over her shoulder. "I was gonna wear a dress, but it's cold…and I didn't want to."

Jason laughed.

The drive to the small restaurant in downtown Paradise Valley was a quiet, comfortable one. Once parked along the well-lit, tree-lined street, the pair walked hand in arm inside of the place. Jason helped Chasity remove her coat and pulled out her chair once they were escorted to their reserved table.

"This place is nice," Chasity observed, looking around, once they were given their menus. The dimly lit room and the soft R&B music provided an intimate mood. The tea light candles set at each table added to it. There was even a small area for dancing towards the back of the room.

"Yeah, I actually came across this place when I was in the area with my parents last semester," he revealed, sitting his glass of water down. "I don't think too many people at school know about it."

"That's because the only places the people from school eat at are those raggedy pizza places," Chasity jeered.

Jason chuckled. "True," he agreed. "I knew when I first saw it that I wanted to bring you here."

Chasity smiled. "Yeah?"

"Yup, a special place for a special woman."

Chasity stared at him momentarily. "Jason, don't be

corny," she teased, with a straight face.

Jason busted out laughing at her blunt response to his declaration. "That *was* pretty sad, wasn't it?"

She giggled. "I'm just messing with you."

Jason put his hands up. "Nope, you're right," he agreed. "I don't know what it is, but I'm actually really nervous around you tonight."

Chasity frowned. "Why?"

"I guess because this is our first official date," he admitted honestly. "It's different than when we're hanging out just casual."

Chasity glanced to see where their waiter was. "What? You've never been on a date before?"

"Not with *you*," he stated, staring at her.

Chasity didn't say anything. She hated to admit it, but she was nervous around him too.

"Are you telling me that you aren't nervous?" he smiled.

Chasity looked at her manicured nails, trying to avoid the question.

"Be honest."

"Okay, maybe a little bit," she admitted finally. "You have a point. I guess it *is* a different vibe."

Jason picked up his glass. "Exactly," he replied. "I mean, I'm sure that you've been on dates before too, so it's not *totally* weird."

I wouldn't know about anything prior. You're my first date, Chasity thought as Jason continued talking.

"Right," she answered, as the waiter approached.

As the evening went on and they ate their dinner, the nervousness they both admitted to seemed to melt away. The conversation between Jason and Chasity was easy and engaging. Jason was both surprised and happy to find that Chasity was, for once, not giving him her usual guarded conversation. She seemed lighter, happier.

"That food was so good," Jason mused, setting his napkin on the table.

"I know, right," Chasity agreed, taking a sip of her virgin strawberry daiquiri. "Now we have to go back to the cafeteria food after this."

Jason shook his head. "Don't remind me," he chortled, looking at her. "So, are you glad that you lost the bet?" he teased. "I mean, of *course* you are. You passed your midterm, after all."

Chasity glanced down at the table. "Can I be honest with you about something?" she asked, catching him off guard.

"Sure," he replied, leaning forward with anticipation.

Chasity hesitated for a moment. "I'm not out with you because I lost the bet," she revealed.

Jason just sat there, listening, his facial expression not changing.

"I'm out with you because...I *want* to be," she continued. "I've been...wanting to go out with you for...um..." Chasity struggled to finish her thought. She couldn't help but feel her walls building back up, she always had a hard time expressing her feelings. "It's not because of the bet, just leave it at that," she finished finally.

Jason nodded. "Can I be honest with *you*?" he asked.

"Sure."

"I already knew that," he stated.

Chasity shot him a challenging look "Oh *really*?"

"Yes," he answered. "Chaz, we've known each other for a little over a year, and I'm pretty sure I know you well enough to know that you don't do *anything* that you don't want to do. Bet or no bet."

True, Chasity thought as she sat there, listening to him continue.

"When I asked you out earlier, I was expecting a 'fuck off, Jason'."

Chasity couldn't help but laugh a little.

"Or some other rude remark," Jason chuckled. The laughter left his face as he felt himself being vulnerable. "When you agreed to this date, it shocked me," he admitted.

"It meant that you *actually* wanted to spend time with me and I think that's what had me nervous."

"What do you mean?"

"Well…I spent all this time trying to convince you that I'm good enough to take you out, and now I actually have to *prove* to you that I am."

Chasity stared at him; she was seeing him in a new light. Sure, Jason had always been sweet to her, was always there when she needed him, and she appreciated him as a friend. But the way that he was being vulnerable with her and the way that he was making her feel without even touching her made her realize that she cared more about him than she wanted to admit to him, or to herself.

"You didn't have to prove anything to me, Jason," she replied.

"Yes, I *did*," Jason insisted. "I wanted you to see that I'm not just this jock who participates in pranks…That I'm not just around you because we're friends or even because I'm attracted to you…I'm around you because…being around you makes me want to be better…It makes me happy."

Chasity frowned in confusion. "You're actually *happy* being around me?" she asked, not sure if she heard him correctly.

Jason too held a look of confusion on his face. "Why are you asking like you don't think I'm being honest?"

Chasity was taken back by his question. She had a reason why she questioned him. She just wasn't sure if she wanted to elaborate on it. "Um…I…" she stammered.

Jason picked up on her hesitation. Seeing her struggle internally made him just want to grab her and hug her. But not wanting to make her even more uncomfortable than she appeared at that moment, he decided against it.

Hearing a familiar slow jam play through the restaurant, Jason thought of the perfect distraction. "You want to dance?" he asked.

"No," Chasity answered, grateful for the change in subject.

Jason smirked as he pushed himself back from the table. "Don't be difficult, you were doing so well," he joked, moving around to her chair.

"Fine," she relented, rising from her seat.

They made their way over to the dance floor and began to slow dance. Even though Jason held her close to him, Chasity didn't feel uncomfortable or awkward. She felt safe, it felt natural.

Chasity, feeling the start of another headache coming on, ran her hand along the back of her neck. *Shit*, she thought. With a quick nap after Malajia stormed out of the room earlier, and aspirin, Chasity thought she had solved her headache problem. That didn't seem to be the case.

Jason, feeling her stiffen in his arms, pulled back and looked at her. "You okay?" he asked.

Chasity ran her hand through her hair. "Can we go?" she replied.

Jason nodded. He was disappointed, but made sure not to show it. Chasity sat down briefly as Jason took care of the check, she rested her elbows on the table and put her head in her hands. *First another headache and now this dizzy shit again!*

As they headed out of the restaurant, Chasity felt that her stride was off. The dizziness, which usually passed within a few seconds, was still with her as she tried to maneuver. *Something's not right*, she warned herself, halting her stride.

Jason, feeling her pull her hand from his arm, stopped and turned around. If he sensed something was off with her back on the dancefloor, his senses were definitely heightened now. It looked like the color had drained from her face. She stared at him, blinking slowly.

Jason stood in front of her and put his hand on her face. "What's the matter?" he asked. His voice or his face didn't hide his concern.

Before he knew what was happening, Chasity had collapsed into his arms.

Malajia sat in the lobby of her dorm, cradling a clutch under her arm while she adjusted the collar of her coat. Checking her watch for the fifth time, she sucked her teeth. *He's twenty minutes late.*

Malajia had been sitting in the lobby for almost a half-hour, waiting on Tyrone to arrive. It was bad enough that he had her waiting, but he didn't even call to say that he would be running late. After another five minutes, she slammed her hand on the arm of the couch that she was sitting on. "If he stood me up, I swear—"

Malajia didn't finish her solo rant session, because the moment that she saw Tyrone walk through the door, a smile broke across her perfectly made-up face. "It's about time," she teased, standing up.

"My fault," he replied, nonchalantly. "You ready?"

Malajia frowned at the urgency in his voice. *Damn dude, no 'you look pretty'? No flowers? You lucky you cute.* Even though his attire of jeans and a blue t-shirt wasn't exactly her idea of first date wear, he was as good looking as she had remembered.

Malajia tried to engage in conversation with Tyrone during the twenty-minute ride off campus. Tyrone didn't say much other than an occasional comment about how sexy she was. While she was flattered, she hoped that he would have more to say than that. Malajia frowned when she noticed they were pulling up to an apartment complex.

"Ummm, is this your place?" she asked as he turned the car off.

"Sure is," Tyrone replied, opening his door.

Malajia stepped out of the car and followed him in silence, scanning the area with her eyes. The apartment complex was small, and resembled a motel. *Maybe he's just stopping to change his clothes,* she thought.

When Tyrone opened the door, Malajia stepped in and looked around the living area as he shut the door behind her. "Nice place," she mused. The décor was simple, but at least it was inviting.

"Thanks," Tyrone smiled, heading over to the couch and flopping down. "Why don't you come sit down?" he asked, patting the cushion next to him.

Malajia shook her head. "Uh no, I'm good," she replied, shifting her clutch from one arm to the other. "What did we stop here for?" she asked, tired of waiting. "Are you changing or something?"

"No." Tyrone looked confused. "Why?"

"I just figured that since we're going out, you'd want to put on something other than a t-shirt," she explained, pushing some of her curled hair out of her face. "But hey, if that's what you like, do *you* boo, let's just be out."

Tyrone still held the same confused look on his face. "Who said that we were going *out* anywhere?"

This time *Malajia* was confused. "What do you mean?" she asked. "You asked me out, so I assumed that we were going on a *date*."

"No, I asked you to *chill* with me," he slowly put out. "I didn't plan on taking you anywhere."

Malajia's look went from calm to angry. "Time out," she said, putting her hand up. "So, when you said 'chill' you meant what? That I was gonna come over here, sit on your couch and do *what*?" she asked, already having an idea of what he was going to say.

"What do *you* think?" he sneered.

"Are you fuckin' kidding me?" she snapped, stomping her foot on the floor.

Tyrone folded his arms. "Don't act like you don't know what this is about."

Malajia snatched open her coat and held it open, revealing her outfit of a short, tight, long-sleeved, black sweater dress with black high heeled boots. "Does it *look* like I'm dressed to sit on some damn couch?" she sneered.

"It *looks* like you're dressed to come sit on my *dick*," he bit back.

Malajia was offended and it showed on her face as she quickly yanked her coat closed. "So you just automatically assumed that I was gonna come over here and fuck you?" she hissed. "After two hours of talking on the phone, and that's *after* I hadn't heard from you in almost a damn month."

Tyrone, who was clearly irritated, rose from his seat. "Whatever yo," he barked. "You chillin' or naw? 'Cause I'm not taking you out."

"I don't know what vibe you got, but I'm not the chick who sleeps with some dude I barely know," she assured, tone angry. "So you can chill by your-damn-self."

"I sure can't tell by the way you dress or how you were talking to me on the phone," he threw back. "You're full of shit, and what *you* won't do, the others girls in my phone will."

Malajia shook her head; she was so disappointed she felt like crying. She put her hopes into a man who turned out to be like many others; someone who just wanted her for her body. Someone who assumed that she was fast because of how she dressed. Someone who refused to see past her exterior.

Malajia held her coat closed as she looked at the floor. "Just take me home," she demanded.

"Take your*self* home," Tyrone refused, pointing the door.

Malajia shook her head. "You're such a fuckin' asshole," she seethed, teeth clenched, heading for the door. Before walking out, she spun around. "And even if I *was* that type of bitch, you could've at *least* offered to feed me first, before trying to get me to suck your dick, you cheap, disrespectful bastard."

Tyrone watched as Malajia stormed out of his apartment, slamming the door behind her.

As soon as Malajia hit the corner of the complex, she let the tears flow. She couldn't believe what had just happened. She'd never been insulted like that before. Through her tear filled eyes, she looked around; she had no idea where she was.

Stupid! You're so stupid Malajia!

Walking to the corner, while continuing to mentally berate herself, Malajia saw a cab and hailed for it. Breathing a sigh of relief when it stopped, she hopped in. After providing her destination, she sat quietly as she wiped her tears with the back of her hand. She stared out of the window while the driver maneuvered the streets.

Chaz was right, Malajia thought. Sighing, she reached for her phone. Noticing several missed calls from Sidra, she frowned and dialed her number. "Yeah Sid, what's up?" she said once Sidra answered. Her voice was low. "Nothing, I'm fine. What's going on? You called me like five times…Wait, what? She's *where*?"

Malajia hurried down the hall of the Valley Memorial Hospital waiting room. She was stricken with panic and guilt when Sidra told her that Chasity was taken to the emergency room. She barely got the full story before she yelled at the cab driver to take her to the hospital.

Sidra, hearing Malajia call her name, looked up and saw her approaching. Malajia took an empty seat next to Sidra and proceeded to remove her coat.

"*What* happened again?" Malajia asked.

Sidra sat the magazine she was reading on the table in front of her. "Jason said that she passed out when they were leaving the restaurant," she informed. "He brought her straight here."

"Is she okay?" Malajia asked.

"She's up, I know *that*," Sidra replied. "They're running a bunch of tests right now, but at least she's awake and aware of what's going on."

Malajia breathed a sigh of relief. "I feel bad," she admitted.

Sidra frowned. "Why?"

"I made a joke about her dying earlier," Malajia admitted, rubbing her arm. "And that was *before* I purposely slammed the door to aggravate her headache."

Sidra shook her head. "You're right, you *should* feel bad," she chided. When Malajia put her head in her hands, Sidra giggled and rubbed her shoulder. "I'm kidding."

Malajia raised her head and ran her hand over her hair, smoothing it down.

"I know your date was cut short by all this," Sidra began. Malajia stiffened, she really didn't want to discuss the evening's events at that moment. "I meant to tell you that you look pretty before you left…a little *cold*," she said, amusement in her voice. "But, pretty nonetheless."

Malajia looked down at her hands. "Thanks," she mumbled.

"So, did Tyrone drop you off here?" Sidra pressed, not picking up on Malajia's sour mood.

Malajia shook her head, not saying a word.

Sidra frowned. "If he didn't drop you off, how did you get here?" she asked.

"A cab," Malajia answered, tone dry.

Sidra looked stunned. She didn't understand why Tyrone put Malajia in a cab instead of dropping her off himself. "But—"

"Sidra, can we not talk about this right now?" Malajia requested, trying to stay calm.

This time, Sidra did pick up on Malajia's mood, and she sensed that it didn't have anything to do with Chasity. "Mel, what happened?" she asked, ignoring Malajia's request.

Malajia just shook her head, letting out a long sigh.

"What did he do to you?"

"He didn't do *anything*," Malajia assured, taking a pause. "It's what he *said,* and what he *expected me* to do that's the problem."

Sidra studied Malajia's expression. She looked sad, she hadn't seen her look that sad in a long time. It didn't sit well with her. "What did—"

"He wanted what damn near *every* guy wants from me," Malajia interrupted, exasperated.

Sidra put her hands up. "I'm sorry," she said.

Feeling bad for snapping at Sidra, Malajia grabbed her hand. "No, my fault. I don't mean to snap at you," she apologized. "I guess I'm just…"

"Surprised?"

"I'm…disappointed, I guess," Malajia clarified. "I thought he could be something that he clearly isn't." Malajia chuckled. "I guess I read too much into a two hour conversation," she joked.

Sidra shot her a sympathetic look. "You don't have to make a joke," she replied.

"Yeah, I *do*," Malajia confirmed, still laughing. "'Cause if I don't, I'm gonna get back in that cab and go burn his apartment down."

Sidra winced. "Now, no need for *that*," she assured.

Chasity laid in her hospital bed, drumming her finger nails on the bed railing while she stared at the wall. She'd been in the emergency room for a few hours and was just transferred to another room.

Jason walked in and sat down in the chair next to her bed. "I talked to Ms. Trisha and she said that she'll be on the first available flight in the morning," he informed, sitting a cup of ice in front of her.

"Yeah, I'm sure she's thrilled to have to fly back from Florida for this," Chasity jeered, rubbing her arm, where an IV was located. "I'm over this shit."

"What did they say when I left?" he asked.

"That they're running tests and that they want to keep me overnight to monitor me," she replied, running her hand through her hair.

Jason nodded. "I'm sure you'll be fine, sweetie," he assured. "Did the others come in and see you?"

"They *wanted* to, but I told them to go home," Chasity answered, voice tired. She looked at him. "*You* can go home too, you know," she put out.

He frowned. "Why would I do that?" he asked. Seeing Chasity pass out in front of him was horrible. Jason had no plans on leaving her side and only planned on walking out of that hospital when it was time to take her home. "They said that someone can stay with you, so we'll be roommates tonight."

Chasity narrowed her eyes. "Fine," she relented.

Jason sat back in the chair. "You want to know what I think?" he asked after some silence.

"Not really," Chasity replied, tone even. "No, I'm messing with you. Go ahead."

"I think you fainted after our date so you wouldn't have to kiss me," he said, amusement in his voice.

Chasity pointed at him. "You figured me out," she joked in return.

Jason laughed a little, reaching for the TV remote near Chasity's bed. "Did the doctors say how long it would take to get your results?" he asked.

Chasity sighed. "Not too long," she replied, voice low.

Jason stared at her, she looked like she was deep in thought. He wondered if it was due to being nervous about her pending test results, or if it was something else.

"Are you scared?" he asked, point blank.

"I'm anxious," she clarified.

Jason nodded slowly. "That's understandable."

"There *is* something about all of this that's bothering me more than people poking my damn veins every five minutes," Chasity began.

Jason sat in anticipation of what she was about to reveal.

"While you were out, the doctors came in, asking all these questions about me and about my family's health history, and I started answering, then it hit me…" she paused as she faced Jason. "I have no freakin' idea about my family history, because I don't know who my biological family *is*."

Jason shot Chasity a sympathetic look. "Damn, I'm sorry Chaz," was all that he could say. He couldn't imagine what was going through her mind.

"I hate that this is on my mind right now," she complained. Chasity tried hard to keep her thoughts and feelings about her adoption buried within the depths of her mind. But she knew that eventually, they would resurface.

Jason sat quietly for a moment. He wasn't sure if he should bring up what he was about to, but he figured, he'd never hid his opinions before, why start now? "Chaz...do you think that maybe you should try to find out who your birth mother is?" he asked, hesitantly. He braced himself for an irate reaction from Chasity.

Chasity hesitated for a moment. "I actually thought about it, after the doctors left," she admitted, much to Jason's surprise.

"Oh really?" he replied.

Chasity nodded. "I'm just not sure if I really want to, though."

"What's stopping you?"

"Feelings getting hurt," Chasity answered honestly.

"Whose feelings?" Jason asked, curious.

"My aunts," she replied.

Jason grabbed Chasity's hand and held it. "I'm sure Ms. Trisha will be supportive of your decision, should you make it," he assured, confidently. "She seems like she just wants you to be happy."

Chasity stared at him. She wasn't so sure that was true, especially since Trisha always tried to dodge and dismiss the topic of her adoption when she brought it up. What Chasity didn't reveal was the fact that she was afraid of her own feelings getting hurt, if she decided to search for the woman who gave her up.

Chapter 19

Emily rolled over and groggily rubbed her eyes as a knock at the door woke her out of her slumber. *Who the heck could it be at this hour?* She thought, glancing at the clock.

"Eight in the morning on a Saturday?" she grumbled, stumbling out of bed, to her door. "Who is it?" she asked, leaning against it.

"It's Mommy," the soft voice on the other side answered.

Emily's eyes widened. *Crap!*

She wasn't expecting a visit from her mother this weekend. She could've screamed, she was so annoyed. Emily couldn't even force a smile as she opened the door.

"Hey sweetie," Ms. Harris beamed, hugging her disheveled daughter.

"Hi Mom," Emily replied, voice dry.

Ms. Harris pulled away and stared at her. "You look tired," she observed.

Emily resisted the urge to roll her eyes. *That's because you woke me up out of my sleep with your stalkerish visit!* she screamed to herself.

"I *am*," Emily replied.

Ms. Harris shrugged, stepping all the way into Emily's room. She sat her overnight bag on Emily's messy bed. "I figured that I would take a trip down and surprise you," she said.

Emily couldn't take her eyes off of the bag. "Um...You're staying?" she stammered, fighting to keep her tone in check.

"Just for the night," Ms. Harris answered, unaware of how horrified her daughter was. "Over at the motel a few minutes from campus."

"Um...okay," Emily slowly put out, sitting on the bed.

Ms. Harris took a seat next to her, much to Emily's irritation.

God! Can I sit down without you being up under me?

"So," Ms. Harris began, looking around Emily's room. "I take it that your room looks like a pigsty because you've been so busy studying," she assumed.

Emily nodded.

"Speaking of studying, how did you do on your midterms?" Ms. Harris asked.

Emily felt her stomach flip. She'd neglected to inform her mother that she failed her midterms. With her mood lower than it had ever been, Emily's concentration and focus had been non-existent. Even though she tried to study, she never could get her head right enough to do so. Her bad grades were part of the reason she barely left her bed since coming back from her last class the day before.

"Um...I did pretty good," Emily lied, avoiding eye contact.

Ms. Harris focused her gaze on Emily. Something seemed off to her. "So, can I see your grades?" she pressed.

Emily felt close to a panic attack as she eyed the torn up score card in the corner of her room. "Uh, I lost the score card, I'll have to go to the Education department to have them give me a new one."

"Oh?" Ms. Harris replied, holding her gaze. "Are they

open on Saturday's?"

"Uh huh," Emily answered, running a nervous hand over the back of her neck.

"Well maybe—"

"Uh Mommy, I'm hungry. Do you wanna go get something to eat?" she quickly put out, hoping that her mother would drop the subject.

Ms. Harris eyed Emily suspiciously. She seemed all too eager to change the subject. But seeing that her daughter looked like she'd barely eaten, she jumped at the chance to feed her. "Okay, go get ready."

Trisha adjusted the blinds in Chasity's room before sitting on the bed next to her. Chasity sat with her head against the headboard as she sipped on her freshly made tea.

"So…anemia," Trisha said, looking at her niece.

Chasity nodded slowly, continuing to sip her tea. Chasity left the hospital earlier that morning, but that wasn't before the doctors informed her that her blood work came back showing that she was anemic due to iron deficiency. Chasity left the hospital before Trisha's plane landed, but made sure to give her the details and paperwork once she arrived at her dorm.

"They're putting you on iron pills?" Trisha asked, eyeing her paperwork.

"Among others."

"So that means that you need to remember to *take* them," Trisha urged, voice stern. "You know how you are with pills."

"Sure do, don't like taking them," Chasity griped, reaching for her prescription bottle. "Those vitamins that you bought me are in my closet on the floor somewhere."

Trisha shook her head. "What are you going to do when you start taking birth control pills?" she asked, putting her hand on her hip.

"I'm not screwing anybody, so I don't need to worry

about that, now *do* I?" Chasity threw back.

Trisha resisted the urge to shake her smart-mouthed niece. "You're lucky you just got out of the hospital, smart ass," she jeered, sitting the papers on Chasity's nightstand. "But seriously, *take* them. I don't want to get another phone call saying that something happened to you. I love you and I worry."

"You don't need to worry, I'll take them," Chasity promised. The sincerity in Trisha's voice when she spoke of her made Chasity hesitate bringing up what she wanted to talk about.

Trisha noticed the blank look on Chasity's face. "You look like something's on your mind," she pointed out.

Chasity sat her cup on her nightstand, then took a deep breath. "Okay, so…there's something that I want to talk to you about," she began.

Trisha raised a skeptical eyebrow. "What? You really *are* having sex?" she assumed.

Chasity frowned in confusion. "Just automatically going to *that*, huh?" she jeered.

Trisha chuckled. "What? I mean I just figured, since you and Jason seem to be around each other a lot—"

"Trish, will you—" Chasity paused in an effort to calm down. "No, I am not having sex with Jason, okay," she spat. "He's just my friend."

Trisha shrugged. "That's not to say that that title won't change," she teased.

Chasity flashed a scowl at her aunt. Trisha made it no secret that she hoped for Chasity and Jason to end up together. She loved how Jason genuinely cared for and looked out for Chasity.

"Focus, okay," Chasity sneered,

Trisha put her hand up in surrender. "I'm sorry, go ahead."

"Okay so…I wanted to tell you that…" Chasity nervously fiddled with her hands. "I want to find my birth mother."

The news took Trisha by complete surprise, but she didn't let it show on her face. "When did you decide this?" she asked.

Chasity studied Trisha's face to see if she could see a trace of any emotion. She saw none. "Last night," she answered. After Jason fell asleep, Chasity spent the majority of the night lying awake in her hospital bed, pondering her conversation with him. She came to a final decision before drifting off to sleep.

"Um…" Trisha took a deep breath. "Why *now*? I mean…What made you—"

And there's the emotion, Chasity thought as she watched Trisha's face go from calm to agitated. "Why does it look like you're getting mad?" Chasity frowned.

Trisha stood up from the bed. "I'm not mad," she bit out. "I'm just confused as to what brought this on all of a sudden."

Chasity fought the urge to snap at her aunt for her insensitive reaction. "I just figured that it's time that I find out who she *is*," Chasity explained. "I want to know where I come from."

"You have a family already," Trisha barked, folding her arms. "Being *adopted* doesn't change that."

"No, I think it *does*," Chasity bit back.

"Chasity—" Trisha snapped, pointing at her stunned niece. "I'm sorry…I'm going to take off, I have a plane to catch and you need your rest."

Chasity was angry, Trisha was deflecting again. "Are you *seriously* brushing me off right now?" she fumed.

"Chasity, I don't have time for this," Trisha fussed. "I'll call you when I land."

"Don't bother," Chasity spat.

Trisha reached for the door. "Fine," she seethed, walking out.

Chasity held her gaze on the door once Trisha shut it. She was so angry, she could have punched a wall. She expected Trisha to be a little surprised, or maybe even a little hurt, but what Chasity got was a plain old nasty attitude. Too spent to do anything else, Chasity just laid back down in bed.

Emily had persuaded her mother to spend all day doing activities in an effort to keep her mind off of Emily's midterm grades. After eating breakfast, going to the movies, shopping for a new coat and taking a long walk through the entire campus, Emily was tired and so was her mother.

"Emily, don't you think we should try going to your department to ask about your grade card?" Ms. Harris asked as the two women walked the path towards Emily's apartment.

Emily fought the urge to suck her teeth. *Geez, she's like a dog with a bone.* "I think they're closed now," she answered, looking at her watch.

Ms. Harris looked disappointed. "What time do they open tomorrow?"

"They're not open on Sunday's," Emily replied, adjusting the pink scarf around her neck.

"Well what about Mo—"

"What time are you leaving again, tomorrow?" Emily quickly asked, voice sweet.

Ms. Harris shot Emily a cool glance. "Are you trying to get rid of me?"

Yes! "Um, no," Emily sputtered. "Just wanted to make sure that you get home before the Sunday traffic gets bad."

Ms. Harris held her gaze. *What are you hiding, child?* "I'm not sure yet."

"Oh," Emily replied, approaching the steps of her building. Her eyes widened when she saw Sidra and Alex walking towards her. *Crap!* she panicked. The last thing her mother needed to see, when she was already on edge about not knowing Emily's grades, was the girls that Emily assured that she wasn't hanging around anymore.

"Hey Em, we were just at your door," Alex smiled, stopping in front of Emily and her mother.

"Hi Alex…Sidra," Emily slowly put out.

Sidra and Alex glanced at each other before turning back to Emily. "Hi Ms. Harris," Alex attempted as Sidra folded her arms.

Ms. Harris looked both girls up and down, not uttering a word.

Sidra glared at the rude woman before her. *Ignorant ass*, she griped internally. Never had she met an adult who was so nasty and for no reason.

"What did you come over for?" Emily asked, pushing hair behind her ears.

Emily's nonchalant tone took Alex back. "Well, I tried calling you over the past few days," she informed.

"Why?" Emily shrugged.

Sidra raised her eyebrow. Emily's tone was starting to get a little nasty. She couldn't figure out if the girl was trying to put on a front for her mother, or if she truly was upset with them.

"First, I wanted to check on you. Haven't seen you around all week," Alex explained, ignoring Ms. Harris's piercing gaze. "Second, I wanted to tell you, since you probably hadn't heard, that Chasity was in the hospital last night."

Not changing her facial expression, Emily asked, "Is she okay?"

"She's fine," Sidra spat out, tired of the attitude. "Maybe you should go over and ask her your*self*."

Emily rolled her eyes. "Well, maybe I'll get over there eventually," she mumbled. "I mean, what's the point? She doesn't like me anyway."

Ms. Harris stood there, a smug look on her face. *Finally, she gets what I have been trying to tell her about those heathens.*

Alex went to say something when Sidra stepped in. "Emily you've been acting weird lately, what's your problem?" she hissed, pushing her ponytail over her shoulder.

Alex put her hand on Sidra's shoulder in an effort to calm her. She didn't want Emily to feel attacked, especially in front of her mother.

Emily swallowed hard. Seeing Sidra's angry face made Emily clam up. She never knew what to do when confronted. Before she could say anything, her mother stepped in front of her.

"She finally realizes that I was right about you girls all along," Ms. Harris sniped, folding her arms.

Alex shook her head as Sidra gritted her teeth.

"You know what, Ms. Harris," Sidra sneered. "Out of respect for your daughter, and because my mother raised me right, I'm going to refrain from saying what I *really* want to say to you."

"I don't care what—"

Emily felt bad as her mother began her tirade. No matter how she was feeling, at the end of the day, she still cared for the girls and she didn't want her mother to push them further away from her. "Mommy, wait—"

"Emily! Don't interrupt me while I'm talking," Ms. Harris boomed.

Emily looked around embarrassed, as her mother's loud voice carried. Looking down at the ground, and without saying a word, she scurried off towards the complex staircase.

"Nice going," Sidra directed at Ms. Harris while walking away with an equally annoyed Alex following.

Ms. Harris stormed into Emily's room, to find her sitting on her bed. "I can't believe—"

"Why do you keep embarrassing me like that?!" Emily snapped, facing down her stunned mother.

"Did you just raise your voice at me?" Ms. Harris fumed, hands on her hips. "Have you lost your mind?"

Emily stared at the floor. "I'm sorry, but I *hate* when you do that," she explained. "You keep embarrassing me in front of my friends like I'm some child."

Ms. Harris folded her arms. "I thought you said that you

weren't friends with them anymore."

Emily's eyes widened. *Oops.* "I um…Well."

Ms. Harris shook her head as Emily continued to stammer. "Lying *again*, huh?"

Emily frowned as she gathered her nerve. "I shouldn't *have* to lie about who I'm hanging out with, Mommy," she said. "I'm eighteen…I just—why do I have to lie to you to live my life?"

Ms. Harris stared at Emily, shocked. She wondered where she got her nerve from. Wherever it was, she didn't like it. Without saying another word, she stormed out of Emily's room, slamming the door behind her. The smack echoing through her small room made Emily flinch, but after her shock wore off, she was relieved.

Emily hurried out of class Monday morning and made her way for the exit doors. She awoke earlier feeling refreshed and relieved. She hadn't seen or spoken to her mother since the woman stormed out of her room late Saturday afternoon. She figured that she might have gone back to Jersey that evening.

I hope what I said to her finally gets her to back off, Emily thought, smiling to herself.

As Emily passed the head office of the Education department, she heard a familiar voice. Stopping, she stood at the door and listened for a moment.

No, it can't be, she thought. When she heard the voice again, she barged through the door and was shocked to see her mother sitting across from her professor, talking to him.

Emily's shocked gaze was met with her mother's angry one. Watching her professor shake her mother's hand, Emily was speechless.

"It was nice meeting you Ms. Harris, and I sure do hope that Emily's grades improve," he said.

"Oh, they *will*. I'll see to that," Ms. Harris assured, voice deceptively calm.

Emily, although silent, was screaming on the inside. *I can't believe she did that!*

When the two left the office, Emily, feeling like she could pass out, leaned against the wall as students disappeared into the classes. She felt like she couldn't breathe. "You—you talked to my—" Emily put both hands on her knees as she tried to compose herself.

"Did you *really* think that I was going to leave here without finding out what your grades were?" Ms. Harris replied, unfazed by Emily's reaction.

Emily looked up at her mother, tears in her eyes. She was embarrassed. "You went to my professor?" she questioned, tone failing to hide her anger. "Behind my back?"

"You're damn right I did," Ms. Harris barked. "I figured that since you seem to be lying about *everything* these days, why not go straight to the source to find out what your grades are? I can't believe that you're down here failing your damn classes. What the hell are you doing?!"

Emily felt her temper rise as her mother continued to berate her like a child. She was humiliated; she felt smothered.

"I can see that I'm going to have to make you come home every weekend again," Ms. Harris ranted. "Clearly, you have too much free time on your hands. If you don't get your damn act together—"

"You're crazy! Just leave me alone!" Emily exploded.

Emily's outburst startled her mother. "Have you lost your mind, girl?" she yelled back. She wasn't about to argue with her child in front of people. "Let's go, right now."

"I'm not going *anywhere* with you!" Emily shouted. "Just leave me alone!" Ms. Harris watched with shock as Emily ran out of the doors.

Emily didn't stop running until she reached her complex. She darted into her bedroom and slammed the door as hard as she could. Emily began pacing while trying to calm herself down. Feeling like she was about to explode, Emily grabbed a pillow from her bed, put it to her face and screamed into it.

Before she knew what happened, she was tearing her room apart as she cried out her frustrations. Her frustrations with her mother, her frustrations with herself. She hated herself for the fact that she didn't stand up to her mother a long time ago. Now it was too late; her mother knew that she had complete control over her and there was nothing that Emily could do about it.

Looking for more items to toss, she ran over to her closet and began pulling things from the top shelf. She sent clothes and toiletries flying across the room. Noticing something, she paused. With a tear streaked face, Emily pulled out the bottle of the drink that Praz had given to her for Malajia, weeks ago. She had every intention of giving the bottle to Malajia, but forgot about it when she hid it during one of her mother's visits. Needing to make her feelings go away, if only for a moment, Emily opened the bottle and began drinking. The strong taste never registered, she was too worked up to care.

Chapter 20

"I can't wait to get home and eat some of that home cooking," Alex mused, tossing some clothing into her duffle bag.

Malajia rolled her eyes. "You hype as shit about eatin' some dry ass turkey," she grumbled, examining her nails. "Thanksgiving isn't until tomorrow, with your greedy ass."

Alex paused from packing and flashed a scowl Malajia's way. "First of all, my mother's turkey is *never* dry, okay heifer," she proclaimed, pointing. "Second, just because *you're* miserable and don't want to go home, doesn't mean that you can come over here damaging everyone *else's* mood."

Malajia's eyes became slits. "Shut up," was all that she could say.

Alex waved her hand. She didn't care what Malajia had to say, she welcomed the Thanksgiving holiday. She was due for a break from classes and couldn't wait to spend time with her family.

Sidra stepped out of the bathroom, holding cleaning supplies. "I swear, I have never hated sharing something so much in my life," she complained, tossing the items on the floor.

"You still whining about that bathroom?" Malajia jeered. "What's wrong? Did one of them leave a finger nail on the sink?"

Sidra flipped Malajia off for her snarky remark. "Shut up, Malajia," she hurled. "And no, it wasn't a *finger nail*. It was hair, tooth paste splatters and trash…smart ass."

Alex giggled. "When we come back from break, why don't we have a meeting about the mess?" she suggested.

"I'm not meeting about *shit*," Sidra refused with a wave of her hand. "I'm tired of talking." Sidra sat on the bed and examined her nightstand. "Alex have you seen my charm bracelet, by any chance? The one with the silver elephants on it?"

Alex looked up from her bag. "No sweetie, can't say that I have," she answered. "Where do you think you had it last?"

"I want to say the bathroom, but I'm not sure," Sidra slowly answered, then looked at Malajia.

"What?" Malajia barked, noticing Sidra's accusing gaze. "I don't have that corny bracelet, okay," she hissed, pointing herself. "I don't even *like* elephants."

Alex laughed at the confused expression on Sidra's face.

The door opened after a light tap was heard. Malajia looked and saw Chasity walk in. "Heeey low iron," she teased.

Chasity fixed an angry gaze. "That's funny?"

"Sorry," Malajia chuckled.

"Whatever," Chasity returned. "I'm about to leave, do you have your room key?"

Malajia checked the pockets of her jeans. "Got it," she confirmed. Malajia had a thought as Chasity walked out of the door. "Chasity," she called.

Chasity pulled her head back inside. "What?"

"Can I come home with you for Thanksgiving?"

Chasity frowned. "Bitch please," she scoffed, closing the door.

Malajia sucked her teeth. "Rude ass."

Sidra opened her suitcase and glanced at Alex. "Alex,

you're not riding with Chaz this time?" she asked.

Alex zipped her bag and shook her head. "I'm riding home with Stacey and her parents."

"Wow, haven't seen *her* around in a while," Malajia commented, looking at her phone. A text message popped up, catching her off guard.

"I know," Alex agreed. "She said that it's because she's been busy with classes. But I think she's been avoiding me."

Malajia stood up and headed for the door. "I'll be back," she announced, walking out.

Sidra followed Malajia's progress before turning her attention back to Alex. "Why do you think Stacey is avoiding you?" she asked, packing her bag.

"I think she still feels guilty about keeping what happened between Victoria and Paul from me," Alex replied. "I think she may think that I'm mad at her."

"*Are* you?" Sudra asked point blank.

"No," Alex assured, standing from the floor. "Speaking of Stacey, I better get down there and meet her."

Sidra nodded as Alex gave her a hug. "See you Sunday," Sidra said.

Alex walked to the door and blew Sidra a kiss with her hand. "Call me."

"Do you want me to drive?" Jason asked, plopping his bag into the trunk of Chasity's car.

Chasity opened the door and tossed her purse in the backseat. "No, I'm good," she assured.

Jason put his hand on the roof of the car. "Okay, suit yourself," he shrugged. "That traffic is gonna be crazy."

Chasity paused for a moment. "On second thought, *you* drive," she amended, gesturing Jason to the driver's side.

Chasity, after finding out that Jason's parents weren't coming to pick him up until later that evening, decided to offer him a ride with her. The two slid into the car and put their seat belts on.

"Thanks for the ride, Chaz," Jason said, pulling off. "I appreciate it."

"Yeah well, there was no need in you sitting on this dry ass campus all night," Chasity replied.

Jason laughed.

"Besides, it's not like you're killing my gas tank. You don't live that far," she joked.

"You can't just say 'you're welcome' huh?" he teased, glancing at her.

"Nah, that would be too nice," she shrugged.

It was silent for moments while Jason maneuvered through the streets. "What are your plans for tomorrow?" he asked. "Going to anybody's house?"

Chasity shook her head emphatically. "Hell no," she bit out. "Last time I went to somebody's house for Thanksgiving, I got in a damn fight."

Jason shook his head as he recalled the epic fight that took place between Chasity and her adoptive mother Brenda the year before. "Just spending time with Ms. Trisha, huh?"

Chasity glanced out of the window. "I have no idea," she answered. "I haven't really spoken to her about too much of anything since I got out of the hospital." She pushed some hair behind her ears. "When she calls, it's just to make sure I'm taking my damn iron pills."

Jason was silent. Chasity told him about Trisha's reaction to her request to find her birth mother. He, like Chasity, was taken back by Trisha's behavior.

"She's still dodging the issue, huh?" he asked.

"Yup," Chasity nodded.

"You gonna bring it up to her again?"

"Yup," Chasity confirmed. "I don't care about her attitude."

Jason gazed at Chasity when he stopped at a red light. She looked sad. "Hey, if you end up not doing anything tomorrow…you *could* spend Thanksgiving with me and *my* family," he offered.

"I'm not your girlfriend, Jason," she declared.

Jason resisted the urge to roll his eyes. "Yes, Chasity, I'm *aware* that you aren't my girlfriend." He pulled off when the light changed. "But if nothing else, you're my friend. And I just want to keep you company…Is that such a bad thing?"

Chasity looked at him. It was a sweet gesture and the way that Jason was looking at her, with hope in his eyes, made her want to melt, but she kept her composure. "Thanks, but I'll be fine," she carefully declined.

Jason's face didn't hide his disappointment. "Okay," he said, continuing his driving. "If you change your mind, let me know."

Chasity stared out the window. She started to feel bad. Jason only wanted to spend time with her, no strings attached. "Look, attitude aside, Trisha probably *does* have something planned for tomorrow," Chasity modified. "But she'll be going out of town on Friday for business, so…" she hesitated momentarily. "If you still want to keep me company…you can come over on Friday…if you want."

Jason nodded as he fought to contain the smile bubbling up. "I'll bring some movies."

Malajia paced back and forth in her room, staring at the message on her phone. *Are you fuckin' kidding me?* she fumed.

Seeing the text pop up from Tyrone's number reading *'can I have another chance?'* threw her for a loop. She hadn't seen or spoken to the man since she left his apartment feeling disrespected.

Malajia's internal vent session was halted when she saw Tyrone's number flash across her screen. "Is this bastard really calling me?" she exclaimed. She had every intention of sending the call straight to voicemail, but her curiosity got the best of her.

"What could you *possibly* have to say to me?" Malajia barked into the phone.

It was silent for a few seconds. "Malajia?" Tyrone questioned.

Malajia pulled the phone away from her ear and stared at it in disbelief. "Yes, it's *Malajia*," she spat, putting the phone back to her ear. "What, you thought you called one of those *other* bitches in your phone?"

"Listen, I know I messed up," he explained. "I acted like a complete jackass."

"You damn *right*, you did," Malajia agreed. "Treating me like some common ho. Boy, you got me chopped."

"Look, I get it, and to be honest, I'm glad you're not like I *thought* you were," he said.

"Yeah, whatever."

"I'm serious," he declared. "I'm tired of these fast ass girls...I really enjoyed the talk that we had that day...I mean aside from the flirting stuff, we actually had a meaningful conversation."

Malajia rolled her eyes, her pacing continuing. *He's full of shit!* Everything in her told her to hang up on the man, but for some reason, she couldn't. "What did you call for, Tyrone?"

"Let me make it up to you, what are you doing now?"

"About to take my ass home for Thanksgiving break," she bit out.

"You getting a ride or taking the train?"

Malajia sucked her teeth. "What does it matter?"

"Because I wanted to swing by and take you to get something to eat," he proposed. "And no, I'm not taking you to my apartment."

Malajia once again rolled her eyes, flopping down on her bed. *He's an asshole. Say no, Malajia, say no*, the voice screamed in her head. "I um..." she let out a deep sigh. "I'm taking the train home and it leaves in like two hours, so wherever you plan on taking me better be close...and quick," she reluctantly replied, ignoring the voice in her head.

A sigh of relief came through the phone. "Cool, I'll be there in twenty."

"Yeah," Malajia replied, unenthused, before ending the call. She tossed the phone on her bed and ran her hands over her hair. Although irritated, a smile came through.

Maybe there's hope.

Mark cracked his knuckles while sitting inside of his car. He'd been sitting in the parking lot of Court Terrace for ten minutes; he was anxious to get on the road to Delaware.

A knock on the driver's side window prompted him to rub his chin. He glanced at the person outside in dramatic fashion before rolling his window down halfway.

"You got the goods?" Mark asked, tone even.

"You got the *space*?" Josh returned.

"Whatchu got?" Mark threw back, eyes facing forward.

"What we agreed on," Josh replied.

Mark fixed a long look on Josh's smiling face, before gesturing to the passenger's side with his head.

"Hop in," Mark ordered.

Josh hurried around the car and jumped in. "Here's the large supreme pizza, you greedy bastard," he joked.

Mark chuckled. "Good lookin', I ain't eat all morning," he beamed, opening the box and grabbing a slice. "Yo, where's David? I'm ready to roll."

"You should know, he's *your* roommate," Josh reminded. "Naw, here he comes."

Mark watched as David ambled through the parking lot, over to the driver's side window. Mark stared at David as he knocked. When Mark didn't roll the window down right away, David sucked his teeth and knocked again.

"You hype as shit," Mark griped, rolling down his window, halfway. "You got the goods?"

"You got the *space*?" David threw back.

"Whatchu got?"

"What we agreed on." David held a smug look on his face as he pulled a bottle of soda from his book bag.

Mark eyed the bottle and frowned. "Man I said *cola*, not

some nasty pineapple soda," he ground out. "And the shit ain't even name brand."

"Come on man, you're lucky I was able to find *this*," David argued. "The vending machine in the building needs to be refilled."

"Dawg, you coulda' ran to the store inside the SDC," Mark threw back.

David sucked his teeth. "Man, I wasn't trying to run all the way over there for a soda," he returned, voice raised.

"So you just gonna stand in my face with this wack ass soda?" Mark scoffed, reaching out and snatching the bottle from David's hand. "Shimmy Sham soda? Nobody even heard of this bullshit."

Josh busted out laughing as he put his seatbelt on.

"How the hell are you gonna make me and Josh bring you food and drinks to get a ride home?" David fumed, shifting his bag from one hand to the other. "You act like you wasn't gonna drive us *anyway*."

"Man fuck outta here, you walk home, glasses boy," Mark mocked, rolling up his window.

David walked over to the back door and began jiggling the locked door handle. "Man you better open this damn door," he ordered.

"Naw bruh, you take this Shimmy Sham soda and hope the bubbles carry your ass down the highway," Mark goaded.

"Mark, stop playing, I'm cold and it's starting to rain!" David hollered.

"Make better decisions next time," Mark taunted, turning the car on.

"Will you let him in, so we can go?" Josh urged, laughter subsiding. "You're such a jackass."

Mark unlocked the door and laughed. Once David got in and shut the door, Mark glanced back at David before nudging Josh. "Look Josh, his glasses all foggy and shit," he mocked.

David jerked his seatbelt across his shoulder. "Just pull

the hell off," he huffed.

Malajia sat across the table from Tyrone and poked at her sandwich. He'd picked her up twenty minutes prior and brought her to a sandwich place around the corner from the train station.

Tyrone picked up on the unenthused look on Malajia's face. "What's wrong, you don't like your sandwich?" he asked.

"It's fine," she mumbled.

"Well, you said close and quick," Tyrone reminded, taking a bite of some french fries.

"You're right, I did," Malajia quickly agreed, pushing the plastic basket away from her.

Tyrone took a sip of his drink. "You wanna wrap that up to take on the train with you?"

"No, I'm done with it," she said.

Tyrone stared at her. "Don't be rude," he chastised. "I paid for the thing, the *least* you can do is eat it."

Malajia shot him a challenging look. "You're calling *me* rude?" she hissed.

Tyrone put his hands up in surrender. "Okay, forget I said that," he quickly cut in. "My purpose of bringing you here wasn't to start an argument. It was a peace offering."

"It's gonna take more than some dry ass sandwich and a pickle to make peace with me after you disrespected me the way you did," Malajia argued, gesturing to her half-eaten sandwich.

Tyrone rubbed his chin, then nodded slowly. "I feel you," he agreed. "I was a jerk and I feel bad, but you need to take some responsibility for *your* part."

"What the hell are you talking about?"

"Malajia, the way you come off—look, you can't blame me for thinking a certain way about you," he reasoned. "No disrespect, but you dress and flirt like you're ready and willing."

Malajia rolled her eyes and sat back in her seat. *So I've been told a million times.* "Look, I might *look* a certain way, but you shouldn't judge me *because* of it," she threw back.

Tyrone opened his mouth to speak, when he noticed some guys at the next table staring in their direction. He frowned at them. "Yo, you staring at *her*?" he barked, pointing to Malajia. "You see her sitting here with me, you just gonna disrespect me like that?"

Malajia was shocked. She put her hand on Tyrone's arm. "Hey, it's not that—"

Tyrone put his hand up at Malajia, signaling her to stop talking while he continued to rant at the on-lookers. "Keep your damn eyes to yourself before I come over there and snatch them out of your head."

Malajia put her hand over her face, she was feeling slightly embarrassed. Not just about the fact that Tyrone went off on the guys for looking at her; but at the fact that he just, without saying a word, made her shut her mouth.

As Tyrone, grabbed a napkin from under his basket, Malajia looked at him. *I should cuss his ass out!* she thought. But despite what she was telling herself, she couldn't. She actually found his aggressiveness attractive. *Well...at least he's protective, that's a good thing. And he looks so cute when he does it.*

Still annoyed, Tyrone balled up his napkin and tossed it into his empty burger basket. "Let's go," he ordered.

Without saying a word, Malajia gathered her belongings and stood from her seat.

Chapter 21

Emily stumbled out of bed Thanksgiving morning and looked around the floor for her slippers. Unable to locate them under the belongings that were strewn across her shared bedroom, she flopped back on the bed.

After enduring a long, uncomfortable ride with her mother from school the day before, Emily, upon entering the house, went straight to her bedroom and locked herself in for the night.

I'm so not looking forward to this holiday. I wish I could've stayed at school by myself, Emily thought, hearing the doorknob jiggle. She sighed when she heard her mother's voice on the other side.

"Emily, you know that I don't like doors locked in my house," Ms. Harris said through the door.

Emily stared at the door and shook her head. "I know, I'm sorry," she meekly put out.

"Save it," Ms. Harris hissed. Ever since Emily snapped at her mother over the woman's visit to her professor behind her back, Ms. Harris made no attempts at hiding her disdain for Emily. "Get up and come down here," she ordered. "We should've started cooking hours ago."

"Okay," Emily replied. "I'll be down in a few minutes."

It was a half-hour later when Emily finally entered the kitchen. Ms. Harris glared. "Took you long enough," she grunted, washing greens in the sink.

Emily rubbed her eyes before grabbing a loaf of bread from the counter. "I'm sorry, I was really tired," she explained.

Ms. Harris slammed the dish towel she was holding, on the counter. "Tired?" she snapped. "I don't know *why*. It's not like you were *studying* or anything."

Emily looked down at the kitchen table while she tore the bread into small pieces. She knew it was only a matter of time before her lousy grades were brought up again. It was bad enough that Emily had to hear about it every day on the phone and endured a verbal lashing about them during the ride home.

"And don't think I forgot about your little outburst."

"Mommy, I've apologized for that," Emily reminded. "I was angry."

"You were *disrespectful*," Ms. Harris amended, tone sharp. "I don't know what you were on, or who told you that it was okay to talk to your mother like that…especially after *you* were the one who lied."

Emily gripped the bowl that she placed her bread crumbles in. In her mind, she was throwing the bowl across the room, but in reality, she just stared at it. "I—I know that I messed up," she sputtered after a moment of silence. "I'm sorry for yelling at you. And, I can fix my grades. I'll do better."

"Oh I *know* you will, you have no *choice*," Ms. Harris assured, folding her arms. "The colleges in this area won't take acceptance with low grades anyway…Well *one* of them will, Community."

Emily felt her stomach drop. "Um…What are you talking about? Why are you looking at other schools?"

"Emily, you're clearly not doing what you're supposed to do down there in Virginia," Ms. Harris said, fixing her gaze on Emily. "You're too busy lying and carrying on, instead of studying and passing your classes like you're *supposed* to be doing."

Is she serious?! Emily screamed to herself. "Mommy—" she took a deep breath in an effort to keep tears from forming in her eyes. "I don't *want* to go to another school...I like my school."

"It's not about what you *like*, it's about what's best for you," Ms. Harris insisted. "You have until the end of this year to get your damn act together, or so help me, I'll see to it that you transfer."

Emily fought the urge to scream as she watched her mother walk out of the kitchen.

Emily pushed herself back from the table and grabbed the bowl of crumbled bread. As she prepared to start her mother's stuffing recipe, she felt herself nearing a breakdown. Her mother was taking control to another level. Emily sat the spoon that she held down, and began searching in an overhead cabinet for something, *anything* with alcohol in it.

Not finding anything, she slammed the cabinet door. Having a thought, Emily jogged up the steps. She ran into her room, shutting and locking the door behind her. She headed over to Jazmine's bed and began searching under the mattress.

Where's your stash, Jaz? She grabbed hold of two items and pulled them from the mattress. Focusing on the two small plastic bottles of rum in her hand, her eyes lit up. *At least her short-lived job at the liquor store was good for something.*

Emily, needing to release the stress building inside of her, opened one of the bottles, and downed the liquid. Realizing that straight liquor was much stronger than the drinks she'd had before, she put her hand over her mouth and coughed.

"How did I get stuck making this dry ass stuffing?"

Malajia griped, sprinkling seasoning into a bowl of crumbled bread, celery and onions.

Mrs. Simmons closed the refrigerator door and regarded her daughter sternly. "Did you just cuss?"

"No," Malajia lied, stirring the contents with a spoon. "Mom, nobody's gonna eat this. They never *do*," she whined, tossing the spoon in the sink.

"Will you stop your damn complaining?" Mrs. Simmons hissed, shuffling one of her younger daughters out of the kitchen. "And people *do* eat the stuffing."

"Mom, every year it sits in a bowl," Malajia argued. "Your recipe is dry and it sucks."

"That was your grandmother's recipe!"

Malajia stared at her mother, expression confused. "That's not even *true*, though," she contradicted. "You got it out of a cook book."

Mrs. Simmons sucked her teeth. "That's not the point," she bit out, with a wave of her hand.

"You just lied that fast," Malajia chuckled. *And people wonder where I get it from.*

"Girl, just hurry on up and make it. People will start arriving soon," Mrs. Simmons ordered, checking on the sweet potatoes and macaroni and cheese in the oven. "We'll have some new guests this year, so behave."

Malajia rolled her eyes. "You act like Sidra's never been here before. She ain't no damn guest."

Happy that their daughters had rekindled their friendship, thus rekindling theirs, Mrs. Simmons and Sidra's mother decided to spend Thanksgiving together this time. Mrs. Simmons offered to host.

"Just hurry up," Mrs. Simmons demanded, peering over Malajia's shoulder. "Malajia where are the carrots? The recipe called for them."

"Mom, *nobody* in this house likes carrots," Malajia protested, exasperated. "You always tryna put carrots in people's food. You know the original recipe didn't call for no nasty carrots."

Ignoring Malajia, Mrs. Simmons opened the refrigerator and pulled out a bowl of carrots that she chopped the previous evening. "Put these in there."

Malajia pushed the bowl away. "No Mom, people aren't gonna blame *me* for that nasty, carrot infested stuffing," she groused, heading out of the kitchen.

Mrs. Simmons laughed. "Girl, stop being so damn dramatic," she called after her. "Malajia Lakeshia, you know you hear me!"

Malajia stormed back into the kitchen, grabbed the bowl from her mother, and as she headed for the counter, accidentally-on-purpose spilled the carrots into the dishwater filled sink. "Oops," she hissed as the bowl dropped in the sink.

Angry, Mrs. Simmons grabbed a towel off of the counter and began swatting Malajia on the behind with it. "You play too damn much!"

Malajia laughed while she covered her behind with her hand, trying to shield the blows. "You mad 'cause your carrots fell in the sink," she mocked, relishing her mother's irritation.

Mrs. Simmons headed back to the refrigerator and after digging around in the crisper, pulled out a bag of carrots. "Now, smart ass, cut these up and put them in there," she commanded.

Malajia's eyes widened. "They all old!"

"Cut em' up!" Mrs. Simmons screamed, making Malajia flinch.

The doorbell rang nearly two hours later, sending Malajia darting for it. "Ponytail!" she cried out.

Sidra rolled her eyes as her parents chuckled. "You're always starting," she griped, stepping inside the house, followed by her parents and two of her brothers.

As Malajia's family greeted Sidra's family, Malajia asked, "Where's Marcus?"

Sidra sucked her teeth. "Girl, he's spending Thanksgiving with that *thing*," she jeered, hanging her coat on the rack.

Malajia giggled. "You still don't like his girlfriend, huh?"

"*What* girlfriend?" Sidra sneered. "They break up like every three days. I swear, the chick loves drama."

Malajia put her arm around Sidra as both girls walked to the kitchen. "Aww, Sidra's cranky because her big brother is dating a fool," she teased.

"Hush," Sidra spat, leaning over the kitchen island. "I talked to Mark today and he told me to tell you to go screw yourself, because you didn't invite him to dinner," she laughed.

Malajia sucked her teeth. "He better leave me the hell alone," she scoffed, leaning against the counter.

"Everything smells good," Sidra beamed, eyeing the dishes full of carved turkey, baked macaroni and cheese, greens, yams, pasta salad, potato salad, and biscuits. Sidra's eyes fixed on something in another dish. "What's that?" she asked, pointing to it.

Malajia rolled her eyes. "Stuffing," she answered, unenthused. "That shit is terrible."

Sidra frowned her face in disgust at the tan, green and orange substance. "Eww, it looks like something my neighbor's cat threw up," she grimaced. "Did *you* make that?"

Malajia turned her lip up. "Fuck no, I ain't make that bullshit," she assured. "Mom tried to get me to do it, but I told her I wasn't for it."

Sidra laughed. "Girl, stop lying. You know you made that vomit," she teased, much to Malajia's annoyance. Malajia stared at the girl as she kept laughing. "Trying to place the blame of that disaster on my second mother. You're so wrong for that."

Malajia slowly folded her arms. "Hey Mom!" she called.

Mrs. Simmons walked into the kitchen, holding a pie

dish. "Sidra, your mother said that you made sweet potato pie?" she said, a bright smile on her face.

Sidra nodded proudly.

"Mom, Sidra was just saying how good the stuffing looks," Malajia lied.

Sidra held a smile on her face as Mrs. Simmons clasped her hands together. "Thank you sweetie," she gushed. "See, I *told* you that people would like it, Malajia."

Malajia nodded enthusiastically. "You did, you sure did," she mocked, examining her nails. "Hey Sid, why don't you taste it?"

Sidra glared at Malajia. "I wouldn't want to mess up the presentation," she declined, teeth clenched.

"Oh no, you don't have to worry about that," Mrs. Simmons cut in.

Sidra snapped her head around and looked at Mrs. Simmons. "Huh?" she replied, wide-eyed. "No, it's fine—"

"Please, I want you to try it," Mrs. Simmons insisted, handing Sidra a small spoon full.

Sidra hesitantly took the spoon. Malajia put her hand over her mouth to keep from bursting with laughter.

"Go on, try it," Mrs. Simmons urged.

"I don't wanna," Sidra whined, voice low. Then gave a nervous laugh when Mrs. Simmons frowned. Sidra stared at the spoon. "Um…what's the orange and green stuff in here?"

"Carrots and scallions," Malajia snickered. "A whole *bag* full."

Sidra looked like she wanted to cry as she placed the substance into her mouth. *Oh God! It's terrible*. In an effort to not hurt Mrs. Simmons feelings, Sidra just stood there, slowly chewing the food, suffering.

Malajia felt like her chest was going to explode as she tried to hold her laughter in. Hearing someone call her name, Mrs. Simmons bolted from the kitchen. Seizing the opportunity, Sidra darted for the trash can and spit the chewed up stuffing out. Malajia finally let her laughter out.

"That was disgusting," Sidra whined, wiping her mouth with a paper towel. Malajia handed her a bottle of water. "How is it crunchy and mushy at the same time?" she fussed, taking a sip.

"I tried to tell her that the stuff was nasty, she don't listen," Malajia said, laughter subsiding.

"You didn't have to do that to me, you heifer," Sidra fumed, pointing at her.

"Oh I *so* did," Malajia laughed.

Sitting by the fireplace in her living room, Chasity propped a throw pillow under her back. With Trisha out with a client, Chasity relished the quiet while playing on her phone. Hearing the front door open, Chasity sighed. "Great," she mumbled.

"What are you up to?" Trisha asked, walking over and sitting on the chaise lounge across from Chasity.

Chasity sat her phone on the cushion next to her. "Nothing," she replied, tone dry. "You working today?"

"Not anymore. I just came from my last meeting of the day," Trisha returned.

Chasity just sat there. The interaction between the two women felt strained. She felt it ever since she brought up her wishes to find her birth mother. "Trish, we need to talk."

"Not now," Trisha dismissed with a wave of her hand.

Chasity frowned. "Why *not* now?"

"Because, it's Thanksgiving and I have a lot to do today," Trisha replied.

"Like *what*?" Chasity asked, confused. "We're not doing anything but staying in the house, and I really wanna talk to you about—"

"Listen, I wanted to talk to you about dinner tonight," Trisha interrupted, scratching her head.

Chasity rolled her eyes. "I'm not going over anybody's house today," she spat. "Can you just listen to me—"

"I invited the family to come over *here* for

Thanksgiving," Trisha interrupted once again.

Chasity raised an eyebrow "*Whose* family?" she hissed.
"Ours."

"You mean *yours*," Chasity threw back, standing from her seat.

"Chaz, don't start this mess today," Trisha chided. "It's Thanksgiving and your grandmother wants to see you."

"I can't believe you did this," Chasity replied, angry.

Trisha watched as Chasity approached the winding staircase. "You can be mad all you want, but you better be on your best behavior tonight."

"Whatever yo," Chasity threw over her shoulder, heading up the steps.

Agitation was frozen on Chasity's face as she cut into the apple pie, which was sitting on the counter. Hearing a noise from the dining room, she spun around, knocking the pie off of the counter.

"Shit," she whispered, bending to retrieve it.

"What are you doing?" Trisha asked upon entering the kitchen.

Chasity quickly stood up from the floor, innocence on her face. "Huh?"

Trisha eyed Chasity suspiciously. "What did you do?"

"What do you mean?" Chasity asked, perplexed.

"You think I can't see that pie on the floor behind you?" Trisha chortled, shaking her head.

Chasity sucked her teeth, grabbing the pie from the floor. "If you already saw it, why go through all the damn questions?" she mumbled.

"You say something?" Trisha challenged, grabbing a serving tray piled high with cornbread, from the counter island.

"You know I *did*," Chasity returned, tossing the destroyed pie in the trash.

"Why are you hiding out in here?"

"Why do you *think*?" Chasity returned, folding her arms.

Trisha rolled her eyes and huffed. Chasity barely said two words to Trisha since that afternoon when she dropped the bomb about the family coming. She almost missed the silence now that her attitude was in full affect. "Chaz, you haven't said a word to anybody since they walked in this house," she nagged.

"You already know I don't like those fucked up ass people in there," Chasity sneered.

"Watch your damn mouth," Trisha ordered. "You need to stop acting so freakin' mean."

"No, *you* need to stop doing stuff like this behind my back," Chasity threw back.

Trisha resisted the urge to continue the back and forth with her stubborn niece. "We have company, stop being rude and come eat with us."

"I don't want to."

"Chasity, don't play with me today!" Trisha snapped, completely over Chasity's attitude. Chasity flinched at the loudness in Trisha's voice. "Now, come on."

Chasity glared at Trisha's departing back for several seething moments, before reluctantly following her into the dining room.

Chasity rolled her eyes and looked at her watch for the fifth time, while listening to the chatter around her. *It's been two fuckin' hours! How long do I have to sit here?* she fumed. She eyed a bottle of wine sitting on the table in front of her and tried to grab for it, but Trisha, who was sitting next to her, grabbed it and moved it out of her reach.

"Stop it," Trisha reprimanded, voice low.

"Tell *them* to stop talking so damn much," Chasity returned, voice just as low. Trisha softy backhanded Chasity on the arm.

"So Chasity, how's school?" Grandmother Duvall asked, reaching for her glass of wine.

Chasity looked up from her plate. "Its fine," she answered through a forced smile.

Her grandmother frowned, picking up on Chasity's bad vibe. "Are you okay?"

"Uh huh," Chasity replied. *Please stop asking me questions.*

"Trisha told me that you were in the hospital," Grandmother Duvall continued. "I've been calling you, trying to check on you, but you don't answer."

Before Chasity could respond, Trisha intervened. "Mom, she's been busy with her studies." Trisha then turned to Chasity. "You *should* return her calls, Chasity."

Chasity rolled her eyes. She was in no mood for lectures from anybody at that table, *especially* from Trisha who wasn't exactly on her good side.

"Aunt Trisha, we should've had dinner at Grandmom's house," Chasity's cousin Melina put out, chewing her food.

Trisha rubbed her forehead with her hand. "Melina, if I *had*, then Chasity wouldn't have come."

"*Exactly*," Melina grumbled.

Great, just what I need. Trisha thought, knowing that Chasity wasn't going to let that comment slide.

Chasity glared at her most hated cousin, a former childhood bully. "Your fat ass is just gonna keep talking while you're chewing like a freakin' horse, huh?" she sneered.

"Can we not do this right now?" Trisha pleaded, putting her hands up.

"*I* didn't start with her," Chasity fussed.

"You've been sitting here with a damn attitude all night," Melina threw back. "You *always* have an attitude. That's why nobody in this family likes your ignorant behind."

"You really think I *give* a shit about *anybody* at this damn table?" Chasity returned. "Including *your* ugly ass?"

Trisha slammed her hand on the table. "Enough Chasity!" she barked, regarding her sternly. "Your grandmother is sitting here."

Chasity looked at Trisha with shock. She'd made it a point to keep her mouth shut just to get through the dinner that she was forced to sit through, and because she refused to let her cousin verbally attack her, she was getting scolded for it.

Upset, Chasity slammed her cloth napkin on the table and rose from her seat. "I'm over this."

Trisha apologized to the family as Chasity stormed out of the dining room. Rising from her seat, Trisha followed her into the kitchen. "Really Chasity?" she scolded. "You couldn't curb that mouth for another fuckin' hour?"

Chasity spun around to face her. "Why are you on *my* case?" she fumed, pointing to herself. "You sprung this 'family thing' on me like *four hours* ago," she reminded.

Trisha folded her arms as she looked away.

"You already *knew* I wasn't gonna be happy. That's why you didn't tell me *before* today," Chasity added. "I'm sure you *just* didn't decide to do this."

Trisha ran her hand over her hair and sighed. "Look, I apologize for putting you in this position," she said.

"Why would you do that to me?" Chasity asked, confused. "After everything that happened last year. Why would you force me to sit in a room with people who I *know* I'm not related to? Hell, they don't even like me."

"That's not true. Melina was just being rude," Trisha placated. "Your family loves you, and you already know that you're your grandmother's favorite."

Chasity ran her hands through her hair, fighting to stay calm. "Stop trying to force these people on me," she fussed.

Trisha threw her hands up in the air. "Fine, Chasity. Go ahead and hide out in here," she snapped, turning to walk out.

Chasity shook her head. "I know what you're doing," she called after Trisha, stopping her dead in her tracks.

Trisha spun around. "And what's *that*, know-it-all?"

Chasity folded her arms. "You avoided me all day

yesterday, you piss me off by crowding the damn house *today*, all so I won't talk to you."

"Why would I do that?"

"Because you don't want me to bring up my birth mother again," Chasity spat.

Trisha's jaw tightened. *Will this damn girl drop this shit?* "I don't have time for this, I have company to get back to."

"Trisha, don't do that," Chasity barked. "Don't brush me off about this."

"God, why can't you let this thing go?" Trisha asked, exasperated.

"Why do you *want* me to?" Chasity threw back. "You're treating me like shit right now because you have a problem with what I want to do. That's not fair."

"Fair? You want to talk about what's not *fair*?" Trisha hissed, moving closer to Chasity. "The fact that I even have to *endure* this mess. I've provided for you since you were a child."

"Yes, I know that."

"*Do* you?" Trisha challenged.

Chasity was confused and it showed on her face. "Are you serious?"

"Yes, I *am*," Trisha seethed. "I do *everything* for you. *Whatever* you want, I give. Money, clothes, trips, a car, a damn condo—"

"I *never* asked you for *any* of that stuff," Chasity hurled.

"I didn't say that you *did*," Trisha threw back. "Everything I did and *continue* to do for you is because I *want* to."

"Then why throw it in my face?"

"I'm not *trying* to," Trisha assured her. "I'm just saying that...after everything, why isn't it enough for you? Why can't you just be happy with the way that things are?"

Chasity stared at Trisha in disbelief. "This isn't about *you*, Trisha," Chasity wailed. Trisha turned away briefly. "This isn't about my relationship with you, or about what you *do* for me."

"That's not what—"

"*Listen* to me," Chasity urged, voice filled with pain. "This is something that I need to do for *myself*...I just thought that as the most important person in my life, that you would be supportive."

"Well...You thought wrong," Trisha sneered. "I'm *not* supportive of this. I don't condone it. Let it go."

Chasity held a fiery gaze. "You *do* know that I don't need your permission right?" she bluntly stated. "I'm nineteen, I can do this with or with*out* your help."

Furious, Trisha's eyes widened. Taking another step forward, standing face to face with Chasity, she pointed at her. "You go through with this search, and we're done," she warned.

Shock and disappointment resonated on Chasity's face as Trisha stormed out of the kitchen. Her aunt, her mother figure, someone whom she considered to be her best friend just threatened to walk out of her life if she didn't comply with her wishes. Feeling betrayed, feeling let down, Chasity felt tears fill her eyes. Not wanting to face anybody, she walked out the back door.

Jason poured himself a glass of juice while listening to his family converse around him. Grandparents, parents, aunts, uncles, cousins and his brother crowded the Adams' large dining room table, Thanksgiving evening.

"So Jase, your dad told us how great you played at homecoming," one of Jason's uncles gushed.

Jason smiled. "I did okay," he replied, breaking one of his mother's homemade biscuits in half.

"Nonsense, he did absolutely perfect," Mr. Adams beamed. "He's a star."

"I'm only as good as my team," Jason said. He prided himself on being modest when it came to his abilities as a football player. Even when his family wasn't.

"Baby, don't be modest, you were great," Mrs. Adams smiled, before pointing her fork in her brother-in-law's direction. "If your uncle would've come down like he was *supposed* to, he would've seen you play for *himself.*"

"Mom, there'll be other games for him to come to," Jason pointed out, voice filled with amusement.

"So Jason, do you have a girlfriend yet?" his grandfather asked.

Before Jason could answer, his mother put her hand up. "He doesn't have time for those fast behind little girls," she scoffed. "Most girls his age only want to latch themselves to a guy like him because they know he'll make something of himself."

"Mom, not *all* girls my age are fast and are just looking for an opportunity," Jason argued. "I happen to be friends with five women who have a lot going for *them...* You've met them."

"I don't remember," Mrs. Adams sneered.

"Yes you do, Mom," Jason returned, shaking his head. His mother had a knack for pretending to forget about any female in his life.

"Anyway Jason, back to my question," his grandfather pressed, shooting his daughter a side-glance. "Do you have a girlfriend yet?"

"No Grandpop, not yet," Jason confirmed. "But I'm working on it."

"No? No jawns?" His grandfather teased, earning a backhand from his wife.

"Dad!" Mrs. Adams exclaimed.

"Wait, did he just say 'jawns'?" Jason asked his father, laugher in his voice.

"I was trying to pretend like I didn't hear that," Mr. Adams laughed.

 Mrs. Adams shook her head, embarrassed.

"Jase, what about the girl that I met last Christmas?" Jason's fourteen-year-old brother Kyle asked. "The one that came with your other friends over the summer to visit. Isn't *she* your girlfriend?"

"Who, *Chasity*?" Jason replied, heart skipping a beat at the mere mention of her. "I *wish* bro. Trust me, I've been working on it."

"Well what's wrong with this girl that you have to *try* so damn hard?" Mrs. Adams hissed.

Jason glanced at her. His mother thought highly of him and she couldn't understand why *any* girl would give him a hard time.

"Is she blind or stupid?" Mrs. Adams ranted.

Jason felt himself becoming agitated. *Don't start, Mom.* Jason didn't approve of anybody talking negatively about Chasity, not even his own mother. "Mom, there's *nothing* wrong with her," he bit out. "She's making me work for her attention, which is what a woman *should* do."

"I *do* remember that girl," Mrs. Adams recalled, pouring herself a glass of wine. "The one with the attitude."

"She didn't give you attitude," Jason contradicted, frowning.

"Mmm hmm," Mrs. Adams grumbled.

Sensing the tension building between his son and his wife, Mr. Adams decided to intervene. "Son, I'm glad that you've found someone who you're interested in," he cut in. "Chasity seems like a good woman."

Aside from meeting Chasity the one time, Mr. Adams had heard all about her from Jason.

"Dad she *is*," Jason confirmed, pouring gravy over his mashed potatoes. "I mean she's stubborn as hell, but I can deal with that. You know I love a challenge."

"I'm glad that you're doing so well Jason," his grandmother chimed in, folding her arms. "The whole family is very proud of you."

Jason, feeling flushed, smiled as he looked down at the table. "Thanks Grandma."

"I mean to think, you're the first one of your generation to go to college," she gushed.

Jason smiled. Her statement was accurate. He *was* the

first one in his generation to go to college. Although his cousins were given the same opportunities, they never had the desire to go further than high school.

"Well, I promise not to disappoint you guys," Jason replied, putting a fork full of food into his mouth.

"Don't worry Jason, you won't," Mrs. Adams boasted.

Jason concentrated on the food on his plate. He had to admit, the pressure that his family put on him was a little overwhelming at times. But, despite what he felt, he never complained.

"Mmm, Mrs. Addison, this stuffing is the best," Alex beamed, stuffing a fork full into her mouth.

"Actually baby, I didn't make it, *Stacey* did," Mrs. Addison revealed.

Alex tossed her fork on the plate. "Well so much for *that*," she joked.

Stacey poked Alex on her arm, laughing. "Real funny."

The small Chisolm household was full of family and friends. Gathered around the dining room table for dinner, the warmth could be felt.

Mrs. Chisolm giggled, scooping baked macaroni and cheese onto her fork. "Thanks again for bringing the stuffing and mashed potatoes over, Adele."

"Oh, no problem," Mrs. Addison smiled. "My family appreciates the invite to dinner this year."

"No need to thank me," Mrs. Chisolm assured, waving her hand. "It was my pleasure." With everything that happened with Victoria, Mrs. Chisolm didn't want Stacey and her family to feel awkward, so she extended an invite for them to have dinner with her family.

Mrs. Addison turned to Alex and Stacey, who were seated next to one another. "I'm so glad that you two didn't lose your friendship with each other over all of that Paul and Victoria madness."

Alex shook her head, resting her elbow on the table.

Great, not even an hour into dinner and somebody brings this up, she thought, putting her head in her hand.

"Mom, not now please," Stacey pleaded, reaching for her glass of soda.

"What?" Mrs. Addison asked with surprise.

"Come on Mom, at the table with everyone here though?" Stacey hissed.

"Sorry, I was just saying—"

"It's okay Stacey," Alex assured, putting her hand on Stacey's arm. She appreciated the fact that her friend was so protective. "I'm fine," she directed to Mrs. Addison. "The bright side of all of this is that I know who my *real* friends are."

"That's my baby, always finding the bright side," Mrs. Chisolm smiled, winking at Alex.

"Oh stop it Ma," Alex blushed.

A knock at the door interrupted the group's discussion. "I wonder who *that* is," Mrs. Chisolm commented.

"*Whoever* it is, they missed all of the mashed potatoes," Alex chuckled when her mother scurried to the door.

"That's because *you* ate it all," Mr. Chisolm teased.

"You *know* it," Alex laughed, pointing to her behind. "I need to feed *this* booty."

Alex's laughter was cut short once she heard her mother's elevated voice. "What are y'all doing here?"

Alex rose from her seat and headed for the door, along with some of their guests. A collective gasp was heard when the group laid eyes on Victoria and her mother standing in the doorway.

"Mrs. James?" Stacey gasped.

"What? No invite for *us*?" Mrs. James sneered at Alex's mother, who in turn shot her a challenging look.

"Are you really surprised?" Mrs. Chisolm returned, holding her hand on the door.

Alex stood in front of her mother. "No disrespect to you Mrs. James, but *this thing* right here needs to get from in front of my door," she demanded, pointing to Victoria, who looked at the ground in shame.

"Alex, you already hit Victoria in her damn face, what *else* do you want to do?" Mrs. James ranted, folding her arms.

Alex was about to respond when her mother moved her aside. "Your backstabbing daughter is lucky that's *all* my baby did to her," she barked.

Alex resisted the urge to smile. Her mother may have had a soft demeanor, but when it came to her children, she had the mentality of a lioness.

As Mrs. Chisolm directed her prying guests to go back into the dining room, Alex continued to stare daggers at Victoria. "Victoria, I'm warning you, walk away."

Victoria went to leave, but her mother grabbed her arm, stopping her. "No, you hold on," she demanded, before facing Alex and her mother. "Look, I know that Victoria made a mistake, but—"

"She was my best friend and she slept with my boyfriend!" Alex snapped, clapping her hands with each word. "There is nothing that she or *you* can say to justify that."

"So what are you gonna do?" Mrs. James asked, angry. "Just completely cut her out of your life? After *years* of friendship?"

"*She* made that decision *for* me when she betrayed me," Alex seethed. "I'm done."

"You should be ashamed of yourself, coming to my home on Thanksgiving with this mess," Mrs. Chisolm added. "You need to back away from my door before it hits you in the face."

Not allowing another word to be said out of either of the uninvited women, Mrs. Chisolm shut the door. "Can you believe that?" she directed at Alex as the two women walked back into the dining room.

"Surprisingly, yes," Alex replied, running her hands through her hair. "Mrs. James has always been that way. She thinks her daughter can do no wrong."

"Forget them," Mrs. Chisolm urged, giving Alex a pat on her back.

Alex sat down and picked up her fork. A frown resonated on her face. "Dad, did you eat my mashed potatoes?"

"Huh?" He looked at her wide-eyed, placing a spoonful into his mouth.

Alex shook her head in amusement.

Chapter 22

Chasity walked into her home from a much needed shopping trip, just in time to see Trisha put her coat on. Chasity rolled her eyes. *Shit! I was hoping I wouldn't have to see her ass before she left,* she thought, turning to head back out the door.

"You're just going to act like you don't see me here?" Trisha hissed, reaching for her suitcase.

Chasity turned back around, walked inside, and shut the door behind her.

"As you know, I'll be tied up in Florida for a few days, so I probably won't see you before you go back to school," Trisha informed, looking at her silver and diamond watch.

Chasity blinked slowly, trying to keep from losing her temper. Trisha was acting like they didn't just have an argument the day before. "You're telling me this for…what?" she sneered.

Trisha glowered. "Lose the damn attitude," she ordered, voice stern.

"No, *you* lose it," Chasity shot back.

"Excuse me?"

"You're standing here acting like you don't know why I'm pissed at you," Chasity argued.

"Oh, I *know* why you're pissed at me," Trisha confirmed. "But I don't have time to go into this with you right now."

Chasity put her hands up. "What *else* is new?" she snarled, heading for the stair case. "Have a safe trip."

"Chasity," Trisha called after her. When she heard the door slam, tears filled her eyes. *I hate being this way to her.* Dropping her suitcase handle, she headed up the steps and twisted the doorknob to Chasity's bedroom, only to find it locked. Sighing, Trisha put her hand on the door. "Chaz, sweetie…I'm sorry," she said through the door.

Standing on the other side of the door, Chasity gave no response.

"I know you don't understand why I don't want you to search for your mother," Trisha continued. "But, I need you to just—" hearing her voice crack, she took a deep breath. "Look, Chasity, I—I love you okay…Always remember that."

Chasity folded her arms, still not saying a word. She didn't care what Trisha had to say at that moment. Her feelings were hurt, and she was angry. Tears filled her eyes, but it wasn't until she heard Trisha leave that she let them fall.

Stretching out on her bed, Malajia let a sigh of delight come through. Having just ended a three-hour-long call with Tyrone, Malajia's mood was at an all-time high. Given his history of letting weeks pass without calling, she didn't think that she would hear from him so soon after his impromptu visit two days ago. So when he called her, she was both shocked and ecstatic.

Geri walked in the room and eyed Malajia suspiciously as the girl began kicking her legs in the air. "Girl, what the hell are you doing?"

Malajia sat up and faced her sister. "I'm minding my damn business," she bit out, smoothing her hair with her hand.

"How are you minding your business on *my* damn bed?" Geri sneered, heading over to her closet.

"Your mattress is better than mine."

"Well, if you stop jumping on the damn thing, then yours would be better," Geri threw back.

Malajia waved her hand in Geri's direction. "Whatever," she ground out. "Anyway, you wanna hear about this guy I'm talking to?"

"Not really," Geri replied, tone dry. She sighed when Malajia sucked her teeth. "What's he like, Mel?"

Malajia smiled. "Okay, so he's twenty-one, tall, dark-skinned, he has a bangin' body and—"

"Not surprised, the first thing you mention are looks, with your shallow ass," Geri teased.

Malajia frowned. "Heifer, I'm not shallow," she protested. "And I mentioned his *age* first."

Geri laughed as she headed for the door, a pair of boots in her hand. "Yeah, okay," she scoffed.

Malajia rolled her eyes. *Always gotta say some smart shit.* "Where *you* going?" she asked, changing the subject.

"I'm going to mind my business," Geri threw over her shoulder, walking out of the room, shutting the door behind her.

Malajia once again sucked her teeth. "That's why those boots don't match your ugly ass outfit," she hissed to the empty room. Looking at her phone, she sighed. Malajia needed to gush to somebody. There was only one person at this point, who she wanted to do that with.

Picking up the phone, she dialed a number.

Chasity had just straightened a center piece on the glass coffee table in her living room, when her cell phone rang. "This better not be you, Trisha," she mumbled to herself, reaching for the phone on the couch. When she saw the name on the caller ID, she rolled her eyes.

"What Malajia?" she spat into the phone.

"Eww, what's *your* attitude all about?" Malajia bit back, face scrunched up.

Chasity flopped down on the couch. "Nothing, what's up?"

"Well, I didn't talk to you yesterday, how was your Thanksgiving?"

"I don't wanna talk about it," Chasity ground out, turning the fireplace on with a remote.

Malajia winced. "*That* bad huh?"

"Yup," Chasity confirmed, tone even.

"You didn't get into a fight with anybody did you?"

"Not *physically*," Chasity vaguely replied. "How was *yours*?"

Malajia pulled the phone from her ear and looked at it in disbelief before putting it back. "Did you just ask me how my Thanksgiving was?" she teased. "I mean, like you *actually* care about it?"

Chasity sucked her teeth. "Don't be a smart ass, you gonna answer or not?"

Malajia giggled. "It was fine," she answered. "Princess Ponytail and her family came over for dinner." Malajia examined her nails. "I made her eat my mom's nasty ass, carrot-filled stuffing," she recalled, laughing.

Chasity's face frowned in disgust. "Ugh," she scoffed.

"She was pissed," Malajia continued, laughter still in her voice. "Anyway, I just got off the phone with Tyrone not too long ago." Malajia paused, waiting to see if Chasity was going to say something smart. When she didn't hear anything, she continued. "We talked for like three hours."

"Oh, he actually called you again, huh?" Chasity sniped.

Malajia rolled her eyes to the ceiling, *And there it is*. "Yes, he *did*. And it didn't take fifty weeks like the *last* time," she added, at an attempt at a joke.

"Wasn't your date with him like three weeks ago?"

Malajia ran her hand along her neck. She tried to put that so-called 'date' out of her mind. She'd even neglected to tell Chasity about it once she got out of the hospital, out of embarrassment. "Yes, it *was*," she replied, unenthused. "But he stopped by our room the day before Thanksgiving to take me to get something to eat…He wanted to make up for—"

"Make up for *what*?" Chasity frowned, interrupting Malajia.

Shit, Malajia thought, smacking her palm against her forehead. She hadn't meant to say that. *Always running my damn mouth.* She took a deep breath. "Look, I'm about to tell you something and I'mma need for you not to judge me."

"Do I even *want* to know what it is?" Chasity sighed.

"Probably not, but I'm gonna tell you *anyway* because…for some reason I feel like I just wanna tell you shit." Malajia took another deep breath. "So, when you made your smart ass comment about him picking me up so late for our date…You were right," she revealed. "I thought I was going out, and he thought I was gonna come to his house to—"

"Fuck him?" Chasity finished.

"Yes," Malajia hissed through clenched teeth. "Anyway, he basically called me a tease and we got in an argument and I left. That's when I found out that you were in the hospital and came straight there."

Chasity was silent

"Um…you there?" Malajia pressed.

"Yeah."

"Why are you so quiet?"

"Because I'm trying to figure out why the fuck you let him talk you into going out with his ignorant ass *again*," Chasity bluntly answered.

"Look, he said he was sorry, okay," Malajia argued.

"That's some bullshit," Chasity threw back.

"Whatever," Malajia grumbled. "That's why I didn't want to tell your ass about it in the *first* place."

"Well, you *did* and now you have to pay the price for that," Chasity snapped back. Any other word that she was about to say was interrupted by a knock at the door. "I gotta go, I have company."

"Who the hell came to see *your* evil ass?" Malajia sniped, feeling salty over Chasity's harsh words.

"Someone who doesn't think I'm a tease," Chasity returned, heading for the door.

"Fuck you bitch," Malajia spat. "Tell Jason I said hi," she added, after a moment.

"How did you know it was him?"

"Who *else* would visit and put up with you?" Malajia chuckled. "Call me when he leaves."

"Yeah," Chasity replied, then ended the call. "Hey," she greeted, opening the door.

Jason held up several DVD's. "I brought the movies."

Chasity moved aside to let him in. "I meant to tell you that you didn't have to bring those. I have a bunch here."

Jason let out a sigh of relief while removing his coat. "Good, 'cause these are wack," he chortled, sitting them on the coffee table.

"You want anything to eat?"

"No, I'm good," he replied. "I'm still full from yesterday...*and* this morning."

Chasity shook her head. "Greedy ass," she teased, sitting on the couch.

"Hey, I'm six-three and weigh two hundred and twenty pounds. You can't expect me to eat like *you*," he laughed back, sitting next to her. She turned the TV on with the remote, and Jason leaned back against the couch cushions. "I think it's supposed to storm tonight," he announced after a few moments of silence.

Chasity shook her head. "No, that's supposed to happen *tomorrow* night," she contradicted.

Jason looked at his phone. "That's not what they're saying," he replied.

"Well, *they* lie about the weather all the time, so, not believing it," Chasity threw back.

Jason shrugged. "How was yesterday?" he asked.

Chasity slowly shook her head. "I really don't want to

get into that right now," she answered, some bite in her tone.

Jason stared at her as she kept her eyes focused on the TV screen. He was already aware of the family showing up for dinner the previous evening, for Chasity had talked to him briefly after she found out. But not hearing from her long after dinner should have been over, his curiosity piqued as to what went down.

"Well—"

"Jason, what did I just say?" she bit out, facing him. Jason put his hands up in surrender.

"Okay," he relented.

Chasity, feeling a little bad for snapping, sighed and turned a movie on.

Several hours, a movie, and a few TV shows later, Chasity stretched, then jumped when she heard a loud thunder clap. "Shit," she muttered, much to Jason's amusement.

"I *told* you," he chuckled as the rain began tapping on the windows.

She made a face at him. "Nobody asked you that," she sneered, rising from the seat and heading over to a window. "You should probably go," she advised, seeing the sheets of rain fall from the sky.

Jason stood next to her. "Can I at *least* wait until it dies down?" he joked. "I could drown out there...or get blown away."

"Remember? You're six-three and weight two hundred and twenty pounds," she reminded. Jason narrowed his eyes at the smart remark. "You should be fine."

"That's real cute," he replied.

Chasity laughed at him, but stopped once the power cut off. "Are you serious?" she huffed. Luckily, the lit fireplace provided them with some light.

"Damn, the power's out on the whole block," Jason observed, moving away from the window. As the rain beat harder and the thunder grew louder, Jason reached for his phone. Chasity checked her phone while Jason spoke to his mother on his.

"Power out on your block too?" she asked, once he disconnected the call.

Jason nodded. "Yep," he sighed, tossing the phone back on the couch. "My mom is freaking out. She hates being in the dark," he said.

"Yeah, I don't blame her," Chasity replied. Being alone in a big, dark house for who knows how long, was not her idea of a good time. She looked at Jason. "You gonna try to go home in that?" she asked.

Jason stared back at her, folding his arms. "Well, I'd prefer to wait it out," he replied. "But I don't want to make you uncomfortable by staying, so if you want me to go, I *will*."

Chasity looked away briefly. Truth be told, she didn't want him to leave. With everything that she was dealing with and now the storm, accompanied by the blackout, she didn't want to be left alone. And she was enjoying Jason's company.

"Do you want me to go?" Jason asked, picking up on her hesitation. *Please say no.*

Chasity looked back at him and shook her head slightly. "No, you can stay and wait it out," she replied, finally.

"Cool," Jason smiled. He was relieved. Not only did he not have to brave the weather, he was able to spend some more alone time with Chasity. "Well, no TV, and I'm sure you don't want to *talk*," he joked. "You got any board games or anything?"

Chasity shrugged. "Who knows," she scoffed. "There may be some in the basement somewhere."

"Well," Jason said, extending his hand out. "Let's go find them."

Chasity let out a loud sigh. "I don't wanna go in that dark ass basement," she whined.

"Oh what? You're afraid of your own house?" he teased.

"No," she pouted.

"Then come on," he urged. "You would know better than me where to find stuff."

Chasity rolled her eyes. "Fine," she huffed, leading the way to the basement. Grabbing a flashlight out of a nearby closet, Chasity opened the door and nudged for Jason to go ahead of her.

Reaching the bottom of the staircase, they surveyed the large, finished basement for boxes. "What is Ms. Trisha gonna do with all this space?" Jason asked, walking around.

Chasity shrugged. "Knowing her, she'll turn it into an apartment and rent it out."

"Would you be okay with that?" Jason asked. "Some stranger living under you?"

"Nope," Chasity ground out. "But I'm sure she doesn't care."

Jason, picking up on the change in Chasity's tone, looked over at her. "What made you say that?"

"Never mind," she quickly dismissed, pointing to a box in the corner. "There may be some games in there."

Jason followed her progress as she began digging into the box. She let out a scream, startling him. "What's wrong?" he asked, shining the flashlight on her.

"I just saw a spider," she panicked, darting away from the box.

He stared at her. "A *bug*? Are you serious?"

"Jason it's not funny, I hate bugs," she hissed, inching her way towards the stairs.

Jason busted out laughing. "Just hold on, I'll kill it."

"Fine, just hurry up," she demanded, standing on a step.

Jason shook his head. Chasity watched him slowly creep to the box. Suddenly, Jason jumped back and exclaimed, "Oh shit!"

Chasity, not waiting to see what had Jason startled, darted up the steps and out of the basement. Jason followed behind her.

"No, what the fuck did you see?" she barked at him as

he shut the basement door.

"Nothing," he laughed.

"Don't play with me boy!"

Jason held his hands up. "Nothing, I swear. I was joking," he promised.

Chasity glared at him, before delivering a slap to his arm. "You play too damn much," she fussed, walking away.

"I'm sorry," he chuckled, following her into the living room.

"Don't make me put you out," she warned, folding her arms in a huff.

"Okay, okay I'm sorry," he insisted. "Such a baby," he teased after a few seconds. Chasity flipped him off in retaliation. He shook his head as he smoothed his shirt with his hands. "Well, no games…You wanna talk now?"

"You need to give me like five minutes." Chasity returned to her seat on the couch. "'Cause right *now* I wanna punch you for scaring me," she added, much to Jason's amusement.

Chasity emerged from upstairs with a blanket. With the power off for almost an hour, a chill was now felt throughout the house. The lit fireplace helped, but not as much as central heat would have.

Chasity sat on the carpeted floor next to the fireplace with Jason and spread the cover out. "I'm over this storm," she complained.

"Hopefully it'll pass soon," Jason consoled, handing her a can of soda. "All that food in your fridge is gonna go to waste."

"Fuck that food," Chasity bit out, opening her can. "I wish this damn storm would've came *yesterday* to sweep Trisha and her damn family out of my face."

Jason shook his head. "What happened yesterday, Chasity?" he asked, point blank. She had been avoiding the conversation all evening.

Chasity sat her drink on the nearby coffee table and sighed. She was tired of keeping her agitation in and needed to talk about it. "Okay," she began, facing him. "So...you already know that Trisha pissed me off yesterday by inviting everybody over here." Jason nodded. "That wasn't the worst part...Trisha and I got into an argument about me wanting to find my birth mother."

Jason frowned. "Why is she arguing with you about it?"

"Because she has a fuckin' attitude," Chasity blurted out. "She feels that I should just be happy with how things are because she does all this shit for me...She's making this whole situation about *her*." She sighed. "It's clear to me that she doesn't give a shit about my feelings." Chasity ran her hand through her hair. "She told me that our relationship would be done if I went ahead with it."

Jason was in disbelief. "That's crazy," he commented. "I don't see her doing that to you. She might feel some kind of way but...naw, Ms. Trisha isn't that vindictive."

"Her sister is, so I wouldn't be surprised if *she* was," Chasity hissed. "I'm just..."

"Angry?"

Chasity shook her head. "I'm hurt," she admitted, much to Jason's surprise. "And I'm disappointed...I don't even know if I want to do it anymore."

Jason placed a sympathetic hand on Chasity's arm. "Chaz, don't let anybody discourage you from doing what you want to do," he advised, tone caring. "Your aunt may be mad about it, but she'll get over it."

Chasity just stared at him. "I don't think it's worth it," she said. "Why would I damage...*further* damage a relationship with Trisha, for someone who clearly didn't care enough about me to keep me?"

Jason saw the sadness on Chasity's face and heard it in her voice. It killed him that he couldn't make things better for her. "I don't know what to say to that."

"There's nothing you *can* say," she replied. "It's not your problem."

Jason sighed. He wondered if he should reach out and hug her, to comfort her. He decided against it, for fear of her reaction. Having a thought, he reached for his phone. "Okay, time to lighten up this mood," he announced, standing up.

Chasity looked up at him confused. "What the hell are you doing?"

Jason played a song on his phone and turned up the speaker. "Come on, dance with me," he suggested.

Chasity eyed him skeptically as she stood up. "No," she said.

Jason shrugged as the familiar R&B song blared. "No? Okay, I'll just lip sync for you," he announced, much to Chasity's astonishment.

"Please don't."

"Look, I'm being nice," he laughed. "I won't subject you to my *actual* singing voice."

"Don't subject me to *none* of this," she joked. Watching Jason dance around while he lip synched the song, was amusing, although she tried not to show it. "You're stupid," she chuckled.

Not fazed by her comments, Jason continued on.

Chasity finally let a laugh come through as he continued. Before she knew it, she had joined him. What could she say, it was one of her favorite songs. Jason relished the carefree way that they were able to dance around together. He was happy that he was able to get her to loosen up, if only for a moment. If acting like a fool helped, he would do it again.

They flopped down on the floor once the song, and their dance session ended. "I wish I had a video of that," he mused.

"Shit, *I* don't," Chasity returned. "I looked stupid."

"No, you looked *happy*," he amended. "It's a good thing to see."

Chasity rolled her eyes. "Uh huh," she grunted, pushing some hair behind her ears.

Jason shook his head and leaned back on his hands. "And you go *right* back to being mean," he teased.

Chasity shrugged. She examined her nails as they sat in the quiet for a few moments. She had to admit that being with Jason at that moment made her feel much better.

"Look, thanks for staying and trying to cheer me up," she hesitantly said. "I know I give you a lot of shit, but…I appreciate it…I appreciate *you*."

Jason stared while she spoke. He took in everything about her; her face, her body, her voice. He began to think about all the times that they spent together. He recalled her smile, her laugh, the way that she could be playful, and the way that in some cases, she let her guard down with him. He recalled the way that she made him feel just by simply looking at hm. He knew that he cared for her, but in that moment his heart jumped as he came to a realization.

Chasity shot him a quizzical look when he didn't speak right away. "You gonna respond? Or are you just going to let me sit here and feel stupid?"

"I love you, Chasity," Jason blurted out. The amusement immediately left Chasity's face, replaced by surprise and confusion. Jason, seeing her reaction to his confession, made him almost wish that he would have kept that to himself.

"What?" she stammered after a few seconds of stunned silence. "You, *what*?"

Jason sat up, wondering if he should apologize, or even try to take his words back. But he couldn't; he didn't want to. "You heard me," he said finally.

"You don't love me Jason," she denied, agitated.

"You can't tell me what I feel," Jason returned, frowning. "It's the truth."

Chasity shook her head. *Shit! Shit! I knew I should've sent his ass home earlier,* she thought. "Why did you have to say that?" she spat out.

"Why are you upset?"

"Because! You just—now I feel all awkward and shit," she barked. "I hate feeling this way."

"Showing your feelings isn't a bad thing, Chasity," he informed, tone stern. "I'm not ashamed of *mine*." Chasity

.B. Vample

sucked her teeth as she stood from the floor. Jason rose to meet her. "So now you're gonna run?"

"I'm *not* running," she frowned.

Jason ran his hand along the back of his neck. "Look, I get that me saying 'I love you' freaked you out, and for that, I'm sorry," he said.

Chasity pinched the bridge of her nose. *Fuck! Now I made him feel bad.*

"I don't expect you to say it back," he said, disappointment in his voice. "But...if you feel *anything* for me, I would appreciate if you would tell me...I just need to know."

Chasity stared at him, unable to speak, unable to think. She'd never been able to express any feeling outside of anger, without feeling weak or vulnerable.

"You may not love me, but...do you at least *care* for me?"

Chasity ran her hand over her hair as she looked at the floor. "Um...I..."

Disappointed, Jason shook his head. "Never mind, Chaz," he bit out, walking away.

Seeing Jason head for the door made Chasity panic. "Jason—I *do* care about you, okay," she uttered, stopping him in his tracks. "I really do, but—"

"But *what*?" he asked, facing her once more.

"I can't—" she pushed her hair over her shoulder, pausing momentarily. "I know what you want, and I can't give it to you."

Jason rolled his eyes. "What? You think after all this time that I just want sex from you?" he asked, insulted.

"No, that's not it," she threw back.

"Then *what* is it?" he asked, taking a step towards her. "Be honest with me."

"I know that you want to be in a relationship with me," she answered.

"What's so wrong about that?" Jason asked, confused.

Chasity struggled to gather her words. "I just...I can't be

in one," she explained. "I don't know *how* to be in one."

It hit Jason at that moment; *she's never had a boyfriend before. She's scared.* "I'm not going to hurt you, Chaz," he promised, approaching her.

She shook her head as she fought to keep her eye contact with him. "I'm not worried about you hurting me," she revealed. "I'm scared that…I'm going to hurt *you*."

Jason shook his head in disbelief as he touched her face. "That's not going to happen." He was confident.

Chasity couldn't concentrate, his touch was distracting her. It was comforting, it was protective, it was loving and she wanted to feel those things, she *needed* to. *You know you have feelings for him too, more than you're letting on.* Chasity couldn't bring herself to say those words out loud. She felt like crying as he stared into her eyes. It was all too much for her to handle.

Not saying another word, Jason leaned in and kissed Chasity. He didn't go as deep with the kiss as he intended; he wanted to see how she would react. It was when she returned his kiss that he grabbed her and held her, their growing passion for each other flowing through them.

Chasity felt her entire body heat up as Jason moved his lips to her neck. She was reacting to his touch, his kiss, in a way that she never thought she could. Laying her on the floor, by the fireplace where they'd spent most of their shut-in evening; Jason let his hands and lips roam over her. His passion was growing at a rapid pace as they undressed each other. He was in the moment, relishing the feel of her, the taste of her; he loved her, and he wanted her more than anything.

Chasity's mind was cloudy. She gripped the covers under her as Jason touched her and kissed her in places no one ever had. Sounds that she never before heard herself make flowed from her. She wanted him just as badly as he wanted her. But her head was telling her not to cross that line, not to lose something that she'd held onto for nineteen years.

Jason, feeling her tense beneath him, stopped short of completely taking her. He looked into her eyes; she looked conflicted, she looked nervous. He touched her face and stroked her hair. "Are you okay?" he whispered to her. She nodded. "Do you want me to stop?" he asked.

Are you really ready to do this? Chasity asked herself as Jason patiently waited for a response. Throwing the reservations in her head aside, and listening to her body and her heart, Chasity shook her head 'no'. Having the confirmation that he sought, Jason told her once more that he loved her, then kissed her as he carefully and gently accepted the gift that she gave to him.

Chapter 23

Chasity sat in the parking lot of Paradise Terrace for what seemed like forever Sunday afternoon, gazing out of the window. Having arrived back on campus nearly a half-hour ago, she couldn't bring herself to get out of the car to make the journey into her building.

She'd been in a haze ever since she woke up in Jason's protective arms just the day before. *What the fuck did I do?* was the question that she asked herself over and over. She remembered waking feeling sore, awkward, and confused. Losing her virginity to Jason was something that she was having a hard time wrapping her head around.

The notification on her phone prompted her to look down at it. Reading the message from Jason, she sighed. No sooner than she closed her message screen, did the phone ring. Chasity saw Jason's name flash across her screen, and waited for the call to go to voicemail. *I just can't, right now*, she thought, tossing the phone into her purse.

Finally stepping out of the car, Chasity made her way to her room. Opening the door, she spotted Malajia laying on the bed, talking on the phone.

Malajia sat up. "I'll call you later," she said into her phone. "Nice of you to call me back Friday," she bit out once she ended her call.

Chasity, not in the mood for Malajia and her nonsense, sighed. "Malajia, don't start," she said, voice low, tired.

Malajia made a face. "Don't come up in here with that attitude," she sneered, pointing. "You were supposed to call me back after Jason left. I was all bored and shit."

Chasity faced Malajia, while leaning against her desk. "You act like you couldn't call anybody *else*."

"Called *who*?" Malajia bit out, standing from her bed. "*Alex*? You wanted me to call *Alex*?"

Chasity shook her head. "Whatever, yo," she ground out.

Malajia flagged Chasity while retrieving a bottle of juice from her nightstand. "I just don't appreciate being blown off, especially since your ass wasn't doing shit."

Chasity was staring off into space, silent.

Malajia paused in mid-sip of her juice and regarded Chasity suspiciously. "What's the matter with you?" she asked, picking up on her mood, her tone and her wandering gaze. "You still pissed over whatever happened on Thanksgiving?"

"Not at the moment," Chasity answered honestly.

Malajia raised an eyebrow. "Hmm," she mumbled. "Anyway, I heard y'all had a big storm up your end that night," she said. "Did Jase get caught in it going home?"

"No," Chasity murmured, looking at her nails. The memories from that night were swirling in her head.

"I don't see how he *couldn't*," Malajia chuckled. "That shit was going all night."

"Uh huh," Chasity replied.

"He probably camped at your place and shit," Malajia teased.

"Uh huh," Chasity repeated.

Malajia frowned. "He really stayed over?" she asked. "I was kidding, but hell, that's good. At least you had some company."

"Yep."

Malajia stomped her foot on the floor. The monotone, one word responses that Chasity was giving were irritating her. She almost wished for the normal snarky remarks. "Damn bitch, what the hell?" she fussed.

Chasity eyed her with confusion. "What?"

"You acting all funny and shit," Malajia pointed out. "Did something happen between the time I got off the phone with you and *now*?"

"No," Chasity lied instantly.

Malajia approached her, narrowing her eyes. Chasity answered that too quickly for her liking. "You look like you wanna tell me something," she said, waving her finger in Chasity's face.

Chasity rolled her eyes and tried to walk away. "Malajia, leave me alone," she grumbled. She shot Malajia a death stare as the girl blocked her path, standing in her face. "Move!"

"Naw bitch, you need to start talking," Malajia pressed.

"Talking about *what*?"

"*Talking* about what got you lookin' all stupid in the face," Malajia threw back, folding her arms. "What happened? Did Jason kiss you or something?" When Chasity's eyes widened slightly, Malajia knew she'd figured it out. "He really *did* kiss you?" she questioned.

Chasity hesitated for a moment. "Yeah," she finally answered.

"Oh!" Malajia was excited. "Well, shit that's a *good* thing," she chuckled. "It's about time. I was tired of waiting on it to happen."

Chasity looked down at her hands as Malajia walked away.

"There's no need to act all weird over a kiss," Malajia teased. "Even though I'm sure it was amazing. He got some nice lips."

"Can you stop?"

"What? I'm just saying," Malajia shrugged. "It's not like y'all got *busy*. It was just a kiss."

God, why can't she shut the fuck up?! Chasity rubbed her forehead but didn't say anything.

Malajia, picking up on her silence, spun around. "Chasity?" she drew the name out slowly, studying her. Chasity's silence spoke volumes. "Is that what—"

"I don't know what you're talking about?" Chasity huffed.

Malajia stood close to Chasity. "Chasity Taj-Mahal Parker, you better spill it."

Chasity frowned. "Did you just fuck up my middle name?"

"Don't change the subject," Malajia snapped, pointing. Chasity glanced down at Malajia's finger before shooting her a warning look. "That look don't scare me," Malajia assured. "Did you and Jason—did y'all sleep together?"

Chasity's eyes shifted. Malajia was standing in her face and it was clear that the girl wasn't going to let up until she had an answer. Chasity couldn't hold herself together enough to lie. "Yes," she hesitantly admitted.

"I don't mean no, 'we just slept in the same bed' bullshit, either," Malajia spat out.

"I know what you meant," Chasity assured her, tone even.

Malajia put her hand up. "Soooo, you're telling me that you had actual *sex* with Jason when he stayed over?"

Chasity nodded slowly.

Malajia was still in disbelief. "*You*, Miss don't-touch-me? Miss stop-staring-at-me?" Chasity rolled her eyes. "Miss virgin? You—*you* had sex? *Really*?"

Chasity let out a sigh. "Yes," she ground out, teeth clenched.

Malajia's eyes and mouth widened as she tried to register what she had just heard. If the extra questions that Malajia had, or the stunned look on her face didn't make

Chasity regret her decision to come clean, the scream of delight that Malajia let out, certainly did.

"Do you *have* to do that?" Chasity barked. When Malajia started jumping up and down while continuing to scream, Chasity nearly snapped. She quickly put her hand over Malajia's mouth. "Malajia, shut up," she ordered. "Shut up," she barked again when Malajia kept making noise. "I swear to God, I will snatch your goddamn lips off your face."

Malajia quieted down and put up the 'okay' sign, prompting Chasity to remove her hand from her mouth. "Okay, I won't scream," she promised. "This is crazy, I'm so hype!" she shrieked, clapping her hands. Malajia then flopped down on the bed and eagerly stared at her roommate. "You gotta give me details."

"Fuck no," Chasity refused.

Malajia frowned. "Either you give me details, or I'mma march my sexy ass next door and tell the other girls," she warned, standing up.

"No, don't do that, I'm serious," Chasity panicked, putting her hand up. She was barely keeping it together as it was, the last thing she needed was everybody in her business.

Malajia sat back down. "Well, get to it, I want details," she pressed. When Chasity glared at her, Malajia sucked her teeth. "Okay, tell you what, I'll ask you a question and you just give me a 'yes' or 'no' answer," she proposed.

Chasity rolled her eyes and folded her arms. "Fine," she agreed, voice not hiding her disdain.

Malajia was excited as she pondered her first question. "Was it planned?"

Chasity frowned. "No," she hissed.

Malajia put her hands up. "My bad, just wanted to know," she reasoned. "Soooo, did it…hurt?"

Chasity wanted to punch Malajia right in her face. *This is what I get for saying anything.* "Yes," she replied.

"But you enjoyed it right?"

"Yes."

Malajia put her finger on her chin while racking her

brain for more questions.

"You don't have too many more of these damn questions," Chasity warned, patience wearing thin.

"Hey, don't rush me," Malajia threw back. "Was there foreplay involved?"

Chasity sucked her teeth. "Come the fuck *on*, Malajia."

"Answer it!"

Chasity rubbed her face. "From *him*, yeah."

"So you didn't give him—"

"No," Chasity immediately denied, earning a laugh from Malajia.

"Well…did you enjoy that?"

Chasity felt hot as she remembered what Jason had done to her. "Uh huh," she answered.

Malajia, noticing Chasity's flushed face and half smile, narrowed her eyes. "You're not about to rub one out right here, thinking about it are you?" she teased.

"Shut up," Chasity snapped. Malajia laughed.

"Okay, okay, just one more," Malajia promised, laughter subsiding. "Does he have a big one?"

Chasity's eyes flashed. "Make me punch you, all right?"

"What? It's my question and you have to answer it," Malajia persisted.

"I'm *not* answering that," Chasity rebuffed.

"Alex!" Malajia screamed.

"Fuck you, Malajia," Chasity fussed.

Malajia stomped her foot on the floor. "Damn it, Chasity." Chasity's refusal to answer her question annoyed Malajia, but secretly, she understood why she did. "Fine, you don't have to say it…I can tell it is anyway," she teased. "He *looks* like he's *gifted*."

Chasity tapped her foot on the floor as she resisted the urge to lunge across the room and gut punch Malajia. *Yes, he sure is, but your freak ass will never know.*

"One more question—"

"No, I'm done," Chasity bit out, heading for the bathroom.

Malajia giggled. "Okay, I'll leave you alone for now," she promised. "Come on, I'm hungry, let's go get the other girls and go grab something to eat."

"I'm not hungry," Chasity ground out.

"Well come with me any-damn-way," Malajia insisted, standing from the bed. "If you don't, they're just gonna ask me where you are."

Chasity sighed as she walked out of the bathroom. She knew that Malajia would bug her if she didn't comply and she wasn't in the mood to argue. "Fine," she relented. "But don't go over there running your fuckin' mouth about this. I mean it."

"Now, would *I* tell your business?" Malajia quibbled, pointing to herself. Chasity jerked her hand up causing Malajia to flinch. "Okay, I won't say anything," she promised.

Chasity eyed her skeptically before walking out the door, with Malajia trailing behind her.

Sidra straightened out several index cards in her hands, then upon hearing Malajia's mouth outside the door, put her head down and huffed.

"Open up! Y'all know who it is!" Malajia shouted, banging on the door.

Sidra rolled her eyes and placed her cards neatly on her bed.

Alex chuckled. "I swear, that girl can wake the dead," she commented, standing from her desk. In passing, she brushed past Sidra's bed, knocking the cards to the floor.

"Alex!" Sidra yelped, looking down at the fallen items. "I just put these in order."

"Ooh sorry girl, you know my butt knocks over everything," Alex joked, opening the door.

"Next time don't take so damn long," Malajia snarled, pushing her way into the room, with Chasity following behind.

"Don't start your nonsense," Alex warned.

"Shut up," Malajia threw back. "Anyway, I'm hungry, let's go eat."

"I gotta re-organize my index cards first," Sidra replied, retrieving cards from the floor.

"I'm sorry for knocking them over Sid. I'll help you," Alex offered.

Malajia shot Alex a glance. "Your goofy ass always messin' up shit," she barked, much to Sidra's amusement.

Alex put her hands on her hips and shot Sidra a side-glance for laughing. "Really Sidra?"

Sidra put her hand up. "I'm sorry, but that was out of nowhere," she laughed of Malajia's comment.

"Hey, why don't we go around the room and ask everyone how their holiday was?" Malajia eagerly suggested, much to the confusion of the other girls.

"You actually want to *hear* about our holiday?" Alex asked, folding her arms.

Malajia shrugged. "I mean, why *not*? I'm sure some stuff happened—"

Chasity slowly turned and glared at Malajia while she continued to speak.

"Happened like *what*? Us eating turkey?" Alex giggled. "Well, aside from Victoria and her moth—"

"Uh huh, that's nice, Alex," Malajia quickly interrupted before turning to Chasity. "Chaz, you got anything to share with the group?"

Chasity stared at her. "No," she spat.

Malajia stomped her foot on the floor. This was killing her. Jason and Chasity sleeping together was the biggest thing to happen in their group in a while and she wanted desperately to say something about it. She glanced down at Sidra, who was searching under her bed. "Sidra what are you doing down there?"

"I think one of my index cards is lost," Sidra answered, lifting up the cover.

"You lost something huh?" Malajia commented. "Say

Chasity have *you* lost anything lately?"

"Stop it," Chasity barked.

"Stop *what*?" Malajia asked, feigning innocence.

Alex sucked her teeth. "Malajia, whatever you're doing to Chaz, cut it out okay," she put in.

"Mind your damn business, Alex," Malajia scowled, reaching for her cell phone. She typed out a text and hit send. Chasity, hearing a notification on her phone, reached for it.

'Why won't you just tell them?' the message read. Chasity frowned.

"Tell who, *what*?" Sidra asked, before Chasity could respond.

Chasity's eyes widened as Malajia quickly glanced at Sidra, who was looking at her phone. Malajia then glanced down at *her* phone. "Shit," Malajia panicked. She hadn't meant to send it to Sidra too. "My bad, Chaz," she directed at Chasity.

"You did that shit on purpose you fuckin' bitch," Chasity snapped, pointing her phone at Malajia.

Malajia put her hands up. "I swear, it was an accident," she explained.

"Wait, who's 'them', *us*?" Sidra cut in, curious.

"Do one of you need to tell us something?" Alex added, interest piqued.

Angry, Chasity walked out of the room without saying another word, leaving Malajia standing there. "Um…I think she went to lay down or something," she nervously put out.

Sidra rose from the floor and folded her arms. "It sounds like a secret is being kept," she observed. "Why did Chaz get mad at you for sending that text?"

"No, there's no secret," Malajia sputtered. "And she's not mad, she's…um...tired."

"What do you know?" Alex pressed, picking up on Malajia's nervousness.

Malajia laughed and waved her hand dismissively. "Oh girl please, I don't know nothin' about nobody having sex—I mean I don't know nothin' about anything," she stammered.

Alex and Sidra glanced at each other before turning back to Malajia and exclaiming, "*Who* had sex?!" in unison.

"I don't know what you're talking about," Malajia lied.

"Malajia Lakeshia Simmons, you better spill it," Sidra demanded.

"Um…I can't. Chaz would kill—"

"Wait, *Chasity* had sex?" Alex questioned, hearing the name. "Wait a minute Malajia, you gotta be lying. She doesn't even like people *looking* at her."

"I didn't even *say* anything!" Malajia exclaimed.

"Oh there's *one* person who she does," Sidra pointed out, ignoring Malajia's protests.

Malajia waved her hands in their faces. "Hello, I didn't confirm anything about Chaz doin' nothing'," she maintained.

The girls faced Malajia, who in turn gulped. Their eyes burrowed through her like lasers. Malajia, feeling the words about to tumble out of her mouth, put her hand over her face.

Chasity, hearing screams from outside her room, knew what Malajia had done. *Fuck my life*, she thought, putting her hands over her face. The sounds of the girls banging on the door almost made her want to cry. She couldn't deal with their questions.

Malajia opened the door. "Move, move!" she barked at the girls.

"Chasity, we wanna talk to you," Alex pressed, voice loud, sticking her head in the door.

Chasity just stared at her, seething.

Malajia moved Alex's hand from the door and slammed it in her face. "Stay your nosey ass out *there*," she hissed, before spinning around and meeting Chasity's fiery gaze. Malajia put her hands up. "Okay, just hear me out—"

"I don't even know why I'm surprised," Chasity spat. "I *knew* you would do this. I should've never told you."

Malajia felt terrible. "Chaz, I'm sorry," she said. "I was

wrong for that."

"Whatever, Malajia," Chasity hissed, folding her arms.

"I figured that it wasn't a bad thing that happened, so—"

"It wasn't your fuckin' business to tell!" Chasity exploded, clapping her hands with each word. "You don't get that."

"I *do* get it...*now*," Malajia replied, sitting on the bed. Malajia paused as she studied Chasity; she was angry, but she had an inkling that it wasn't just because of what she did. "Are you okay?" she asked, finally.

"Is that a *joke*?" Chasity snarled.

Malajia shook her head. "No, I'm being serious," she confirmed. "I'm not talking about you being okay with me running my mouth...Are you okay with what happened, *period*?"

Chasity ran her hands through her hair, sighing in the process.

"I know I fucked up just now, but you really look like you need to talk and I want to listen," Malajia pressed. "I swear to God, I won't say anything this time," she promised. "You can slap me if I do."

"You promise?" Chasity jeered.

"No. Your slaps hurt," Malajia chuckled. "But seriously...Are you okay?"

Chasity hesitated for a moment as she looked at her phone. Another message popped up. "I don't know," she answered honestly.

Malajia frowned in concern. "You don't regret doing it, do you?"

"I don't know," Chasity repeated.

"Oh," Malajia gasped. "Well, how does *he* feel about that?"

"I don't know."

"What do you mean, you don't know?" Malajia asked. "You talked to him right?"

Chasity shook her head. "Not since he left yesterday morning."

Malajia didn't get to respond because a knock at the door interrupted her thoughts. "Go away Alex, she doesn't wanna talk!" Malajia hollered at the door.

"It's Jason," the deep voice announced from the other side.

Chasity's eyes widened as Malajia looked back at her. Malajia frowned in confusion when Chasity shook her head 'no' while frantically waving her hands.

"Are you serious?" Malajia whispered as Chasity dashed for the bathroom. Rolling her eyes, Malajia walked to the door and opened it a crack. "Hey Jase," she smiled.

Jason forced a smile, but it was clear that he wasn't in a happy mood. "Hey, is Chasity here?"

"Um…No, she's not," Malajia lied. "I think she went to the SDC or something." Seeing the somber look on Jason's face made her feel terrible. "I'll tell her you stopped by when she gets back."

"Thanks, I appreciate it," he replied, before walking away. Malajia watched his progress until he turned the corner, before closing the door.

"Chasity, what the hell was that?" she questioned when Chasity walked out of the bathroom.

"What do you mean?"

"Don't play stupid," Malajia returned. "Why are you avoiding Jason? That's not cool."

Chasity sucked her teeth. "I'm *not* avoiding him," she lied, looking down at her phone as another notification came through.

Malajia narrowed her eyes. "No?" she pressed, snatching the phone from Chasity's hand.

"Are you crazy?" Chasity barked, reaching for it. "Give me my damn phone."

Malajia held it out of her reach, then began looking at it. "Look at this," she growled. "Missed calls from Jason, Saturday and today," she continued scrolling. "Text message, after text message…he's asking you why you're not talking to him in these damn messages," she observed, tone scolding, shoving the phone back in Chasity's hand.

"Look, I'll deal with this in my own way all right," Chasity huffed, slamming her phone on her desk.

Malajia folded her arms. "And what way is *that*? Avoidance?" she threw back. "God knows you're good at that, but it don't make it right."

Chasity just stared at Malajia as she continued to scold her on her behavior. Deep down, she knew that Malajia was right.

"What if that was *you*?" Malajia continued. "What if he was avoiding *you* afterwards? What would *you* think? How would *you* feel?"

Chasity rubbed her forehead with her hands. "That he used me," she mumbled.

"*Exactly*, so stop acting like a jackass, put your big girl panties on, deal with *whatever* you need to deal with, and *talk* to the man," Malajia chastised.

Chasity stared at Malajia for a few seconds in disbelief. "Did you just check me?" she asked, pointing to herself.

"You damn right. You're being a complete asshole," Malajia threw back. "Now stop it."

Chasity sighed. "I'll talk to him," she promised.

"When?"

"When I'm ready."

Malajia rolled her eyes. "Yeah well, you better be ready *soon*," she warned.

Chapter 24

Ms. Harris pulled into the parking lot of Emily's apartment complex and put the car in park. She glanced over at her daughter, who was peering out the window, a blank expression on her face.

"You've barely said two words since Thanksgiving," Ms. Harris badgered.

Emily took a deep breath. After drinking the liquor that she found in her sister's stash on Thanksgiving, Emily spent the majority of that day, and the rest of the break in her room, wishing that she had more.

"I don't really have anything to say," Emily said after a few moments.

"Well, the silent treatment is *not* appreciated," Ms. Harris spat, regarding her daughter sternly. "You may not have liked what I said—but you don't get to be disrespectful."

Emily let out a loud sigh. *How is me being silent disrespectful?!* "I just…have a lot on my mind," she put out, voice low as she opened the door.

"I don't care *what's* on your mind. You better fix your

attitude."

Emily rolled her eyes when her mother wasn't looking. She was over her mother at this point. The woman had the gall to tell Emily that she was going to make her change schools. She was trying to control who she hung out with, hovering over her like a cloud, and yet she still expected Emily to smile and be nice.

"I'll talk to you later," Emily grumbled, stepping out of the car. "I'm sure you'll call me like five minutes from now."

Ms. Harris's eyes widened at Emily's smart remark. "Emily Kelly Harris!" she boomed.

"*What*?!" Emily snapped, looking back at her mother. She immediately regretted her outburst. "I'm sorry, I gotta go," Emily sputtered. She grabbed her bag out of the trunk and headed for the steps, leaving her stunned mother in the car alone.

Emily pushed open her room door and tossed her bag on the floor. Sitting on her bed, she put her face in her hands, trying to block the thoughts in her head. *Just tell her to back off, Emily*, she thought. She raised her head and looked over at the stack of books on her desk. She immediately felt the pressure of the week's upcoming classes looming over her.

Emily eyed the red light flashing on her answering machine. She pressed play and listened.

"Hey girl, it's Alex. Just calling to check on you to see if you were back yet. Hope that you had a nice holiday. I tried to call your house, but your mom kept saying that you were busy...go figure. But when you get in, just call me so we can hang out for a little bit. Miss you."

Emily listened to the message again, then deleted it. She'd been alienating herself from the girls and she hated herself for it. "I miss you guys," she admitted out loud.

Chasity tied the belt on her coat as she stepped out of her room. On her way down the hall, she heard a door open and a voice shout her name. Rolling her eyes, she turned around to face an approaching Alex.

"What?" she spat.

"You think that ducking us yesterday was going to stop us from asking you about what happened?" Alex replied, folding her arms.

"What do you want me to say?" Chasity shrugged. She was in no mood to have it out with Alex. She was already stressing over the fact that she would eventually come face to face with Jason.

"Obviously, what happened was a big deal, and I just want you to talk about it," Alex pressed. "I mean, I'm sure there are some feelings—"

"Alex, save whatever lecture you're about to give me," Chasity interrupted.

"I'm not giving a lecture," Alex assured. "But I *am* curious…Does this mean that you two will *finally* stop playing and be a couple?"

"See, *this* is why I didn't want you to find out about this," Chasity snapped. "I knew that y'all would start this shit."

"Start *what*?" Alex asked, surprised at Chasity's outburst. "I just figured that since you slept with him, then you might as well stop lying to yourself and *be* with him."

"Leave me the hell alone," Chasity hissed, walking away. Alex stood there, stunned.

Chasity was still fuming as she made her way to the science building. She stopped in her tracks when she saw Jason leave the same building. "Shit," she said to herself when he locked eyes on her. She hadn't planned on talking to him this soon.

Jason approached her, a stern gaze fixed on his face. "I need to talk to you for a second," he urged, adjusting the book bag on his shoulder.

Chasity tried to maneuver around him. "Not now, Jason," she refused.

He stopped her by grabbing her arm. "Yes *now*," he insisted, holding his gaze.

She sucked her teeth; there was no avoiding the inevitable any longer. "Fine," she replied.

Jason directed her to a spot under a large tree, away from the crowds of other students. Standing in front of her, he folded his arms. "Why haven't you returned any of my phone calls?"

"What are you talking about?" she asked, feigning confusion.

Jason rolled his eyes. "Chasity, don't play stupid with me," he bit out. "I'm sure you've seen my calls and texts," he declared. "Why are you avoiding me?"

"I'm *not* avoiding you," Chasity threw back.

"Stop lying!" he hollered, patience gone. The loudness of his voice startled her. She had never heard him yell before.

Chasity pinched the bridge of her nose. "Look, I just needed some time to think, okay," she put out after a few seconds.

Jason was clearly agitated. He was certain that after the night that the two shared, after he confessed his love for her, that Chasity would finally be at a place where she wouldn't feel the need to keep a wall up around him. But when she stopped answering his calls after he left her house that following morning, that certainty was gone.

"Chasity, what's wrong?" he asked, tone matching his attitude. "Are you upset over what happened between us?"

"No," she lied.

He clenched his jaw. "Can you *please* just be honest?"

"I'm just—I can't…" Chasity looked at the ground for a moment. Her thoughts, her emotions, were all over the place. She, like Jason, thought that she would feel more open to him once she awoke the next day. But fear made her walls build back up. *I'm sorry Jason*, she thought. "I wish that it never happened," she regretfully put out.

Jason frowned in confusion. "Are you serious?"

No. "Yes," she replied, despite what she felt. "I'm sorry Jason, I—"

"What, do you regret admitting that you care about me *too*?"

Chasity felt like crying. Jason was standing before her, looking like she had stabbed him. "I wasn't lying when I told you that I care about you," she admitted. "But…"

"Why did you sleep with me?" Jason asked, point blank. "If you're regretting it now, why even let it happen?"

"Um…I guess I just needed to…take my mind off of everything that I was dealing with," she slowly answered.

Jason shook his head. "That's bullshit and you *know* it," he barked. "There is no way in hell that after nineteen years of saving yourself, you would give it up just to release some damn stress," he pointed out. "You're lying to yourself and to *me,* and that's not fair."

Chasity knew that he was right, but for the sake of protecting herself, she had to keep her lie up. "I don't know what you want me to say, Jason," she said.

"You're really just gonna stand here in my fuckin' face and keep lying to me?" Jason was furious.

"It is what it is," she bit back. "I'm sorry."

Jason stared at Chasity in disbelief as she walked away from him. Angry, confused, and hurt, Jason headed off in the other direction towards his dorm.

Jason sat at his desk, staring at the complex problems in his notebook. Advanced Calculus problems were normally a breeze for him, but ever since his confrontation with Chasity the day before, he hadn't been able to focus on anything else but her. Reaching for his pencil, he sighed. "Come on Jase, focus," he urged himself. He rolled his eyes when he heard a knock on his room door. "What?" he called.

Mark barged through the door, smiling. "Whatchu doing?" he asked.

Jason fixed an angry gaze on him. "Did I say you could come in?"

Mark shrugged. "Since when do I ever wait for an invitation?" he threw back, unfazed by Jason's attitude.

Jason sucked his teeth. He was in no mood for Mark's nonsense. "What do you want, Mark?"

"Just wanted to see if you want to go play some ball," Mark replied.

"No, I *don't*," Jason bit out, turning back to his book. "I have homework to do."

Mark sucked his teeth. "You corny," he huffed, turning to walk out. Having a thought, he spun around. "Oh and congrats man."

Jason was confused. "Congrats on what?" he asked, eyes not leaving his book.

"I heard you and Chasity finally got it in," Mark returned proudly.

Jason's head snapped towards him. "What?" he barked. He was amazed at how quickly the news spread throughout the group.

Mark, oblivious to what Jason was going through, kept talking. "I mean, it's about *time*," he joked. "I'm surprised she even let you tap that, as evil as she—"

"Get the fuck out my room," Jason ordered, pointing to the door.

"Damn, chill yo," Mark protested, holding his hands up. "I was jokin', no disrespect. Hell, I figured you'd at *least* be happier about it…You chased her ass for over a year."

Jason stared at Mark, eyes blazing, if he didn't get out of his room Jason was going to punch him. "What part of 'get out' don't you get?" he fumed.

Mark shook his head as he walked out.

Annoyed, not so much by Mark's simple words, but at the fact that he was so caught up in a woman who clearly didn't return his feelings, Jason tossed his pencil down and shoved his books away from him. He put his head in his hand and sighed. Chasity had become someone who caused him sadness when he thought of her, even though he didn't want that to be the case. He never thought that after making love to the woman of his dreams that he would begin to resent her.

I can't do this, I need to know once and for all.

Jason picked up his phone and dialed a number.

Standing in the commons area outside, between both his dorm and Paradise Terrace, Jason paced in the chilly night air, waiting for Chasity to emerge. He'd called her after Mark left his room; he couldn't function until he spoke to her again.

Chasity walked outside and came face to face with Jason. She was surprised when she saw his name flash across her phone screen. After their exchange, she was sure she wouldn't hear from him for at least a week. "Hi," she softy put out.

"Hi," he returned. "We need to talk."

Chasity looked down at the ground momentarily. "I know," she admitted. "I lied to you the other day," she blurted out.

Jason frowned. "About what, exactly?" he asked, some bite in his voice.

She took a deep breath. "I didn't sleep with you because I needed to forget about my problems," she admitted, "I did it because…I wanted to…and I don't regret it."

Jason's face relaxed a bit. He was happy to hear that. Maybe now they could actually move forward.

"But—"

"But what?" he cut in, frowning once again.

"I…I don't want to be in a relationship," she revealed.

"With me?"

"With *any*body," she clarified. "Look, I know that you want us to be together. I know that's what you've *always* wanted." She pushed some hair behind her ear, looking away from Jason's piercing gaze. "I'm sorry Jason. I don't mean to hurt you, but I can't be with you."

Jason watched her struggle internally as he ran his hand

over his head. "What are you afraid of?"

Chasity slowly shook her head and folded her arms as she fought to keep her fears in check. *I'm scared that I won't be able to make you happy*, she thought. "I'm just not ready for a relationship," she put out.

Jason felt his frustrations ease up as he stared into her eyes. He felt the sincerity in her words. "Chasity, the last thing that I want to do is pressure you into doing something that you don't want to," he responded, tone calm.

"I know that."

"But…" he paused, wondering if he could even say what he was about to. While he respected the fact that she didn't want to be in a relationship with him, he couldn't put aside his feelings for her. "I meant what I said when I told you that I love you…I want to be with you and knowing that's not a possibility now or even *ever* isn't something that I can get over right now." He rubbed his face as he felt a knot form in his throat. "So…because of that…we can't be friends anymore," he revealed.

Anger resonated on Chasity's face. "What did you just say?"

Jason shook his head. "I'm sorry, I just…being around you right now, hurts like hell."

Chasity was visibly upset. "Do you have *any* idea what you're doing to me right now?" she barked. "This is the same shit that my fuckin' aunt pulled because I wouldn't do what she wanted me to do…and now *you* turn around and do the exact same thing."

"That's *not* what I'm doing," he protested.

"That's *exactly* what the fuck you're doing!" she yelled. "Jason can't get what he wants from Chasity, so Jason goes and throws a fuckin' temper tantrum."

Jason shook his head. "Do you have *any* idea how much I want to just grab you right now and hold you? How much I want to kiss you? How much I want to—" He rubbed his hand over his head as he fought to contain his emotions. "You think I want to see you looking at me the way you are now? You think I want to upset you?"

"Why are you doing it?" Chasity asked, voice trembling.

"Because *for once* I have to put myself and *my* feelings first," he explained. "I can't *just* be your friend anymore…at least not right now."

Never in a million years did she think that Jason would ever go to this extreme. His friendship was something that she cherished. His conversations, something that she looked forward to, his presence, something that she needed. "You're being stupid," she threw back, tears in her eyes.

He shook his head as he tried to contain his own pain. "You may be right," he admitted. "But it's how I feel…I'm sorry."

"Save your sorry," Chasity hissed, storming off.

Jason followed her progress as she hurried into the building. Part of him wanted to go after her, hold her and say that he would take her any way that he could get her. But the other part of him realized that this was the best way for him to deal with everything. He just couldn't be around her without being *with* her. It wasn't in him anymore.

Chasity opened the door to her empty room and slammed it shut behind her. She sat back at her desk, the place she was sitting when Jason called her to meet him. She turned her laptop back on and as she went to type; she felt her emotions boil over. Putting her face in her hands, she broke down crying. She was both sad and angry. But she couldn't figure out if she was angrier at Jason, or herself.

The sound of Malajia walking in made her suck up her tears and wipe her face. "Chaz, can I use your laptop when you're done?" Malajia asked, plunking her book bag down by her bed.

"Uh huh," Chasity put out.

Malajia spun around, removing her coat. She stared at Chasity's back. Her voice sounded different, and she didn't put up an argument about letting her use the laptop. "Uhhh, you feeling sick or something?" she teased.

Chasity, not saying a word, put her hands over her face again. *Stop it Chasity! Stop fuckin' crying you weak bitch!* she screamed to herself.

Malajia, hearing a sniffle, approached. "Are you okay?" she asked, the humor leaving her voice.

Chasity stood up and made an attempt to head for the bathroom to stop Malajia from seeing her cry, but Malajia blocked her path. "Can you get out of my damn face?!" Chasity erupted.

"No, not until you tell me why you're crying," Malajia threw back, voice filled with concern. Chasity rarely cried in front of anyone; Malajia knew it had to be something serious. "What happened while I was gone?"

Chasity tried to fight it, but she couldn't; the tears just kept flowing. "Jason doesn't want anything to do with me anymore," she put out.

Malajia's mouth fell open. "What do you mean?"

"What I *said*," Chasity barked.

Malajia put a hand up in surrender. "Okay sweetie, try to calm down," she urged, rubbing Chasity's shoulder.

"I can't be with him how he wants me to and now he doesn't want to be my friend anymore."

Malajia was in disbelief. She knew that there was some tension between Jason and Chasity after they'd slept together, but she never thought that their friendship would end over it. "Chaz..." Malajia paused, she really didn't know what to say. "I'm sure he's just upset right now—"

Chasity didn't want to hear none of what Malajia was about to say. "Malajia, don't!" she abruptly interrupted. "Don't try to justify, to reason, *nothing*," she said. "This is my fault, I shouldn't have let this go this far," Chasity cried, wiping her eyes with the back of her hand. "Everything is always my fault."

"This is *not* your fault," Malajia consoled. "Don't do that to yourself."

"Just leave me alone," Chasity sniffled, moving around

Malajia to get to the bathroom.

Malajia brushed over her hair with her hand, sighing in the process. Two of her friends were hurting and there was nothing that she could do about it. She knew the friendships that everyone shared with Jason and Chasity wouldn't be the same.

Chapter 25

"Guys, this is ridiculous," Alex griped, poking at her meatloaf. "I hate not having the whole group together."

"I know," Sidra agreed, slicing into her lasagna. "I miss Jason fooling around, I miss Chasity's smart mouth...I even miss Emily's whining."

In the weeks after Jason and Chasity's friendship split, the two distanced themselves from the rest of the group. Now, only two weeks before the end of the semester, the once vibrant group was feeling the strain of their absence.

Alex sighed as she thought of Emily. She'd barely seen the girl, let alone talked to her. All of Alex's phone calls and pop up visits went unanswered.

"Man, Jason is so different now, it's like he's just...broken," Mark put in, reaching for his hoagie. "He don't be laughin' at my damn jokes no more—"

"That's 'cause your jokes ain't *funny*," Malajia sneered, interrupting him.

Mark shot Malajia a glance, but for once decided not to engage her. "Whatever yo," he hissed to her. "Bottom line is that my friend is all jacked up and it's *y'all* friends fault," he spat, much to the annoyance of the girls. "Why did Chaz break him down like that?"

"Are you kidding me?" Alex ranted as Sidra and Malajia stared daggers at Mark. Having gotten the full story of exactly what transpired between Jason and Chasity a while ago, everyone, for the sake of their friends feelings, tried to keep their opinions and point of views to themselves...until now.

"Look boy," Alex hissed, pointing to Mark. "Jason isn't the *only* one who's suffering, okay." Mark rolled his eyes. "I watch Chasity pull away more and more every day. *She's* hurting *too*."

"It's her fault, she *should* suffer," Mark grumbled, folding his arms.

Josh shook his head. "You always gotta start something," he commented to Mark.

"What?" Mark asked, shocked. "Am I *wrong*?"

"Yes, you're *completely* wrong, you asshat," Malajia ground out.

"Was calling me an asshat necessary?" Mark threw back.

"Absolutely," Malajia countered, folding her arms.

"This isn't on her," Alex cut in. "She didn't break him down. She was honest about not wanting to be in a relationship, and Jason went and threw a temper tantrum because he couldn't get his way." Alex looked to Malajia and Sidra for backup. "Am I right?"

"Well, I wouldn't go *that* far," Sidra softly put in. "I don't think that Jason threw a temper tantrum. I think that at the time, he thought he was protecting his heart."

Malajia waved her hand at Sidra dismissively. "Come on with that fussy bus shit," she grunted.

Sidra frowned in confusion. "What the hell is a fussy bus?"

"A bus that has fussy, mushy bullshit on it," Malajia barked, in an effort to justify a remark that made no sense.

"Shut your simple ass up," Mark threw out, tired of hearing Malajia talk. He then turned his attention to Alex. "At least *Sid* isn't on the man-bashing boat," he commented.

"I'm *not* man-bashing," Alex threw back.

"Bullshit," Mark countered. "So you're gonna sit here and tell me that you wouldn't have done the same thing if you were in Jason's position?" he challenged.

"No, I would *not*," Alex assured. "I would *never* stop being friends with someone just because they don't want to be with me romantically. That's petty."

"So, if you were in love with *me*—"

"Boy, don't nobody want *you*!" Malajia snapped, face scrunched up.

"I was making a *point*, you ass crack!" Mark shot back. Malajia sucked her teeth. "I'm saying though, if you were in love with me and I told you that I didn't want to be with you, *after* you told me how you felt and *after* we slept together, you wouldn't be mad and say 'stay the hell away from me'?" he asked.

"No," Alex confirmed, annoyed.

"Alex, you lyin' like shit," Mark threw back.

"Boy, stop trying to act like you're deep," Malajia spat at Mark, gathering her books.

Sidra, having had enough of the arguing, put her hands up. "Okay you guys, arguing over this situation isn't helping," she pointed out. "Bottom line, both of our friends are hurt, both are upset and both have pulled away from us. As people who care about them and miss them, we need to think of something to do to bring everyone back together."

Malajia slammed her hand on the table. "I got it," she announced, grabbing everyone's attention. "Let's go on a trip for winter break."

"What kind of trip?" Sidra asked, intrigued.

"Well, it's winter…how about skiing?" Malajia suggested.

Mark nodded, rubbing his chin in the process. "Not a bad idea, big head," he responded. "You're not entirely useless *after* all."

Malajia flagged him with her hand. She was too excited about her idea to argue with Mark. "I'll start checking out some resorts."

Alex tapped Malajia on the shoulder. "Excuse me, I don't have money for that," she reminded.

Malajia wasn't trying to hear of any excuses. "Alex, you been slinging them dry ass pizzas *all* semester. I'm sure you got a few extra bucks," she snarled, putting her hand in Alex's face.

Alex stared at Malajia in silence for a few moments. "You get on my damn nerves," she bit out finally.

"So, how are we gonna get Chaz *and* Jason to go on this trip?" Josh asked.

"We'll figure that out later," Malajia replied.

"What about Emily?" Alex asked.

"What *about* her?" Malajia ground out, earning a backhand to her arm from Alex.

"Look, I love Emily to death, but there is *no* way her mother is gonna go for that," Sidra pointed out. "You remember how she reacted when the girl went to Florida."

Alex sighed. She knew that the girls were right, but she would tell her about the trip anyway.

Malajia, on her walk back to her room after her last class of the day, was letting her mind wander. In talking about the relationship between Jason and Chasity earlier with the others, she started thinking about her own potential relationship. *I haven't talked to Tyrone in a while,* she thought, reaching for her phone. Smiling, she dialed his number.

When her call went to voicemail after one ring, she frowned. "Let me try this again," she said to herself, hitting the redial button. After the third time calling, he finally picked up.

"What, yo?" Tyrone bit out.

Malajia frowned. "Damn, hello to you *too*?" she threw back, voice not masking her agitation.

"What do you want?" he spat.

"You don't have to be so fuckin' rude," Malajia barked. "I just called to talk to you, it's been a while."

There was a pause on the line. "Who you cussin' at?" he asked, bite in his voice.

"*You!*" Malajia snapped. "You're acting like an asshole."

"'Cause you blowin' up my damn phone like some stalker," Tyrone threw back. "I'm tryna study."

Malajia was in disbelief. This Tyrone was the same one who made her feel like garbage on their first outing together. The Tyrone she wasn't fond of.

"You know what, forget I even called," Malajia snarled.

A sigh came through the line. "Look, I'm just trying to study so I can pass this test, I'll call you back—"

"Lose my number," Malajia interrupted, voice filled with anger. Ending the call, she felt her blood boil. She couldn't believe how nasty he got over a simple phone call. *Fuck him*, she fumed to herself as she continued her pace into the dorm.

Malajia made her way up to her floor, only to be greeted at her door by Alex and Sidra. "What are you doing?" she asked, eyeing the two suspiciously.

"We're going to talk to Chaz about the trip," Sidra answered.

Malajia tossed her phone in her bag, "She's not in there," she informed. "She's in the library, doing research on her paper."

"How do you know?" Alex frowned.

"'Cause apparently I'm a stalker," Malajia bit out.

Sidra frowned in confusion. "What are you talking about?"

"Nothing," Malajia dismissed. "I asked her when I was about to leave for class earlier. I figured she would be a while."

"Are you okay?" Sidra asked, noticing Malajia's attitude. "You seem upset about something."

"I'm fine. Come on, let's go bug her," Malajia quickly put out, before walking off with Alex and Sidra trailing behind. *I'll deal with my own feelings later.*

Enjoying the secluded quiet of the private library room, Chasity flipped through the borrowed books strewn across the table while taking notes. Her peace was short-lived when she looked up and saw the girls walk into the room.

"God, not now, I'm busy," Chasity spat out.

"Shut up, you act like you don't need a break from that boring ass paper," Malajia threw back, taking a seat across from her.

"We won't be long," Sidra promised, sitting down next to Malajia. "We just want to talk to you about something."

Chasity rolled her eyes as she sat her pen on her book and leaned back in her seat. "Come on with it," she urged, hoping to get the conversation over as quickly as possible.

Taking the last seat across from Chasity, Alex shook her head. "You know, for someone who barely speaks to us nowadays, you could stand to be a little nicer," Alex hurled, irritated. Upset or not, Alex hated the fact that Chasity had reverted back to her old anti-social ways as a method of coping.

Chasity folded her arms while shooting Alex a glance. "I *am* being nice," she contradicted. "I haven't told you to go fuck yourself...*yet*."

Malajia snickered at the agitated look on Alex's face.

"Okay, okay, no need for the hostility," Sidra cut in, putting her hands up.

"What do y'all want?" Chasity sighed, running a hand over her ponytail.

Malajia leaned forward. "Okay, so the others and I were talking earlier and we thought that it'll be fun if we go skiing during the break," she revealed.

Chasity nodded slowly. "Oh okay," she replied. The girls smiled, hope lit up their eyes. "Have fun."

Malajia sucked her teeth, tossing her hands up in the process.

"I knew that was too easy," Sidra chuckled.

"Chaz, you're *going*," Malajia ordered, pointing at her.

"No I'm *not*," Chasity refused.

"Come on, it'll be fun," Alex put in. "Everyone is going."

Chasity rolled her eyes. *That's the damn problem.* "*Emily* ain't going a damn step," she jeered.

Exasperated, Alex let out a loud, quick huff. "You're being ridiculous," she charged.

"How?" Chasity calmly returned, staring defiantly at Alex. "Because I don't want to go skiing?"

"No, because you're pushing the rest of us away, all because you're mad at *one* person," Alex argued. Sidra put a hand over her face and shook her head. She knew this wasn't going to end well. "I understand that your feelings are hurt, but what you *and* Jason are doing to the rest of the group is petty."

Chasity narrowed her eyes. "Go fuck yourself, Alex," she hissed, much to Alex's shock.

"And there it goes," Malajia commented. This was not how she wanted this conversation with her roommate to go.

"That was uncalled for," Alex seethed.

"Somebody tell this self-righteous bitch to stop talking to me," Chasity ordered the other girls as she looked at them.

"Alex, go step out," Sidra softly commanded. "You've said enough," she added once Alex shot her a shocked look.

Alex stood up and walked out in a huff; Chasity followed her progress with her eyes. Once the door shut, Chasity turned her attention back to Sidra and Malajia. "Either of *you* have an unwanted opinion to express?" she ground out.

"*I* do, but you probably won't listen to it anyway," Malajia returned, examining her nails.

Sidra shook her head. "Listen Chaz, Alex misses you…we *all* do," she said, voice soft and caring.

Chasity rolled her eyes. "I haven't gone anywhere."

"Maybe not *physically* but—" Sidra paused. "You know

things are different…Are you really okay with how things are? Are you okay with not hanging with us, not talking to us anymore?"

Chasity sighed as she ran her hand along the back of her neck. She had to admit, the way that she was handling her feelings wasn't the best way, but it was *her* way. "No, I'm not okay with it," she answered, finally.

"Then why are you *doing* it?" Malajia asked, folding her arms on the table top. "You got us all walking on eggshells and that's not cool…especially for *me*, 'cause *I* gotta live with your non-talking ass."

Chasity resisted the urge to chuckle at Malajia's words. "Falling back is just how I deal with things," she shrugged. "I don't know any other way."

"Well, you better *think* of another way, and fast," Malajia commanded, standing from her seat. "I've given you *enough* space. I'm two seconds from sitting on you until you start talking."

Chasity frowned. "You wanna rephrase that?"

"No, I know how it sounded," Malajia joked, walking out of the room.

Sidra giggled as Chasity shook her head. "Chaz…we love you and we're here for you," Sidra assured. "So, just call us, okay?"

"I'll think about it," Chasity replied, reaching for her pen.

Sidra stood from her seat. "You might get mad at me for saying this, but I think that you and Jason really need to talk again," she advised.

"No, I think we've said all that we needed to say."

"He loves you, girl," Sidra replied, adjusting the purse strap on her shoulder. "People do irrational things when their feelings—"

"Are you finished?" Chasity bit out, interrupting Sidra. She didn't need to hear any lectures about Jason. She'd been thinking about him enough.

Sidra sighed. "For now," she relented, leaving Chasity

to her books and her racing thoughts.

J.B. Vample

Chapter 26

Jason adjusted the strap of the gym bag on his shoulder as he walked inside Court Terrace late in the afternoon. Besides his school work, the gym had become his distraction. He spent over two hours each day among the weights and machines, just trying to keep his mind off of Chasity.

Taking a sip from his water bottle, Jason opened his room door and tossed his bag in the corner. As soon as he closed the door, there was a knock. Jason opened the door, perplexed at the smiling faces of Mark, Josh, and David.

"What's going on?" Jason asked, curious.

"Damn dawg, I know you ain't been around us like that lately, but you *could* invite us in," Mark griped.

David shot Mark a side-glance as Jason raised his eyebrow. "Don't get us kicked out before we even get *in*," David mumbled, pushing his glasses on his nose.

Mark waved his hand dismissively at David in retaliation.

Shaking his head, Jason signaled for the guys to come in. "How've you guys been?" he asked, closing the door behind him.

"We've been good," Josh answered, taking a seat at Jason's desk. "Would be nice if *you* were around though."

Jason sighed as he folded his arms. "I know," he agreed. "I've just had—well, you know."

Mark just nodded. "You know what, let's go grab a pizza off campus," he suggested. Mark figured the best way to break the news about the ski trip would be over full stomachs.

"Naw, I'm cool," Jason declined, running his hand over his hair.

"Come on Jase. It's been a minute since all us guys hung out," Josh pressed.

"Dawg, even if we gotta drag your ass out of this room, you're coming *with* us," Mark added, shaking his hand in Jason's direction.

Jason chuckled after glaring for several seconds. Threats aside, Jason did want to get away from campus. He was tired of hiding.

"Let me grab a shower and I'll meet y'all in the lobby," Jason relented, opening the door.

"See, a little threat goes a long way," Mark boasted as he and the guys walked out the room.

"Yeah, I wouldn't go *that* far," Jason chortled.

"Man, nobody takes anything you say seriously," Josh joked as the door closed behind them.

"Josh, tell the waiter to hurry up with those pizzas," Mark demanded, reaching for his cup of soda.

Josh cut his eye at him. "Don't be a jackass today," he threw back. A half-hour later, the guys, with Jason in tow, sat in a booth at the Pizza Shack, waiting on their food to come out.

Jason shook his head at the banter. "Thanks for the invite out, guys," he said, before taking a sip of his drink.

"No problem," David smiled. "We wanted to talk to you about something anyway."

Jason stared in anticipation. "What about?"

Mark eagerly rubbed his hands together. "So, I decided that we should go skiing over the break," he revealed, a big smile on his face.

David looked confused. "Wasn't skiing *Malajia's* idea?"

"Nobody asked you for the specifics," Mark barked, pounding his fist on the table.

Josh let out a sigh and Jason rubbed his forehead. "Am I going to have to be subjected to these outbursts all night?" Jason bit out.

"Naw, ignore him," Josh returned, Mark sucked his teeth. "Except about the *skiing* part. Mel brought that idea up yesterday. I think she already started looking for some cheap resorts."

Jason thought for a moment. "That could be fun," he mused.

"So, are you saying that you're gonna go?" Josh asked, hope in his voice.

Jason opened his mouth to speak but was interrupted by Mark. "Of *course* he's going," Mark declared confidently. "How can he pass up this opportunity?"

Jason stared at Mark. "I don't know what you're on tonight, but you need to leave it alone," he joked at Mark's eagerness. "But yeah, I'm down to go. I need to have some fun."

"That's great," David beamed, as the waiter sat the two pizzas that they ordered on the table. "The girls will be ecstatic."

Mark sucked his teeth as he shot David a glare. "Yo, who the fuck says *ecstatic*?" he fussed. "You always gotta be on some nerd shit."

David rubbed his face vigorously. "God, can you go five minutes without making a damn comment?!" he boomed.

"Guys." Josh tapped his hand on the table. "We're not here to argue over dumb stuff, we're here for Jase…So kill the nonsense."

Mark mumbled something under his breath as he reached for two slices of pizza.

Jason looked down at his slice momentarily. "So…are *all* the girls going?" he asked after a few moments.

Mark, Josh and David glanced at each other. They knew which 'girl' he was referring to. "Um…the girls tried to get Chaz to go…She told them no," Josh hesitantly put out.

Jason let out a sigh. *Damn,* he thought. He'd heard that Chasity distanced herself from the group just as he did. He mostly fell back because he didn't want to crowd her or make her feel awkward when the group hung out together. He sacrificed his time with them for her, not realizing that she was going to fall back too.

"How *is* Chasity doing, by the way?" Jason asked. "I know at least Malajia still talks to her, being her roommate and all."

"Um…" Josh scratched the back of his head. "We hear that she's feeling just as you do. If that makes sense."

"It does," Jason confirmed. "Do the girls blame *me* for this whole thing?"

"Well—"

"*Alex* does," Mark bluntly stated, interrupting Josh's pacifying words.

Jason chuckled. "Not surprised," he joked. "No, I get why though. Their friend is pulling away because of *me*."

"I gotta ask you this, man," Mark began, with a seriousness that nobody expected. Jason gestured for him to speak. "Do you regret pulling the friendship rug out from under her?"

"Well, damn," David commented as Jason pondered Mark's question.

"To be honest," Jason began, thinking. "Yeah…I do."

"Oh really?" Josh questioned.

"Yeah, I admit that I might have reacted a little childish," Jason confirmed. "But it's what I felt at the time."

"That's a *good* thing," Mark smiled, throwing his arms up. "Shit, go tell Chaz that, so you can start being friends again...and we can stop tip toeing around y'all ignorant asses...Y'all fuckin' up the group and shit."

Jason shook his head. "Naw, it's not that simple," he replied. Jason knew that Chasity probably wouldn't take him back as her friend after he pulled what her aunt tried to do too. Then there was also the fact that he still loved her and wanted to be with her, and she didn't return those feelings. He might have regretted ending their friendship, but he was still battling with his emotions. "I can only hope that she gets to a place where she's okay to be around everybody again...including *me*."

"So does this mean that you're done avoiding everybody?" Mark asked.

"I'm here *now* aren't I?" Jason returned.

"Fair enough," Mark threw back, raising his drink. "To a damn good ski trip with lots of drinks."

"Except for the drinks part, I second that," David chortled, lifting his glass to Marks'.

Mark immediately moved his hand away. "Man, fuck outta here," he griped.

"You not gonna toast me, bro?" David laughed.

"Naw, you not agreeing to the drinks, so I don't want your glass touching mine," Mark fussed.

"You guys are simple," Jason commented, picking up his slice of pizza. For the first time in weeks, he had something to look forward to.

Sitting on her bed, Emily stared at the clear glass bottle, filled to capacity with Praz's special red drink where it stood on her dresser. She'd been staring at it for the past fifteen minutes. Having received it from the well-known campus drink maker a day ago, Emily was having second thoughts about even asking for it.

What was I thinking? she asked herself. Emily recalled her need for something to take her mind off of the finals that she completely bombed on just days before. Feeling down and out, she caught up with Praz, and, using the excuse that she needed to trade it for a tutoring session, nervously asked him to make her one.

"Pour it out, Emily," she coaxed herself as she stood from the bed. Hearing a knock, she stopped in her tracks. "Um...who is it?" she asked, looking at the door.

"It's Alex."

Crap! Emily panicked. Snatching the bottle off of the dresser, she searched around for a place to hide it. The last thing she needed was for Alex or anybody for that matter to know that she'd taken up drinking to cope with her stress. "Just a second," she called to the door, shoving the bottle in the top of her closet. She took a deep breath and opened the door.

Alex smiled once she came face to face with Emily. "Hey sweetie, long time no see," she mused, stepping inside.

Emily returned Alex's smile with a small one of her own.

Alex scanned the disheveled room with her eyes. She'd never seen Emily's space so messy. "Have you started packing yet?" she asked, moving several clothing items aside and sitting on Emily's bed. "Winter break starts in a few days."

Don't remind me, Emily thought. The last thing she wanted to think about was spending another break at home, in the house with her prying mother and annoying sister. "Um, no not yet," she replied, voice low.

Alex rubbed her hands down her jeans repeatedly. "So, I'm sure you're aware that I've been calling to check in on you," she put out. Emily looked down at her floor momentarily. "I'm worried about you...we *all* are."

Emily sighed. "I'm sorry that I haven't been answering," she apologized. "I've just been stressing out over—never mind, it's not important."

"Em, if something is bothering you, of *course* it's important," Alex pressed. "Distancing yourself from the group won't help you." She ran her hand over her hair. "Between you and Chasity, I'm gonna have a conniption."

"Wait, what's wrong with Chasity?" Emily asked, concerned. She'd been out of the loop so long, she wondered what she'd missed.

Alex waved her hand in Emily's direction. "It's a long story that I'll tell you about later," she promised. "But in the meantime, I want to talk about *you*."

Emily folded her arms as she stared at the designs on her socks. "There isn't much to talk about," she lied. *Besides the fact that I'm failing my classes, my mom is threatening to pull me out of this school, oh! And I've developed a taste for drinking alcohol.* Emily thought.

Alex sighed, she knew that Emily wasn't being honest, but decided for once, not to press. "Well, one reason I came over was to tell you in person about the ski trip that Malajia planned," she revealed. "She managed to find a cheap package, last minute."

Emily's eyes and ears perked with anticipation. "Oh, that sounds like fun," she said, a smile on her face. Then just as quickly as the smile appeared, it faded. She knew that going was out of the question.

Noticing the sullen demeanor, Alex stood from the bed. "I know you feel that asking your mom is pointless," she began. "But...I think you should *try*. This trip is what we all need to bring the group back together. We miss you and we want you to be there."

Emily pushed hair behind her ears. "I *do* wanna go," she sulked.

"Well...maybe you'll be *able* to."

Emily shook her head. "I doubt it."

Alex sighed again. "Okay, well, I gotta go start packing," she stated. "So I'll call you later...or call *me*."

Emily simply nodded as Alex walked out of the room.

Once the door closed, Emily rubbed her forehead with her hand. "I hate my life," she grumbled, heading over to the closet to retrieve her hidden drink.

"Dad, I don't understand what the problem is," Malajia hurled into her cell phone. "You know you have the money, so just send it to me already, so I can book my trip."

"Malajia, this family doesn't have extra money lying around just to pay for some fluke trip that you planned," Mr. Simmons returned, voice stern.

Malajia rolled her eyes. She didn't need any lectures from her father, she only wanted him to put the five hundred dollars that she needed into her bank account. Securing a weekend reservation at a small motel for the weekend after New Year's, Malajia was excited when everyone, including Alex paid their fees in full. But she never anticipated to be the last one still with a balance.

"Dad, nobody asked you all that," Malajia hissed, pacing the room. "Just take the secret stash out of Mom's drawer and put it in my account." Malajia pulled the phone away from her ear as her fed up father began yelling at her.

"Malajia! I swear to God, I will throw all your shit out on the lawn if you ask me about some damn money *one* more time!" he boomed through the line. "All you do is get on my damn nerves and make a bunch of C's and you got a nerve to ask me for five hundred dollars!" Malajia rolled her eyes. "I'll give you five hundred kicks up your ass! *That's* what I'll give you!"

Malajia sucked her teeth as the verbal tongue lashing continued. "Dad you hype!" she bellowed into the phone. She flopped back on her bed and kicked her legs in the air. "Oh my Goooooood!" When she heard a knock at the door, she sat up and tossed the phone on the bed. "Come in," she called.

Sidra walked in. "Hey, I wanted to see if you want to take a break from packing and come to lunch with me," she proposed. Sidra frowned once she heard a muffled male voice. "Who is that?"

Malajia rolled her eyes. "My dad is on the phone," she grumbled, pointing to her cell, which was lying face down on the bed.

Sidra looked confused. "Why aren't you talking to him?"

"Because he's cussing me out and I don't have time for that bullshit," she returned. After hearing more hollering, Malajia grabbed the phone and put it to her ear. "Dad! Why are you still yelling though?...I gotta go...okay fine, bye."

Sidra laughed as she sat on Chasity's bed. "Why is he cussing you out?"

"'Cause he don't want to give me five hundred dollars to cover my room," Malajia replied, scrolling through her phone.

Sidra frowned. "But don't you only owe *one* hundred?"

Malajia quickly shook her hand in Sidra's direction. "That's not the point," she deflected, much to Sidra's amusement. "The point *is* that he should stop being a jerk and just give me what I ask for."

"And you wonder why you're always getting cussed out," Sidra pointed out. "*I* can lend you the hundred to cover the rest of your balance. My parents gave me a little extra."

Malajia made a face. "Don't rub it in."

Sidra stood from the bed. "Forget it," she spat out.

"I'm joking," Malajia said. "So sensitive...I'll take it, thanks."

Sidra tilted her head, noticing Malajia's somber look. "Mel, don't worry about paying me back right away if you can't," she said.

Malajia frowned. "Huh?"

"I'm just saying. You look like you're depressed over it."

Malajia shook her head. "Girl please, I'm not worrying about that," she assured. The truth was that Malajia was still upset over Tyrone. She hadn't bothered to call him ever since he snapped at her a little over a week ago. Although she had

no interest in speaking to him, even going as far as blocking
his number for the first few days after the incident, she still
wished that she knew what his problem was with her. "You'll
get it back when we meet up for the trip,"
she added. "Dad's *gonna* give me that damn money or I will
show my whole entire *ass* at the family Christmas dinner."

Sidra shook her head. "Girl, bring your simple self to
lunch with me," she ordered, laughter in her voice.

Malajia shrugged as she stood from the bed. She glanced
at her phone one last time before shoving it into her jeans
pocket and walking out the door behind Sidra.

Chasity stuffed the last of her bags into the trunk of her
car. After a long, trying semester, she couldn't wait to put
some distance between herself and Paradise Valley
University. She gave the packed trunk one last look over
before shutting it.

Hearing a familiar voice call her name, she closed her
eyes. *Shit!* she thought, turning around and coming face to
face with Jason.

"Hey," he said, a slight smile on his face.

Chasity looked at him momentarily. "Hey," she returned.
The tension between them was thick. Having successfully
avoided talking to Jason for weeks and only seeing him in
brief passing, Chasity hoped to continue that streak by
leaving campus two days earlier than the rest of the students.

Jason shoved his hands in his coat pockets. He looked
nervous. He *felt* nervous. He hadn't been this close to Chasity
in a while; he wanted to hug her, to kiss her. Being this close
brought back memories of the night that they shared, a night
that he wished he could relive over and over again.

"So um…leaving early huh?" he asked. "I saw you
putting your bag in your trunk when I was on my way over."

Chasity nodded. "Why *are* you over here anyway?" she
asked, tone not masking her contempt.

Jason wasn't surprised by the bite in Chasity's voice, in

fact he expected it. "I came to see you," he answered honestly.

"Without calling first?" she returned, folding her arms.

"Well, I didn't think that you would answer," he replied. "So, I figured that I would take a chance and just come over."

Chasity rolled her eyes. "Jason, we're not friends anymore, remember?" she hissed. Jason looked at the ground momentarily. "There's no need for you to come see me. We have nothing to talk about anymore."

Jason sighed. *This is all my fault*, he thought. "Look Chaz, I know that I handled things—"

"Can we not do this?" she interrupted. Chasity, feeling her emotions bubble up, wanted to get away from him as fast as possible. "What's done is done."

Jason felt like breaking down as he watched Chasity walk to the driver's side of her car. "Chasity, I miss you," he blurted out. His words, stopped her in her tracks. "And...I don't want us to end this way."

Chasity shook her head. *I miss you too*. Despite how much she wanted to tell him that, especially when he was standing before her, vulnerable, she couldn't bring herself to say it. "Bye Jason," she said. "Have fun on your trip."

Jason ran a hand over his head as he watched the sleek black car pull off. "What the fuck have I done?" he asked himself before heading back to his dorm.

Chapter 27

Malajia drummed her fingers on the dining room table, staring out the window at the dusting of snow covering the lawn.

I'm so damn bored.

Having been home for winter break for a few days, Malajia was already missing her friends…one in particular.

Picking up her phone, she dialed a number. "Good morning sunshine!" she bellowed into the phone once the person answered.

Chasity, who was laying on her side, trying to catch some sleep, rolled over on her back as she cradled the phone to her ear. "What, Malajia?" she ground out.

Malajia sucked her teeth. "You know what? You're an ignorant ass roommate," she barked. "With your attitude having, non-talking, self."

"Feel free to move out," Chasity shot back, looking at her nails.

"Shit, you got me chopped," Malajia threw back. "You got all the rich appliances."

Chasity rolled her eyes. "You called for a reason, right?"

"Yes…I'm bored," Malajia joked. "And, I wanted to check on you, even though you're treating me like shit right now."

"I'm fine," Chasity replied, tone even.

"We *both* know that's not true," Malajia contradicted. "I saw Jason the day that you left and he told me that y'all spoke…briefly."

"So?"

"*So*, I know it must've been weird for you, after everything," Malajia pressed.

"Nope, I'm good."

Malajia let out a loud sigh. "You know what, I'll fix your ass," she said, putting her phone on speaker and scrolling through it.

"What are you talking about?"

"Don't worry about it," Malajia deflected. "You going anywhere today, or tomorrow?"

"Probably not, why? What the fuck are you up to?"

"I'll call you back," Malajia said, before abruptly ending the call. After getting the information she needed from her phone, Malajia headed into the living room. "Dad, can you drive me to West Chester?" she asked.

Mr. Simmons, who was enjoying a football game on television, sent a fiery gaze Malajia's way. "Are you out of your damn mind?"

"Yeah, it was worth a shot," she mumbled. "Can you at *least* take me to the train station? And give me money for a ticket?"

"Malajia, get out of my face," Mr. Simmons spat out, reaching for his can of beer on a side table. "I just gave you money the other day…You're not going to keep spending our money on pointless things for *you*."

"It's *not* pointless, I'm going to visit a friend," Malajia argued. "I'm trying to be a good person and go spend time with my roommate, who is really sad right now and you're holding up the process." Malajia stared in anticipation of what her bothered father would say. It was a stretch, but she prayed that it would work.

"If I give you this damn money for this train…you better stay your ass over there for a few days because you're on my last nerve."

Yes! Malajia rejoiced internally. "Oh you ain't say nothin' but a word brotha," she smiled.

"What did you say?" Mr. Simmons frowned.

Malajia's smile quickly faded. "Nothing, Father," she joked.

Mr. Simmons shook his head. He always wondered where his middle child got her silliness from. "You got fifteen minutes to get your stuff together."

"I only need *ten*," Malajia replied, darting for the steps. In her haste, she tripped over a throw rug and bumped into the side table, spilling the beer that her father just sat back down.

"Damn it, Malajia!" he boomed, jumping up.

Malajia ran up the steps, laughing "Mom! Dad spilled beer on the carpet," she yelled.

"You—" Mr. Simmons was so annoyed, he couldn't even finish his words.

Staring at her e-reader, Chasity adjusted the throw blanket over her legs. Her attempt at an escape through the words on the bright screen wasn't working, her mind was too cluttered. Chasity was plagued with thoughts of her strained relationship with her aunt, and her failed friendship with Jason.

She'd been thinking of him constantly. She just couldn't shake the images of him. Feeling herself tear up, Chasity sat her e-reader down and put her hands over her face. A knock at the door startled her. Wiping her eyes with the sleeve of her sweater, she stood from her seat and headed for the door.

Laying eyes on the visitor, Chasity's eyes widened. "What the fuck are *you* doing here?"

Malajia's smile faded as she put her hand up. "A simple,

'hello' would've done just fine," she sneered, moving around Chasity to step inside. "Evil ass."

"How are you just gonna show up at somebody's damn house unannounced?" Chasity harped, slamming the door.

Malajia spun around to face Chasity as she removed her coat. "Nice sweater," she complimented of Chasity's cream turtleneck sweater. Chasity pointed to the coat hanger by the door, which Malajia walked over to and hung her coat on.

"And I already knew you were gonna be home…Remember, you told me earlier on the phone that you wasn't doing nothin'."

Chasity stood there in disbelief. The lengths that Malajia would go, to get on her nerves. "And just how long do you think you're staying here?"

"Until my dad stops wanting to choke slam the shit outta me," Malajia joked, sitting her overnight bag on the floor near the couch.

"Oh, so I guess you'll be moving in, huh?" Chasity threw back, sarcastically.

Malajia's eyes widened. "Ooh, ooh, can I?" she asked, clapping her hands together in excitement.

"Fuck you and no," Chasity hissed, sitting on the couch.

Malajia sucked her teeth. "Just kill my damn hopes and dreams," she mumbled, sitting next to her. "So…what we doin'? You got any drinks?" Malajia asked after a few moments of silence.

"Trisha has some wines from places that she's been to, locked in a case in the basement somewhere," Chasity stated dryly.

"Off limits?"

"As long as it's locked," Chasity returned, tone not changing.

"Damn it," Malajia complained. "Where *is* Ms. Trisha anyway?"

"Traveling on business or for pleasure…Who knows, I don't give a fuck," Chasity grumbled.

Malajia looked over at Chasity, who was staring blankly

at nothing. The light from the fireplace and dim lamp illuminated her sad face. "Sis...seriously, are you cool?"

Chasity took a moment to answer. "No," she answered honestly, which took Malajia by surprise. Chasity then turned to Malajia. "You?"

Malajia was taken back by that question. *How did she know?* She sighed and shook her head. "No."

"I figured," Chasity replied.

"How so?" Malajia asked, moving hair from her face.

"You've had a salty look on your face for like the last two weeks of school."

Malajia frowned. She knew exactly what Chasity was referring to. "Then why didn't you say any-damn-thing?" she snarled. "Shit, I needed to talk about some stuff."

"In case you haven't noticed, I haven't been in the talking mood," Chasity returned.

Malajia waved her hand at Chasity dismissively as she adjusted herself on the couch. "Well, since I'm here, you're gonna listen to me."

Chasity threw her head back in exasperation. "God, please," she groaned, knowing how long the conversation could possibly be.

"Yep, so you better crack that wine case open right now, 'cause I'm about to be all up in my feelings," Malajia teased.

Chasity folded her arms to her chest. "I don't have a key to it," she replied.

Malajia sucked her teeth. "I'm sure there's one downstairs," she assumed, standing from the couch. "I'll be right back."

Chasity followed Malajia's progress as she disappeared through the dining room.

Malajia reappeared, a bottle and two glasses in hand, after ten minutes. "Ta da," she beamed.

Chasity frowned. "Where did you find a key?"

"What key?" Malajia shrugged.

"What did you do, Malajia?" Chasity asked, eyeing her friend suspiciously.

"I picked the lock, duh," Malajia returned, sitting back down in her seat. "Now let's get to drinking."

Chasity frowned in disgust as she watched Malajia fill both glasses to capacity with the warm, red wine. "I don't like wine," she complained.

"It's either *this* or that corn liquor I saw down there," Malajia proposed, handing Chasity a glass.

"There's no damn corn liquor down there," Chasity laughed.

"Maybe there *is*, maybe there *isn't*," Malajia vaguely replied. "You wanna take the risk and find out?"

"Naw, I'm cool," Chasity complied, taking a sip.

Malajia took a sip herself and gathered her thoughts. "So…Tyrone is a certified asshole," she divulged.

Chasity shook her head as she tried to adjust her pallet to the bitter taste of the wine. "You're *just now* coming to that conclusion?"

Malajia narrowed her eyes. "Don't be a smart ass," she chided. "Anyway, when I called him like two weeks ago, he completely blew up at me," she continued. "Talking about I'm blowing his phone up like a stalker and shit. I only wanted to *talk* to his ignorant ass." She paused for a second. "It's like he only wants to talk to me or see me when *he* wants to. But when *I* want to, it's a problem."

"Malajia, I honestly don't know why you're wasting your time on this jackass."

Malajia shrugged as she took another sip. "I like him."

"*Why*?" Chasity was confused.

"Look, you don't get it, but he can be such a sweetheart at times, but other times…" Malajia sighed, "he's an asshole…I was just hoping that the good in him outweighed the bad, you know?"

Chasity shook her head emphatically. "No, I *don't* know," she responded truthfully. "As far as I know, he's been a jackass from the jump. I'm pretty sure even with all your stupidity, you can do better."

Malajia looked at her. "What if I can't?" she asked, with

a seriousness that Chasity wasn't expecting.

"What does *that* mean?" she asked, curious.

Malajia shook her head, realizing that she was going deeper into the heart of things than she wanted to. "Nothing. I blocked his number so he's done," she quickly dismissed.

Chasity squinted at her. "Uh huh," she replied, not wanting to press the issue.

"So," Malajia began, taking another sip. "This stuff tastes like ass," she commented.

The offhand remark made Chasity nearly spit out her drink while laughing. She coughed as she sat the glass on the coffee table. "Stupid," she chortled, examining her sweater for red droplets.

Malajia sat her glass down. "So…you gonna talk about Jason now?"

"Do I *have* to?"

"Yes," Malajia insisted. "You got some of this wine in you, so you'll start being honest about your feelings soon enough."

Chasity shook her head. *This girl is gonna get on my nerves all night if I don't say something.*

"Do you miss him?" Malajia asked point blank.

"Yes," Chasity answered.

"Are you ever gonna be friends again?"

"I don't know."

Malajia frowned in concern. "Do you regret sleeping with him?"

"No," Chasity answered after a few seconds.

Malajia thought about what question to ask next. "Are you still mad at him?"

Chasity thought for a moment. "No."

"*Really?*" Malajia was shocked. Judging by how she heard that Chasity reacted to being face to face with Jason before leaving school, she was sure that she was still harboring bad feelings for the man. "Then what's the attitude for?" she asked. "What are you mad at?"

Me, Chasity thought. "I'm done talking about this," she

deflected.

Malajia let out a huff. "Fine, just one last question," she insisted, much to Chasity's annoyance. "Are you gonna come on this ski trip with us?"

"No." Chasity's response was instantaneous.

Malajia threw her head back and groaned loudly. "Come *on*!" she belted out. "You can't leave me there with Alex!"

Chasity giggled. "You'll be fine."

"No, I *won't*. I—" A loud noise from the basement startled both girls. "What's up with this spooky ass house?"

"Shut up, something probably fell," Chasity reasoned, rising from the couch. Malajia watched as Chasity headed for the basement. She refused to go with her, but once she remembered something, she darted off the couch.

"Malajia! What the fuck?" Chasity yelled as Malajia ran down the steps.

"Huh? What's wrong?" Malajia asked, feigning innocence.

Chasity spun around and pointed to the broken glass on the wine cabinet door. "You really wanna do this right now?" she seethed.

Malajia craned her neck to see. Eyeing the glass on the floor, she struggled to find something to say to justify the scene. "Okay fine, I broke it by accident," she admitted.

"What? How did you do *that*?" Chasity barked.

"Well…I had to get the wine out *somehow*," Malajia explained.

"I thought you picked the lock."

"Oh come on, I don't know how to pick a lock," Malajia shot back.

"Un- *fuckin*- believable!" Chasity fumed after staring at the stupid look on Malajia's face for a few seconds. "You better find a damn glass shop, like now," she ordered, moving past Malajia and heading up the steps.

Malajia sighed. "It isn't even that noticeable," she mumbled.

"*Now*, Malajia!" Chasity thundered, causing Malajia to flinch.

Jason stared out of the living room window, watching the rain fall. Although the sound of it was soothing to him, it did little to take his mind off of his problems. His father calling his name snapped him out of his trance.

Jason turned around, face void of a smile. "You called me?"

Mr. Adams chuckled. "Just checking on you," he replied. "You've been staring out that window for the past half-hour."

Jason ran his hand over his hair. "*Have* I?" he asked.

Mr. Adams studied his son; he seemed tired. Not to mention he'd been hibernating in his room since he returned home on break. "What's going on with you, son?"

"I just have a lot on my mind right now," he replied.

"Do you want to talk about it?"

Jason stared at his father. He needed to talk to someone about what he was feeling, but he didn't know where to start.

Sensing Jason's inner struggle, Mr. Adams held a concerned look upon his face. "Jason, whatever it is…you can tell me."

"I um…" Jason hesitated for a moment. "I messed up really bad."

Mr. Adams's eyes widened as he prepared himself for the worst. "Did you kill somebody?"

Jason was taken back by the question. "No, of *course* not."

His father put his hands up. "I had to go to the worst possible thing first," he explained. "Did you fail a class?"

"No."

"Did you get somebody pregnant?" Mr. Adams paused, waiting for the response.

"No, sir."

He breathed a sigh of relief. "You want to tell me what

it *is*? Or do you want me to keep guessing?"

Jason stalled for a moment. "Dad...I think that I may have lost the woman that I love," he finally admitted.

Mr. Adams took a long look into his son's eyes and saw confusion and pain. Glancing out of the window, he noticed that the rain had stopped. "Come with me," he said as he made his way to the door.

At first Jason looked confused, but soon after, he followed suit.

Mr. Adams stepped onto the football field at Jason's former high school ten minutes later. "Good thing they don't lock the gate," he mused, tucking a football under his arm.

Jason adjusted the black gloves on his hands. *What the hell did he bring me here for?* he quietly wondered. "Dad, it's freezing out here," he grumbled. The last thing he wanted to do at that moment was play football.

"It's not so bad," Mr. Adams contradicted, removing his coat.

Jason rolled his eyes. "Dad, what are we doing out here?" he asked.

Mr. Adams tossed the ball in the air and caught it. "I figured that you needed to get out of the house for a bit," he explained. "To get some fresh air in you…also to keep your mother out of earshot," he said. Jason chuckled. "I figured that you needed a man to man talk."

Jason managed a smile. His father was always so attentive to the needs of his wife and sons. He could only hope that he would be the same way when the time came. Jason removed his coat and held his hands out for his father to toss the ball.

"So," Mr. Adams began, tossing it. "What happened?"

Jason caught the ball, then immediately tossed it back. "I um…okay so, I mentioned that I loved someone and I'm guessing that you're aware that that woman is Chasity," he revealed.

Mr. Adams nodded. "I figured," he replied. "What makes you think that you've lost her?"

Jason hesitated. He wasn't sure if he wanted to go through the details of what transpired. But his father went through the trouble to get him to open up, and he was the one person that Jason felt he could talk to about anything.

"Okay so…over Thanksgiving break…when I went over her house…" Jason took a deep breath. "Long story short, by the end of the night I ended up telling her that I loved her and we slept together."

Mr. Adams looked at him. "Oh," he said, giving the ball another throw. He knew his son was no virgin. He remembered the conversation that he had with Jason when he found out that he had lost his virginity at the age of sixteen. He also knew that his son was not the type to sleep around, so if he had sex with Chasity, then his feelings for her must be real.

"And…she was a virgin," Jason added.

Mr. Adams eyes widened. "Oh!" he was shocked.

"Yep," Jason confirmed.

"Are you sure?"

Jason shot his dad a knowing look as he tossed the ball back. "*Trust* me, I'm sure," he assured.

Mr. Adams caught the ball and signaled for Jason to continue.

"Anyway afterwards she…she pushed me away Dad," Jason vented. "I mean, she ignored my phone calls, she pretended not to be home when I came by…When I finally *did* talk to her, she told me she didn't want to be in a relationship with me."

"Did she say that she wanted a relationship *beforehand*?"

Jason shook his head. "No…I just thought that maybe she *wanted* to be in one but was apprehensive—I guess I misread her signals." He let out a sigh. "Anyway, I realized that I wanted more from our relationship than she was willing to give me and I ended our friendship."

"Wow," was all that his father could get out as he adjusted the knit cap on his head.

"Yeah, *exactly*," Jason agreed. "And now, I miss her, but I'm pretty sure that she's fine with never talking to me again."

"So, you wish that things could go back to the way they were?" It was more of a statement, than a question.

"I mean…no, not really," Jason admitted. "I still want more, but…I also don't *not* want her in my life because she can't give me that…or she *won't*." Jason put his hands on his head. "I'm so damn confused."

Mr. Adams approached Jason. "Your confusion is understandable," he assured. "I get why you did what you did. You were disappointed and hurt. And when we're hurt, we make irrational decisions."

"Tell me about it," Jason griped. "I blew it."

Mr. Adams put his hand on Jason's shoulder. "I honestly don't think that you *did*," he replied. "I think you should try to talk to her again…She may be a tough one, but if she's anything like I *think* she is, she'll give you another chance."

Jason shrugged. He wasn't so sure that his father was right. "I'll try, I guess," he replied.

Mr. Adams adjusted his hat once again. "I've never seen you this affected by a woman before, not even with Paris."

Jason shook his head as he briefly thought of his ex-girlfriend from high school. "Naw, this is *nothing* like what I felt with Paris," he clarified. "This thing that I feel for Chasity is totally different."

Mr. Adams eyed his son proudly. "Then…don't give up on her," he advised.

Jason forced a smile. "Thanks for the talk."

Mr. Adams smiled back. "Any time," he replied, giving Jason a pat on his back. "Come on, let's go grab some burgers."

"Mom said you need to cut down on the red meat," Jason chuckled, retrieving his coat from the wet grass.

Mr. Adams put his coat on. "What your mother doesn't know, won't hurt her," he joked as they headed off the field.

Chapter 28

"Ma, that gingerbread house is looking good," Alex mused, sticking her finger close to a gumdrop that her mother had just carefully placed. She giggled as her mother delivered a light tap to her hand.

"I already had to ban your brother and sister from the kitchen while I finish this," Mrs. Chisolm teased. "Do I need to do the same to *you*?"

Alex put her hands up and laughed. "No ma'am," she assured. "I'm on my way to work anyway."

"Really? You worked six days straight already." Mrs. Chisolm failed to conceal her disappointment.

"Yeah, well, people are hungry for diner food I guess," Alex joked.

"You shouldn't have to do that," Mrs. Chisolm sulked, retrieving a few more gumdrops out of a bowl.

"Well, I need stuff for school. Not to mention I have the ski trip coming up after the holidays," Alex placated. "Remind me to thank Aunt Karen again for lending me the money for my room."

"Oh please, that was no loan," Mrs. Chisolm replied with a wave of her hand. "She owed me a favor. So you have that free and clear."

Alex smiled, but she still sensed that her mother was troubled. "You know that I don't mind the work, Ma," she replied. She gently tapped her mother on her arm. "I'm okay."

"Okay, well, you just be careful out there. People are crazy you know," Mrs. Chisolm cautioned.

"They can't be any crazier than what I've already encountered," Alex chuckled, heading out of the kitchen.

The bitter cold air hit Alex as she stepped outside of the house. "This cold is just disrespectful," she vented to herself, bundling the collar of her long, brown coat to her neck. She waved to a few of her neighbors in passing as she made her way off of her small block. Hearing her name, she paused and spun around. "You've got to be freakin' kidding me!" Alex raged, seeing Victoria crossing the street. "It's too damn cold for this, Victoria," she hissed.

"I promise I'm not stalking you Alex," Victoria explained, putting her hands up. "I was on my way to see—"

"Who, *Paul?*" Alex spat out.

Victoria looked at the ground momentarily. "No...I was on my way to ask about a job at the corner store," she clarified. "I'm gonna need one now that I decided not to return to school."

Alex was taken back. "What do you mean you're not returning to school?" She might not have liked the girl, but Alex didn't want her to miss out on an opportunity to complete her education.

Victoria shrugged, staring at the ground. "My grades are really bad...I—I can't focus so I decided to take some time off."

Alex shook her head. She knew that once Victoria stopped trying, that meant she was giving up. "Go ahead and throw away your opportunities because you can't *concentrate.* That's on *you.*" she bit out. "I gotta go."

Victoria watched as Alex moved around her to continue on her way. "Alex, I didn't mean to hurt you," she blurted out.

Alex stopped in her tracks, letting out a loud huff as she spun around. "Save it, you freakin' liar," she snarled. "You plotted and schemed behind my back, you lied to my face. You *did* mean to hurt me."

"Alex—"

"Girl!" Alex erupted, stepping close to Victoria's face. "I let you off easy when I slapped you before. *Please* don't make me drag you down this cold ass street."

Victoria adjusted the earmuffs on her ears. "If that would make you feel better, then go ahead," she challenged.

Alex pondered the thought, then waved her hand dismissively. "You're not worth the sweat that I would break to carry it out," she smirked. Victoria's eyes filled with tears. "I hope you both have a miserable ass life for what you've done to me."

"I'm so sorry," Victoria cried.

Her tears were lost on Alex, who stared at Victoria with cold brown eyes. "Go to hell," she sneered before walking away.

Adrenaline on high, Alex's pace quickened. She could've exploded at that very moment. She wished that she could vent to one of her friends during the twenty-minute walk to her job. "I need a damn cell phone," she hissed to herself.

Sidra searched through her drawers before heading over to her suitcase where it lay open on the floor near her bed. "Where the hell *is* the damn thing?" she asked herself as she sat on her bed and tossed her arms in the air. She sighed once she heard her name being called from downstairs. "Coming!" she called, heading out of the room.

"What's wrong, Princess?" Mrs. Howard asked, noticing the somber look on her daughters face.

"I can't find my cell phone case," Sidra replied, adjusting the bangle bracelet on her wrist.

"Where did you last see it?"

Sidra shrugged as she watched her mother spread wrapping paper out on the carpeted floor of the living room. "I could have sworn that I last had it in my bathroom at school," she tried to remember. "I remember taking it off to wipe my phone off."

"Well, I'm sure it'll turn up," Mrs. Howard assured. "It's not like you to lose anything."

"Tell me about it," Sidra muttered. She surveyed the piles of gifts strewn about the floor. "You and Daddy were feeling extra generous this year, huh?" she joked.

"Girl yes," Mrs. Howard chuckled. "And now I regret it because I have all of this wrapping to do at the last minute."

Sidra shook her head. With Christmas approaching in only two days, she knew that her perfectionist of a mother was stressing over her gift wrapping. Aside from her skin tone, height, and beauty, Sidra also inherited her mother's need for perfection. "I can help with that," she offered.

"As much as I *need* it, I need you to help me with something else."

Sidra folded her arms and stared at her mother in anticipation. "Okay."

"I need you to go to Patty's house and pick up my casserole dish," Mrs. Howard replied, tearing tape out of its holder.

Sidra sighed; a trip to Mark's house was not something that she felt like doing. "Mama, you have a million other dishes in there," she whined, pointing to the kitchen.

"Not like *that* one," Mrs. Howard returned, voice stern. "Now come on, I need it for the dinner that I'm making tonight."

Sidra resisted the urge to roll her eyes. "Okay fine, I'll go," she relented before turning on her heel and heading for the coat closet. "There better be something good in those boxes on that floor for me, since I'm being subjected to this," she mumbled to herself, walking out the door.

As Sidra stepped into the driver's seat of her mother's car, she retrieved her cell phone from her purse and dialed

Mark's number.

"Yo bee," Mark answered.

Sidra rolled her eyes. "You really need to stop calling people 'bee'," she scoffed, starting the ignition. Mark sucked his teeth loudly. "Anyway, are you home? Mama wants me to pick up the casserole dish that your mom borrowed."

"Yeah, I'm here, ain't doin' shit," Mark replied. "Since you coming over, bring me some food. I know your mom cooked last night."

"She *did*, but there are no leftovers."

"Then you can't get this dish," Mark shot back.

"Boy, stop playing," Sidra barked. "I already don't feel like coming there, don't annoy me."

"You think I'm playing," Mark said after a few seconds of silence. "Mom isn't here, so *I'm* the only thing standing between you and this dish that everybody's so hype about."

Sidra rolled her eyes as Mark continued to speak. *I'm gonna kill him one day, I swear*, she thought.

"So, you might as well pack up some of that potato salad that I *know* she made, along with those ribs, that chicken or whatever *else* is there," Mark ordered.

Sidra sat in seething silence for a few moments. "Are you freakin' kidding me?"

"Nope," Mark laughed.

"Very well," Sidra complied, much to Mark's delight. Sidra stormed out of the car and into the house. "Mama! Mark is being greedy and told me he won't give me your dish if I don't bring him some food!" she yelled into the kitchen.

"Snitch!" Mark hollered into the phone.

Sidra laughed as she handed Mrs. Howard the phone. "Ha ha!" Sidra teased.

"Mark—"

"Mama, I didn't even say that," Mark lied nervously, interrupting Mrs. Howard. "You know how dramatic your daughter is."

"No, I know how dramatic and hungry *you* are," Mrs. Howard returned, laughter in her voice.

"I'mma make sure the dish is ready when she gets here," Mark promised.

"Um hmm," Mrs. Howard jeered. "You still want a plate?"

"Yes ma'am."

Mrs. Howard giggled as she handed the phone back to Sidra.

"Ah ha, you got in trouble," Sidra mocked.

"I'm still gettin' a plate though," Mark returned, voice filled with disdain. "Just hurry up. Josh and David are coming over to play video games and I wanna eat my food before they get here and start looking all in my damn face and shit."

"How are you going to be stingy with food that isn't even *yours*?" Sidra laughed.

"Just come on!" Mark snapped.

"Yeah, yeah, you just watch your tone brother." Sidra shook her head in amusement as she hung up the phone. "Mama, you might as well put more of that food in a container," she suggested. "All of your greedy sons will be there."

Emily stared blankly at the tape in her hand. Having been subjected to helping her mother wrap gifts for the past hour and a half, while having everything that she was dealing with on her mind, Emily's mood was low.

"Emily, hand me the tape," Ms. Harris commanded, holding her hand out.

"Sure," Emily mumbled, handing the plastic holder to her mother.

After securing the paper with the tape, Ms. Harris proudly examined her work, before glancing at Emily. "Emily, what's with the sour face?" she asked.

Emily looked up, confused. "I'm sorry?" she queried.

"You've been moping around this house ever since you've been home."

That's because I don't want to be here! "I'm um...I guess I'm just tired," she replied, using her go-to excuse.

"Well, you need to get it together," Ms. Harris urged. "Nobody wants to be subjected to your attitude for the rest of the break."

Emily sighed. *I'm tired of being stuck in this house! I want to go skiing!* With the trip a little over a week away; Emily couldn't dare bring it up to her mother. Her grades taking a major dive, along with her mother's utter dislike for the group was sure to garner a quick 'no'.

"By the way, when are your final grades coming in?" Ms. Harris asked, adjusting several ornaments on the family Christmas tree.

Crap! "Um...soon I guess," she put out hesitantly.

Ms. Harris shot her a glance. "Don't think you're going to get away with hiding your final grades like you did your midterms, either," she began.

Emily put her hands over her head as her mother continued talking. "I know, I know," she grumbled. Relief soon came once the phone rang. *Thank God!* "I'll get it." Emily made a mad dash for the cordless phone. "Hello?"

"Hey sweetie," a male voice answered.

A broad smile appeared on Emily's face; she hadn't heard from him in a week. "Hi Daddy."

"Who is that?" Ms. Harris asked, curious.

Emily rolled her eyes when she was sure that her mother wasn't looking. *Can't even talk on the phone in peace.* "It's Daddy," she replied, before heading upstairs to her room.

"Sorry about that," Emily apologized, shutting her room door. She flopped down on the bed and sighed.

"It's okay," Mr. Harris assured. "How's your break so far?"

Emily laid her head on her pillow. "Its fine," she sulked.

Mr. Harris noticed the tone in his daughter's voice. "You don't *sound* like things are fine," he pointed out. Mr. Harris could always sense when things weren't right.

Emily once again sighed. She hated to talk about her

mother behind her back, especially to her father. Her parents had just started being civil towards one another before she went off to college. After a nasty divorce, them being cordial was a relief to their children. Emily had been careful to keep the conversations that she shared with her father on the positive things, but she was starting to feel that there wasn't much positivity in her life anymore. For her own sanity, she needed to vent. "Daddy, I'm starting to feel…smothered," she revealed.

"Your mother still has that vice grip on you guys, huh?" Mr. Harris concluded, knowing his ex-wife all too well.

Emily shook her head. "Not them…just *me*," she clarified. "I feel like I can't breathe sometimes…I mean, I love her, but she stresses me out," she added, careful to keep her voice low.

"I agree that your mother, although a good woman overall, can have the tendency to…how can I say this?" he wondered. "To make you guys her *entire* world…I mean you're grown and she still acts like she can't function if you're not around."

"Yeah," Emily agreed, voice somber.

"At least you're at school the majority of the time."

Emily shook her head. "If she has her way, I won't be there for much longer," Emily groused.

"What do you mean?"

Emily stared up at the ceiling. "Daddy…" she wondered if she should even say anything else, afraid of how he would react. "I don't know what happened…I guess I let myself get so stressed…my grades are messed up."

"How bad?"

"I mean, they're lower than they *should* be," she temporized. "In all honesty…I'll have to fight hard next semester to keep from being put on academic probation."

"Wow Emily," he commented.

"I know," Emily agreed, feeling ashamed. "Everything is messed up. My grades, the relationship with my friends—I feel like I can't enjoy my college experience." She felt some tears forming in her eyes as all of her stress came to a head. "I hate that I can't stand up to her," she sniffled. "I mean…I can't even get up the nerve to ask her if I can go on this ski trip that my friends are going on next week."

"Emily, you're eighteen years old," Mr. Harris pointed out, voice stern. "You can let her know what you want to do, in a respectful manner."

Emily wiped her eyes as she sighed.

Mr. Harris paused momentarily. "Maybe you need a break from her," he vaguely put out.

"You mean while I'm at school?"

"No…I mean even when you're *not* at school," he corrected. "Maybe you should come out to North Carolina and live with *me.*"

Emily's eyes widened at the offer.

"You can still go to your same school," he added. "You'll have your freedom…Now, you *will* need to bring those grades up," he put out. "But I'm confident that you will."

Emily put her finger on her cheek as she pondered the offer. *It would be nice spending more time with Daddy and he's so much more laid back than Mommy.* Emily didn't want to be wild, she just wanted freedom; the freedom that an eighteen-year-old college student was entitled to.

"Daddy, thank you for the offer…" Although she saw hope with the possibility of moving with her father, she still couldn't see herself abandoning her mother, which is exactly how Ms. Harris would see it. "I don't think that will be necessary."

A sigh came through the phone. "Can't say that I'm not disappointed," he admitted. He always wished that he could spend more time with his children. But him living in a different state, and always working, made it difficult. He'd hoped that Emily moving in with him would give him that chance. "But, if you ever change your mind, you're always welcome," he assured.

"I appreciate it," she replied, tone somber.

"I *can* help you with your ski trip dilemma right now, though," he declared, peeking Emily's interest.

"How?"

"I can always tell her that I want you to come visit me that weekend."

Emily smiled at the possibility. "Do you think it'll work?"

"Trust me, it will." His voice was full of confidence. After the two discussed some details, Emily stood from her bed. "Put your mother on the phone so I can work this out."

Emily ran out the door and made a dash downstairs. She handed her mother the phone and eagerly listened to the conversation that was taking place. When her mother hung up and looked at her, Emily fought to keep her excitement to a minimum. "Um…what did Daddy say?" she asked innocently.

"Looks like you're going to North Carolina next weekend," Ms. Harris spat.

Emily smiled. *Yes!* she thought. As her mother disappeared into the kitchen, Emily clasped her hands together. She couldn't wait to call the girls to let them know the good news. *Finally, things are looking up.*

Chapter 29

Mark ran out of his bedroom and started banging on the walls. "Wake up, wake up!" he hollered, running down the hall. Entering the guest room, he peered at David and Josh sleeping in the double beds. A sly smile crept across his face and he ran and jumped on the beds.

"Dude, what the hell is wrong with you?" Josh barked, throwing a pillow at Mark.

"It's Christmas!" Mark hollered in David's ear.

"Move," David grunted, shoving Mark away. "What are you, five?"

Mark flagged David with his hand. He didn't care what David had to say, he was excited for Christmas, just as he always had been. "Why did y'all even come over here if you're not excited?"

Josh and David stared at Mark with confusion plastered to their faces. "'Cause you *asked* us to," Josh reminded, rubbing his eyes. After coming over late the previous evening, once he finished helping his father do inventory at the family car shop, Josh was hoping to sleep in a little later than six in the morning.

"That's irrelevant," Mark scoffed. "Just get up and come the hell on before I open y'all damn presents."

Josh perked up, "We have presents?" he smiled.

"Oh, *now* you happy and shit," Mark griped, walking out the room. "Mom! Josh said he don't want his present," he shouted as he ran down the steps.

"You play too much!" Josh hollered after him, heading out of the room.

David, still groggy, just reached for his glasses on the nightstand. "I don't know why I keep coming over here," he grumbled. "Fool probably can't even spell 'irrelevant'."

Mark, in the process of running for the couch, tripped over a throw rug. He let out a yelp as he fell into the Christmas tree, knocking it over.

Mrs. Johnson darted out of the kitchen door. "What the hell was that?!" Seeing her son laying on the floor with the tree on top of him, she sucked her teeth. *This boy is always doing some dumb shit!* "Goddamn it Mark!" she snapped.

Mark picked himself up from the floor. "How's it *my* fault that the rug was flipped up all stupid," he threw back. When he caught his mother's death stare, he swallowed hard. "I'm just gonna pick this up," he promised, pointing at the fallen tree.

When Mrs. Johnson went back into the kitchen, Mark looked over at Josh, who was holding his stomach, laughing hysterically. "You laughing kinda hard over there, you pizza slinging bastard," he snarled, standing the tree upright.

"Call me what you want, but you looked stupid as shit when you slid across that floor," Josh laughed. "Where did that scream come from?"

"I was scared as shit," Mark admitted, hanging some ornaments.

"Clearly," Josh chortled, laughter now subsiding.

David made his way down the steps. "What was that noise?" he yawned.

Mark shot him a glare. "You all late and shit," he sneered, inciting David to make a face at him.

"Mark busted his ass," Josh informed, laughter bubbling back up. Mark flopped down on the couch, a salty look on his face.

Mr. and Mrs. Johnson emerged from the kitchen, cups of coffee in hand, and gave the guys the go ahead to begin opening gifts.

"Ahhh, y'all watches corny," Mark teased, watching David and Josh beam over the expensive sport watches that they received.

"Why do you always have to start with them?" Mrs. Johnson hurled, eyeing her son with disgust. "One of them is going to punch you right in your face one day."

"Pay him no mind, Mom," Josh dismissed, giving her a kiss on the cheek and Mr. Johnson a hand shake. "Thanks for the gift."

"Don't be kissin' on my mom, man," Mark barked.

"Will you shut up?" David fussed. Mark had been working his last nerves since the previous evening and he wished *for once* the man would keep his comments to a minimum. "Anyway, thank you both," he said, ignoring the glare that Mark was shooting him.

Mrs. Johnson waved her hand dismissively, "Don't mention it, you two have always been like sons to us," she gushed. She loved the fact that Mark was still friends with the same people from childhood. Being an only child, she knew that her son always wanted siblings. Even though they couldn't provide blood ones, he at least had them through friendship.

Mark eagerly opened his gift. "Yeeeeeessss," he rejoiced, throwing his head back in dramatic fashion.

"Good, you have a new laptop," David observed. "Now you can stop trying to use *mine*."

Mark shot him a glance. "Dawg, nobody be tryna use that old laptop you got," he threw back.

David's jaw clenched as he stared at Mark with anger.

"Why are you looking at me like I stink, weirdo?" Mark asked, confused. "You must be smelling those glasses."

David was seething as Mr. Johnson tried desperately to contain his laughter.

"How your glasses got morning breath?" Mark added. Annoyed, David jumped up from the floor and began chasing Mark around the living room "Mom! Mom, David's running through the house," Mark hollered as he ran into the kitchen with David following.

Mrs. Johnson shook her head. "I don't know where that boy came from, sometimes," she said, tired.

Malajia, feeling something close to her face, jerked awake. "What the hell are you doing?!" she snapped at her eleven-year-old sister, Dana.

"Get up, it's Christmas!" Dana screamed in Malajia's face.

Malajia gave the girl a little push. "It's too early for you to be in my damn face with your hot breath," she hissed, pushing the covers off of her.

Dana darted pass Malajia and ran out of the room. "Mommy! Malajia cursed at me," she screamed, running down the steps.

Malajia threw her head back and groaned loudly. "I swear to God, I can't wait to get out of this damn house next week," she grunted to herself, making her way to the hall bathroom.

Emerging from the bathroom ten minutes later, Malajia headed down the steps and laid eyes on her family sitting in the living room, congregating around the Christmas tree.

"I swear, if I have to share *any* of those presents with these raggedy sisters of mine, I might as well take my sexy behind back upstairs," Malajia scoffed, plopping down next to Geri.

"Please," Maria teased. "There's *nothing* sexy about you right now."

Malajia rolled her eyes, smoothing her disheveled hair down with her hands. "Just waking up, messy hair and *all*, I look better than you on your *best* day...freak," she threw back.

"Okay, nobody wants to be subjected to this nonsense right now," Mr. Simmons cut in, voice stern. "Malajia chill out."

Malajia regarded her father with shock. "*She* started it," she threw back.

Mr. Simmons tossed Malajia a small box. "Shut your big mouth and open your gift," he ordered.

Malajia reached for the package and shook it. "And what is this? A gift card to nowhere?" she groused.

"It's something that you've been getting on our nerves about," Mrs. Simmons added, adjusting her youngest daughter on her lap. "Girl, where is all of this energy coming from?" she commented to the squirmy little girl.

"You fit a new family in this box?" Malajia muttered.

"Hey, cut the crap, smart ass," Mr. Simmons demanded, pointing at her. "You aren't exactly a joy to deal with *yourself.*"

Malajia rolled her eyes as she ripped the paper from the box.

"It's a phone!" Dana revealed, voice excited.

"Thank you, oh queen of ruining surprises," Malajia drawled sarcastically. Her eyes brightened when she laid eyes on the new phone that she had been eyeing for months. "Yeeeesss, now I can stop using that raggedy phone that Dad gave me before I left freshman year." Malajia glanced up at her father and dissolved into laughter at the angry stare that he was shooting. "I'm just messing with you Dad," she teased. "You're so sensitive…and old."

"Keep it up," he warned, tossing her another gift. "I'm still waiting on a paternity test to see if you're my child," he joked. "If it comes back negative, you're being put out, right on your ass."

Malajia waved her hand at him dismissively. "Please," she returned, ripping open the gift. She let out a scream. "You got me the crystal case too! My phone is gonna be pretty. It's gonna be preeeetttyyyyy," she sang, placing the delicate red case on to her new phone.

"Ooh, can I see it?" Maria asked, holding her hand out.

Malajia slowly placed the phone near Maria's face, then as Maria went to grab for it, she quickly moved it out of reach. "Nope," she laughed, much to Maria's embarrassment.

Maria stood up in a huff. "I hope it breaks," she threw over her shoulder, heading for the kitchen.

"You mad your phone old," Malajia taunted, jumping up to follow Maria.

Alex laid on the couch, curled into the fetal position. "My stomach is killing me," she groaned, face buried in a throw pillow.

Mrs. Chisolm giggled. "Child, I told you about eating all that cheesecake." She gave Alex's shoulder a rub as she handed her a cup of tea.

Alex slowly sat up and grabbed the cup from her mother's hand. "Thanks Ma," she smiled, taking a careful sip. "It was so good though."

Her mother shook her head. They had been invited to dinner at the Addison home the previous evening, and Alex overloaded on the smorgasbord of desserts that were prepared. Alex, full and tired from working a double the night before, returned home and crashed, dead asleep until her younger siblings practically dragged her out of bed that morning to open Christmas gifts.

"Well if it isn't cherry cheesecake girl," Mr. Chisolm teased, walking out of the kitchen.

"Very funny, Dad," Alex grimaced, sitting the cup on the coffee table.

Mrs. Chisolm playfully tapped her husband's leg. "Don't pay him any mind, honey," she said. "Here, open your gift," she urged, handing Alex a present.

Alex reluctantly grabbed the box. "Guys, I thought I told you that you didn't have to get me anything this year," she said, eyeing the neat wrapping. "I know that money's tight."

"Alex—"

"No, seriously," Alex persisted, interrupting her father's stern tone.

"Alex stop," he demanded. Alex immediately complied. "Now, I know you worry about this family," he said sincerely. "But that is me and your mother's job, not *yours*."

Alex let out a sigh. *I can't help it,* she thought. She always felt that it was her responsibility to help pick up the slack.

"You need to concentrate on *you*. The money you make is for *you*," Mrs. Chisolm stated. "So stop stuffing your tips in our drawer...I know you do it."

Alex let out a little laugh. "I'll try," she joked.

"Besides, things should be better because I'm going to start my little catering business that I've always wanted," Mrs. Chisolm announced, much to Alex's delight. "I have a few events set up over the next few weeks. I mean, it's nothing big but—"

"That's great Ma," Alex smiled, giving both of her parents a hug. She knew how much her mother loved cooking and knew that she would be great at catering.

"We can start sending you a few bucks here and there while you're away," her mother added.

Alex quickly waved her hand. "No, don't worry about me, I'm fine. My job up there holds me over."

Mr. Chisolm shook his head. His daughter was stubborn, but he admired her. "Will you at *least* accept your Christmas gift?" he chuckled.

"Sure *can*," Alex beamed, smile bright. She quickly ripped the wrapping paper off and opened the box. "Ooh a cell phone!" she shrieked.

"I know it's not a fancy one like your *friends* have, but I figured that you needed one. I know you're tired of using calling cards," Mr. Chisolm explained.

Alex gave her father a kiss on his cheek as she cradled the silver flip phone in her hand. "I love it, thank you," she said, voice filled with gratitude.

"Oh and here is a card with some money for you to take on your ski trip," Mrs. Chisolm quickly interjected. "Shut up," she urged when Alex went to protest.

Alex laughed as she gave her mother another hug. "Yes Ma'am."

Standing in the dining room watching his family open gifts in the living room, Jason took a sip of his hot chocolate. He smiled, watching his brother jump up and down while holding the new video game system that he received.

"Don't hurt yourself," Jason joked.

"He better *not*, or his game will be returned for money for the medical bill," Mrs. Adams assured.

Jason smiled briefly, but it quickly faded before he headed for the dining room table. He'd awoken that morning with a headache. His head was full of thoughts and visions of Chasity, thoughts that he tried to get rid of, at least for a few hours while he tried to enjoy time with his family.

Opening his gifts preoccupied him for a moment, but it lasted just that long. Sitting down at the table, he sat his cup down and ran his hands over his hair, sighing loudly. *Ugh, God please fix this. I can't take it anymore!*

Jason was in deep thought when his mother walked in and put her hand on his shoulder. "Jason?"

"Yeah Mom," he sighed, lifting his head up.

"Are you okay, honey?"

"I'm fine," he lied.

Mrs. Adams sat in the seat next to him. "You don't *seem* fine," she observed. "You've been looking sad ever since you got home."

"I just have some stuff on my mind, that's all," he replied.

"Well, do you want to tell me about it?" she pressed.

"Not really," he answered honestly. He knew that if his mother had any idea that his mood was out of whack because of Chasity, her already ill-feelings for the girl would intensify.

Mrs. Adams stared at her son, eyeing him with suspicion. Jason rarely let things affect him, and in her mind there was only one reason why her son was moping. "Who hurt you baby?" she asked, voice stern.

Jason rolled his eyes. "Mom," he groaned.

"Was it that girl?" she asked, putting her hand on his wrist. "Look Jason, if she's causing you this much heartache, then stop dealing with her, you hear me?"

"Mom, don't start," he hissed. "It's not Chasity, so just relax," he lied.

She folded her arms as she shook her head. "You can't lie to me Jason," she pointed out. "You never *could.*"

Mr. Adams, who had been standing in the dining room entry way, frowned in concern. Judging by the look on Jason's face, he was getting agitated. He knew it wasn't a good idea for his wife to pry into their son's romantic life, let alone talk down about the woman that he had fallen for.

"Nancy," he called.

Mrs. Adams turned and faced him. "What?"

"Leave the man alone," he said, gesturing his head towards the living room. "Come on and open the rest of your gifts."

Mrs. Adams shot him a frown, but in recognizing the authoritative tone in his voice, and the look on Jason's face, she realized that she was probing too much. "Fine, I'll back off," she agreed. "For *now.*"

"That's all we can ask for," Mr. Adams chuckled as his wife walked past him.

Jason looked up at his father, who gave him a knowing nod. Jason flashed an appreciative smile. Once his father was out of the dining room, he grabbed the phone from his robe pocket
and headed out the back door for some fresh air and privacy. He scrolled through his phone to see all of the 'Happy Holiday' messages from his friends, all except one.

"Just call her Jason," he prompted himself.

Sighing, he dialed Chasity's number and put it to his ear. He waited as the phone rang several times before going to voicemail. He was in no way surprised when she didn't pick up. He took a deep breath. "Hey Chasity, it's Jason," he began. "I was just calling to wish you a happy holiday...and I wanted to know how you were doing." *You're rambling bro.* "Anyway, I miss talking to you and..." He let out another sigh. "I guess I'll see you back at school in a few weeks...and Happy New Year, Chaz."

Jason disconnected the call and shoved the phone back in his pocket. The ski trip couldn't come quick enough for him. He needed some fun in his life, now more than ever.

Chasity removed the phone from her ear and looked at it. She sighed, seeing the missed call notification from Jason. She pushed a button, replaying his voice message. Rubbing her forehead with her hand, she put the phone back to her ear. It was the fourth time that she'd listened to it.

Her aunt's footsteps were approaching the den, forcing Chasity to abruptly hang up the phone. She rolled her eyes when she heard Trisha call her name. *Go the fuck away!* she thought.

"Chasity," Trisha called again, voice a bit more stern. *Take the damn hint.* Chasity sighed, still not answering.

Trisha put her hands on her hips and frowned; Chasity was facing the bay window and not her. "Pebbles," she barked.

Chasity's head snapped around. "What did you call me?" she hissed.

"I *thought* that might get your attention," Trisha replied, folding her arms to her chest. She knew how much Chasity detested her childhood nickname.

Chasity rolled her eyes. "Yes, Trisha?" she sneered.

Trisha stepped into the den. "So what, you think it's okay to ignore me?" she ground out.

Chasity shrugged. "It's either ignore you or be a snapping bitch, which one would *you* prefer?" she bit back.

Trisha rolled her eyes as she sat down on the ottoman next to Chasity. "*Neither,* but if I had to choose, I'd rather you *talk*," she replied. "You haven't said anything since you mumbled a 'thank you' for your present earlier."

"I don't want to go skiing," Chasity threw back, irritated.

"The trip is a peace offering. I'm trying to make things right," Trisha argued. She knew that she would be taking a chance that Chasity would reject her Christmas gift of an all-expense paid ski weekend at one of the top resorts in New York, but she had to admit, she hoped that she would be more appreciative.

"Oh, you want to make things right?" Chasity sniped.

"Yes."

"Are you sure?"

Trisha rolled her eyes at Chasity's smart tone. "What do you want from me?" she snapped. "I'm trying—I've *been* trying. You won't talk to me."

"I'm not *talking* to you because I'm *mad* at you," Chasity snapped back. "You hurt me."

Trisha looked down at her hands in shame.

"You made me feel like shit, all because I want to find out where I come from...well, I *did*."

Trisha looked up, confused. "What do you mean you *did*?"

Chasity shot her a glare. "Don't do that," she bit out. "Don't act like you're all concerned and whatnot...No, I don't want to find my so-called mother anymore. It's not worth wasting my time. She probably doesn't want to see me anyway...and my feelings have been shitted on enough."

Trisha felt like the most horrible person in the world. Not only for how she treated Chasity recently, but for things that she couldn't bring herself to share with her, things she wouldn't dare to. "I am so sorry," Trisha apologized, voice full of emotion. "I was being selfish...I thought that I was going to lose you and—"

"Why would you think that?" Chasity asked.

Trisha shook her head. "You wouldn't understand baby," she replied, tears filling her eyes. "I just—I don't know. But I'm sorry I hurt you. I'm sorry that I told you I would cut you out if you went ahead with your search...I was just—" Trisha let out a sigh. "I would *never* cut you out of my life," she assured.

Chasity just stared at Trisha as she kept talking.

"Truth is, I miss you," Trisha admitted. "I miss talking to you, you know. You're—you're my best friend. I miss our relationship and I'm trying to get that back."

Chasity looked away. She had to admit that she missed her aunt too. It was taking so much energy for Chasity to stay mad at Trisha, when what she really wanted to do was sit down and tell her everything that had been going on with her.

"Okay," Chasity said after a moment. "I'll try to get over it."

Trisha smiled as she wiped her eyes with the sleeve of her sweater. "Really?" she asked, voice filled with hope.

Chasity nodded, reaching for a folder holding the ski lodge information. After glancing at the details earlier, she'd thrown it on the floor upon entering the den.

Trisha reached her arms out to hug Chasity but was stopped by a hand.

"What? I can't get a hug?" Trisha asked, shocked.

"I have one question first," Chasity replied, tone even.

"What's that?"

"You picked this place, do you have any idea who runs it?"

Trisha looked confused. "No, I don't."

Chasity frowned. "Are you sure?"

Trisha put her hands up. "One of my clients recommended the place. They're wealthy and love to travel, so I took their word for it," she assured. "I really don't know what you *think* I know, but whatever it is, I *don't*."

Chasity stared at her. She had no idea if Trisha was lying or not, but she didn't have the mental energy to harp on it. "Okay fine," she relented hesitantly, before allowing Trisha to embrace her. Beaming, Trisha exited the den in search of some dessert for the two of them.

Chasity, hearing an alert on her phone, picked it up and looked at it. She shook her head as she read the text message from Malajia. *'You need to stop playing and come on this ski trip next weekend, bitch.'* Chasity didn't even bother to respond, she would never hear the end of it if Malajia found out that she was actually going skiing that same weekend, but not with *them.*

She did, however look up the lodge information that Malajia had included in her text. Looking at the pictures of the rooms, Chasity frowned her face in disgust. "They're gonna be pissed," she said to herself.

Malajia told Chasity that where they were staying was cheap and in Chasity's opinion, she could definitely see why. *They actually thought that I was gonna stay there?* Chasity let out a groan. "God, these people irk my face," she huffed, dialing a number. She rolled her eyes as she waiting for someone to answer. "Can I speak to Derrick?...Tell him it's Chasity." Chasity examined her nails while she waited. "Yes, it's really me," she said when the person answered. "I'm fine...No, I didn't call for small talk…I need you to do me a favor."

Chapter 30

"Wooooo! We're on our waaaayyy!" Mark hollered, tossing his overnight bag into the trunk of his car.

"Easy Mark, we have a long ride ahead of us," Sidra reminded, settling down in the front seat.

"You can't stop me from being hype," Mark groused, stepping into the driver's seat. "I'm not to be censored."

"Shut up," Josh laughed. "Nobody wants to hear your nonsense for this three-and-a-half hour drive to New York."

Mark flipped Josh the middle finger. Mark didn't care what they said, he'd waited weeks for this trip and now the day of, at eleven in the morning, they were finally on their way.

"Anybody know how Malajia's getting there?" David asked, putting his seatbelt on. "I would've thought that we would pick her up."

"No *you* would've picked her up," Mark contradicted, starting the car. "I told her whining ass that I wasn't driving to no damn Baltimore, then going all the way back up to New York," he added, voice filled with disdain. "Shit, she ain't my girl, and we *ain't* fuckin'." His crude remark earned him a stern backhand from Sidra.

"Don't be disrespectful," she scolded. Rolling her eyes at the smirk on Mark's face, Sidra turned towards the backseat and faced David. "Anyway, she went to Philly last night, and spent the night at Alex's house."

"I'm sure she loved *that*," Mark laughed, knowing how much Alex got on Malajia's nerves.

"Jason is driving his father's car to the motel, so he's picking the girls up as we speak," Sidra said, ignoring Mark's comment.

Mark waved his hand dismissively. "Enough of this chit chattin' bullshit about Malajia," he griped. "All I know is that she better have picked a good motel." He punctuated his comment by putting sunglasses on his face.

David sucked his teeth as Mark pulled out of his parent's driveway. "What's the point of the sunglasses?" he scoffed.

"To block out the glare from them lenses on *your* glasses," Mark threw back, earning a snicker from Josh, a glare from David, and a head shake from Sidra.

"This is going to be a long ride," Sidra sighed.

"I swear to God, this is the last time I spend the night at your house, Alex," Malajia ranted, zipping her overnight bag with a hard yank.

"I didn't even do anything to you!" Alex exclaimed, slinging her bag over her shoulder while standing on the porch of her Philadelphia home.

Malajia stood up right and grabbed her bag. "You was snoring all damn night, waking me up and shit," she nitpicked. "*And* you ate all the damn bacon this morning."

Alex was confused. "First of all *I* wasn't the one snoring, that was *you*," she threw back, pointing to a disbelieving Malajia. "And second, you said you didn't *want* any bacon."

"You knew I was lying. You know I love bacon," Malajia snapped, stomping her foot on the ground.

Alex stared blankly at Malajia for several seconds before shaking her head. "Girl, you don't have to worry about coming back over here," she returned. "You're a pain in my *entire* ass...and it's big, so you know that's saying a lot."

Malajia rolled her eyes as she moved hair from her face. "Where's Jase?" she grumbled. "He said he was around the corner. He's already late."

Alex smirked. "Let me call him and see," she said, retrieving her cell phone from her purse.

Malajia sucked her teeth as she watched Alex dial. "You hype as shit you got a cell phone," she teased, much to Alex's annoyance. "Why you got that old ass flip?"

"Malajia! I swear to God—" Alex's outburst was interrupted by a familiar car pulling in front of her house. "You're lucky Jason's here."

"No *you're* lucky," Malajia countered. "I was about to snap that flip in half." As Malajia walked to the car, she noticed a figure in the passenger seat. Her eyes widened. "Emily?!"

Smiling, Emily rolled down the window. "Hey, Malajia."

"What the hell are *you* doing here?" Malajia asked as Jason stepped out of the car.

"I'm coming skiing with you guys," Emily beamed.

Malajia was confused. "How did you get your mom to let you from under her dress long enough, to go?" she mocked.

Emily shook her head, suppressing a giggle.

"Malajia, talk in the car, it's freezing out here," Jason urged, placing the girls' bags into the trunk of the car.

Malajia sat in the backseat, a confused look held on her face. "So how—"

"Her father helped her by telling her mom that she was going to stay with him for a few days," Alex cut in.

"Yeah, so I took the train here to Philly and Jason picked me up and...here I am," Emily smiled, holding her arms up.

Malajia shook her hand in Emily's direction as Jason pulled off. "No, you put those arms down," she hissed, much to Emily's amusement. "You didn't tell me, I don't appreciate not knowing shit."

"You're so damn dramatic," Alex ground out, opening a pack of cookies.

Malajia's head snapped towards her. "And how the hell did *you* know?"

"She *told* me," Alex revealed, taking a bite out of the oatmeal raisin cookie.

Alex remembered the excitement that she felt when Emily called to tell her that she was going. She was not only excited for herself because she was able to spend some much needed fun time with Emily, but she was even more excited for Emily to get out of the house and be free, at least for a few days. "She wanted it to be a surprise for the rest of you guys."

Malajia rolled her eyes. "Fuck y'all surprises," she spat out, holding her hand out. "Give me a damn cookie, Alex."

Alex cut her eye at Malajia before slamming a cookie in Malajia's hand, breaking it in the process. "You're on my last nerve."

Malajia ignored her as she took a bite. She scrunched her face up. "What the—raisin?" she complained. "Eww, where's the damn chocolate chips?"

"Malajia, for the love of God, give your mouth a rest for *two* seconds, *please*," Jason cut in as he maneuvered through the streets.

"I wish she *would*," Alex added. "You should've gone to Sidra's last night." She retrieved another cookie. "But you just *had* to play around and miss that last train to Delaware."

Unfazed, Malajia folded her arms and sat back in her seat.

Jason rubbed the back of his neck. "Malajia, are you sure that you gave me the right address?" he asked, voice tired.

Having driven for over three hours, he was hungry and agitated.

"Yeah, I'm sure," Malajia confirmed, looking at her

phone. "Have I showed you guys my new phone?" she grinned, holding it up in plain view. "Isn't it pretty?"

Jason rolled his eyes. "Malajia it's a phone with red crystals on it, why would I *care*?" he hissed.

Malajia lowered her hand and sucked her teeth. "Don't get all cranky with *me* 'cause Chasity ain't here."

Jason gritted his teeth. Malajia sure knew how to push a button. "No, I'm *cranky* because I'm pretty sure you have us lost, not to *mention* you've been talking ever since you stepped foot in the damn car."

"How you gonna say 'not to mention' then mention it?" Malajia returned.

"Malajia, stop annoying him and check the address again," Alex cut in, noting the taut look on Jason's face.

Before Malajia could check the papers in her hand or respond, her phone rang. "What Mark?" she answered.

"Where the hell y'all at?" Mark asked.

"On the road fool," Malajia returned. "What do you want?"

"We're like ten minutes from the motel," Sidra could be heard saying over the speaker.

Malajia sucked her teeth. "See Jase, we're still on good time, the others are like ten minutes away," she announced.

"Well, we stopped and ate first," Sidra revealed. "We sat for like forty-five minutes."

Malajia frowned. "Let me call y'all back." Malajia searched through her folder full of the trip information once she hung up. She scanned the paper with her eyes, then winced. "Oops," she said.

"Oops, what do you mean *oops*?" Jason asked.

"Um…okay sooooo…" Malajia scratched her head, hesitating. "I *may* have told you Gilmore Drive and it actually says…*Greyson* Drive."

Jason quickly updated his GPS information. "Malajia—" Jason fumed once the new information popped up on the small screen. "We're like forty-five minutes *past* Greyson."

"I could've *sworn* it said Gilmore," Malajia defended.

"What, you can't read?" Alex bit out, shooting Malajia a glare. She'd had to use the bathroom for the past half-hour, but didn't want to hold the group up by stopping.

Malajia narrowed her eyes at Alex. "I can read just fine you big-faced mop," she threw back. "Your hot ass breath probably made the words move."

Emily, who was drinking some water, almost spit it out trying to hold in a laugh at Malajia's comment. Even Jason cracked a smile.

"Oh for real?" Alex scoffed at her amused friends.

Finally arriving at the address, Jason's group stepped out of the car and stretched. "I gotta use the bathroom," Alex complained, doing a dance.

"Eww, you didn't need to announce that," Malajia sneered. "You probably got the bubble guts, eatin' all those nasty ass oatmeal cookies."

Alex, fed up, reached for Malajia's scarf. "I'm so over you right now."

Malajia quickly ducked. "You mad you got the shits," she taunted.

Retrieving their bags from the trunk, the group headed inside the motel to find Mark's group standing in a huddle, annoyed looks on some of their faces.

"What's wrong with *y'all*?" Jason asked, confused.

"Yeah, why aren't you in your rooms?" Alex asked.

The others were distracted by the fact that Emily was there. "Emily, you made it," Sidra mused, hugging her. Parting from her embrace, the smile left Sidra's face as she pointed to Malajia. "You screwed us, Malajia."

Malajia was shocked. "What did *I* do?"

"This place is ass, yo," Mark spat. "It smells like a musty basement, there's hardly nobody in here and we're like an hour from an actual ski resort."

"What do you mean an hour?" Jason asked. "You mean this isn't *on* one?"

"Did you see any ski lifts on your way here?" Mark returned smartly, folding his arms.

Jason shook his head. He was so preoccupied with getting out of the car after driving over four hours, he hadn't paid attention.

Alex, who couldn't hold it any longer, took off in search of a bathroom as the others continued to gripe.

"Look, you guys are exaggerating," Malajia assumed. "It's probably not that bad."

"Do you *not* see this lobby?" Sidra barked, pointing to the surroundings.

Malajia scanned the area with her eyes. The outside looked kept enough to her, but she had to admit that the inside looked old, dark, and dismal. From the wood panel walls, the shag carpeting, and the dull lighting, to the furniture that was clearly in need of some reupholstering.

"There is a whole stuffed raccoon on the front desk," Sidra added. "This place is making me itch."

Malajia looked at Josh and David, who weren't saying anything. "What do *y'all* think?" she asked. "We know that Sidra is bougie and Mark complains about every-damn-thing."

Josh shrugged. "I mean, it's not the *best* looking place, but I'm not picky." Josh wasn't one to complain.

"Nobody cares what Josh has to say, this place is some bullshit," Mark barked, earning an eye roll from Josh. "And why did you pick a place so damn far from a freakin' resort?"

"Have y'all even *been* in the damn rooms yet?" Malajia asked, ignoring Mark. "Or have you been standing here bitchin' this whole time?" Judging by the looks on their faces, Malajia had her answer. "Come on, let's just see what they look like."

"I don't wanna," Sidra whined. As far as she was concerned, it didn't matter what the rooms looked like, she was already turned off by the lobby.

Alex returned from the lobby bathroom. "They actually have carpet on the bathroom floor," she chortled.

"Eww," Sidra complained, stomping her foot on the floor.

"Guys, that man behind the counter is staring at us, lets figure out what we're doing," Jason advised.

After retrieving their keys from the unenthused desk clerk, the gang hesitantly made their way to their rooms.

"Oh God," Sidra griped once she opened the door to her and Malajia's room. "This is so gross." She drew the words out slowly.

Malajia held a look of disgust on her face as she eyed the room. *I'm not fuckin' sleeping here*, she promised herself.

"Those covers look worn out, and that bathroom is just nasty," Sidra groused. "I don't even want the *wheels of my suitcase* touching this floor."

Malajia was embarrassed. Having been the one to book the rooms for everyone, she felt responsible, but didn't want Sidra to know that. "Look, it's not that bad," she lied.

Sidra shot her a venomous look. "Malajia, I will punch you in the fuckin' boob," she warned. Malajia successfully contained her laughter, holding a blank look on her face. "How does tissue get stuck to the damn light fixture, huh?" Sidra asked, pointing to the fixture in question.

Malajia glanced up. "I don't know how you want me to answer that," she replied, tone even, after a few seconds.

Sidra felt like she was about to snap, but her words were interrupted by a scream. Both she and Malajia ran out of the room to find Emily and Alex sprinting down the hall.

"What happened?" Sidra asked.

Alex had her hand on her chest, trying to catch her breath. "We just saw a huge flying bug in there," she informed, pointing in the rooms direction.

"To hell with this, I'm not sleeping here," Sidra promised.

The guys, who had been on the floor above them, emerged from the elevator. "You ladies okay? We heard a scream," David asked, bundling the collar of his coat to his neck.

"There's a mutant bug in our room," Alex jeered.

"I'll be at the car," Jason seethed, heading back for the elevator.

As the others followed suit, Malajia looked at Mark who was glaring at her. "What?" she frowned.

Mark put his hand up. "No words…Just *no* words," he fussed, walking off.

"We need to get our damn money back, and *you* need to make sure that happens," Sidra hurled at Malajia once the gang congregated out in the parking lot.

"I don't know if I can do that," Malajia replied, placing her gloves on her hand. "If we had *any* chance of a refund, we would have had to cancel like last night."

"I don't get why you would *pick* this place," Mark threw at her. "Who plans a ski trip at a place where there's no actual *skiing*?"

Malajia, tired of being scolded and picked on, frowned. "You know what, fuck y'all," she snapped.

"What was *that* for?" Alex asked, in disbelief of Malajia's outburst.

"'Cause, y'all snappin' at me and shit about booking this place and *none* of y'all bothered to look at the information that I gave you."

"You said that you stayed at this place before, so we trusted you," Sidra pointed out.

"Girl, I never been to this rural ass part of New York before," Malajia revealed. "You actually *believed* that shit?"

Jason frowned. "What was the point in lying about it?" he asked, voice full of agitation.

Malajia shook her hand in his direction. "That's irrelevant," she threw back. "Bottom line is that *nobody* questioned the fact that you only had to pay *two hundred* dollars apiece to spend a weekend in New York, as expensive as it is out here. So y'all just as stupid as *I* am right now."

The group stared at her in disbelief. "Un-fuckin-believable," Jason grumbled, running his hand over his head.

"Yep, it sure *is*," Malajia agreed, looking at her phone.

"So, does this mean the trip is over?" Emily sulked, pushing hair out of her face. *I can't believe I went through all of this just for this trip not to happen.*

"Looks like," David concluded, shoving his hands in his pockets.

"Damn that," Mark said, folding his arms and leaning against his car. "I'm driving to that rich resort we saw on the way over here and bumming in *somebody's* room this weekend."

"Boy, nobody is gonna let your black ass sleep in their room," Malajia mumbled.

Mark cut his eye at her. "You don't get to talk to me right now."

Malajia made a face as she continued to look at her phone.

"Malajia, find the room agreement so I can look at it," Sidra ordered. "There has to be a loophole in there somewhere that'll allow us to get our money back."

"Okay now, Miss future lawyer," Malajia mused, doing a dance.

"Just find the damn email!" Sidra yelled.

In searching for said email, Malajia came across one from a contact that she didn't recognize. She frowned as she read the email. "What the hell?"

"What?" Alex asked, peering over her shoulder.

Malajia put her hand up to stop any further questions as she continued to read. "Yo," she said, voice filled with shock. "We have rooms booked at the Pine Hill ski resort here in New York," she announced to the stunned group.

"Wait, what?" Jason questioned, unsure if he'd heard correctly.

"Yep," Malajia confirmed, showing the group her phone.

"How? *Why*?" Alex asked, confused.

"Does it *matter*?" Malajia drawled, losing her patience.

"Our weekend is still *on*."

"But *how* were we booked for these rooms though?" Sidra pressed. "*You* obviously didn't book them, with your non-planning butt."

Ignoring Sidra's snide comment, Malajia shrugged. "Hell if *I* know, I just know that some guy named Derrick P sent me an email from a Pine Hill email address and it has our names with reservations."

Unconvinced, Sidra took Malajia's phone and called the resort. "Looks like she's right," she informed after ending the call with a concierge.

"See, *told* you," Malajia smiled.

Sidra looked at the email date. "Mel, you got this email *days* ago," she pointed out, shoving the phone into Malajia's hand. Malajia was silent as she looked back at her phone. "You could've confirmed this and we would've had time to get our damn money back from this raggedy hell hole."

"Are we gonna keep standing around talking? Or are we gonna get in the car and go to the *good* resort before the raccoon from that desk comes and get us?" Mark cut in, tired of standing around.

With Mark's question, the group scurried back to the cars and pulled off.

Chapter 31

Chasity's leg bounced up and down in a nervous rhythm as she stared down at the menu in front of her. She'd been sitting at a table at one of Pine Hill resorts exclusive restaurants for nearly fifteen minutes.

Why the hell am I here? Why did I agree to this? she asked herself. She'd been asking herself the second question ever since she arrived at the resort earlier that morning with Trisha.

Looking at her watch, she let out a sigh and having a change of mind, stood from her seat.

"You can't leave yet, I just got here," she heard a male voice say, causing her to sit back down. Her eyes followed the older, dark haired, brown-skinned gentleman's progress as he walked around the table and took a seat across from her. "You look pretty," he smiled.

"Took you long enough," she hissed, ignoring the compliment.

The handsome man rubbed his chin, nodding slowly. "I apologize," he stated, voice sincere. "I got held up in a meeting."

"Sure you did," Chasity sneered, folding her arms on the table.

Signaling for a waiter, the man cleared his throat. "I hope you saved your appetite, the lobster dish is amazing here," he mused.

"I don't like lobster," Chasity spat, eyes fixed in an angry gaze. "I guess I shouldn't be surprised that you wouldn't know that. It's not like you know *anything* about me really."

The man sighed. "Chasity—"

"What's wrong? You don't like hearing that?...*Dad*." Chasity's hazel eyes bore through him like a laser.

Derrick Parker ran a hand over his short, neatly cut hair. He knew when he asked his estranged daughter to dinner, he would get attitude. He expected it. What he didn't expect was for her to agree to see him in the *first* place. "I'm sorry about the lobster thing," he apologized, putting his hand up. "Order whatever you want, it's all good here."

Chasity rolled her eyes as she sat back in her seat. "Whatever," she mumbled. "I'm not hungry."

"You're eating something *anyway*," he ordered. "I'll get you the shrimp pasta, I *do* remember that you like shrimp."

Chasity shrugged while staring at the expensive painting on the wall next to her, not bothering to respond.

After Derrick gave the waiter instructions, he turned back to Chasity, who looked unenthused. "So, how are you?"

"Fine," she threw back instantly.

"Your grades?"

"Fine."

He closed his eyes momentarily. *The girl still has that attitude*, he thought, rubbing the bridge of his nose with two fingers. "Are you actually going to participate in a conversation with me?"

"Why do I *have* to?"

"Because I want to know what's going on with you," he responded. "A father deserves to know what's going on in his child's life."

"*Father*?" Chasity scoffed.

"Look, I know that I haven't been around that much—"

"That's an *understatement,*" she bit out. "It was bad enough you barely paid attention to me when you were living at home full time, but then you started that back and forth mess, leaving me alone with *her.*"

Derrick looked down in shame. "I know."

"You *knew* how she treated me. You *knew* she hated me and you just—you ignored it, you ignored *me,*" Chasity recalled, voice filled with anger.

"I didn't mean to."

Chasity sucked her teeth. "Yeah okay," she hissed. "I bet you were real happy when you got this position out here…It gave you the excuse that you wanted, to just take off permanently."

"It's true, I *was* happy about the job," Derrick admitted. "I have always wanted to manage a hotel. And I admit that I *was* eager to leave. But that was because of Brenda, not *you.*"

"Dad, come on, don't start lying because I'm sitting in front of you," she bit back. "If that was true, then you would've tried to contact me. The *only* reason why I knew you worked here was because right after you left, I looked you up."

"I *wanted* to contact you, but I figured that you wouldn't want to talk to me," he replied, sadly. "I figured that there was too much damage in our relationship."

"We *have* no relationship," she corrected.

Derrick sighed as he leaned forward. "Chasity you have to know that while you were growing up, I tried to have a relationship with you, but…" he rubbed his face with his hands. "It was like Brenda was keeping me from doing so. Like she didn't want me to bond with you."

"What kind of crap is that to say to me?" Chasity threw back. "You think that's an excuse?"

"I didn't say that I was *proud* of it," he responded. "I know that growing up with your mother was hard for you and I'm sorry that I wasn't there for you when I *should've* been."

Chasity sat back in her seat and folded her arms. "Did you know that your joy of an ex-wife told me in front of the *entire* family that I was adopted?"

Derrick looked confused. "Wait, *what* did you say?"

"Yeah," she confirmed. "That was a nice thing to find out on Thanksgiving," she added, voice filled with sarcasm.

"Wait—Benda said that you were adop—adopted?"

Catching the look on Derrick's face, a look that mixed stunned and confused, Chasity narrowed her eyes at him. "That's what I just *said*," she reiterated, angry. "Why are you looking at me like that?"

Derrick squinted. "So…Brenda told you that she wasn't your mother?"

"Um, that's what *adopted* means," she returned sarcastically. "So apparently, you aren't my damn father, for real."

Derrick sat in stunned silence as he held his gaze on Chasity. His eyes glazed over briefly before he rubbed them. "Um…I'm sorry that you had to go through that." He paused momentarily. "She—she's not right in the head, and hasn't been for a long time."

Chasity rolled her eyes. *Yeah, no shit.*

Derrick pinched the bridge of his nose as he sat back in his seat. "Um, I'll call Brenda—I have to talk to her to see what her damn problem is," he stammered. "I haven't talked to her since the divorce was finalized."

Chasity shook her head as she watched Derrick. He seemed distracted, which in her opinion, was typical. "If you have somewhere to be, then go," she ground out, pushing her chair back from the table.

Derrick looked up at her. "Chasity—"

"No, it's cool, I'm over this anyway," she assured him, voice filled with angst. "I only agreed to see you because you did me a favor."

Derrick stood from his seat as Chasity stood from hers. "I'm sorry, I—"

Chasity rolled her eyes. As far as she was concerned, she didn't want or need to hear anything else that Derrick had to say. "Thanks for putting my friends up for the weekend," she mumbled, retrieving her purse from the arm of her chair. "Have a nice life."

Derrick watched with sadness as his only child walked out of the restaurant. Letting out a long sigh, he reached for his cell phone and dialed a number. He gritted his teeth as he waited for the answering machine message to cease. "Hey it's Derrick. You need to call me back ASAP."

"Now *this* is my kind of place," Sidra smiled, setting foot in the lobby of the lavish Pine Hill resort over an hour later. The lobby of the massive resort was like paradise compared to the worn down motel that they'd left. The décor was extravagant, from the marble concierge desks, the expensive paintings hanging on the walls, the crystal chandeliers hanging from the tall ceilings, to the plush cream chairs in the lounge. The marble fountain in the middle of the room added a calming effect, which seemed to be appreciated by the many guests that were navigating the space.

"Whoever Derrick P is, remind me to thank him," Alex said, voice filled with awe.

"Nobody finds it weird that this unknown person put us up in this place?" Jason asked, scratching his head. While he was grateful, he was still confused.

"Are you really complaining?" Mark scoffed, snapping his head around. "We in here free and shit."

Jason shot Mark a glare. "I'm not complaining, and you're entirely too hype in my face," he groused.

"Whatever yo, let's go get our rooms," Mark advised, paying Jason's aggravation no mind.

After checking in, the group huddled around, room key cards in hand. "Okay it looks like we have four rooms with double queen beds, so pick your roommate," Alex suggested.

"I call Sidra!" Malajia quickly announced.

Alex put her hand on her hip. "You don't have to be that loud," she scoffed.

"You mad 'cause I don't wanna be your roommate,"

Malajia mocked.

"Let's go get settled," Josh suggested, tired. "They said they'll bring our bags to the room, right?"

"Yep," Mark answered, rubbing his hands together. "Last one upstairs gotta tip the bag man," he blurted out before purposely bumping David as he took off running, causing David to stumble into a nearby bag cart.

"Oh *come* on!" David hollered, watching his friends run away laughing. "He plays too damn much," he seethed, straightening out his shirt.

Chasity flipped through the TV channels as she settled back on a lounge chair in her suite. "Ain't shit on this damn TV," she mumbled to herself, clicking the off button. She reached for her e-reader, and just as she was about to escape into the world of her latest book, the door opened.

"That heated pool is amazing," Trisha mused, plunking her bag down on the floor. "You should go down and get in."

"No, not really in the mood to swim in the winter," Chasity drawled sarcastically, eyes not leaving the tablet in her hand.

Trisha smirked. "The pool is *indoors*, smart ass," she chuckled, tightening the strap on her sarong.

"Still," Chasity shrugged, tone dry.

Trisha walked over to Chasity and stood next to her, arms folded. She stared at her, waiting.

Feeling eyes on her, Chasity looked up and frowned slightly. "Why are you staring at me?"

"Are you going to tell me how it went?" Trisha asked.

"Tell you how *what* went?" Chasity asked, confused.

"Dinner with your father."

Chasity's eyes widened. "How did—"

"He called me," Trisha revealed, sitting on the edge of an adjoining chair. "He actually called me after you spoke to him on Christmas."

Chasity looked away. She'd neglected to mention

anything to Trisha about meeting with her father, she just didn't feel like any pep talks.

"By the way, that was a nice thing that you did for your friends," Trisha smiled, giving Chasity's knee a pat. "Asking your father to get them rooms for the weekend. I'm sure they appreciate it."

They don't know that I asked him and that's how I want it. "Uh huh," Chasity replied.

"So?" Trisha pressed. "How was it, meeting with him after all this time?"

"I really don't want to get into it."

"*Can* you?" Trisha pleaded. "I know it took a lot for you to do that. And…I just want you to talk about it with me."

Chasity pondered whether to hold her feelings in or not, but seeing the hopeful eyes of her aunt, made her decide on the latter. "It *went*," she put out, sitting her e-reader on the small wood table next to her. "It was weird."

Trisha shot her a sympathetic look. "I'm sure it *was*," she replied. "But I know that he was grateful that you went."

"He might've reneged on his favor to me if I *hadn't*," Chasity griped.

"No, I don't think that he *would've*," Trisha replied. "He would've done that for you *anyway*, he just wanted to see you."

"It's crazy 'cause, I was talking to him about Brenda and about how she told me that I was adopted and he got all weird after that," Chasity recalled.

Trisha felt her stomach drop, but held a blank look on her face. "*Did* he?" she asked. "Did he um, have anything to say about it?"

"No," Chasity fussed. "He just stared at me all crazy. Then he kept saying that he needed to talk to Brenda. Like, why would I give a shit if he needs to talk to her?"

Trisha ran a hand over the back of her damp neck. "Um, I'm sorry," she sputtered.

"What are *you* sorry for?"

"That you had to go through that," Trisha clarified.

"Listen, I know you don't want to hear this, but despite everything, your father loves—"

"You're right, I *don't* want to hear that," Chasity abruptly put out. Trisha looked down at her hands. "Let's just drop it."

Trisha nodded slowly. "Um, okay," she agreed. She was secretly grateful that Chasity ended their conversation about it. She needed time to gather all of her thoughts. "So…what *else* has been going on with you?" she asked, changing the subject. "Now that we're on good terms again, I have a feeling that I missed out on some stuff."

Chasity's eyes shifted. "No, there's nothing going on," she lied.

Trisha sat back and folded her arms. Eyes fixed on Chasity with a skeptical look. "You're not good at lying you know," she said.

"Sure I am," Chasity joked.

"Not to *me* you're not," Trisha threw back. "Come on, something's up, I can tell. You might as well spill it."

Chasity tried to think of something to say, some lie to tell to satisfy Trisha's need for an update on her life. But as she thought, and as Trisha stared at her in anticipation, she realized that her secret was something that she could no longer keep from the one person that she used to tell everything to.

"Um…I'm not a virgin anymore," Chasity hesitantly put out, unsure of what Trisha's reaction would be.

Trisha's eyes and mouth opened wide. "Say *what* now?" she asked, unsure if she heard correctly.

"You know you heard me," Chasity replied.

Trisha put her hand over her heart as she took a deep breath. At nineteen, Trisha knew Chasity wasn't a child and that sex for her would eventually happen, but to hear her actually say it almost knocked the wind out of her. "Was it Jason?" she asked after getting her thoughts in order.

"Yeah," Chasity nodded.

"Oh," Trisha breathed. "I mean, I know I made jokes

about it happening and I know that you two were close but…oh."

"Are you disappointed?" Chasity asked, sensing Trisha's struggle to grasp what she had just told her.

"No, sweetie, I'm not disappointed," Trisha promised. "I'm just a little shocked, that's all," she admitted. "You never told me that you two were in a relationship."

"That's because we're *not*," Chasity said.

Trisha frowned. "Really?" she asked. "Why not? I would think that if—"

"It just *happened* and—" Chasity ran her hand through her hair. "I think—no, I *know* that Jason thought that afterwards we would be in a relationship but—"

"*You* didn't want one," Trisha concluded.

Chasity looked away momentarily. "Honestly, I don't know *what* I want really," she admitted. "I mean, I know what I feel, but just can't—It's complicated…*I'm* complicated."

Trisha stood up and moved to sit on the arm of Chasity's chair. She put her arms around her troubled niece and leaned her head on her hair. "You're not complicated," she assured. "You just have a hard time getting a grip on your feelings. I know that Brenda and Derrick didn't really encourage you to express them when you were growing up, so now…you run from them."

Chasity just stared out ahead of her as she listened to Trisha's words.

"Also sex can confuse things. Especially if you were already confused about your feelings beforehand," Trisha added. "Did you use protection?"

"Yes," Chasity answered.

"Good." Trisha breathed a sigh of relief. "The last thing you need is to be confused *and* pregnant." She gave Chasity's arm a rub. "Sweetie, if you know how you feel, then you need to talk to Jason. I'm sure *he's* confused too."

"I can't do that."

"Yes you *can*," Trisha insisted, voice stern. "What, do

you think you're going to scare him away?"

That's exactly what I think. "I don't know," Chasity answered.

"Look, I can tell that he really cares for you," Trisha said. "And if he didn't run after *first meeting* your evil behind, trust me when I say, he's not going anywhere," she teased.

Chasity managed a smirk. She felt a little better, she realized that talking to Trisha usually made her feel that way. It was like the woman knew her better than anyone. "Okay, your bathing suit is getting my shirt wet," she joked. Despite her aunt's comfort, Chasity had had enough of the pep talk.

Trisha stood up and gave Chasity's arm a tap. "Smart ass," she laughed.

Chapter 32

"Another club soda please," Jason asked the smiling male bartender. Jason waited as his order was fulfilled. Having unpacked nearly a half-hour prior and needing a little bit of quiet time away from his roommate Mark, Jason took a much needed walk around the resort before settling at a small bar.

"Thanks man," Jason replied, before taking a sip. As he sat the glass back down, he felt a tap on his shoulder. Turning around in his seat, he nodded. "What's up, Mel?"

"Sidra's getting on my last damn nerves, so I needed to get out of the room," Malajia chortled, taking the seat next to him.

"Going anywhere in particular?" he asked, taking another sip.

Malajia shook her head as she adjusted the hoop earring in her ear. "Nah, I was just gonna wander around to see if I can find any rich men who won't mind spoiling a young chick," she joked.

Jason shook his head in amusement. "So silly."

Malajia giggled. "Anyway, I saw you over here…You

treatin' for drinks?"

He smiled. "Sure, why not?" he agreed. "Knock yourself out with a soda."

Malajia turned her lip up. "Soda?" she scoffed. "Man, I'm talkin' 'bout a *real* drink. Some liquor."

"Malajia, that's never gonna happen, they'll card you," Jason pointed out, tone even. "And you'll be thrown out."

"Honey, with this makeup, this hair, these boobs and these tight ass jeans I got on, they ain't carding *shit*." Malajia was confident as she spun around in her seat. "Watch me work."

Jason sat in anticipation of the show that Malajia was about to put on.

Malajia signaled for the bartender, who smiled brightly as he leaned over the counter. "I'll take a vodka and cranberry please," she crooned.

"Sure thing," the man replied.

Malajia glanced at Jason and winked. Jason took a sip of his soda and watched.

"Can I see some ID?" the man asked.

Jason nearly spit out his soda as he tried to hold in his laughter at the stunned look on Malajia's face.

"Huh?" Malajia stammered, eyes wide.

"Can I see some ID?" the bartender repeated. "Hotel policy."

Malajia huffed as she puffed out her chest. "Look here...*Travis*," she spat, eyeing his name tag. "Do I *look* underage to you?"

Jason shook his head. "Yeah, go ahead and piss him off."

Malajia's eyes shifted as the bartender held a stern gaze on her. "I mean—look—shut up *Jason*," she snarled when Jason started laughing.

"That soda sounding pretty good right about now, huh?" Jason teased.

Malajia folded her arms and sat back in her seat, defeated. "A ginger ale, please," she mumbled.

"Right away," the bartender chuckled. "Nice try, by the way."

"Yeah, yeah," Malajia grumbled. "And put that on the rocks."

"You couldn't just say 'ice'?" Jason mocked.

"Mind your business," Malajia sneered.

"I can't get over how nice this place is," Sidra mused to Josh, walking alongside him.

"Yeah," Josh agreed as he kept in stride. Feeling hunger pangs, the two of them decided to take an excursion in search of a restaurant.

"I have no idea where I want to eat," Sidra said, looking around at the court full of restaurants. "There's so many choices."

"What do you have a taste for?" Josh asked, glancing at her.

Sidra looked at the ceiling. "I have no idea," she laughed.

Josh shook his head. "Not surprised," he commented, earning a playful backhand on his arm. "I'll be right back."

"Where are you going?" Sidra frowned, following his progress.

"To find a bathroom," he replied, continuing his pace.

Sidra folded her arms as she let out a sigh. She waited for another minute before her stomach started making sounds. "Ugh, I can't wait, I need a cookie or something," she said to herself, turning to walk in the other direction.

Just as Sidra spun around, she collided with someone. She let out a scream as the guy reached out and held both of her arms to steady her.

"I'm so sorry," he apologized. "Are you okay?"

Sidra, feeling like the wind had been knocked out of her, put her finger up. "Just…give me a second," she sputtered. When she finally composed herself, she smoothed her sweater down and flung her ponytail over her shoulder. "I'm fine," she said as she locked eyes with the culprit.

He smiled as she stared at him, her eyes were practically bulging. "You have beautiful eyes," he said of Sidra's grey eyes.

Sidra blushed, looking at the floor momentarily. *God, he's so handsome*, she thought, glancing back up at him. Her eyes took in his tall frame, his smooth dark complexion, his short cut hair; black as coal. *And he can dress too*, she thought of his black business suit and shoes.

"Thank you," she returned finally.

He put his hand up. "Again, I'm sorry for the collision," he said. "I should've been looking where I was going. Too busy on this phone," he added, gesturing to the black phone in his hand.

"It's okay, I'll live," she assured him with a wave of her delicate hand.

He put his hand on his chest and let out a huge sigh. "That's good to know," he teased. He found himself staring at Sidra; he found her beautiful. "What's your name, if you don't mind me asking?"

I don't mind you doing any-damn-thing, she thought then frowned slightly, shocked at her own inner thoughts. "Um, it's Sidra," she revealed, holding her hand out. "Sidra Howard."

The man gently grabbed her hand and held it. "Miss Sidra, I'm James, James Grant."

Josh, making his way back from the bathroom, stopped when he saw a random guy holding Sidra's hand. He frowned. *Who the hell is that dude, and why is he touching her?* Protection mode kicked in as he hurried over.

"Everything okay over here?" he asked Sidra once next to her.

Sidra snapped out of her daze. "Huh?" she said, focusing. "Oh, yeah Josh, I'm fine," she assured him.

Josh stood there, waiting to see if Sidra was going to explain who this clearly older man was. "Ummm, so…who are *you*?" he asked, when Sidra failed to explain.

James looked over at Josh, eyebrow raised. The tension between the two men could be felt immediately. A smile broke across his face after a moment. "I'm James," he introduced, extending his hand.

Josh briefly glanced down at it before shaking it. "Josh," he returned, tone dry.

"I'm sorry, I bumped into your girlfriend and—"

"Oh, Josh isn't my boyfriend," Sidra quickly put out, much to Josh's annoyance. "He's my best friend."

Josh resisted the urge to roll his eyes at the title. She had no idea that her words had cut him like a knife. *Ouch,* he thought. *I hope to change that in the future, though.*

James on the other hand, seemed delighted with Sidra's response.

Sidra glanced at Josh, then back at James. "James, I wish I could stay, but I have to get going," she said, tone not hiding her disappointment.

James, quickly reached into his jacket pocket and pulled out a business card. "Please take my card," he offered, handing it to her. "I'd love to talk to you again…or even see you."

Sidra glanced at the card and smiled brightly. "You're a lawyer?" she asked, noticing the title.

Josh rolled his eyes. "Sid, we really gotta go," he urged. *The sooner I get you away from this suit, the better.*

"Yes, I *am*," James confirmed, ignoring Josh. "I work at a law firm in DC. I'm here in New York for the weekend to work with one of my clients."

Sidra was clearly impressed; wanting to be a lawyer herself, this was an added bonus. "I'm here for the weekend *too*, with my friends," she cooed. "We're on break from school so—"

Josh loudly cleared his throat.

Sidra successfully contained her irritation. *Damn it*

Joshua! "Yeah, I really need to go." She reached for a pen in her purse. Josh and James watched as she wrote her number on the back of James's business card and handed it back to him.

Acknowledging the invitation to call her, James nodded before saying his goodbyes and walking off.

Josh folded his arms and glared at the side of Sidra's head as she followed James's progress through the crowded floor. "Are we gonna go eat, or are you gonna stare some more?" he hissed.

Sidra's head snapped around. "I *wasn't* staring," she lied.

"Yeah, sure," Josh threw back, toned filled with sarcasm. As far as he was concerned, if he never saw James again, that would be perfectly fine with him.

Malajia, used her phone to take several pictures of the hotel décor as she sauntered through the lobby floor. "I just wanna live here," she mused to herself, snapping a picture of herself in front of a painting on a wall.

After hanging out with Jason for nearly an hour, they parted ways, with Jason going in search of something to eat, and Malajia left to wander around. Intent on checking out more amenities of the hotel, Malajia made her way to the front desk.

"Hey, can you tell me where the pool and hot tubs are?" Malajia asked the desk clerk.

The young woman looked up from her computer. "Sure, I can," she beamed. Just as she was about to provide directions, an older gentleman approached behind the desk and whispered something to her. Nodding, the young woman asked Malajia to give her a moment and headed away.

Malajia stared at the man who was now in front of her. *He's so damn sexy with his old ass*, she thought, twirling some hair around her finger.

"I apologize for the interruption," he said, looking at her. "How can I help you?"

Malajia took in the man's smile, his handsome face, his brown skin, his hazel eyes, and his neat suit. She could tell that he was much older than her, maybe by twenty years give or take. *You can take my number down and call me.* "Um— yeah, can you tell me where the pool and hot tubs are?"

"Sure, there are some on every floor, what floor are you staying on?"

Malajia was so preoccupied by this man's eyes that her mind drew a blank. "Uh…" she gave a nervous laugh. "I don't remember at the moment."

The man chuckled at the young woman before him. "No problem, I'll look it up," he assured, typing on the computer screen in front of him. "What's your name?"

"Malajia Simmons," she blurted out instantaneously.

The man looked up at her. "Did you say Malajia Simmons?" he asked.

Malajia shot him a skeptical look. "Yes," she drew the word out slowly. *Shit, what did I do?* she panicked.

"Oh, no need to be alarmed," he said, sensing her hesitation. "I just realized that you're one of my daughters' friends," he said.

Malajia frowned in confusion, she'd never seen this man before in her life, and for the most part she knew the majority of her friends' parents. "You might have me confused," she laughed.

He looked up once again and shook his head. "No, I don't think so," he insisted. "You're part of a group that checked in earlier right?"

Malajia held the same confused look on her face as the man ran down the names of the rest of her friends. "Wait, how do you know—"

The man extended his hand. "*I'm* Derrick P," he revealed. "As in *Parker.*"

Coming to a realization, Malajia's mouth fell open. "Wait a minute." She put her hand up as she tried to compose her thoughts. "*Who's* your daughter?"

Chasity, having just put the top back on the tray of leftover room service, reached for her glass of juice and took a sip. Pushing the tray table aside, she looked over at Trisha, who just emerged from the adjoining room.

"Are you sure you don't want to come to the restaurant with me?" Trisha asked, retrieving her purse from a chair.

"No, I just ate," Chasity said, pointing to the tray.

Trisha shrugged, obviously disappointed. "Well, okay," she said. "I'll probably hit up a few shops when I'm finished. You want me to pick up anything for you?"

Chasity shook her head. "Nope."

Trisha walked over and gave Chasity a kiss on the cheek. "See you later, and behave yourself."

"I'll try," Chasity joked. Once Trisha left, Chasity rose from her seat and headed for the adjoining bedroom, intending on taking a nap. She spun around when she heard a knock at the door. "Did you leave your room key?" she chortled, heading over and opening the door. The amusement on her face changed to shock once she saw who was on the other side. "Shit," she griped.

"Surprised, huh?" Malajia returned, pushing past Chasity to enter the suite. "Imagine how *I* felt, finding out that *you* were here."

Chasity rolled her eyes, and shut the door while Malajia continued to talk.

"I feel some kind of way, why didn't—" Malajia cut her words short as she glanced around the massive one bedroom suite. "Damn this room is nice," she commented.

"How did you find out I was here?" Chasity asked, folding her arms.

Malajia looked at her. "Your *father* told me," she sneered, folding her arms in return.

Chasity's eyes widened. "Who?"

Malajia sucked her teeth. "Don't play stupid," she spat,

approaching. "Mr. Derrick P? As in *Parker*?"

Chasity rubbed her forehead. "Shit," she mumbled.

"And by the way, your dad is fine, girl," Malajia cooed.

Chasity frowned in disgust. "Eww," she scoffed.

"Since he's technically not your real father, can I get his number?" Malajia joked.

Chasity's eyes became slits. "Don't make me punch you," she warned.

Malajia giggled as she unfolded her arms. "I know what you did for us," she said, voice sincere.

"He told you?"

"He did," Malajia confirmed with a nod.

Chasity shook her head. "I told him not to," she griped. Chasity wasn't one for doing things for recognition or praise.

"Why do you want to *hide* it?" Malajia asked, perplexed. "You did something amazing for your friends and trust me when I say, we appreciate it, because that place that we booked was some bullshit."

"Yes, I know," Chasity replied, voice filled with laughter. "*Clearly* none of you did your research."

"Girl, who you tellin'?" Malajia agreed with a wave of her hand. "They was cussing my ass *all* the way out."

Chasity shook her head.

"So, you turned *us* down for a ski trip, but you ended up here *anyway*, huh?"

"It was a Christmas present from Trisha," Chasity explained. "I *had* to come."

Malajia tossed her arms in the air. "Well, now that we're all here in the same place, you might as well come on down and hang with us," she insisted.

"No," Chasity shot down.

Malajia let out a groan. "Why *not*?" she barked. "Come *on*, you know you *want* to. Stop being anti-social."

Chasity rolled her eyes. "Malajia, I just... I just don't want to."

Malajia ran her hand over her hair as she sighed. *Time to get sentimental on this heifer*. "Look Chaz, I know we've said this before but…we miss you," she said, tone caring. "I know you think that you not being around doesn't mean much to anybody, but it *does*." Malajia sighed. "Truth is…this trip just isn't the same without you. *We're* not the same without you."

Chasity just stared at Malajia as she continued to speak, expression blank.

Malajia studied her friends' face, trying to find a trace of any emotion, but she got none. Nevertheless, she wasn't about to give up. "I know that you're in your feelings right now, but…you can't continue to penalize *us* for that," she pointed out. "Jason finally realized that, and now *you* need to."

Chasity looked away momentarily. "I know," she answered finally.

Malajia shot her a stunned look. "Wait, you actually *agree* with me?" she asked in disbelief.

"*Shocking* isn't it," Chasity joked. She'd been feeling guilty for freezing out the group over her issues with Jason. But her pride wouldn't let her admit that…until now.

"Hell *yeah*, it is," Malajia laughed. "With your stubborn ass." Feeling the tension ease, Malajia walked over to Chasity with her arms out. "Come on, give me some love Satan."

Chasity put her hand out. "No, it's cool. No need for all that."

Malajia smacked her hand down. "Shut up, shut up," she said, wrapping her arms around a reluctant Chasity, who after a brief moment, hugged her back. "Okay, get off me."

"I knew that wouldn't last too long," Malajia teased. "Now come on bitch, let's go see the other girls," she insisted, gesturing toward the door.

"Fine," Chasity sighed, reaching for the doorknob.

"You might as well smile, 'cause they gonna be hype to see you," Malajia advised, noticing the taut look on Chasity's face.

"Yeah whatever," Chasity sneered.

Malajia stopped suddenly. "Wait, is that the mini bar?" she asked, pointing to a dark wood shelf filled with small bottles. Chasity nodded as she shot Malajia a skeptical look. Ignoring Chasity's look, Malajia walked over to the bar and grabbed five mini bottles of liquor from it.

"Malajia!" Chasity called out.

Malajia looked up, innocence on her face. "What?"

"Don't go fuckin' overboard."

Malajia sucked her teeth. "All right, fine," she huffed, putting one of the bottles back in place. "Alex don't get none," she said, stuffing the bottles in her purse, before walking out the door, leaving a disgusted Chasity to trail behind.

Sidra sat on her bed. Recalling her chance meeting with James earlier that day, she smiled. She couldn't get his face, his body, or the sound of his smooth baritone voice out of her head. After having lunch with Josh earlier, Sidra retreated to the room to daydream. *Damn, I should've kept his card*, she thought. Then quickly dismissed it. *No, then I would be tempted to call him like, now.* The door opening stirred Sidra out of her thoughts.

"Girl, that nap was everything," Alex mused, walking in with Emily following close behind. "I can't believe I was *that* tired."

"Yeah, well we had a long day," Sidra replied, rubbing her arm.

Alex shrugged as she flopped down on Malajia's bed.

Sidra looked at Emily. "Em, did you check in with your mother?" she asked.

That question took Emily back. "Um…no."

"Not trying to get in your business, but you may *want* to," Sidra insisted. "You remember what happened when you didn't contact your mom during spring break…she went looking for you."

Emily put her hand on her chin. *Good point.* "I'll call her tomorrow," she promised. The last thing she wanted to deal with on her first day in New York was a conversation with her smothering mother.

"Ooh, I met someone today," Sidra gushed, unable to hold it in any longer.

Alex leaned forward in anticipation. "Yeah?"

Sidra nodded. "Yes, his name is James and—" hearing the door open, she rolled her eyes. The interruption annoyed her, she was about to burst.

"I knew I heard Alex's mouth," Malajia joked, walking in.

Alex sucked her teeth. "I wasn't even loud," she returned, perplexed.

Malajia flagged Alex with her hand. "Guess who *I* found?" she vaguely announced, much to the confusion of the other girls.

"What? The rest of your shirt?" Sidra jeered, pointing to Malajia's breasts that were *very* noticeable, thanks to her push-up bra and low cut top.

Malajia made a face at her. "No, but I found the horse you got your ponytail from," she bit back.

Sidra narrowed her eyes, but resisted the urge to say anything. There was no need in defending her hair. Everyone knew it was real.

"Anyway," Malajia began, changing the subject. "Come in here, Lucifer," she called out the door.

The three girls' eyes brightened as Chasity walked through the door. "Chasity!" Sidra squealed, darting over to give her a hug.

Alex's smile was ear to ear. "What are you doing here?" she wondered, embracing Chasity once Sidra let go. "I thought you didn't want to come."

Chasity couldn't respond initially; all of her focus was on Emily. "How the hell did *you* get to come here?" she asked, shocked.

Emily giggled as she walked over and gave Chasity a hug. "I can thank my dad for that."

"I hear *that*," Malajia beamed, happy to have all the girls in one room again. "Dads are just coming through all around, isn't that right Chaz?"

Chasity cut her eye at her. "Malajia, don't," she spat.

"Wait, what's going on?" Alex asked, putting her hand up.

"Derrick P is Chasity's dad," Malajia revealed, ignoring Chasity's protest. "She asked him to give us these rooms."

Chasity rolled her eyes. "You talk way too much," she hurled at Malajia.

"Oh get over it, these heifers need to know what you did for them," Malajia returned. "Just shut up and bask in the gratitude."

Chasity's eyes met the three girls standing before her. They were filled with shock and most of all, appreciation. Sidra threw her arms out. "Awww, I knew you loved us, thank yoooouuu," she gushed, moving in for another hug.

"Oh God, no, I've had enough hugs for one fuckin' day," Chasity protested, backing away.

"Just let it happen, just let it happen," Sidra teased, embracing the unenthused Chasity anyway.

"Thank you Chaz," Alex smiled. "I keep saying that you're more—"

"Alex, don't start with your mushy mess," Malajia intervened, with a wave of her hand, once she noticed the uncomfortable look on Chasity's face. "You ruining the moment and shit."

Alex placed her hands on her hips. "How is being gracious—"

"'Cause it just *is*, okay," Malajia snapped.

Alex shook her head. "You got issues," she directed at Malajia, pointing. "You need prayer."

Malajia smirked.

Chapter 33

"Yo, if *one* more person steps on my damn boots, I'm smackin' em," Mark groused, wiping his new boots off with his hand.

"You ain't gonna do shit," Jason laughed, signing the papers for his rental ski equipment. Saturday morning brought the guys out early to take advantage of the fresh snow on the slopes. But first, they needed equipment.

"I wonder when the girls are gonna come down," David wondered, eyeing a key chain on a small rack.

"They're probably still sleeping," Josh put out, pulling his knit cap down on his head. "We had a long night."

Mark laughed. "They got their asses busted in spades," he bragged. Turning to Jason, he gave his arm a light backhand. "Why didn't *you* play last night?"

Jason rubbed the back of his neck. "Man, I was tired."

Mark twisted his lip up. "Nah, I think you were scared to see Chaz and shit," he mocked. He remembered the stunned look on Jason's face when he told him, before heading back to the girls' room the previous evening that Chasity was at the resort and what she did.

Jason shot Mark a glare. "Shut your loud, wrong ass up," he snapped, snatching his receipt off the counter. "Like I said, I was tired."

Jason didn't want to admit it, but Mark was right about him being nervous to see Chasity. He didn't know what she would say, what he himself would say. He figured he would sleep and wake up with fresh thoughts on how to approach her.

"Whatever yo," Mark ground out, putting sunglasses on his face. "Let's get out there so I can show my skills in front of some of these fine ass women."

As Mark walked out the rental shop with the three guys trailing behind him, he heard groans. "What's all the non-verbal commentary for?" he hissed, spinning around.

"That question made no sense," Jason put out, tone even.

"You know what I meant," Mark barked, pointing.

"Why are you so mad?" Josh chuckled.

"'Cause, y'all always talkin' shit," Mark grunted, kicking some of the fresh white snow with his foot. "*Especially* David."

David looked confused. "I didn't even say anything!" he exclaimed. "Don't start with me today, bro."

Mark was about to fire off a remark, but a tall, slim figure walked pass him, catching his eye. "Hey sweetheart," he crooned, tilting his glasses.

The girl, who was walking with some friends, turned around and flashed a smile.

"Hey now, why don't you come over here and let me show you how to ski," he proposed, tone lowered as he licked his lips.

Mark's antics were amusing to the guys, who just tried to hold in their laughs.

The girl shook her head. "I already know how to ski," she informed. "My boyfriend taught me."

Mark's smile faded as he pushed his glasses back up on his nose. "Oh a'ight," he dismissed as the girl continued on her way. He slowly turned around to face his friends who were snickering before breaking out in laughter. "Oh that's funny?" he griped.

"Absolutely," Josh teased. "That's what you get for always trying to play Mr. Smooth."

Mark rolled his eyes. "Shut up," he grunted. He turned to David who was still laughing. "You laughin' kinda hard over there Dave."

Mark's attitude only made the situation funnier for David. "That was hilarious," he concluded.

Mark folded his arms. "At least I'm out here *trying* to get a girl," Mark spat out. "Jase, you acting all depressed and shit. And Josh, your face is stuck so far up Sidra's ass that you missin' all the opportunities."

"Unlike *you*, I'm not out here looking for some random girl to bang," Jason threw back, unfazed by Mark's irritation with him.

"And my face isn't—"

"Yes the fuck it *is, Joshua*," Mark snapped, cutting off Josh's protest. Josh flagged him with his hand. "And *you*," he began, pointing at David. "You *need* to be out here lookin'."

David folded his arms. "And why is *that,* oh smart one?" he mocked.

Mark smirked. "I'm sure you're pretty tired of jerkin' off to that eye chart in your room," he jeered. Josh put his hand over his mouth to keep from laughing at Mark's ignorance. David, wasn't amused, and it showed in his face as his jaw tightened. "He be having his glasses on his shlong and shit."

"Something is seriously wrong with you," Jason concluded, shaking his head. Mark certainly knew how to push David's buttons; if it had been *him*, he would've punched Mark a long time ago.

Mark laughed as David stood there seething. "He be all into it, lookin' at that chart moaning and shit, talkin' 'bout, big E, big Eeeeee."

Having reached his limit with Mark's stupidity, David

grabbed some snow off the ground and threw it at him. Mark's laughter abruptly ended as he felt the cold snow hit his face. Fuming, he bent down to retrieve some snow. Before he could stand up, David ran and tackled him to the ground.

"Seriously guys?!" Josh wailed, watching his friends tussle on the ground.

"David chill!" Mark yelled, smashing a handful of snow on David's head.

"I'm tired of your mess," David seethed, trying to push Mark's head down in the snow.

"Y'all chill," Jason barked as he and Josh moved to break the two up.

Chasity moved some hair from her face with one hand, while holding a cup of hot chocolate with the other. "I don't know why I agreed to come out here. I hate the cold," she griped.

"As soon as we hit those slopes, we'll warm up," Alex mused as she, along with Malajia, Chasity, and Sidra walked along the path towards the ski rental place. Alex was excited; she couldn't wait to try her hand at skiing.

"I can't stay that long, I promised Trisha I would go shopping with her," Chasity informed.

Malajia looked over at her. "Ooh, can I come?" she asked, voice full of hope.

"No," Chasity immediately put out. Malajia sucked her teeth.

"How are you just gonna ditch us?" Sidra asked with amusement, smoothing some hair up into her bun. "You're so rude."

"Shit Chaz, I don't blame you," Malajia put in before Chasity could respond. "For a shopping trip, *I'd* ditch y'all asses too."

Whatever the other girls were about to say next was

halted as they laid eyes on the commotion several feet in front of them.

"What's going on over there by the rental place?" Alex asked, craning her neck. Two guys were wrestling in the snow, while two others were trying to break them up.

"Somebody's fighting, it looks like," Sidra replied as the girls moved closer. Seeing who the culprits were, the girls were shocked. "What the hell?" Sidra shrieked, spotting Mark and David on the ground. "Are you two fighting?"

"Of course *your* dumbass would be involved." Malajia gestured to Mark. "You probably started it."

"He *did*, as always," Josh confirmed, helping a snow-covered David off the ground.

"He's lucky I didn't bury his annoying ass in that snow," David seethed, brushing himself off.

"You wasn't gonna do *shit*, witcho weak ass," Mark taunted.

David tried to jerk his arm out of Josh's grip. "Get off me, Josh!" he raged.

"You guys are so damn embarrassing," Sidra fussed, placing her hands on her hips. "You know better than this."

While the bickering continued around them, Jason and Chasity managed to lock eyes with one another from where they stood, several feet apart. It was the first time in a while that they were able to even look at one another. Jason, taking in her beauty and remembering the night that they shared before things got crazy, smiled at her. Chasity remembered the same thing, smiling back briefly before shyly glancing down at the ground.

Chasity heard Alex call her. She tried to ignore her, but couldn't drown out Alex's loud voice.

"Chasity!" Alex yelled.

"What!" Chasity snapped, turning to face her.

"Your phone is ringing," Alex pointed out.

Looking in her purse, Chasity pulled the phone out and put it to her ear.

"How did you not hear that?" Alex asked as Chasity walked away. "That ringtone is loud."

Chasity flagged Alex with her hand as she moved to find a quiet spot away from the arguing, Jason followed Chasity with his eyes. He wanted more than anything to go over and talk to her.

"Jase!" Mark's loud voice interrupted Jason's musings.

"What?" Jason snapped, angry for the interruption.

"David over here lyin' talkin' about he had me in a headlock," Mark rambled, full of animation. "Tell them you ain't see that shit."

Aggravation was clear on Jason's face as he stared at Mark. *He made me look away from her for this?* "Dawg, leave me out of y'all bullshit," he hissed.

Mark flashed a frown back. "What's *your* attitude for?"

Jason halted his retort when he saw Chasity approach the group. Mark's nonsense was the last thing on his mind right now.

"Guys, I gotta go," Chasity announced to them. "I'll be back later." She then directed her attention to Mark and David. "You two stop acting like you're fuckin' twelve before I have Derrick kick you out," she bit out before walking away, leaving the two guys looking like they had just been scolded by their mother.

"Chaz, hold on a sec," Jason called after her. Chasity stopped walking and turned around as he approached her.

"Yeah?" she replied, staring up at him.

Jason looked like he was nervous. "I um—I wanted to know if…."

"I gotta go, okay?" she put out, sensing his hesitation. Jason nodded, relegated once again to watching her walk away.

Sidra shook her head as the commotion died down. "You guys have succeeded in pissing me *all* the way off, right now," she ranted. She hated when the guys acted juvenile, especially in public.

"Everything's good now Sid," Josh assured her. "We can

still salvage what's left of this morning and go skiing."

"I don't want to go anywhere but back to the lounge right now," Sidra returned.

Josh sighed. Sidra getting worked into a bad mood wasn't anything new. "Well, how about we just—"

"James," Sidra breathed, noticing him approaching the rental place.

Josh tossed his hands in the air, agitated. *Oh come on! Not this damn guy again.*

"Who the fuck is *James*?" Mark mumbled in a quiet aside to Josh and David.

"Nobody," Josh grumbled, sticking his hands into his coat pockets. He stood there with a scowl plastered to his face, watching Sidra talk to him. He didn't know the man, but he despised him.

Malajia, on the other hand, was glad to see the man that Sidra gushed about the night before. *Okay Sidra, he's a sexy thing,* she mused.

"I'm glad I saw you," James smiled. "I was going to call you later tonight, but since we're here, would you like to go have lunch with me?"

Sidra's heart jumped. "Um…" she glanced over at Malajia and Alex who were staring at her, smiling.

"Girl you better *go*," Malajia urged.

Sidra giggled as she faced James. "Um…sure that'll be nice," she shyly accepted.

Josh, having heard the proposal and acceptance, cleared his throat. "Uh, Sid, I thought you were going back to the lounge," he reminded her.

"I changed my mind," Sidra threw back, unaware of what Josh was feeling.

Delighted, James extended his arm for Sidra to grab hold of and the pair walked away.

"Look at that," Malajia said. "The ponytail done came out here and found herself a man." She smoothed some hair out of her face as she looked at the others. "Okay, so what are *we* about to do? It's cold as shit and we're just standing around."

"You guys still wanna ski?" David asked, now fully calm.

Jason shook his head. "No, I'll catch you guys later," he said. He was much too preoccupied to hang out any longer. "I'm heading back to the hotel."

"Hold up Jase, I'll walk with you," Alex said, following him.

Mark sucked his teeth. "They dry yo," he griped. "Come on y'all, let's go snow tubing."

"Nobody feels like that right now," Josh protested. His mood was now just as shot as Jason's.

Mark shot Josh a glance. "Oh, now *you* got an attitude," he mocked.

"Leave me alone Mark," Josh growled, folding his arms

Mark smirked, knowing full well where Josh's change in attitude came from. "You mad as shit Sidra is smitten with him," he teased.

Malajia tossed her hand in the air. "Oh God, boy don't start your shit again," she griped. *Damn, we just got David calm and now he's about to start with Josh.*

Josh glared at him. "You don't even know what 'smitten' *means*," he shot back.

"I do *so* know what *smitten* means and Sidra is *it* with *James*," Mark teased.

Josh put his hand up as he turned away. "Mark man, drop it," he warned.

"Smitten," Mark taunted. Josh's jaw clenched in anger, giving Mark the fuel he needed. "Smitten...smitten...smiiiittttteeeennnn."

"You know what—" Josh erupted, reaching for Mark's collar. Malajia quickly stepped in between Josh and a laughing Mark.

David grabbed Josh's arm and pulled him away. "Come on Josh, walk it off," he urged.

Once the two were out of earshot, Malajia turned around and smacked Mark on the back of his head. "You play too damn much," she scolded. Mark just sucked his teeth, rubbing the spot where he was hit.

Emily stared at the phone in her hand. She'd been staring at the thing for the past fifteen minutes. *God, I don't feel like making this phone call.* After hearing what Sidra said the night before, Emily knew that she had to check in with her mother.

"Come on Emily, just get it over with," she huffed, dialing. Placing the phone to her ear, she bit her already short nails as the phone rang.

"Emily, sweetie," Ms. Harris gushed through the phone.

Emily forced a smile. "Hey Mommy," she said, playing with the strings of her sweatshirt hood. "I just wanted to call and check in."

"Well, thank you for that," Ms. Harris returned. "I was just about to call your father to see how your trip was going."

Emily rolled her eyes. *Of course you were*, she thought. "Everything's going fine," she promised.

"What time is your train getting in tomorrow?"

Emily bit her bottom lip momentarily. "Uh, I'm not coming home tomorrow," she revealed.

"And why *not*? I thought that you were only staying the weekend."

Emily rolled her eyes as her mother ranted. "Mom— Mom, can you please—" Emily felt like throwing the phone when her mother wouldn't stop talking. Just knowing that she was going to have to go back to that nagging, in less than two days was making Emily's stomach hurt. "It's just an extra day," she cut in. "At least I'm having a good time. Aren't you happy about that?"

There was a pause on the line. "What is *that* supposed to mean?" Ms. Harris barked.

Emily put her hand over her forehead. "Nothing Mommy, I'll see you Monday okay," she quickly deflected. "Love you." Emily didn't give her mother the chance to respond as she quickly ended the call.

Emily put her face in her hands and tried to calm herself down. A conversation that took less than ten minutes, erased the peace that she felt for a whole day. Emily glanced up at the dresser, spotting two of the mini bottles of liquor that Malajia had brought into the room the previous evening.

She rose from the bed and walked over to the dresser, retrieving one of the bottles. She stared at it for several seconds, before deciding against drinking it.

"Just go find the others to get your mind off *her*," she told herself. She sat the bottle back down, then quickly picked it back up along with the remaining bottle and stuffed them into the pockets of her sweatshirt.

Chapter 34

"So…you ready to try this?" Alex asked the gang as they stood atop a small snow-covered hill.

"I was *born* ready," Mark boasted, pushing his sunglasses up on his nose. After a failed attempt at skiing the day before, the gang finally decided to try some snow activities. The powdery white slopes were filled with professional and amateur skiers, parents pulling their children on snow tubs and teenagers snowboarding. The atmosphere was as bright as the sun in the sky.

"Always with those sunglasses," Sidra teased, smoothing her hand over her bun. "Maybe you should put on the *actual* ski goggles."

Mark waved his hand at her. "Man, I don't need no damn goggles," he refused. "They ain't cool anyway."

Sidra looked down at the skis strapped to Mark's boots. "And when was the last time you went skiing?" she asked.

"Why you all up in my business, Sidra?" Mark snarled, much to Sidra's amusement.

Josh shook his head. "He's going to bust his ass right in this snow," he grumbled.

Mark shot him a glance, then looked at Sidra. "Princess, how was your lunch date with James yesterday?" he asked, much to Josh's annoyance.

Seriously dude?! Josh had successfully avoided Sidra the rest of the previous day, for he knew that she would just go on and on about her little date with James. Sitting around listening to his crush talk about another man was not high on Josh's list of things to do.

Sidra smiled. "It was nice. We—"

"Would you say that you're *smitten* with him?" Mark pressed, smirking at Josh.

Sidra was confused. "You've never used the word 'smitten' in your life," she chuckled at Mark.

"Sid, ignore him," Josh spat, adjusting his glove. Sidra just shrugged.

"All right, y'all talking is irritating, are we going snow tubing or not?" Malajia huffed. She'd been itching to get down the hill for the past ten minutes.

"Y'all go ahead with the tubes, I'm gonna ski," Jason said. Having been skiing several times with his parents, Jason was eager to show off his skills. He looked over at Chasity, who was standing next to Malajia. He didn't get a chance to see her after she left to hang out with her aunt the day before. He wished that he would have talked to her when he first laid eyes on her, but now with everyone around, standing on top of a snow-covered hill, it wasn't the best time to have a deep conversation about the state of their friendship.

Chasity briefly caught his gaze and looked away. She was secretly relieved that Trisha held her up the rest of the evening by dragging her to every tourist spot in town. Chasity knew that a conversation with Jason was inevitable, but she needed to get in her head what she wanted to say to him first.

"Come on, enough bullshittin' let's get down this slope!" Mark bellowed, grabbing a handful of David's coat.

David, who was sitting on a sled, tried to jerk his arm away. "Man, let go," he barked. "I gotta get situated on this thing."

"No time," Mark urged, as the two men went sliding down the hill. David's panicked yells could be heard as they slid.

"You guys be careful!" Sidra yelled after them. "Mark plays entirely *too* damn much."

Emily put her hands over her mouth. "Oh my God," she shrieked as she watched David swerve on his sled and nearly hit someone, but missed just in the nick of time.

Mark's laugh was louder than ever as David began screaming.

"Help! I can't stop sliding," David shouted.

Jason sighed loudly as he positioned himself at the edge of the slope. "I *knew* that I would end up saving someone's ass today," he huffed, tilting himself down the slope.

"Maybe we should go after them," Alex suggested, keeping a careful eye on the guys ahead of her.

Malajia carefully sat inside of the black rubber snow tube in front of her. "Shit, they'll be a'ight," she bit out nonchalantly "If I get *my* wish, Mark will fall off a damn cliff."

Sidra placed her hands on her hips, flashing Malajia a scowl. "You shouldn't say things like that," she chided.

Malajia's head snapped towards Sidra. "*You* shouldn't wear a bun with your head that small," she joked, moving her hand across the snow. Her laughter turned to panic as she felt the tube slide. "Shit, I'm not ready yet!" she shrieked.

"Hope you don't fall off a cliff," Sidra threw back, folding her arms.

Malajia, desperate to stop her sliding, reached out and grabbed the first arm that she could get ahold of; Chasity's.

"Girl! Get the fuck off me," Chasity barked, jerking her arm.

"*I* die, *you* die best friend," Malajia taunted, giving Chasity's arm a yank, pulling her into the tube and sending both girls sliding down the hill, screaming.

"Damn it," Alex fumed, stomping her foot on the

ground. "If it's not Mark trying to kill somebody, it's *Malajia*." She then carefully tried to climb down the hill.

"Alex, you can't go down there without any skis," Sidra warned as Alex continued to inch her way down the hill.

"No, I got this," Alex assured. Suddenly she slipped and fell on her butt. "Whoa!" she hollered as she began sliding down the hill on her behind.

Reacting quickly, Josh jumped down the slope on his snowboard. Trailing Alex.

"Ooooohhhh," Sidra panicked as she watched her friends careen down the slope.

Emily, eyes wide, placed her hands on top of her head. "What can we do?" she asked.

"Pray," Sidra answered.

"Chasity how do we stop this thing?!" Malajia wailed, keeping a tight grip on Chasity as their tube continued down the slope.

"*I* don't fuckin' know," Chasity barked, nudging her off. "You always doin' shit without thinking it through." She moved hair out of her face. "And you always gotta drag *me* with you!"

"You yelling at me isn't going to solve our problem, now *is* it?" Malajia hurled back.

Chasity checked her reply once she noticed that their tube was approaching Mark, who was skiing with ease in front of them. "Shit," she panicked. "Mark look out!"

"Mooooooovvvveee," Malajia urged, waving her hands wildly in the air.

Through the wind, Mark could barely hear. Glancing behind him, he saw the girls fast approaching. "What the hell?" he muttered, confused. His eyes widened once he realized what was about to happen. "Oh shit!" he panicked. Not thinking straight, Mark's first instinct was to run, and he soon realized that trying to run in skis was a bad idea. He immediately tripped and fell in the snow. "Ow!" he bellowed.

"Fuckin' idiot," Chasity commented, grabbing the handle of the tube. Malajia grabbed the handle on her side and they tried to shift the tube, but failed. Mark tried to roll out of the way, but it was too late. The tube had collided with him.

"Y'all play too much," Mark griped, wiping snow from his face. He grabbed his side and winced. "Who kicked me?"

"My bad," Malajia chuckled, struggling to get out of the tube. "Thanks for stopping us though," she teased, brushing snow from her jeans.

"Fuck y'all," Mark hurled, still laying on the ground. "I lost my damn sunglasses."

"Boy, nobody cares about those cheap ass sunglasses," Malajia scoffed with a wave of her hand.

"Who tries to run in skis anyway?" Chasity laughed.

"Lookin' all stupid and shit," Malajia mocked.

Mark sat there seething quietly as the girls continued to tease him.

David, who was clinging to the sled for dear life, careened down the hill. "I can't stop this thing! I can't stop it," he panicked.

Jason, who was skiing next to him, fought the urge to laugh. "David, give me your hand," he urged.

"I'm not taking my hands off this thing. Are you crazy?" David bellowed.

"I need something to work with here, man," Jason replied. Glancing off to the side, Jason noticed a small snow bank approaching.

"Help!" David wailed.

Jason carefully bumped into David, sending him in the direction of the snow bank. Jason stopped and watched as David, sled and all, crashed into the pile of soft snow, bringing his ride to a halt.

"You okay?" Jason yelled over to David, watching his

shaken friend struggle to sit up.

David sat up momentarily, smiled, and flashed the thumbs up sign before flopping back into the snow.

Jason chuckled. Scanning his surroundings with his eyes, Jason saw Malajia and Chasity standing a few feet away talking to Mark, who was laying in the snow. He watched Chasity extend her arm out to help Mark up, only for him to pull her down in the snow with him. Fuming, Jason took off in that direction.

"What the hell is your problem, you jackass?" Chasity fumed, flinging snow in his face.

"*That's* for laughing," Mark threw back, shielding his face from more snow being thrown at him by Malajia.

"You're such a damn troll," Malajia griped, kicking snow at him.

"Aye Mel, why you always gotta go overboard?" he ranted. "That got in my eye!" Before Mark or anybody else could say anything, Jason skied over, stopping short and sending more snow flying in Mark's direction. "Damn it!" Mark yelled, dusting himself off.

"I hope the snow melts and *cleans* your black ass," Malajia hissed at Mark, folding her arms.

Jason removed his skis and bent down to help Chasity off the ground. "You okay?" he asked her.

"Man she good, it's just *snow*," Mark dismissed, flagging Chasity with his hand.

Jason's head snapped in his direction. "I wasn't talking to *you*!" he hollered. Mark flinched at the bass in Jason's voice.

Malajia busted out laughing. "Ahhh, you got screamed," she mocked, moving hair out of her face.

Mark narrowed his eyes at Malajia before grabbing some leftover snow from his coat and tossing it at her mouth.

"You asshole!" Malajia screamed in between spitting the snow out.

Jason and Chasity shook their heads at the scene. "So stupid," she mumbled.

"Tell me about it," Jason agreed. He looked back at her. "You okay?" he repeated.

"Yeah, I'm fine," she assured him.

Mark glanced up at Malajia. "Mel, stop standing there with snow on your lip and help me up will you?" he demanded.

"Get out my damn face," Malajia bit back. "I hope you get frost bite on your ass."

"Come on, my bad about the snow in your mouth," Mark pleaded, holding his hand out. "This shit is cold, bee."

Malajia sucked her teeth. "Don't call me 'bee'," she sniped, reaching for his hand. "You wanna help me, help *you,* fool?" she barked, tugging his arm.

"I'm *trying,*" Mark promised, struggling to get up.

"Take them goddamn skis off!" Malajia wailed, then screamed as Mark accidentally pulled her down on top of him. "Oh come on!"

Jason opened his mouth to say something, but someone bumping into him stopped his thought process. Turning around and glancing down, he saw Alex sitting there. "What the hell?" he laughed, reaching for her arm.

"I tried to stop her, but I didn't want to hit her," Josh informed, bringing his snowboarding to an abrupt halt.

"I just slid all the way down here on my ass," Alex groaned as Jason pulled her from the ground.

"Why would you do that?" Chasity chuckled.

"It's not funny. I was trying to help *you* guys," Alex hissed, brushing snow out of her wild hair.

"How you mad at *us?* Nobody told you to slide down here like that," Malajia argued from the side. "Mark, I swear to God, if you don't take those damn skis *off!*" she yelled, smacking him on the leg as she struggled to get off of him. She then tugged at her coat in frustration. "Why we got on these thick ass coats?!"

Mark busted out laughing as he laid back in the snow.

"My ass is cold," Alex complained, rubbing her behind.

Chapter 35

"Why is it that we can never get through any activity without some sort of catastrophe happening?" Sidra wondered, sipping on a cup of hot chocolate.

"'Cause we always bring stupid people with us," Malajia commented, gesturing to Mark who was taking a bite of a muffin.

"That explains why *you're* here," Mark threw back, earning a middle finger from Malajia.

With their disastrous skiing episode over with, the group was trying to salvage what little time they had left together, sitting in a private fireplace-lit lounge within the hotel.

"I don't *wanna* go back home tomorrow," Malajia whined, slamming her hand on the cushy cream couch where she sat. "My bratty ass sisters are gonna be all in my face and shit for the rest of the break."

Alex laughed. Malajia never ceased to express her displeasure with being home. "Relax Mel, we only have two weeks left before we get back to campus," she informed.

"Nobody asked you for a countdown," Malajia spat out, reaching for a cookie from a large tray on a wood table next to her.

"This hotel is off the chain. They hooked us up with the treats," Mark mused, reaching for another muffin.

"Shut your greedy ass up, talkin' about some damn treats," Malajia jeered. Mark ignored her as he concentrated on his food. Malajia then turned her attention to Chasity. "Chaz, you think your sexy father will put us up for another night?"

Chasity took a pause from sipping her hot cider and glared at Malajia. "Don't make me slap you," she warned, earning a giggle from Malajia.

Emily was quiet as she sat on one of the chaise lounges. Her mind was plagued with thoughts of having to return home tomorrow, a place that she had grown to despise. She blew into her cup of hot tea before taking a sip.

"Yo, Em, what kinda drink you got?" Mark asked, reaching over to grab her cup.

"No!" Emily shrieked, quickly moving the mug out of his reach. Her reaction stunned Mark, who quickly put his hands up in surrender.

"Boy, keep your damn hands off people's stuff," Alex barked, tossing a balled up napkin at Mark who in turn sucked his teeth.

"I wasn't *really* gonna take it," Mark grunted. "And why you all up in the mix, frosty ass?"

Alex held a scowl on her face as laughter resonated around her. "Shut up," she sniped, leaning back in her seat.

"My bad, Em," Mark apologized, taking another bite of his muffin.

Emily forced a smile and nodded, going back to sipping her tea. Her reaction was not intentional, but if Mark would have sipped her drink, he would have tasted the vodka that she poured into it. Unable to relax the last few hours, Emily gave in to temptation and opened one of the mini bar bottles. *Just keep quiet and nobody will know*, she thought.

"At least Sidra is leaving here with a man," Malajia gushed, nudging Sidra who was sitting next to her.

Sidra blushed as she placed her hand over her face.

"Stop it Malajia," she giggled. "He's not my man."

"*Yet*," Alex teased, giving the embarrassed Sidra a poke on the arm.

Josh fidgeted in his seat. *Here they go bringing up this fool again.* "Can we talk about something else?" he grimaced, folding his arms.

Sidra looked over at him. "Everything okay, Josh?" she asked, concerned. His mood had been off to her lately.

Josh gave a nervous laugh. "I'm fine," he assured her. "Just tired, that's all."

Mark snickered. "Josh throwin' a temper tantrum and shit," he mocked.

"Shut up," Josh spat, tossing a small pillow at Mark.

As the conversations around him continued, Jason saw the perfect opportunity to speak to Chasity alone, He rose from his seat and walked over to her. "Hey, can I talk to you for a minute?" he whispered.

Chasity glanced up at him. "Yeah," she said, setting her mug down on the end table next to her. The pair took off for a quiet area.

Malajia sucked her teeth as she saw a call flashing across her screen. "He better kiss my ass," she muttered, turning her phone off. That had been the fourth time that Tyrone had called her in the past few days, and she still had no intention of talking to him. She'd neglected to block his number again when she switched phones.

"What are you complaining about *now*?" Mark asked, face scrunched up. "Be happy *somebody* is calling that raggedy ass phone."

Malajia folded her arms as she sat back in her seat, glaring daggers at Mark. "Stop worrying about who's calling *me* and worry about those raggedy girls who *aren't* calling *you*," she shot back. Mark waved his hand at her dismissively. "It's a shame, you pay them and they *still* don't give you no play."

"I don't pay for my women, baby," Mark boasted, pointing a finger at Malajia.

"Please, you *have* to be paying them," Malajia insisted. "I mean, they must get *something* in return for putting up with those two little unsatisfying minutes in the backseat of your raggedy ass car."

David spit out a mouthful of his cider at Malajia's comeback.

Mark smirked and nodded. *Good one*, he thought. Malajia never let him down with the comebacks.

Jason and Chasity had located a quiet corner outside of the lounge. They were nervous and guarded, and it showed in their expressions and body language. "So…how have you been?" Jason asked after a long pause.

Chasity folded her arms. "I've been all right," she answered. "You?"

Jason hesitated; he wondered if he should come clean about how bad he'd been feeling since their split, or if he should play it off. "I've been…not so good," he admitted finally.

Chasity looked away briefly. He felt that same as *she* had.

"I miss you," he said, voice sincere.

Chasity sighed. "I miss you too," she admitted. Her admission took Jason by surprise.

"You do?" he asked.

Chasity nodded. "Look…I was mad at you for ending our friendship, but—"

"I didn't *want* to," Jason said. "I was just angry at you…hell, I was angry at *myself*."

"Why were you angry at yourself?"

Jason ran a hand over his hair. "For misreading you," he answered honestly. "I wanted what I wanted so bad and I just couldn't see past it."

"Jason, you didn't misread everything," Chasity assured him. "I *do* care about you."

"But not enough to want to be with me," he finished.

Chasity let out a sigh and Jason gently touched her arm. "Look, I get it."

"No, no you *don't*," Chasity vaguely replied.

Jason frowned slightly. "Tell me what I'm not getting Chasity," he pressed.

Chasity felt like stomping her foot on the floor. Here Jason was standing before her, looking for answers, looking for some clue to her inner most feelings, and she was fighting against letting them out. "I just…"

Jason closed his eyes and rubbed his forehead when she hesitated. "Can you just answer me this one question?" he asked, tone serious.

Oh God, what now? "Okay," she replied.

Jason paused for a moment, unsure if he really wanted the honest answer that he sought. "Do you *ever* see yourself being with me?" he asked. "If your answer is no, I promise you, I'll never bring it up again," he assured. "I'll just have to deal with it. But I can't continue to hope for something that may never happen…I don't have it in me."

Chasity stared up at him as that question roared in her head.

"I deserve to know that," he added. "I mean…*do* you?"

Chasity felt herself tear up as she thought of what to say. She didn't know if she should do what she normally did and run from the situation, or if she should stand and face it. "Yes," she answered finally. "I see myself being with you."

Jason fought hard to keep his relief from showing on his face. But on the inside he was doing backflips. "Really?"

Chasity nodded as a tear fell. She wiped it with the sleeve of her sweater. "Just not—I just can't—" *I'm just scared.*

Jason sensed her inner struggle. "Just not right now," he finished for her.

Chasity slowly shook her head. "I'm sorry," she said, voice sincere.

Jason smiled as he wiped a tear from her cheek with his

hand. "It's okay," he promised. "I don't want to rush you into something that you're not ready for…I get the feeling that I did, when—"

"You didn't rush me," Chasity immediately cut in, knowing what he was about to say. "Like I said before, I wanted to."

Jason nodded. He was relieved to hear that. If he thought for one moment that Chasity felt pressure from him to have sex, he'd never forgive himself. He wasn't that type of guy. "Can we start off by at least trying to be friends again?" he asked after a moment.

"Yeah, we can do that," she agreed.

Jason's smile was bright, brighter than it had been in a long time. Even though he had no idea how soon it would happen, he had hope for a future with Chasity. For the mean time, he was satisfied with having his friend back, or at least trying to. "Am I allowed to hug you now?"

Chasity let out a small laugh. "Sure," she said, before he enveloped her in a warm, loving embrace. Chasity closed her eyes as she held onto him. This was the most at peace that she had felt in long time.

As they parted, Chasity stared at him, taking in everything about him. Every moment that she shared with him flooded her mind. The first time they met, the times when he protected her, times when he comforted her, when he made her feel like she was the only person in his world. He had the ability to make her feel vulnerable and safe at the same time. The way that he professed his feelings for her. He was selfless when it came to her. Jason made her feel something that she'd never felt before, something that she feared, but deep down, had always wanted to feel. Chasity, in that instant, came to a realization. *I love him.*

Knowing that the feelings she'd questioned, the feelings that she fought hard to keep buried had surfaced, she wondered if she could bring herself to even tell him. She wondered if she could ever put aside her fears and insecurities to allow herself the chance to be happy with him.

Jason had no clue what was going on inside of Chasity's troubled head as he took hold of her hand. "I guess we should get back to the others," he suggested.

Chasity nodded slightly, squeezing his hand as she allowed him to lead her away from their secluded corner. "Yeah, I guess we *should*."